MADS RAFFERTY

HEIR OF BROKEN KINGDOM

Copyright © 2024 by Mads Rafferty

All rights reserved.

No part of this book may be reproduced in any form or by any electronic or mechanical means, including information storage and retrieval systems, without written permission from the author, except for the use of brief quotations in a book review.

The characters and events portrayed in this book are fictitious. Any resemblance to places, events or real people, living or dead, are entirely coincidental and not intended by the author.

Cover Designed by Thea Magerand.

Edited by Makenna Albert.

Published by Mads Rafferty.

ISBN: 978-0-6458037-5-4

❦ Created with Vellum

Trigger Warning

Please read with care, this book touches on the following topics.
Domestic violence, abuse, suicide ideation, torture off-page, grief and loss, explicit sexual scenes, fantasy violence, and gore.

*To those with battle scars internal or external,
I see you and the beauty of them.*

And to those with a father who doesn't deserve the title, this one's for you.

ALORIAH
SECTOR 3
SECTOR 6
SECTOR 7
SECTOR 2
SECTOR 4
SECTOR 5
CAPITAL
PALACE
SECTOR 1
MASON RIVER
DEYANIRA MOUNTAINS
MERMAID TERRITORY
CARDANIA
WITCHES TERRITORY
EARTH COURT
EDEN
WATER COURT
AIR COURT
ENTRILE
ESSENCE COURT
FIRE COURT
ORNX
AZALEA
AERIAL LEGION
WARRIOR ISLAND

Chapter One

Who would have imagined that the world burning to the ground would be such a beautiful sight? That the very thing we've ruined ourselves to protect would look so breathtakingly gorgeous as it's destroyed?

Aloriah is burning.

Dying before our very eyes, and there is nothing anyone can do to stop it.

Ashes flutter in the wind. Tendrils of black smoke curl around the ruined buildings.

As the land I've fallen in love with erupts into nothing but orange flames, I cannot help the desolate feeling that sinks into the bottom of my stomach as I realize I never got to say goodbye. Not knowing I should have savored the last breath of fresh air I inhaled, that I should have reveled in the soft grass as it cushioned my feet, rejoiced as my body basked in its deep pool of magic before everything divine was stripped away.

Taking a deep pull of air, I pause.

I should be able to smell the undeniable scent of burnt

flesh and char as the innocent people of Aloriah are torched to death. Hear the screams of those running in the streets as they plead for mercy. I should be able to feel a strong tether where my soul lies, the bond connecting our two hearts and souls, and yet there's nothing.

I should be down there, spending my last moments fighting a fruitless battle that we will never win. Instead, I float, dangling in the black depths of this abyss. Unable to do anything as my Fae sight locks onto every graphic detail of humans, Fae, and magical creatures being slaughtered.

The human lands remain nothing more than a charred kingdom. The Deyanira Mountains are not a beautiful shade of forest green but a black smear, as dark as the one I float through.

The blazing fire of destruction swept through the Fae courts as if they were merely flecks of bark, leaving nothing behind of the once bustling cities. Cardania, the capital city of the Water Court, is now nothing but steam, its glorious water long gone.

I swing my fist, throwing hit after hit after hit.

Yet no matter how much strength I throw into my punches, the loss of gravity fights against me, making every swing of my fists slow.

Glass separates me from my home—from my love, Knox. Not even sound breaks the barrier as it shimmers in front of me, the invisible barricade reverberating with the hits I can't feel.

It's as if I've become nothing, not existing in any time or place.

And then suddenly, terror clutches me in its talons, shaking my body violently as my mouth gapes open on a silent scream. My voice tries to escape past the ward holding me captive as a dragon flies below me. Black shadows cling to its unnaturally large body, indicating its allegiance.

The demonic dragon swoops, flying faster than any creature I've witnessed before, its wings beating erratically as it climbs the impossibly high altitude, not stopping until its glowing red eyes connect with mine.

It stops mid-air. The corner of its large, leathery mouth lifts, curving as if to smirk at me. Before I can process the haunting gleam shining in its eyes the dragon tucks its wings in tight and drops. Plunging faster than light itself for the burning city of Azalea below.

The dragon's jaw opens, teeth glinting, and tongue slithering, as its eyes narrow on its prey.

My pulse turns erratic, skittering between the lines of death and life as my throat issues a blood-curdling scream. My vocal cords strain on the warning, and I plead with the forgotten gods to save what I cherish most.

Instead, I remain suspended, hovering between time and space as my efforts go unheard.

A lightning bolt of shock cracks through my body, so fierce my head rears back with the force. My hands fly to my chest as if they can stop my heart from falling out of its cage, as if they can push all the air back into my lungs. Yet they cannot stop my heart from cracking and crumbling under the weight of gut-wrenching agony.

My eyes stay unblinking as the demonic dragon sails past, slowing in front of me, its eyes glinting with triumphant glee as Knox's head dangles from its razor-sharp teeth.

I dive within myself, roaring as I discover my magic well frozen, the shimmering gold asleep once more. I beg for it to awaken and avenge his death.

But like before, my pleas go unanswered.

Tears roll down my cheeks with abandon as I sob, unable

to tear my gaze away from Knox's lifeless, vacant sapphire eyes.

Two shadows form, darker than the night itself. Their gray robes flutter in the wind, blending with the clouds of smoke dancing in the air.

As the two shadows tower over me, rage contorts my features and engulfs my body, so strong it pulses through my bloodstream.

They did this.

A lone finger lifts, poking out beneath the heavy robes. The finger points directly to my heart as it taps the glass.

It's such a light tap. No sound is created, the glass never moving, and yet the force of it creates a crack. A small blip compared to the large size of the glass and yet that one singular tap will be my undoing. I can feel it within every fiber of my being that the end is near, that death hovers nearby, Knox calling my name on the other side as he waits for me to join him.

Until that, too, is ripped away from me.

The darkness around me begins to rumble—gleeful for what's to come.

The two before me tap the glass once more and rip everything away from me.

The city below cracks, the glass barrier shattering, and instead of the smell of death and smoke-filled air rushing in, I'm met with nothing but an endless black pit. The yawning darkness of the universe itself.

The last thing I see is Knox's unseeing sapphire eyes and a demonic army swarming the city I've come to call my home. Then I'm plummeting to a space with no end in sight.

Falling with no world to catch me.

Chapter Two

Knox takes a step back as my eyes flutter open.

His hands hover in the air, still curved from where they were cupping my cheeks just a mere moment ago.

The horror I find dancing in his eyes is nothing compared to the bottomless pit in my stomach that I haven't been able to shake. The utter agony my heart has endured from watching the dragon tear Knox's head from his body as my mind replayed the image, over and over and over.

Gratitude lies heavy between the bond, sizzling over the power of Knox's mind and his ability to flick through my emotions like a book. If I had to verbally explain what I saw and felt, I wouldn't have been able to make it past the first sentence.

Knox's gaze flits behind me, his hands falling helplessly to his sides as he steps forward on wobbly legs. "You must know who that was. You have the power to see!"

A chill snakes down my spine at the plea in his voice, the utter terror dancing at the edge of his words.

Turning in the meadow, I face the seven mermaids in the

watering hole. My eyes land on the white-haired mermaid's glowing red eyes—identical to the demonic dragon's—in time to watch her shake her head.

No.

"We can't see past their shadows. The dark magic they possess is unlike anything from this world. It blocks our sight."

I take a tentative step forward, cocking my head to the side. "What *can* you see?"

"The same as you—death."

"Naia," Knox growls.

My brows rise in shock at finally learning her name, only to drop the moment Naia narrows those red eyes on him.

"We don't take orders from Fae. You may be a king in the eyes of your people, Holloway, but we are not yours to rule."

A muscle ticks in Knox's jaw. "I wasn't the only one who died in that vision. It was everyone and everything, *including* your pod."

A flash of sadness flits across Naia's eyes before her internal walls rise, her voice somber as she says, "I know." She slides her gaze to me, pity marring her words. "You won't like the answers we have for you, child."

Child.

In her eyes, we are all children. I remember the shock I felt when she deemed Hazel one too, being that she is older than one hundred and fifty years. If that's the case, I must be no more than an infant to her. An infant with an immense amount of pressure weighing on her young shoulders.

Regardless of her opinion of me, I was the one who had the vision, and deep within my heart I know there must be a reason for that.

"I will do anything to save this world. *Anything*."

After all, I gave up my life for this world, for this land

Heir of Broken Kingdom 7

and its magic. I gave up my very breath to save the Tree of Life. If it weren't for Knox's sheer will and the stubbornness in his hold on my soul, I wouldn't be standing here right now, chasing another faceless enemy.

Naia dips her chin, the turquoise jewel on her forehead glinting off the moonlight. "Travel to the human lands and you'll find the answers you seek."

I'm unable to stop my head from rearing back as if her words were a physical blow.

Knox's warm hand links with mine, his support felt through my soul as I shake my head. "Why would I need to go back? In the dream, it was magic and demons that destroyed Aloriah, not humans."

"That is where our vision wished to take you. We may see all but that does not mean the universe whispers its plans to us," Naia says, eerily calm.

"We will stay hidden," Knox whispers beside me, no doubt feeling my stampede of emotions.

"No one enters the human lands without his knowledge."

Knox, as hopeful as ever, turns to Naia. "You said the human lands. You never said anything about the human king."

"Nothing will stop that monster from coming after me once word gets out that I'm in his lands," I argue.

My lips curl in disgust at the idea of another choice being made for me. Another aspect of my life that I don't have control over. I wanted to have time to decide my fate, to have a say in whether I returned to the human lands or not. Whether I decided to face *him*.

An image of my father sneering at me flashes across my mind.

Terror locks my body as I whisper, "He will kill me."

"He won't come within breathing distance of you," Knox

swears. His hand tightening around mine as if the notion will stop my father from taking me away.

"If he wants me dead…I'm dead. And there will be nothing anyone can do to stop him."

Knox may be the most powerful Fae. He may be a king and he may have an army at his disposal, but nothing is stronger than the force of the king's despicable mind.

"Are you sending her to her death?" Knox grits out.

Naia slides her gaze to Knox, the move predatory. "I suggest you think your questions through before throwing accusations at the ones who are trying to help save her life." To me, Naia reiterates, "You will find what you seek most in the human lands."

Knox's brow quirks. "Care to share what, exactly, we are searching for?"

Amelia, Naia's second, snaps, "She will know when she sees it, boy."

"Do I have a choice?" I dare ask.

The red-haired second snorts. "Not unless you want us all to be charred."

Knox's back stiffens. "You think the threat of the Fae and human race being destroyed is humorous?"

A purring female voice rises behind Naia, drawing our attention to the violet steel eyes. "I think you forget we're immortals far too often, Holloway."

"Immortals that can be killed by fire. Water won't save you this time, Alentia. It'll just delay your fate."

Naia ignores the sparring match of words and cuts off Alentia before she can retaliate. "You have a choice. No matter what it feels like, you always have free will; we are never truly placed in a position of limited options. However, whether you choose to face this threat is up to you. But the lives of many hang in the balance of your decision."

I may be many things, but selfish isn't one of them. I won't kill innocents out of fear of facing what lies in the human lands. I won't turn my back on this. If I did, I would become the very thing I despise most—my father.

Knox looks at me expectantly, prepared to support me regardless of my answer.

I clear my throat, lowering my head to hide my grimace. "I'll leave as soon as I can."

The words taste like poison on my tongue, one that will kill me slowly with every step toward the life I fled. I can't douse the dread coiling around my heart, nor can I hide it from my eyes.

"You were given the dream for a reason. Don't doubt that child."

With no riddles to help me or words of psychic wisdom, I swallow thickly, making to leave.

"Delilah." Naia's voice drifts toward me once more. She's moved forward, separating herself from her pod.

I squeeze Knox's hand, telling him with my eyes to stay back. Gratitude fills my heart as he waits for me in the tall grass, trust running through the bond.

Kneeling on the riverbank's edge I dip my chin, bringing my head forward as Naia does the same. To my surprise, she doesn't stop before me. Instead, she moves past my face until her cold, wet lips brush the shell of my ear, her voice barely above a whisper even to my Fae ears.

My brow furrows at the message she wants to hide from the others and before I can ask any questions, she disappears, her head submerging beneath the water. Naia's pod follows suit, leaving ripples of water in their wake.

Knox comes to a stop beside me when I make no move to stand. His hand slides across my back, his touch sending warmth through my chilled bones.

"You don't have to go. I can go in your place."

I whip my head to him. "Yes, I do. You know I have to."

I would *never* send Knox in my place, not when I know what's to come…what we need to fight against.

Shrugging helplessly my voice wavers. "I was hoping they would say it was a dream…something as simple as a nightmare. Not—"

"A premonition," Knox finishes for me. He tears his gaze from the swimming hole, his sapphire eyes softening as they connect with mine. "You're not alone, nor are you the same girl who entered these lands months ago. He can't hurt you now, Delilah."

I may have grown stronger with the cards I was dealt walking into these magical lands, but when I think of my father, that terrified little girl within me takes control and the years of abuse berate my mind, reminding me exactly what he's capable of.

I don't voice that my father's mind games and words are just as deadly as his fists. Unlike a bruise, they are permanent scars.

"I possess magic, Knox. Not only that, but I'm now Fae…the two things he despises most. He hated me before, could barely tolerate my presence, and now this." I wave my hands around my body. "He will kill me the moment he lays eyes on me."

The fear of my body turning back into a human's vanished the moment Knox watched my memory of the night Easton was taken from me. Witnessing golden magic explode from within me before I ever entered the Fae lands.

No longer do I have to worry about losing my strength and magic. However, I may just get myself killed because of it.

Knox kneels, cupping my cheeks. His eyes blaze with

fierce protection. "I won't let him lay a finger on you ever again, Angel."

"You can't leave your people after everything. There's far too much to do, too much work—"

The corner of his lip twitches. "I don't know if you've noticed this, Angel, but I rule Azalea and the Essence Court. I have the power to choose what tasks I assign myself." When I don't laugh at his attempt to lighten the situation, his mask drops, letting me see the vulnerability in his eyes. "Where you go, I go."

I open my mouth to spew more nonsense, any excuse that comes to mind of why he can't come, but I fall short. His words break through the fear squeezing my heart. I don't want him to go for a multitude of reasons, but mainly because I don't want to go myself.

And doesn't that just make me a coward?

"You are *not* a coward."

"Get out of my head," I grumble.

Knox's smirk turns feline. "Unfortunately, I can't do that. Being that we're mates and all."

Mates.

The invisible bond tying our two souls, our hearts, tugs. Reminding me of its presence every time I hear the word. As if the bond itself is proud that it was forged. It will take time to adjust to the overwhelming feeling it brings. Pure, unconditional love. We may not have said those words to each other, but they are felt. Every time I stare into his striking sapphire eyes, I feel it consume my entire being.

I rub a hand over my chest as if I can make the larger-than-life feeling lessen. "We have to tell them everything," I say softly, changing the topic. "I can't ask for their help without doing so. It's unfair to make them walk into the situation blind."

It's also unfair that the Fae and human races don't know their days are numbered and that they should cherish every breath they take.

Knox runs his fingers through my hair. "About the premonition or about who your father is?" he asks gently.

With my heart in my throat, I say, "Both."

Knox nods. "What did Naia say to you?"

Plucking a blade of grass, I begin tearing it into small pieces. "She gave me a location. I take it that's where she wants us to go."

Knox stands, offering me his hand. "And where are we off to?"

Taking a deep breath, I lift my chin, willing strength into my heart. "Sector Four."

The sense of peace I feel that rushes down my spine as Knox and I approach his estate is a small blip compared to the heaviness weighing down on me.

Tristan and Malik, the night guards, step aside as the heavy gates groan, opening on their own.

My heavy footfalls should lighten as I approach what my heart now knows to be my safe haven. Yet with every crunch of gravel, anger fills my veins. The choice of whether I return to the human lands or not has been made for me—regardless of what Naia said.

Sector Four may not be near the capital, but the man who sits atop the throne sees all, and I will have to do everything within my power to not be seen by him or his spies.

"I'm sorry," Knox whispers.

"What do you have to apologize for?"

Knox steps in front of me abruptly, his chest heaving as if

he was running from the dragon that is fated to sink its teeth into his neck. He brushes his fingers across my chin and pulls my gaze to his. "I'm sorry that I can't fix the situation…that I can't take away the pain radiating through your heart."

I lower my eyes, unable to face him as I voice the thunderous fear that continues to strike me. "I don't think I can do this. I don't think I'm strong enough."

"You can and you are." Knox bends to my height. "Do you know how I know that?"

I shake my head, suddenly too tired for words.

"Because you're Delilah Covington, one of the strongest people I know. You *saved* the people of Aloriah and the entire Fae race, along with the creatures who dwell in these lands and magic itself." His thumb brushes across my bottom lip before he lifts my head, forcing me to stare at him again. "If you can do that, you can face *anything*."

I breathe in his words as if the very air he spoke them with can fill me with strength.

Knox leans forward, brushing his soft lips against my forehead. The tenderness and care in that one kiss is enough to break through the fear holding my heart prisoner.

"Bond or not, Delilah, I would choose to go anywhere with you. I couldn't imagine a day that goes by where I don't see your eyes." Knox rests his forehand against mine, his warm breath brushing across my lips. "Wherever you go, whatever you must face, know that I'll be right beside you. You don't have to tackle life alone anymore, Delilah. I will always be there for you, and we will face whatever life decides to throw at us together, as one."

My heart skips a beat as my eyes glisten for another reason other than dread.

"As one?"

"As one," he vows.

The smoldering heat pouring off him in waves makes me lick my suddenly dry lips. The words he spoke, the *vow* he's promising, shines in the depths of his eyes.

"As one," I repeat, with the conviction of his heart thumping down our bond.

Knox closes the gap between our lips, searing me with a kiss so scorching my arms tingle, goosebumps lining my skin. I rise on the balls of my feet and throw every ounce of heat into the touch. Knox's tongue begs for entrance at the seam of my lips until I open and then he's dancing, consuming, and nipping as if we have all the time in the world.

His palms travel up my body until he cups my face, cradling me ever so softly as if I'm the most prized joy in his life.

He kisses me as if I'm something worth savoring.

Time to face the music.

Pulling away reluctantly, Knox slides his warm palm down my spine, coming to rest atop my lower back as he guides us forward. We both pause at the sudden moment of silence on the other side of the wooden door before a deafening scream ensues.

Barging through the front door, Knox and I stop on the threshold, taking in the chaos we have stumbled upon.

Flames curl around Harlow's hands and forearms, pointing the deadly magic at none other than Nolan. The promise of death that lies in her eyes as she glares at him is one to fear. Especially as a ball of flame forms between her palms, her lip curling back with a feral snarl.

Ace's hand rests on the pommel of the sword strapped to his hip. He stands protectively in front of a frazzled Hazel, who flits her eyes back and forth as if watching a game. Ace's brother, Axel, stands in front of them both, always the protector of his twin. A shimmering iridescent shield of air wraps around them like a bubble.

"Extinguish the flames, Harlow!" Axel screams.

Ignoring him, Harlow's flames burn brighter than the stars themselves as she strides toward Nolan. "Say that again and you'll see just how *unstable* I truly am."

Despite Harlow appearing to be seconds away from scorching Nolan into nothing but ash, he ignores the terrifying half-witch and instead sneers at Lenox. "You don't know that! We know nothing right now!"

"Nothing? *Nothing?*" Lenox booms. "It's happening again. Or is your head so far up your ass you can't see that?"

Nolan's neck flushes crimson. "I'm thinking logically. Unlike some."

Knox whistles, trying to gain his court's attention and failing miserably.

What happened? Last we saw they were all celebrating.

Knox rolls his eyes. *You thought we were hot-tempered before? That was nothing compared to when we are at our peak.*

With a simple flick of his wrist, the doors behind us slam so hard the marble tiles beneath my feet shake, the vibrations jarring my bones. The sound is so powerful it makes my ears ring. His court's wild gazes snap to their king.

Despite the flick of his wrist, I have the overwhelming feeling that the movement was all for show. Knox doesn't have to lift a finger to possess or control his magic.

Knox slides his hands into his pockets and leans against the doorframe. "Now that I have your attention, care to tell me why everyone is acting like infants?"

The look that passes over his court's faces has me straightening. Especially as they all snap their mouths shut, magic vanishing without a trace.

A muscle ticks in his jaw. "I understand that tensions are running high. It will take everyone time to adjust to regaining their full powers once again. However, that doesn't excuse your silence."

If possible, the room grows quieter.

"Spit it out," Knox demands. "Before I place a truth spell over you all."

"They've disappeared," Ace blurts, his cheeks reddening with embarrassment as everyone groans.

Knox snaps his gaze to his second-in-command, demanding answers from the other twin. "Who?"

Axel steps forward, holding his hands behind his back. He seems to take a moment to compose himself before declaring, "The demonic army."

Knox visibly recoils, as if the words themselves will make the dark creatures appear. "The queen ordered her men to disperse them."

"Her guards arrived at the replica of the Tree of Life to find it deserted," Harlow fills in. "None of her spies or men can find a single demonic creature in any of the courts."

I look toward Nolan, my heartbeat slowing as his facial muscles strain to keep a tight leash on his emotions. I soften my voice as if I can make the question easier to answer. "What of the people in the in-between?"

Nolan's sister and mother.

Axel also looks to Nolan before facing me. "Only a handful escaped before the rest disappeared. Those who left the in-between made it to Cardania's borders. They've opened up shelter to them all and by the records they shared this morning, only a hundred returned."

My eyes flare. "How could thousands of demonic creatures and Fae simply disappear? There was no massacre this time. The magnitude of power needed to make them vanish is—"

"Otherworldly," Lenox finishes for me.

"We got it wrong."

It's not the words that make me turn; it's his tone. Knox's face has turned ashen. He can't even face his court as he speaks, his eyes remain glued to the marble-tiled floor.

"What did we get wrong?" I ask hesitantly.

"It wasn't Emmalyn summoning the demons."

She let me kill her.

Knox's confession from earlier rushes to the forefront of my mind. The truth of it rings through my very soul.

"Emmalyn was a puppet, used so no one with the power of mind reading could see who was truly doing the bidding." Knox spits the next words. "Emmalyn was never in charge."

Undulated agony rips through my body, along with horrendous thoughts crafted from Knox's fear.

I failed.

I was wrong again.

I wasn't good enough to save my people.

It's never enough. Nothing I ever do is enough.

My people are doomed if I remain their king.

Knox's thoughts infiltrate my mind, each one more gut-wrenching than the last.

I rest my hand gently on his arm as if the touch can soothe and heal the pain in his heart, the thoughts pelting his mind. I will him to see him through my eyes. To see the strong warrior who is forever putting his people before himself. The king who loves his people with a violent passion. The man that I am proud to call my mate and friend.

Warmth flows back toward me down the bond.

Axel's voice is abnormally soft as he says, "We don't know that, Knox."

Swallowing thickly, I turn away from Knox. The least I can do is face his beautiful court as I rip out their hopes and dreams by letting them see their fate...the death sentence waiting for us all.

"Yes, we do."

Knox runs calloused fingers down my forearm, entwining our hands as we face the truth of the matter together—as one.

"I've been receiving visions—premonitions—in the form of dreams. They've all been accurate...every single one of them." Pulling in a deep breath, I tighten my hold on Knox's hand as I crack open the door to my memories, leaving a small gap for him to enter. "Tonight, I received this one."

The world as we know it burning to the ground flashes across my eyes. The dream that's lingered, refusing to escape my mind since it happened. The nausea it initially induced rises once more as I helplessly watch the dragon murder Knox.

My eyes flutter open as the vision goes dark, ending with me falling...being sucked into the depthless pit of the universe, floating toward no one and nothing.

With her blue eyes filled with horror and sorrow, Hazel whispers, "Oh, Delilah."

The severity of the vision hits its mark. The truth of our imminent death lies at our feet.

Harlow's hand grips the hilt of her dagger strapped to her thigh. "I will personally break every bone in its hideous body before that gods-awful creature lays a talon on you."

Knox swallows thickly as his hand twitches at his side. As if he wants to reach for his neck to check that it's still intact.

What does that do to someone's psyche? To not only witness their gruesome death but to know that it's coming?

Despite the gray sheen to Lenox's skin, when he steps

forward, his tone is firm, full of strength I can't command myself to feel. "What can we do? We know it's coming, surely, we can stop it."

Axel's eyes don't leave Knox's throat, as if he can still see the moment it was ripped from his body.

"We spoke to the mermaids—"

Harlow's eyes widen. "They're helping you again?"

"We weren't the only race to die in that vision. It was every living creature on the continent. Mermaids included," Knox says roughly, echoing the same words he spoke earlier.

Harlow's small frame straightens. "What did they say?"

The fear that flashes across her face drives a cold spear down my spine. If Harlow is frightened, the one who laughs while standing before demonic creatures…then we all have something to fear.

Knox turns, his sapphire eyes sweeping me head to toe as if assessing and marking the amount of pain that lies within my heart. His hand tightens in mine as if he can stop me from falling apart.

"They're sending us to the human lands," he tells his court.

Axel's steely forest-green eyes fly to mine as shock mares his features. Understanding passes between the two of us before he straightens, preparing for the fight ahead.

If anyone knows the weight of Knox's words, it's Axel. The one who suffered from his mother's cruel hands, similar to how my father treated me. I knew it when I first met him, my body instinctively recognizing a kindred spirit when it saw one.

Axel and Ace may be twins and they may have the same fierce jawline, green eyes, straight nose, and honey-tanned skin, but that is where the similarities end. Axel's as black as the winged tattoo on his neck and Ace is as light as Lenox's brown eyes. The two share a bond that only they will fully understand, yet they did not have the same childhood. Axel has been and will always be Ace's protector, taking the punches of not only life but of his mother's fists.

Harlow pulls out a dagger and waves it around haphazardly before cleaning her nails. "What's the big deal? It'll be nice to leave these lands. We've been stuck in them for nearly one hundred and fifty years."

Nolan's gaze narrows on us. "What aren't you telling us?"

Hazel bites her bottom lip to stop the unshed tears from falling, as she knows what's to come.

I close my eyes like the coward I am as I force the words out. "My name is Delilah…Covington." Ignoring the gasps that fill the foyer, I swallow the thick lump in my throat and push myself to continue. "Heir to the throne of Aloriah, I am the human king's daughter."

To my surprise, Nolan turns on Knox. "You knew and didn't tell us."

"It wasn't my story to tell," Knox says simply, ignoring his outburst.

Lenox's roguish features turn pained. "Why wouldn't you tell us? Do you not trust us?" His question is directed at me, eyes swimming with such deep emotions they pin me to the spot.

The large Fae may have a sharp bone structure and dark locks that make him appear to be a warrior crafted by the forgotten gods themselves, but behind the larger-than-life male is a heart just as deep and full as his build.

"Of course I do," I say, my hand over my heart. "It had nothing to do with trust and everything to do with shame." Catching my voice before it cracks, I go on. "The king is a monster who not only leads his kingdom with cruelty in his heart but rules his court and household with the sheer strength of his fists." My heart pinches. "The king made his own daughter bleed every day."

Knox lays his hand on my back as if he can't physically stay away from me when I'm hurting.

"He beat me every day, sometimes to within an inch of my life. Others were not so lucky to escape." My eyes instinctively flit to Ace, the doppelgänger of Easton. I rip my eyes away as I hurt my own heart with the sight. "Easton was my best friend and my fa—the king killed him in cold-blooded murder."

I choke on the title. He doesn't deserve to be called my father. I will never call him by such again.

"He detests magic. The second I cross into his lands and the whispers begin of his daughter not only having elongated ears but wielding magic…he will kill me on sight."

"We'll kill him first," Lenox sneers.

"No, we're not going to kill him," I whisper.

Harlow's brow arches in astonishment. "And why not?"

"We're going to do something far greater." I look to Knox's court, my friends…my newfound family. And ask them what I never could ask of Easton. "We're going to overthrow the king and make him live out his days in misery."

Chapter Three

"I'm going with you," Hazel declares, the steely tone and conviction shining in her eyes leaving no room for arguments.

I'm not going to be able to change her mind.

I shrug helplessly. "I don't know what the human lands will look like when we cross the border. We will be going in blind."

What I'm trying to say and fail to utter is I don't know if I'm sending them to their deaths or not.

"Have you received any reports on any creatures entering the human lands?" Knox asks Axel, but Axel's focus isn't on the words his king mutters. No, his eyes are still glued to Knox's neck, to that spot where the dragon sunk its razor-sharp teeth and pulled until—

"Axel?" Ace prompts his brother.

Axel lifts his eyes, yet they're dazed. "What?"

"Have there been any reports of creatures entering the human lands?" Knox repeats.

Axel's mouth opens, only to stutter and slam shut as his eyes lock onto his King's neck once more.

Heir of Broken Kingdom

"From what we've gathered no one has breached the border, all too consumed with their magic returning. I'll place orders to stay away until we have come to a peaceful agreement with the current standing human king," Nolan chimes in, saving Axel from his stupor.

I don't dare tell him that there won't be a peaceful agreement. The king would rather have his head torn from his body before making treaties with Fae.

"Very well."

Hazel's copper-red hair sways as she shakes her head. "I don't care what we encounter in the human lands, I'm not letting you face this alone, Delilah."

"Neither will I." Ace steps forward, resting his hand on Hazel's lower back.

A cocky glint enters Harlow's eyes. "If he despised magic before, just wait until he meets us."

My heart trips over itself before melting into a puddle on the floor as every one of Knox's court—my friends—steps forward. Dipping their heads as they offer their company and services.

In keeping me alive.

"This is all very touching." Knox clutches his heart, warmth shining in his eyes. "However, we do have a court and city to run. We can't all leave."

Harlow shrugs, her red streaked hair swaying with the movement. "The less human filth I have to deal with, the better."

"Humans aren't all that bad," I tease, biting back a laugh.

I was getting worried for a moment when Harlow became sentimental. After all, if the half-witch was worried about our lives, it would be a testament to our doom.

Her chin lifts. "They're quite dramatic and stupid. If I had the short lifespan they all do, I wouldn't be flinging myself through useless wars."

"Glad I can count on you, Harlow," Knox says dryly, a ghost of a smile dancing across his lips.

Harlow clicks her tongue. "Pleasure is all mine, Your Majesty."

Axel clears his throat. "I understand my duties." The second-in-command's forest green eyes flick to his twin. Fear flashes in their depths, there and gone in an instant. "But I'd like to join you," he says, more an order than a request.

The only thing that will ever come before his title, before his duty, is his brother.

Knox's mouth opens to speak, his brows dipping as he frowns.

Don't make him stay, I plead, grateful for our mating bond and the ability to speak privately whenever we please. *Don't force them to separate, not when we're facing the end.*

Firstly, we're not facing the end, and secondly…

"Lenox will take over while you're gone."

Surprise flashes in Lenox's amber eyes, accompanied by a whirlwind of vast emotions. Doubt, worry, joy, pride. With his hand over his heart, Lenox dips his head in a small bow. "It would be my honor."

"It's not permanent, you fool," Harlow snickers. "Rise."

Lenox's cheeks flush. "I know that. I'm just happy to help."

Harlow must have missed the emotions that took over Lenox, and I wish she hadn't. If she saw how he truly felt in that moment, worthy and seen by someone he looks up to, I know she wouldn't have teased him.

"Very well. Nolan, you'll continue with your work—"

"I'm coming too," Nolan grumbles. "I don't trust Delilah to stop our burnt fate."

I'm momentarily astonished that he would so bluntly utter those words until I realize I'm thinking about Nolan, a man who will never think I'm good enough, similar to my father.

"You're talking about the person who saved your life," Harlow sneers.

Nolan's mouth tightens. "Once. We don't know if she will turn human once she crosses the border."

Endless groans and curses fill the foyer.

"Forever the pessimist," Harlow mutters.

Care if I tell them? Knox asks on the bridge.

I wave my hand. *Please for the love of gods, shut him up.*

Knox clears his throat, dropping another bombshell. "Delilah was never human."

Nolan scoffs, mumbling, "And I don't have elongated ears."

Ignoring Nolan, Knox goes on. "When Delilah turned, there was a blast of golden light. This occurred in the *human* lands, not the Fae."

Hazel's blue eyes bore into me as if she could watch the memory herself if she stared long enough.

Ace tilts his head. "Golden light... Are you saying she had magic in the human lands?"

"Not only did she have access to her power in the human lands, but she turned there." Knox angles his jaw to face me, his eyes perusing my body. "I believe the trauma she endured was too much for her mind and her magic took over. Why it was concealed in the first place remains a mystery." Knox snaps a look at Nolan. "Satisfied yet?"

Nolan has the wits to pale.

Knox's eyes harden further. "We need someone to rule over the armies. The demonic creatures could return at a moment's notice."

Nolan straightens. "I understand. However, I'm coming."

I'm jarred by his indifferent, cold tone. I've heard him speak that way to me and even his own court members, but never to his king.

Lenox glares at him out of the corner of his eyes. Axel takes up a defensive position in front of Ace and Hazel.

Harlow openly groans and rolls her eyes. "For gods' sake, can you ever not piss off anyone?" she spits.

"Forgive me for not wanting to leave the lives of my mother and sister in the hands of a flimsy premonition from a girl who's only known about magic for a second!"

Hazel bristles, her lip curling on a low snarl. Ace's protection shield snaps around the pair of them, while Axel's added wall of air makes the trio impenetrable.

Lenox's neck flushes red. "She's saved your life once and will most likely do so twice. Delilah was the one who received the premonition, not you."

I worked alongside Knox for three months, I bled and fought for the people of Aloriah, and I broke the entrapment spell that was placed over their Fae courts for one hundred and fifty years. I returned their magic at full force and Nolan *still* does not trust me.

My earlier thoughts are confirmed. If my destruction of the curse didn't change his view of me, nothing ever will.

And I am done chasing men for validation.

Harlow's steely eyes narrow into thin slits. "Why don't you call her by her name? Lest I remind you, she is not a *girl*, she is a woman," she seethes.

Nolan scoffs. "Hold your tongue with your woman this and woman that."

"How *dare* you speak to me like that!"

"Nolan," Axel growls in warning.

"Your mother and sister would be dead if it weren't for Delilah," Harlow snaps.

Electricity zaps up and down Nolan's arms, sparks jumping between fingertips as if he holds a thunderstorm within the palms of his hands. "You are to *never* speak of my mother and sister."

"But you can speak of your king's mate with disrespect?" Lenox cuts in, molten fire brimming in his eyes.

"Not with my life! She's a—"

Knox's wings flare. The windows behind me shatter. Glass explodes throughout the foyer as the leash on Knox's temper snaps.

Shards harmlessly bounce off the wall of air around me, and then shadows erupt from the edges of the room, flying for his court. One by one they turn silent as a shadowed hand slams over their mouths. Nolan's is the first to close, the shadowed hand cutting off his sentence, his skin bulging around the shadows with the tight force Knox holds against him.

"Considering emotions are heightened at the moment, I'm going to give you leeway and ignore your disgusting words and behavior." Knox's sapphire eyes darken to a near black. "But mark my words, this does *not* mean I tolerate it." Knox strides forward. Each step is as menacing as the last, exuding power and regal grace. It isn't until he stops an inch from Nolan's face do his shoulders begin to quake with the restraint needed to hold back the floodgates on his power and emotions. "If you ever speak of my mate with such disrespect again, I will have no qualms about you losing your tongue."

Nolan's face pales, and those wide hazel eyes move to mine, blinking rapidly as if to apologize. It feels as if Nolan is constantly apologizing to me. I know we have more pressing matters than a Fae's bad temper, yet I can't shake the pleading look in his gaze.

I try to put myself in his shoes, knowing that if it were

Easton, Annie, or Knox, I would do anything possible to get them back, no matter who I hurt in the process.

Without taking my eyes off Nolan I talk down the bond.

Let him come; it's his family. Allow him to feel useful and worthwhile. Otherwise, it will drive him insane having to stay back.

Knox's bewildered eyes snap to me.

He doesn't deserve to come, not with the nonsense he spews.

He shouldn't lose the opportunity to seek answers about his family because he doesn't trust me.

Deep down, Knox knows this to be true too. He simply can't see past the protection the mating bond and his heart demands.

Ignoring the six shadowed hands and their victims, I turn away, throwing over my shoulder, "Nolan can come. Lenox and Harlow are quite capable of taking care of things themselves."

Whether my statement is true or not I find I can't force myself to care. Nor do I begin to worry about overstepping my boundaries. Not as the dream—premonition—replays through my mind on an endless loop.

At the end of the day, if we all perish, it won't matter if I spoke when I shouldn't have, and I certainly won't come between someone trying to reunite with their family members.

The weight of the world is placed on my shoulders again, weighing heavily upon me as I climb the stairs to Knox's room. Using what little remaining energy I have left; I begin to pack.

Quiet footsteps pad behind me before Knox leans in the doorway of his dressing room, crossing his muscular arms over his chest as he stares down at me.

Even drained, my body welcomes the sight, my blood humming with warmth.

"You don't need to pack right this moment."

"Yes, I do. We all need to."

I grab carefully folded tunics and pants, courtesy of Knox's starlight workers, whom Hazel and I originally presumed possessed shadow magic. Knox corrected me one night explaining the rarity of the sisters.

Quadruplets said to be made by the stars themselves, were abandoned at the local priestess's resident's tower. All four Fae possess starlight magic, rare though not uncommon in the northern hemisphere Fae's. Their tell is their raven-black hair, which, upon closer inspection, appears to hold the stars of the night in its strands, sparkling and twinkling as it sways.

Some gossip that starlight magic is similar to the mermaids', and that the stars whisper the secrets of the universe to them. However, others believe their power is more comparable to Knox's, dealing with the shadows of the world.

I for one have never seen them perform magic other than to conceal themselves, since they prefer to remain invisible while they work, and when I asked Knox exactly *what* starlight magic was, he simply gave me a devilish grin and dared me to ask them.

The quadruplets are always kind but their presence is unnerving to be around with how they stare blankly at you, blinking ever so slowly as if their eyes hold the universe within them.

Knox didn't mention how the four unique sisters came to work for him, but I've never been more grateful for their invisible and yet felt presence. They always seem to know exactly what you need…sometimes even before you know yourself.

Gently placing the clothing items in the luggage laid out in the middle of the room presumably for Knox and myself, I note the small tremble in my fingers at what knowledge the sisters must possess.

Knox kneels before me. Despite his earlier statement, he lifts the next set of items and places them gently in the luggage. "When do you want to leave?"

"I know there is work to be done in the cities. You have the meetings with the Queen of Air to reinstate the courts. I presume there are many wards to be restored and there's the matter of breaking the news to the families of those from the in-between all over again. Not to mention—"

Knox cups my cheeks, forcing me to slow. "I will see to it that my affairs are in order. You just tell me when you want to leave."

"But how—"

The corner of his lip twitches. "I'm not sure if you're aware, but I have this wonderful ability to speak into the minds of people, no matter how far they may be. Orders are easy to give."

Right. Of course. I force the words to tumble from my lips before I lose my nerve and feel guilty. "Before dawn. I want to cross the border before the sun rises, under the cover of darkness."

I just want to get this over with.

Knox smirks. "The princess sneaking back into her own lands." When I don't return his teasing smile, Knox drops the contents in his hands, not bothering with the mess he spills.

"Angel, take a moment to breathe."

All the air residing in my lungs escapes me in one harried whoosh. "I can't."

His gentle fingers caress my cheeks. "Why not?"

"I can't let the thoughts take control of my mind." *Or the nerves to take my heart prisoner.* There's no need for me to mention that…because he already knows. We're entwined now, forever linked to one another. He can feel the bustling tension running throughout my body, where it'll grow to the point of a tidal wave, and I'll be unable to do anything as it sweeps me away.

I don't miss the irony of the premonition confirming my worst fear of being lost forever.

Knox cradles my face in his hands, forcing our eyes to connect. "I won't let you get swept away. I meant it when I said as one," he whispers. "I won't let it happen…I refuse to let you disappear."

He cannot keep a promise if he is dead.

It seems Knox doesn't want to think about that tidbit of information. I know he can see it in my eyes, the seed of doubt already planted that I won't be able to save him. It's why no matter the conviction in his promise, I cannot help but fear he will not be able to keep his vow, despite how much he cherishes them.

Pausing, I dare ask, "Are you not afraid?"

"Of course not, I'm the most powerful Fae in all the lands."

The longer I hold his gaze, the more his emotional armor seems to crumble, pooling at our feet.

He clears his throat, his Adam's apple working overtime. "Of course, I am." He rubs his neck. "You'd have to be a fool to watch that premonition and not be. But I'll find a way to come back to you. I always will."

He says the last part with such conviction it almost provides my heart with a false sense of hope.

Almost.

Being sucked into the nothingness felt so surreal my heart floated away from my body to protect me and it's having a hard time coming back down to reality. Or perhaps it abandoned me the moment I saw Knox's decapitated head. I don't blame it for not wanting to beat without him.

Thought after thought pelt the forefront of my mind.

What if I lose him?

What if I get lost myself, knowing that he will never come for me?

Is the demonic army lying in wait? If so, what are they waiting for? Where exactly are they hiding? Why take the Fae with them?

Gods, what if Nolan is never reunited with his family?

What if he's right? What if I send them all to their deaths?

My thoughts cease, pausing to allow one that isn't my own to pass through.

Angel, look at me.

The deep husky voice jars me from my fears. I allow the courage and strength he sends down our bond to float through my body.

"That's it, Angel, come back to me," Knox murmurs.

His gentle strokes and touches along my skin coax my heart to slowly come down to Aloriah once more.

It isn't until I'm fully connected do I feel it all. I gasp in shock, my eyes growing impossibly large. The tidal wave crashes over me, making tears well in my eyes as Knox's sapphire ones soften. It makes me wonder if a part of Knox's heart floats away when mine departs.

"There she is."

I take a stuttering breath, rubbing circles over my chest to ease the pain.

"I'll make a deal with you," he says softly. "If we're unable to stop it, stop them, I'll come with you. I'll float with you through the depthless pit of the universe. For eternity, for however long it consumes us. We'll go together, as one."

I shake my head, the tears that were pooled in my eyes now cascading down my cheeks. Knox's thumb captures each one.

"I will go to the end of the world for you, Angel. Don't rob me of what I want. I'm not requesting, I'm vowing to follow you to the end of the universe."

I don't dare utter anything other than what I feel in my heart.

"As one," I whisper.

"As one."

Chapter Four

Piercing golden eyes stop me in my tracks.

The brush in my hand hovers over a silky, raven-black coat of fur, puffs of air from a thick black snout blowing the loose strands back into my face. The air ruffles my brown waist-length hair, making it flutter around my fighting leathers.

Aurora stomps her front right paw, digging her claws into the soil.

The connection between our souls tightens. Similar to the mating bond, though not as strong, Aurora and I can feel each other's emotions and communicate through them.

A wave of fierce loyalty and protectiveness crashes over me as wisps of tenderness and affection rush for my heart. Sinking deep within myself, I run through the garden in my mind with a carefree smile plastered on my face.

I find comfort and safety in books, the way in which my mind can escape reality and enter a world of my choosing. Every day I've spent time building the garden in my mind to welcome a similar feeling. In this particular garden, there is no fear, anxiety, or imminent thoughts of death. I have created a sanctuary for myself. At the edge of the garden, I rush for the large wooden door, opposite to the one that holds the fierce bond between Knox and me, and fling open the doorway to my and Aurora's soul bond, pouring the love and tenderness I feel down the small riverbed, a pathway made of floating stones.

I began crafting the space shortly after she was attacked by the vulgar city warriors in the Fire Court. I wanted to show her what it felt like to be safe…what it felt like to create your own haven.

"She's proud and grateful to have you as her soul pair."

Hazel's voice pulls me from the garden, plunging me back into reality.

Blinking rapidly, I take in Aurora staring at me. Standing to her full height, she's a magnificent sight to behold.

Being a female griffin, she's smaller than Ace's soul pair griffin—Zephlyn—but that doesn't diminish her strength and ability.

The griffins in Aloriah are enlarged lions with beautiful, feathered wings. Aurora towers over my five-foot-nine frame, the tip of my head only coming to rest by her shoulders. Hence why most griffin and dragon handlers possess wings—it makes for grooming and saddling the majestic creatures an easier feat.

The aerial legion was created centuries ago, during the time in which the seven archangels roamed the Fae lands. It was built to aid the Fae that were sent into battle, fighting alongside the archangels in the callings they received to help those in dire need.

The dragons and griffins fought alongside the Fae and though the majority of Fae can fly, it grew to be a tradition, one of a well-oiled contraction where the three creatures worked together seamlessly.

Aurora snaps her head to Hazel, surprise flashing in her golden depths before she turns back to me and puffs air out of her snout as if to agree with the sentiment.

"How do you know?" I ask.

Hazel's smile grows as she stares at Aurora, the freckles smattering her cheeks rising with the movement. "I can hear her. Animals need to feel comfortable for an earth Fae to hear their inner dialogue."

It completely slipped my mind that Hazel possesses the ability to communicate with animals. I turn to Aurora in awe.

"Can soul pairs hear each other's thoughts?" I ask Hazel.

Hazel comes to stand beside me, stroking Aurora behind her ear and eliciting a deep purr from the griffin. "No, they're just incredibly in touch with themselves and those around them. Especially their soul pair."

The corner of my lip tugs upward. "Intuitive and perceptive?"

"In simple terms, yes. Some say that griffins and dragons contain psychic powers and can read people."

My gaze slides to Hazel. "Speaking of soul pairs, I hear congratulations are in order."

Hazel's cheeks flush as red as her hair. "Thank you."

My voice grows somber. "I'm glad that you were able to find happiness again and with someone like Ace. You two deserve each other, along with all the happiness in this world."

"Me too," Hazel says solemnly. The reminder of her daughter Luna and the pain of her loss flashes across her face. Until she cranes her neck as Ace calls her name from across the front yard. With a simple kiss on Aurora's snout, Hazel is off, bouncing over to Ace and Zephlyn, that carefree smile plastered across her face once more.

"I want all the details later!" I call out, elated to be able to return the teasing sentiment she gave me for months over Knox.

My gaze lingers on the happy pair, giggling and wrapping their arms around one another, before it strays, roaming the front yard where the rest of the court lounges by their personal belongings. Magic swirls in the air, electrifying the ocean breeze, courtesy of Lenox, Harlow, Nolan, and Ace as they tease one another.

It's a sight to behold, witnessing the Fae's magic be returned to them. I thought I knew power when I entered these lands all those months ago, but it is nothing compared to the astronomical amount they possess now.

There's so much magic within just this small group that I am almost afraid to be standing amongst them in case I get hit by one of Lenox's flying flame arrows or a lightning strike from Nolan.

They're all galivanting in the yard, acting as if this might not be the last time they step foot on these grounds. The last time they will ever see their home. The last time they'll see Azalea. The last time some of them will see each other.

They all saw the premonition…how can they carry on as if we don't know the end is near?

The premonition was so real I still feel the remnants of it hours later.

And it's because of that lingering feeling that I tip my head back, close my eyes, and cherish the cool air I breathe, the stars sparkling in the late night sky, the soil beneath my boots, and the sounds of those around me not screaming for mercy but squealing with joy.

I inhale the rich spring smells, cherishing my Fae hearing for picking up on the ocean waves crashing against the seaside cliffs below and as I flutter open my eyes, I catalog every minuscule detail of the place I have come to love—the home I wished upon stars for.

I memorize the seven archangel statues that are placed around the front courtyard to overlook and protect the home that has housed the Essence Court royals for centuries. The cream-white paint coating the historical walls that will hopefully stand to hold another thousand years' worth of memories, and the gray brickwork that trims the standing mansion. The sound of the wrought iron gate squeaking at the front entrance as it opens. The large double mahogany doors that barely anybody uses in favor of teleportation. The way the moon illuminates the mammoth of a house at night, shining on the glass doors lining the various terraces.

"Continue thinking like that and you'll summon your death," Knox growls.

I startle at his piercing rumble. The cocky bastard may be a weapon in himself with his large size and rippling muscles, yet his training has taught him how to be as silent as a cat and sneak up on his prey.

Knox chooses when he wants to be heard.

"You frightened me!" I scold.

"Your thoughts frighten me."

My voice grows soft. "Knox—"

"No," he cuts me off. "If you leave these gates believing you will die, you will not return, and I refuse for you to kill us both. We deserve a long life together, Angel."

As one, he whispers down the bond.

As one, I parrot, hoping to ease the tension lining his body.

Knox is right. The dread coiled in my gut will only get me killed, along with those I care about.

Aloriah and this planet included.

"I'm sorry," I whisper.

"Don't apologize for your fear. You have every right to feel it. Just know that I'll be here to remind you every step of the way who you truly are and what you're capable of."

A small smile touches my lips. His faith in my abilities makes my anxiety lessen a claw in my heart.

Leaning forward, his lips brush my forehead. "You must be strong as you face this, but on the days where you cannot find the courage, I'll be strong for the both of us."

This man is going to make my heart implode.

Rising on the balls of my feet, Knox meets me halfway, lowering his head so I can place a featherlight kiss against his lips. I revel in the electricity that flows between us, passion and heat that expands between not only our bodies and mating bond, but our minds, hearts, and souls.

"Thank you," I whisper.

Knox rests his forehead against mine. "Are you ready?"

"As I'll ever be." It's not a lie, because I don't think I'll ever be ready to face this.

Knox's hand travels down my forearm, linking our fingers as we stride to the others. Lifting his free hand, shadows swirl, scattering from his palm before encasing the pile of luggage. One moment, darkness overtakes the pile, and in the next, it simply disappears, gone in the blink of an eye.

I gasp. "How—where—" Knox smirks as I stare in awe. "Where does it all go?"

Knox strides to where the luggage was a moment before, pulling me along with him before he pauses, bending as he carefully plucks a rock off the ground.

"Hold out your hand."

Dumbfounded, I follow his lead and quizzically hold out my palm.

Knox gently places the rock in my hand. My brow furrows at the care in which he treats the rock, seeing nothing out of the ordinary. Until my Fae sight takes over, zeroing in on every minuscule detail.

Where there should be a crumbling gravel courtyard rock are instead bags upon bags of luggage. Every single piece that was just sitting here a mere moment before.

I gasp, then immediately slap my hand over my mouth, frightened of my breath blowing everyone's belongings away. "You shrunk it." My gaze darts between Knox's cocky smile and the items.

Lenox whistles. "Wait until you see Knox in action! Now that his power has fully returned to him, we all need to remain on his good side."

"Who said you were on my good side?"

Lenox's smile drops the instant Knox's face remains impassive. The energy between the two Fae grows taut until the corner of Knox's lip twitches, a dark chuckle rumbling from his chest.

Lenox's relief is tangible in the air.

Harlow rolls her eyes. "With a mouth like yours, it's a wonder as to why you're ever on his good side."

"We can never have a nice moment with the two of you," Axel mutters.

Lenox scoffs. "That was all Low and Knox!"

Axel winks, mouthing, *Good side.*

Cutting off Lenox's protests, Knox teases, "We will enjoy the memory of your humor for the road but it's time to leave."

Lenox mutters under his breath as he stalks off to say goodbye to the twins, Nolan and Hazel. I don't miss the carrots he sneaks to Zephlyn as he hugs Ace.

Harlow saunters over to us. Her honey-brown eyes dart between the both of us, her lips pinching before she jumps, flinging her arms around our necks and pulling us down to her small height.

"Please don't die," she whispers solemnly.

The vulnerability shocks me for a brief moment. I'm frozen until my body kicks into gear, and I wrap my arms around her. Ignoring Knox's words of encouragement earlier, I memorize Harlow's heart-shaped face. The way her eyes crinkle in the corners when she bestows upon us her dazzling smile, the way her lips twitch when dishing out her sultry words. I catalog it all to memory and cling to her a little tighter.

"We'll see you soon, Low. Don't burn my court down while I'm gone," Knox teases, trying to lighten the mood despite his wavering voice.

She nods her head hastily as if the movement can make his statement true. Harlow takes a deep breath before ripping herself away. "Don't bring any humans back with you," she declares before stalking away.

I'd be offended, yet I dare say her remarks are to save face and make light of the farewell. To lessen the guilt Knox feels over his decision to leave Lenox and Harlow behind.

Lenox's amber eyes are full of pain and fear as he slowly approaches. I allow him to wrap his large frame around mine, squeezing gently. "Please take care of him," he whispers in my ear.

My throat burns as I nod and pull away, allowing the two men to have a moment alone before we leave.

Knox's words trail me as I stride toward Aurora.

"The moment you hear anything about where they've disappeared to, I want you to contact me. I trust you, Lenox. You can do this."

Knox is full of wise words this evening, and it amazes me every time how well he reads others, seemingly being able to say exactly what the person needs to hear.

I'm beginning to piece together just how powerful Knox's

abilities are. It was mentioned before, but to watch his powers start to blossom after all the years they've been silenced is a beautiful thing.

What a powerful gift for a king, to be able to communicate with his court members in their minds from the other side of the country.

For my own peace of mind, I triple-check that the latches and satchels are correctly strapped to Aurora's back before mounting the glorious griffin, her black coat blending into the darkness of the night. I can't say the same for Zephlyn, whose stark white coat shines as bright as a star.

Initially, we planned only for Aurora to join us, considering the others knew how to *use* their wings and don't need a flying creature to travel. However, when trying to get the griffin out of her sleeping quarters early this morning, Zephlyn blocked the door, refusing to budge. Ace and Knox agreed to bring him—Ace out of wanting to be with his soul pair, and Knox wanting to give his court member and friend time to spend with his soul pair…in case of the unfortunate event that my premonition comes to fruition.

Reaching behind me, I pull a carrot free from one of the satchels and give it to Aurora. She gobbles it down in one bite.

"Now remember that humans are fragile little pests. You must handle them with care." Harlow waves her hand in the air. "Like a wine glass."

I choke out a laugh, devoid of humor. "Thanks, Low."

She simply shrugs. "You're Fae now. You're not weak." Her eyes widen as she claps her hands. "Ooh! And bring me back a corsage dress from Sector Three! They have the most delightful patterns."

Nolan rolls his eyes. "We're not going shopping, Harlow."

"Sector Three is still the district of textiles but I think Nolan is right," I shock myself by saying.

Lenox moves forward and wraps an arm around Harlow, cutting her off before she can spew more things to annoy Nolan.

"Send us memories, will you?" Lenox's eyes light up with excitement. "I want to know what the human lands look like now."

Nolan throws his hands in the air. "Is everyone ignoring the fact that we're going because death is waiting around the corner to claim us all?"

Harlow claps her hands together in front of her chest. "Oh, Nolan, thank you for reminding me! My clumsy woman brain forgot why you were all departing!" The sarcasm that oozes from her makes my lips twitch despite the topic at hand.

"At least I'm going to fight. When my children ask me what I did to save the world, I won't have to answer them with a measly *staying back to clean*."

Harlow's eyes narrow into small slits. "Don't forget to strike with the pointy end of the sword again." She doesn't stay to watch Nolan's cheeks flush pink, nor to watch us leave. In true Harlow fashion, she spins, strutting inside the house with a resounding slam of the door.

Lenox, however, never leaves the front courtyard, even as we take off and the house grows as small as a blip. I swear I can still see his large hand waving, his worried gaze taking in all our forms as if it's the last time he will ever see us.

Flying away from Azalea and the Essence Court with a sour taste in my mouth, a hollow pit in my stomach, and a heavy heart, I breathe in the fresh air to try and calm my frayed nerves. Despite the deep breaths, I can't shake the longing in my heart and soul as it begs for me to return to the city I've come to love.

My heart thumps wildly in my chest until Knox comes up beside me. His large iridescent wings beat in a steady rhythm, looking to all the world as if flying is easier than breathing.

As one, our minds, souls, and bodies move in sync as we extend our arms, reaching for each other until our fingertips graze, that all too familiar electricity heightening.

I cling to Knox, my heart settling at the touch of his skin.

We fly for hours—Knox having decided against teleporting to reserve our energy for the unknown—gliding over mountaintops and through dense clouds. The streams of water running through the city of Cardania as we pass over lull me into a calm state. Preparing my heart for the imminent border, the mountain lines marking the end of the Fae lands and the beginning of the human ones.

The beginning of my end.

Aurora banks sharply.

The sudden movement jolts my body to the side. Clinging to Aurora's harness, the only thing stopping me from falling thousands of feet, my nails create half-moon dents in my palms with the strength needed to hold on.

Aurora drops, making my stomach plummet from the sheer plunge, only for her to rise, climbing higher than before. The maneuver places me back in her saddle.

Knox swoops beside me, his gaze wild as he searches the grounds below. "She must see something we can't." Knox's face turns ashen when Zephlyn swoops next to Aurora, his hackles raised.

Hazel clings to Ace as he calls over the treacherous winds, "He won't let me steer him back!"

My hands shake as I pat Aurora, sinking my fingers into the thick silky fur as I scan the horizon. The moon has begun to fade, the sky lightening to a pale navy blue as the unmistakable Deyanira Mountain ridges rise before us, growing with the shortening distance.

Nolan and Axel move into formation, flanking the back of Aurora and Zephlyn as Knox flies at the front, his impenetrable shield protecting us as we fly.

"Knox!" I call, as Aurora's hackles rise, her low growl mingling with the rushing water of the Mason River.

The glint of gold has my heart dropping and my pulse skyrocketing. I shake my head profusely, praying the movement can erase the sight. Acting on instinct, tingles race up and down my frame, my magic and mind protecting me as it makes my body wholly invisible.

The shock running through my system doesn't allow me to react to the fact that Knox disappears before my very eyes too, my golden magic racing down the bond and joining our two hearts, protecting him. My mind is solely focused on the thousands of soldiers lined along the Mason River. The army set up between the two mountain peaks, blocking where the river flows between the human and Fae lands.

Gold and black stains the land, as if a plague.

Knox's voice floats through my mind. *Is that…*

The king's army? Yes.

The fastest way to travel to the human lands from the courts for those without wings is by the Mason River and the king has blocked it. Is it to stop the Fae from entering, or to stop the humans from escaping?

The closer we fly to the Deyanira Mountains, to the thousands of men stationed at the border, the more my body seems to pull back, my muscles growing taut as they try to flee.

Bile rises in my throat, acid coating my tongue as the men begin to take formation, rotating shifts as a new day rises. The night shift heads for the thousands of tents lined along the riverbank while fresh, starry-eyed soldiers take up a spot along a makeshift wooden platform—*impossible.*

A wooden bridge stretches across the vast river, a few feet over the rushing water, tall enough to accommodate rainwater and yet low enough to stop any boats that wish to pass. In the last three months since my departure from the human lands, after floating along the Mason River myself, a bridge as large as Knox's garden has been built.

Thousands of men with swords, blades, knives, and crossbows stand at attention along the bridge, every eye focused on the water ahead and the forests to the sides.

The king moved quickly.

Groans at my back have me craning my neck. I frown as Axel and Nolan scowl down at the twitching movements of their limbs. As if they can't control the convulsions. Hazel gasps, her features twisting in pain as her stomach is yanked backward by an invisible force. She clings to Ace, his body spasming in Zephlyn's seat. Even a low whine comes from the white griffin, making Aurora's head snap between the creature and the impending mountains.

Knox's pain-filled groans fill my mind, pulling my attention to my mate flying in front of all the others. My invisibility flickers, Knox's body flashing in and out as his body crumbles into a ball of pain.

"Knox!"

Not a moment after the scream rips from my throat does my body do the same as his.

Agony consumes me. I cry out as I curl into a ball, trying

Heir of Broken Kingdom 47

to make myself as small as possible, as if it can stop my body from convulsing and shaking.

The suffering grows to an unimaginable height, and my magic withers, screaming at me to move, to run, to escape… but I can't. All I can do is hold on as the pain overtakes my body.

Knox's protection shield drops a moment before mine snaps and breaks away.

Wincing, I lift my pounding head and search for Knox. His anguished scream has me reeling, pushing through the insufferable torment as I grip Aurora's harness. My very bones protest as I haul myself into a sitting position.

Then a moment of silence falls over us all like a blanket.

The pain stops.

Pausing for a moment to give us all a second to breathe… before it shoves its final dagger into our hearts.

Knox drops from the sky, clutching his chest as he wails in agony.

A cry of shock flies from my mouth, not only at the sight of Knox dropping mid-air but for my magic. The beautiful golden well near my sternum, beside my heart, is simply gone, my power taken—ripped from me.

The unbearable pain and agony of its sudden silence is enough to steal my breath. Enough to make me collapse. Enough to make my body betray me.

I barely turn my head to the side in time, my cheek instead of my nose dropping against the hard leather of Aurora's harness. I lay on top of her, unable to move, utterly helpless as I watch Axel, Nolan, and Zephlyn—Ace and Hazel on the griffin's back—plummet from the sky.

Dread slices through my heart as I race through my mind, through the beautiful garden I've begun to build, and fling open the door between Knox and me. The smile that covers my face as I take in the beautiful flowers dotting the bridge and the plunge below to the ragging waterfall drops the moment my eyes lift to find his mind quiet…shrouded in shadows.

Our mating bond silent.

Aurora's roar is full of one thing—terror.

I manage to clutch her fur, my fingers clinging onto her for dear life as she drops faster than ever before. My vision swims, the edges blurring as shadows crawl for me.

I shake my head to try and fight them off, only to lose.

Darkness consumes me as Aurora howls.

Chapter Five

Wetness trickles down my cheeks and nose. A weight presses on my chest. My ears pop, allowing the quiet whining to fill them.

The sensation of falling won't stop, my mind spinning as a layer of fog drifts through, dense enough to make me forget where I am. Fluttering open my eyes, I'm met with deep golden ones that seem to plead with me. I try to lift my arm to pat Aurora, only to find it's far too heavy to move.

Panic settles in her golden eyes.

I'm surprised to find my throat dry as I wheeze, "What's wrong?"

Aurora boops me, her nose nudging my head to the side. My vision blurs from the quick movement, the dense forest floor and canopy of trees multiplying.

Why is she worried about the forest?

When my leg twitches, spasming on its own, I manage to lift my heavy head, finding my legs dressed in my fighting leathers and boots. The heavy shoes tethering me to this world.

Why am I dressed like this?
This isn't my room.
Why am I in my fighting leathers?
Why can't I remember?

A large shadow lies to my left. It takes a few rapid blinks to clear the dullness from my mind and the blurry vision clinging to the corners of my eyes. My brows furrow as I try to place what it is.

It's shaped like a person.

My eyes snap open wide, memories assaulting my mind.

Knox.

Scrambling to sit upright, my body fights against me. The pain from before ripples in, consuming every nerve ending as the adrenaline wears off. Aurora places her head on my back, gently pushing me forward to the unmoving figure.

I clamber not only on the forest floor but in my mind, in my soul, as I yank on the silent mating bond.

"Knox," I plead, my voice shaking.

My chest caves in with a sob when I see he's face down on the ground. Every second that passes where he doesn't move is another dose of fear consuming my body, propelling me forward. I turn his body over, groaning at his heavy weight.

The only thing that holds my heart together is the moment his chest rises, slow and shallow. I run my fingers down his unmoving face, tracing his soft skin and sharp lines.

With every stroke of my fingers, I beg him to wake, going so far as to grab his shoulders and shake with the little amount of energy I can gather, a strength that surprises me.

Aurora stalks away, her steps slow and weary, and I follow her movement with my eyes toward four other large figures lying on their backs. They're unmoving, yet their chests rise steadily. Zephlyn's large body is wrapped around them, protecting them even as his eyes lie closed.

Aurora licks each of their faces, puffing air out of her snout onto them to bring them to consciousness.

My heart catches.

The utter exhaustion tells me enough of what happened. *How* we all miraculously fell thousands of feet to the forest floor without severe injuries or death.

Aurora flew us to safety.

Aurora, who's smaller than most griffins, caught another griffin and carried six Fae adults.

A tear runs down my cheek as gratitude swells within my chest, along with a swarm of strong emotions. They swim in my eyes, in every inch of my body and Aurora's shallow blink tells me that despite not being able to feel the bond that lies between us, silent along with the mating bond, she understands.

She knows with just a look how thankful and indebted I am to her selfless act.

Holding onto Knox with a death grip, I gaze at our surroundings. The dense forest is different from the Fae lands, somehow not as bright, the canopy of trees and land missing the magic that makes the Fae forests beautiful.

Magic.

The reminder of it sends a chill down my spine and tears pool in my eyes as the stark realization jolts the breath from my lungs. Because instead of my golden magic twirling, dancing and shining in my well...it's frozen, impenetrable.

"No," I choke.

I begin shaking Knox in earnest, begging him to wake.

Groans surround me, gasps and cries, yet I only have eyes for Knox. Aurora's steps are silent as she pads back over, her presence only known when a large shadow falls over me. Lying beside me in silent support, she peers up at me with a soft vulnerability.

"It's okay, he'll wake up soon," I tell her, yet I say the words more to comfort myself.

Axel gasps. "No. Not again, we just got it back!"

Hazel's small fearful voice makes me turn. "Is it—"

"Our magic is gone," Nolan states coldly.

The slowness it takes for the others to drag themselves into seated positions tells me everything I thought was true. The bone-jarring pain was caused by our magic being stripped away.

"Magic wards," I whisper. "There's no other explanation. My magic is still there, it's just…frozen." I turn back to Knox, his head lying in my lap as I brush my hand through his raven-black hair. Staring at his peaceful face, I hold onto the sight, knowing that when he awakes, he will be in agony. "Why is it taking him so long to wake?" I murmur to no one in particular.

Axel crawls to me—to his king.

His brows furrow at his still form. "He is the most powerful Fae. The amount of pain he must have felt…"

My chest feels as if it's cleaving in two. "Knox, baby, wake up."

Axel moves away, leaving me to Aurora and Knox as he talks to Hazel, Ace, and Nolan. Their whispers drown into a quiet drone of mumbles.

I keep checking the bridge between our minds and the quiet mating bond that should be lively with his joy and laughter, his emotions and thoughts. Where his voice should be filling the space, teasing me endlessly for being so worried about an immortal Fae, it's as silent as my mind.

But the premonition made one truth as clear as water: Fae may be immortal, they may live for thousands of years and they may be one of the strongest creatures to roam the Fae lands, but they are not indestructible. They bleed and feel pain just as much as any human. They are not impenetrable beings. They simply delay the inevitable.

Despite the conviction in my epiphany, I still pause, waiting for Knox to smirk, goading me about how he is the most powerful Fae king in all the lands.

Yet none of that happens, even as his eyelids begin to flutter.

Knox's jaw falls open, his arms coming up to cradle his body as a deep, gravelly wail tears from his throat. He rolls toward me and curls into a ball. His chest rises and falls rapidly, sharp breaths escaping through gritted teeth. His voice cracks as he screams again.

My heart plummets at watching him suffer. I rub my hand up and down his back as if it can ward off the agony he feels. The worried glances adorning his court's faces have the fear within me rising.

"What do I do?" I ask.

Throughout my life, I have felt unmistakable hopelessness as I watched my people suffer from the cruel ruling of the king. Yet the despair I feel in this moment doesn't begin to compare.

"My magic," he sobs.

"Wards were placed over the border. It froze our powers," I whisper.

I may not be able to hear his voice through the bonds, but that doesn't mean I don't know Knox and what he needs.

This very situation is what Knox trained and prepared me for, to not rely on my magic. To not allow it to become my crutch and let the twenty years of combat training and swordsmanship trickle into nothing but a distant memory. What he didn't prepare me for, however, is the gaping hole in my chest. Without my magic, it feels as if I'm missing an intricate part of my body, a vital organ.

My eyes linger over Knox's chest. If I feel as if I'm missing an intricate part of my very being, I cannot imagine the utter agony coursing through him.

I wonder if he feels as if his very soul was ripped from him.

I know the look all too well that falls over Knox's eyes. *Failure.* "All of our belongings, food, water…everything we need was shrunk—"

Nolan scoffs. "Now you can't unshrink it. Lovely."

Before he can utter any more of his venomous words, I snarl, "If you have nothing helpful to contribute then I suggest you refrain from speaking."

"Go scout the perimeter and make sure our king isn't more vulnerable than he already is," Axel orders.

He rolls his eyes. "Of course, I'm the one you send off."

Nolan leaves, muttering a string of curses under his breath. The set of tattooed wings spanning across the front of Axel's neck moves as he grinds his jaw.

I run my fingers down Knox's face gently, relief flooding me as I find his eyes closed once more, his features slack from pain. It's better for him to remain asleep as his body works through the agony.

With a small wince, I lean over to Aurora, where even during sleep, exhaustion wracks her features. Careful not to disturb her, I unclip the satchels from her harness and pull the bags over to my empty side.

"Lucky, we have this," I murmur. Sorting through the contents, I separate the canteens and food. "We have enough water to share for roughly two days if we are careful with the rations. The food, however, will be a problem."

Staring at six apples, a handful of carrots, freshly cut lamb wrapped in linen, and an assortment of nuts, I slide my ice blue eyes to Aurora. "The food was packed for her," I explain.

Ace jumps up, rushing over to Zephlyn's sleeping form, shockingly next to Aurora.

When did he move next to her?

Unstrapping the satchels attached to Zephlyn's harness, Ace comes back, dumping the contents next to my pile. Apples, oranges, and cut meat tumble from the leather bag.

Ace's gaze roams over the food. The skin between his brows crinkles, a deep groove forming as he frowns in concentration. A lump builds in my throat. Easton had a nearly identical concentration face; I used to tease him endlessly about the adorable expression.

"I don't think this will be able to sustain us for more than a day…not while our bodies recover from losing our magic," Ace says.

Axel steps forward as second-in-command, the tension from moments before rolling off his shoulders as Axel does what he does best. "Once Nolan returns, I'll order him to scour the area and search for food while Aurora and Knox rest."

I don't question why he doesn't offer to complete the task himself, not with the way his eyes cannot seem to stay focused on anything other than his king sleeping in my arms.

"I'll search for fresh water." Hazel's eyes snap to mine, already knowing that I was going to protest. "I know better than anyone here how to find fresh water. I practically became an expert at it for Luna."

My heart catches at the name of her daughter. The innocent little girl that was taken—ripped from Hazel's arms the very first day the demonic creatures descended upon the Fae courts and attacked.

I dip my chin, resigned to the fact that Hazel asked me to stop coddling her. Despite the instinct to protect her, I know she's right. My fear of losing my only friend, Easton, has been the driving force behind my fear of something happening to Hazel.

"I'll go with her," Ace adds softly, making the worry in my chest disperse.

Thank you, I mouth.

Aurora whimpers, fear chasing her in sleep until I rest my back against her large form, and her whines slowly drown into nothing. I drag Knox closer to me, settling him between my legs. I hope he remains unconscious until the pain ebbs away.

Ace and Hazel take off in various directions of the quiet forest. The following silence is deafening.

Digging my fingers into the forest floor, I lean my head back on Aurora and close my eyes.

I'm back, Easton.

Nolan appears through the tree line hours later. The grim expression marring the blonde Fae male is enough to make Axel jump to his feet and my back straighten.

"What is it?" I whisper, cautious of Knox asleep in my lap.

Nolan juts his chin to the space beside me. "How many weapons do you have in your satchel?"

I note the tension in Nolan's shoulders, how he can't seem to keep his attention on me as I speak. In fact, he can't focus on any one thing.

He's watching the forest.

"Why?" Axel asks warily, his eyes tracking Nolan's as if he can spot the threat his friend found.

Nolan shares a look with Axel, the fleeting moment there and gone before Nolan turns to me.

"The forest is littered with the king's men, I dare say scouring the area for us…for any Fae that manages to cross the border and move through the wards." Nolan's jaw clenches before he can't contain his anger and spits, "Your father is throwing a hunting party."

My canines flare on a low growl. "That human is not my father."

The growl costs me. Knox's eyes flutter open, the glassy sapphire gaze locking on me. "Angel."

Ignoring Nolan and the ever-present irritation the sight of his face invokes, I focus on Knox. "How are you feeling?" I ask, my heart aching that I'm in a position where I must ask the question out loud.

I wish more than anything in this moment that I could feel him through the bond and know exactly what he needed and hear his cunning drawl in my head telling me to stop fussing over him. I never thought I took the ability of our communication for granted, but now I know that I have.

Knox's face flushes, lips flattening into a thin white line as he pulls himself up. "As if a dragon landed on me." Looking from Aurora and Zephlyn's sleeping forms to Axel's grim face he asks, "What did I miss?"

"The king's men are covering every square inch of this forest and mountain. Littering it like a pack of wolves." Axel takes a deep breath, cutting a quick glare in Nolan's direction. "Nolan was just asking Delilah how many weapons she has."

Quickly retrieving the satchel next to Aurora, my brows

furrow. How much energy did she use? I understand Zephlyn's need for sleep—being a rare griffin with magic is a blessing in the aerial legion. That blessing, however, is the very thing that caused him to drop out of the sky like a dead weight. He'll need just as much, if not more, rest than the others as his body recovers from his loss of power.

But Aurora is just resting from the strength she exerted in saving us. I'm grateful, but I can't stop worry from filling my chest, wondering just how far she pushed herself to do so.

Swallowing thickly, I force myself to focus on one problem at a time, pleading with my anxiety to work with me and not against me. Turning back to Knox while ignoring the insistent glare Nolan sends my way, I dump the weapons between the four of us.

Carefully picking up the dragon pommel sword before anyone else touches it, I sheath it at my back. Right now, I'm grateful to have the gift Knox gave me and the sword that represents Easton in my possession.

After handing Knox my next best sword, Axel and Nolan each take one for themselves, inspecting the blades through a warrior's eye. There are three blades left, enough for Ace and Hazel too.

But I wish I had brought more armory.

"The one time I hand over my damned sword," Nolan grumbles under his breath, his eyes flitting to Knox's pocket where the shrunken weapon lies. At Axel's glare, one that would make most men scurry away, Nolan amends, "I suppose this will do."

"It's not as if we're not weapons ourselves," I remind him. "Losing our magic doesn't lessen the enhanced senses of the Fae body."

Axel assesses the sword he picked. "We have the upper hand with strength. However, they have the numbers—"

A bloodcurdling scream pierces the air, silencing Axel.

I know that scream. The sound has haunted my memories and chased me through sleep ever since I heard it in a shared memory.

Hazel.

Chapter Six

Instinct has me propelling forward, the pain that was lingering long forgotten as I snatch the spare blade from the ground. I don't bother wasting time to see who follows, not while her terrified scream still rings in my ears.

Where's Ace? Is he still with her?

I suppose Axel had the same thought, his powerful legs pushing him to run faster as if the very wind carried us. I would believe it was Axel's doing, manipulating the air around us with his power, yet none of us have access to magic.

Perhaps Mother Gaia herself is assisting us, gifting light and air as we save Hazel from whatever horrid act made that sound rip from her throat.

Despite the loss of magic, we still possess the bodies of honed immortal weapons. Enhanced strength, speed, sight, scent, and hearing. Using those gifted senses, I push myself, the forest blurring around me, the canopy of trees blending into a green canvas. Swirls of brown and green mingling as if

I were running through an artist's shop, the paint leaking together.

The pain is still trying to swallow me whole, yet the adrenaline coursing through my bloodstream allows me to keep pace with Axel.

Without magic it feels impossible to locate her, the forest carrying her scream across hundreds of miles.

It isn't until the rushing of water joins her pleas do we find her.

Under different circumstances, I might have been inspired and would have been in awe of the breathtaking view.

Hundreds of purple water lilies float through a calm waterhole stream, bumping into green lily pads, while dragonflies from all colors of the rainbow buzz between the florals. The narrow stream flows around endless rocks and boulders. Yet the loud sound comes from a waterfall, which only aids the stream's beauty. Trickling over the cliffside into various small pools before running down into the stream, the water is surprisingly blue. A shade of blue, so light, you could place your hand in the water and not tell the difference between air and water.

I'm not surprised Hazel found it, though I cannot say that to her.

Axel and I skid to a stop, dirt spraying beneath our boots.

"Wait!" I hiss, flinging my hand out and catching Axel's arm. As if I could stop him from inflicting the carnage I know is simmering beneath his skin toward the soldier holding an iron dagger to Ace's throat.

Ice runs down my spine.

Black and gold, the house colors of the king.

Hazel dangles upside down behind him, her ankle held by a snare while crimson red blood runs down her pale thigh. Tears stream down her face as she stares at her mate.

Axel's hand moves before I can blink, whipping out a dagger so fast that the next thing that happens is impossible, or it should be.

Iron wraps around Axel's wrist before he can fling the blade at the soldier's skull.

I'm unsure whether Axel's sharp cry is one of outrage or pain until iron wraps around my throat. A collar, choking off my air supply.

"I assure you this is not a wise decision. In fact, I assure you it is the least intelligible decision you will ever make in your pathetic life because if you do not remove that dagger from his neck at once, you will no longer have one," Axel growls, viciously low.

The human soldier cocks his head, his beady eyes hollow and dead as if no life beats behind them.

Why is he not scared?

Axel takes a menacing step forward. "Lower the blade if you cherish your life."

"I'll take that under suggestion." A gleeful, cunning smirk spreads across the soldier's face as he places a finger to his lips, feigning to ponder. "Motion rejected."

A cold, humorless rumble floats from Axel. "Stupid waste of a human."

"Won't be saying that in a moment." The soldier winks.

Before I can unsheathe my dragon sword, iron clamps down on my wrist and a blade slashes the extra sword from my hand. Iron daggers are placed against Axel's neck as he stares helplessly at his brother.

"We have you outnumbered, Fae," he spits.

The undeniable sound of the dragon sword being unsheathed behind my back makes my eyes flare with rage.

Don't look at my face, don't look at my face, don't look at my face.

I shake my head, letting the long brown strands of my hair obscure my features.

"We're going to be eating well tonight, lads! A thousand for each Fae!"

Chuckles go up around the forest. My stomach sinks at the noise, indicating just how many there are.

The one with a blade to Ace's neck drops his smile. "Cuff the abominations."

My body physically jolts forward at the word. *Abomination.* It's exactly what the king would spew when magic or creatures were mentioned alongside the Fae. I see the soldiers of Aloriah still follow the king's word blindly, as if the world was created within his very hands.

A low growl rumbles from my chest before I can stop it. How could these soldiers follow the king so blindly and listen to his preposterous orders? Is it worth the supposed safety offered to the families of those with men and women in service?

"I will gut you if you so much as touch them," I snarl.

The soldier at my back shoves me forward by the iron collar, only to haul me back, a short and quick shaking that makes my head snap, my neck cracking at the odd angle.

"I'll take pleasure in tying you up. Perhaps I'll tape that mouth of yours." A dirty finger slides down my cheek, over the strands of my hair.

The moment I feel the hand on my shoulder slip, I make my move and reach for the dagger hidden within my leathers at my calf. I wrap my hand around the hilt and lift it with a snarl, my canines flaring.

My arm pulls back to give the soldier a scar worth their laughter, only for four more hands to latch onto my skin and clothes. Another yanks me by the collar once more. The sudden intrusion has me crying out in shock at just how many soldiers are behind me.

The owner of the finger comes to stand before me, his lips thinned into a tight line. The thunderous expression that crosses his features is one I know all too well, and it shouldn't be a shock to me, but it is.

After feeling impossibly strong for a few passing months, my body snaps back to what it's once always known—hypervigilance. As if the fear never truly left, it just sank lower within my body, biding its time. But I certainly feel it now.

My body locks up, my heart pounding as I wait for the inevitable.

The soldier's hand pulls up and then comes down hard, striking my cheek with a loud clap. My head snaps sideways.

I already know that he didn't hit me hard enough to split my cheek, and how sad is it that I know the differences in hits and what type of harm they cause my body?

Axel cries out beside me, writhing at the ground beneath him. A few more soldiers join to hold him back. I swallow thickly, avoiding his eyes as I lift my head to the soldier who is now grinning from ear to ear.

"Well, well, what do we have here?" He clicks his tongue. "Never thought I'd see the day. How sorrowful, to have such potential only to wash up as this filth on our border."

"What is it, Jared?" the one at my back asks.

Jared.

I mark the name like a promise. One that I should have made to myself and the little girl within me long ago. That those who hurt me will not simply walk away.

Jared grins. "Forgot about four thousand, boys. This one is worth thirty."

A mammoth of a man steps out from the shadows of the forest, his brows drawn and gait steady as his eyes lock on me. The size of the soldier makes me physically cower away, even with the Fae strength coursing through my muscles.

He stops a few feet from me, placing his fat fingers on his hips. "I'll be damned." A coy smile grows across his lips. "The traitor heir."

Traitor.

Cheers and whistles ring out around the forest as soldiers celebrate their new capture.

A shuttering breath escapes my dry throat, my skin flushing hot to the point sweat glides down my neck. A different kind of hurt and panic overtakes my body. Betrayal. Hot, burning betrayal at the bounty the king has placed over my head.

The man I share blood with…has marked his own as a traitor.

Thirty thousand. That's all I'm worth to him.

I suppose it's a mercy in itself they're not killing me on sight.

Although, the more I ponder, the more I realize there is no mercy to be found in that. The king wants me alive to do his own bidding. To act out whatever punishment he deems suitable. After all, when it came to my mother and me, he never ordered others to do his dirty work. No, he *reveled* in acting out our punishments. He enjoyed marking and maiming us.

The dirt-covered soldier holding the iron blade to Ace's throat chuckles darkly as he drags the blade up to the underside of his ear. "This one's ears will make a fine decoration. Perhaps for the mantel."

Axel growls, resulting in more swords digging deeper into his back. Despite the blades, Axel keeps thrashing, kicking up dirt and leaves as he grits his teeth and roars in outrage.

"Control him!" Jared barks.

More soldiers appear from the tree line, adding more blades and bodies to the pile on Axel.

Jared flicks a blade in his hand, pointing it at him. "Move another inch and this flies through your head."

He heaves in rage, blood running down his face.

The mammoth of a man whistles, the sound traveling far and wide, and it doesn't take long for the remaining soldiers who had kept hidden in the shadows of the forest to come out, enthusiastic to play and toy with their captives.

Fifty-three men now stand around us. Blades and weapons are poised, aiming for at least one of us.

I am blessed enough to only have three arrows pointed at me.

The murderous rage gleaming in Axel's eyes answers the question I already know the answer to. We are completely surrounded…with no way of escaping.

I shake the desolate thought away. Knox and Nolan will come for us. Aurora and Zephlyn. Knox's shadows alone can take out—

There's no magic.

Panic sinks its claws into my heart, overruling my body as I realize where these soldiers will take me.

The amount of pain Knox is in… He could barely lift his head, let alone a sword. Knox is a mighty warrior, but he is in no fighting condition and these men, how they wish to claim their prize money, makes vomit rise in my throat.

Jared's smile turns serpentine. "Round them up, boys! We have a fortune to collect!" He unsheathes the dagger strapped at his waist, pointing it at my face. "Let me have this one."

Grunts and growls fill the once peaceful watering hole as soldiers begin pushing us north—toward the capital.

This is it. The king is going to kill me. These soldiers are going to walk me to my death.

They may as well place a noose around my neck. Anything would be merciful to handing me over to the king.

Panic takes away all logic as I begin to thrash. The blade against my neck slices me with the sudden movements. Metallic stuffs itself down my nostrils as I begin to hyperventilate.

"No, please," I beg.

Though it's useless, my anxiety speaks for me, spewing words before I can stop my tongue from moving.

"Don't do this. Please don't do this!"

Five soldiers make their way for me, their eyes narrowed. Traitor, they called me. Despite leaving to find hope for the people of Aloriah, he has marked my absence as a traitor's workings.

Vengeance burns in their gazes. The closer they near, the faster my vision fades, black closing in. Fear builds to an unimaginable height, growing with every shallow wheeze.

I'm not ready to see him.
I can't handle it if he hurts me again.
I'm not ready to die.

I scream, the sound a death cry on my lips as I lunge, ready to fight my way out of here. The five guards pounce, pinning me to the ground. With the ruckus, more emerge from the shadows.

"Don't touch her!"

Axel's growl pierces through the fog threatening to overtake my mind, yet the rest of his words die on the tip of his tongue as a guttural roar silences the forest.

With my head pinned to the dirt along the riverbed, I let my gaze drift to the canopy of trees as a large black mass hurtles over me. It lands at my feet with such force the ground rocks and shakes, making pebbles and stones fly into the stream.

Aurora roars.

The majestic body looks as menacing as a warrior's nightmare—hackles raised, muscles poised to fight. With her mouth extended and her canines glinting in the daylight, her roar travels for miles.

Fearful screams fill the forest, and I can imagine why.

This is the first time this generation of humans has witnessed griffins. The creatures they've been told were extinct for over a hundred years are here in the flesh, and they aren't meeting the sentient beings. They're meeting the warriors, the true beasts a griffin can become, and why the Fae chose the animal as their aerial legion.

The legends must seem like inconsequential bedtime stories compared to the actual glorious creature with predatory eyes.

The soldiers flee once they behold the griffin, and it's almost enough to make my chest heave with relief.

Yet not all have fled.

Jared, with his dagger still drawn, turns ashen, his jaw dropping to the floor. The wicked smile has been wiped from his face.

The moment those golden eyes connect with the crimson trickling down my neck, rage contorts the griffin's features, and she pounces for the insipid men still pinning me to the ground.

The first to go is the one holding the blade to my neck.

There is nothing the soldier can do as she pounces and rips into him. Her razor-sharp teeth tear his arm from its socket.

A flurry of activity whizzes past Aurora, a blur of silky white fur as Zephlyn takes out three archers aiming for Aurora. The enormous griffin, as white as the divine magic that used to flow through our veins, becomes splattered with blood as he takes out the four remaining archers, leaving the human soldiers to fight hand-to-hand combat against the mythological creatures.

The soldiers at my back make the mistake of releasing me as they try to fight off Aurora.

She spins, thick crimson blood dripping from her teeth. She doesn't even appear to be tired, as if she didn't fly us all to safety mere hours before.

The men who recklessly lift their blades against her meet their end swiftly.

She swipes a claw, gutting the closest soldier from his belly button to his neck within the blink of an eye. The other soldiers halt, second-guessing their strength against an immortal creature.

Unfortunately for them, Aurora doesn't believe in second chances.

Blood splatters across my face as she rips into them with a guttural roar, yet hers isn't the only one I hear.

Knox and Nolan emerge from the forest at my back, their bodies rippling with a vengeance so palpable the air thickens. Knox only has eyes for me, while Nolan's fills with a hunger for blood as he takes in the chaos.

Knox's nostrils flare—perhaps from the scent of my fear or blood—before a growl of rage just as feral as Aurora's ripples out of him.

We may not be able to hear each other or feel the bond, but that doesn't mean it isn't there. That the care or fierce protection for one another disappeared. It's all there, simmering within our hearts.

Knox's fury proves just that.

He lunges, his powerful muscles straining as he lifts his sword high above his head and brings it crashing down upon Jared, the one I marked for retribution. Satisfaction curls around my heart as Knox slices the last remaining soldier holding me to the ground in two.

Zephlyn, done with the archers, stalks forward, his stark blue eyes narrowed into small slits. The ferocious snarls emanating from his sharp mouth send even a trickle of fear through me. Especially as his eyes connect with Hazel dangling from the ankle snare, and Ace's neck dripping with blood. The foolish soldier stays frozen, his iron blade still held against the griffin's soul pair.

The soldier at least has the wits to pale before finally dropping the blade and running. He doesn't take more than three steps before his life ends.

As Knox rips the sword out of the dead soldier and brings it up for his next victim, the last remaining humans begin to run.

But we're faster.

Axel hunts the men who held Ace with a vengeance, vibrating with rage as he kills the soldiers without mercy. He cuts out the tongues of those who laughed about using his twin's ears as a piece of decoration, while those who held Hazel in the snare drop to the ground, Ace landing blades in the center of their backs.

Nolan corners a man, making the soldier soil himself as he stares at him like he's his next meal. "This can either be quick or…" He cocks his head. "We can have a little fun with it."

The soldier's head flies side to side as if pleading for his life can save him after he reveled in our capture.

Removing another one of his blades from a soldier's neck, Knox wipes the blood on the dead man's clothing before striding toward me. He bends in front of me, quickly snatching my dragon pommel sword.

Flipping it in the air, he stretches the pommel to me. The

moment I wrap my hand around the golden hilt, Knox pulls, the momentum helping me to my feet.

Looking at him, you wouldn't know that just mere hours ago he was in a ball on the forest floor, screaming and writhing in pain. He appears perfectly fine, more than fine; he stands tall as a powerful Fae warrior. Yet as his muscles strain in helping me rise, I don't miss the flash of pain he shows me, the vulnerability he allows me to witness.

I rush for Hazel as Ace cuts her down with a soldier's discarded blade and puts an arm around her. Needing to feel that she's breathing and safe once more I wrap my arms around her, noting how hard she tries to hide her shaking. Giving her a tight squeeze, I let go as Ace pulls her into him. His gentle hands caress Hazel's cheek before kissing her ever so gently.

The relief that washes over Hazel's face is clear as day, the tension leaking out of her body visible.

Knox guides me toward Nolan and the last remaining soldier. Aurora follows and stays glued to my side, and I'm sure it will be a while yet before she leaves me alone. After the ordeal, I can't say I blame her.

Watching as the soldier withers in fear, I can't force myself to feel empathy or pity, not when he was one of the men laughing and joking at our demise. It takes a sick sort of human to take pleasure in the downfall of others. Fae or not, this man's true self was shown within those moments.

I should know...I used to find the king smiling when he spilled my blood with his fists.

"I-I'll tell you y-you everything I know!" His eyes flick to me, pinning me to the spot. "Princ-cess, please."

Aurora and Knox's deep warning growl has him leaning away.

"You didn't view me as your princess moments ago! You were going to send me to the gallows," I spit.

Nolan takes a step closer. "I say we gut him like the coward he is."

"No!" the soldier screeches. His complexion paling to a green tint.

I look straight into the eyes of one of the king's men, a soldier who signed up to execute the hatred the king inflicts upon his people. That fact settles into my stomach like a heavy stone. The duties he finds noble, the laws and values he represents, disgust me.

With the knowledge that he will share our location with the next soldier he comes across, I turn away.

The words are heavy as I force them out of my mouth. "Dispose of him."

I'm no better than the king by ordering it but I must protect—

"I'll tell you what he's doing with the children in the sectors!"

My head snaps to him, bile burning my throat as I march back. "What did you just say?"

The soldier gulps, yet his gaze is steady on mine, unwavering. "I'll tell you what he's doing with the children if you promise not to kill me."

I promise no such thing as I mutter, "Go on."

"He plans to create children of war."

I blink. "That's impossible. Everyone would riot. *Everyone.*"

"You haven't been here in months, Princess. It's already happened with Sector Seven. He's started training already."

The bombing.

The sector the king destroyed within mere minutes because the rebels were gaining a footing there and people were beginning to wish for change. The king killed the notion instantly.

But everyone died in that bombing. Eleven thousand people were murdered.

"Impossible," I breathe.

The man who calls himself a soldier lowers his head as if he feels shame. "They evacuated the children before executing the citizens they deemed useless." The persuasion in his next words stops my heart from beating. "Sector One is next."

Chapter Seven

"He's bluffing," Nolan scoffs.

But I saw the truth in his beady eyes. "No, he's not." Knox's hand rests on my lower back for support as I turn to the others. "Before I left, the king bombed Sector Seven. He murdered eleven thousand people." I face the soldier. "Or so we thought. Where has he been keeping the children?"

The man snaps his mouth shut, gulping.

Unsheathing the dragon pommel sword, I let the tip of the silver rest against his jugular. "Speak," I command.

Regardless of what the king has labeled me, I am still a princess of these lands. Of this army. Of this soldier. And the truth in the matter gives me the courage to demand what we need. *Answers.*

The guard blanches. "He'll kill me."

I take a step forward, the tip of my sword never leaving his neck as I bend to whisper in his ear. "The moment you become useless to these Fae, they will kill you without a second thought. I suggest you continue being useful to them and speak."

The soldier's nervous gaze darts around the group of powerful Fae at my back.

"The king didn't kill everyone in Sector Seven. He took those he deemed worthwhile. Those that could offer services he needed...the most reputable swordsmanship and those with the largest collections. They also collected all the armory and weapons before burning it to the ground."

When the news broke, I was so distraught I didn't question why the king would destroy the sector that produces his weapons. Now I know. He took what he needed and burnt what he didn't. People included.

Axel takes a step forward. "And the children?"

The soldier jumps at the ice in Axel's voice, cowering further into the tree trunk. "Taken into the heart of the capital's mountains for training," he rushes out. As if the speed of his words will decide his fate.

All this time... For *months*, innocents have been locked away just a mere two days' ride from the capital. If I had known—

"Why? He has a large army as it is."

"Loyalty," Ace whispers.

The guard dips his quivering chin. "He's created orphans who must rely upon him. Codependent. There's no one more loyal than a child who needs you."

His men are already loyal to a fault. So why does he need the children?

I clench my hands to stop their shaking. "The rebellion. What have they been up to?"

"No one wants to lose their child, Princess. No one even dares to whisper about it."

They've done nothing.

My heart drops, sinking to my stomach like a rock.

He crushed them, utterly destroyed the souls who dared to

hope and aid in the rebellion. Those who dared to dream of a better life, *a better world.*

I stumble backward, running my fingers through my hair in frustration.

The soldier begins shaking in earnest. "Gods have mercy on us," he breathes, his brown eyes locked on my elongated ears.

"I'm done listening," I snap, quickly turning away before the soldier can see just how much his reaction frightened me.

Aurora comes up beside me, her heavy paws leaving imprints beside my boot marks. My protector and soul pair.

I should thank her, pat her even, but I can't find the energy and I think she can sense that. It feels as if I'm dragging my feet up the hill as I leave the others to deal with the soldier. I've heard enough. If there's any more information to glean, Nolan will extract it. Intimidation is what he's best at after all.

Devastation doesn't begin to explain what's wreaking havoc on my heart. The war my emotions are knee-deep in. I thought I would be done feeling this way after I broke the entrapment spell, after facing *demons*.

How can I face those creatures, with hearts as wicked and dead as their souls, and yet be afraid of one man?

Tiredness overtakes my body, spreading so quickly I'm shocked I don't drop to the ground.

Helplessness is a feeling I am all too familiar with, the lack of control that makes my chest burn and my hands clammy.

Yet it still hurts, more so now that I have tasted freedom.

I knew not to get attached and yet I did anyway. Now that I have tasted what it feels like to have happiness and joy in my life, I do not want to go back.

But deep in my heart, I know those are naïve feelings.

The king is a fisherman with his hook lodged in my heart, and he has the power to reel me in whenever he pleases.

"Angel."

Quickly spinning, tears well in my eyes and before they can drop, I'm in Knox's arms, wrapped in his warmth. Just in time to allow the tears to cascade down my cheek onto his chest.

"How many people have died and suffered since I've left?"

Annie.

The breath is stolen from me. "He's labeled me as a traitor. What if he took Annie to punish me? What about my mother?" I begin to sob in earnest. *How could I have not thought of them? How could I have been so selfish?* "What have I done, Knox? What if my actions sent them to their deaths?

Knox's large palm cups my cheek, holding me to his chest as he murmurs into my hair. "This is what he wants, Delilah. He labeled you as a traitor to elicit this response when you returned home. To punish you emotionally when he can no longer physically." His voice lowers, dripping with malice. "He's playing a game."

"I've always been a piece on his chessboard. An object to move as he pleases."

Knox's eyes soften. "Not anymore."

I want his words to be true, but I can see even Knox believes they're false. The king may not be able to order me around on which clothes to wear, what to eat, who to train with, and when to speak. He may no longer be able to strike me...but he can still hurt me. Even from thousands of miles away.

"I need to start thinking like him." I swallow the thick

lump in my throat. "If I want to win whatever game he's decided to create, I need to play."

Knox's grin is borderline murderous. "Good thing I'm an excellent chess player."

I shake my head as my lips threaten to tip into a smile.

How does he do it? How can he soothe the ache in my heart so quickly? How does he make me forget what's at stake, the pressure and responsibility hanging on our shoulders? Even for just a moment, it's a precious gift.

Knox slides his hands into his pockets. "So, Angel…what will our first move be?"

Gazing into his sparkling sapphire eyes, I allow my mind to roam.

Dropping the short leash of control I have over my endless well of panic, the very thing I fight against daily, I allow thoughts to bombard my mind. Allow a tendril of that nervous, buzzing energy to fly through hundreds of different scenarios, showing me everything that could possibly go wrong.

I suppose anxiety is useful for one thing…yet it doesn't seem like a fair trade.

Rising on shaking legs, I say, "We stop what no one else will."

Nolan stalks through the bushes below, his presence snapping me away from the hundreds of thoughts spiraling through my mind. As he climbs the hill, he wipes the dripping blood off his sword.

I slam my eyes shut at the sight, breathing in and out deeply. *He was a bad man.* I'm not sure who I'm trying to convince because that statement isn't enough reason to take a life.

"A lot of people are going to die in this fight, aren't they?"

Silence is my answer and yet the response is loud and clear.

I've never killed anyone, never taken a life. I'm not sure if the demonic hounds and soul eater count, being that they were from another world. Their summoning also ensured they never truly died. Even Knox and Aurora had killed Emmalyn, not me. Despite training for this exact purpose for twenty years, my stomach turns queasy at the thought, and that instinctual bodily reaction confirms that I am nothing like the monster who sits on the human throne.

Ace and Hazel are the next to climb the hill, hand in hand, while Axel stalks behind them, eyes darting in every direction.

"Did he say anything useful?" Knox asks his second.

The quick glances that are traded between each other have my back snapping upright. I steel my heart for another beating.

"They've already begun extractions on Sector One. They're planning to attack in five days," Axel answers solemnly.

My mind whirls, calculating distances, timeframes, and how far the initial attack will be. I'm yanked down to the present as I find everyone's attention on me, including Knox. This may be Knox's court but we're in the human lands. Even Nolan is staring at me as if he's awaiting orders.

As if I rule the lands.

I *hate* the feeling.

Whether that's because of my perception of rulers or not, all I know is that the sticky sensation that fills my veins when I picture myself ruling the human lands is not a pleasant one.

I used to dream about being queen. Of the moment I could restore humanity in the palace, to give the citizens the life they deserved. To fix everything he has broken.

Now I know that it would be cruel to sit atop the throne. To rule over the people who are trying to heal from my father's brutal acts.

The Covington touch is cursed.

"I need to get a better look," I mutter.

Ignoring their eyes boring into the back of my skull, I turn away and start to climb the nearest oak tree. Gritting my teeth, I force the pain to ground me, the pressure keeping my flighty heart from soaring.

It's a feat to ignore my thoughts, to cease the whirlwind of words that threaten to carry me away. It takes every ounce of determination to keep my mind focused on my feet and the movement of my body. It isn't long before I stop, my head and muscles pounding as I pop through the leaves.

Mountains.

Endless ridges and steep mountain summits, for endless miles as far as the eye can see.

In between the highs and lows of what Mother Gaia has created lie trickles of water flowing from the Mason River. Some drift into large swimming holes, others into streams and small puddles. Dense forests lie on either side of the water, covering the bottom of the mountains with a thick canopy of trees and wild fragrant flowers.

Birds fly high in the sky, drifting from treetop to treetop as the sun begins to lower, setting the water in a vibrant pink hue.

A feeling akin to anger begins to build in my chest, making my veins sizzle as I stare at the beauty the king sheltered me from. As the minutes pass and I look at everything I've been missing out on all these years, that anger shifts to resentment.

It isn't until the sun truly begins to fade do I spot it, the small blip in the far-off distance—smoke.

The burning fires in citizens' homes as they scrap what little food they have together to create an assortment of dinner.

Sector One.

I would never have been able to spot the smoke if it weren't for the Fae sight. The copious amount of mountain peaks that surround it tells me everything I need to know— Sector One is a far way off. Pressing time needed to travel that we don't have to waste, that the innocent people of Sector One don't have to spare.

Climbing down, I stalk toward Knox's court, noting the hushed voices and whispers that cease as I come to stand next to Aurora. I check to see if she's up for this.

The vengeance I find reflecting back in her golden eyes makes my lips tug into a smile.

Sinking my fingers into her silky strands, I turn to the others, letting her strength and support ground me. "We're a two-day hike from the center of Sector One. Water isn't an issue since there are streams all through the mountains, but food will be harder to source." I snap my mouth shut on a frown. "Where did Nolan go?"

Ace cocks his head. Following his line of sight, my lips twitch. Nolan comes up the hill, perspiration marring his skin. His arms are laden with the dead soldiers' weaponry.

"Figured we could use some extra steel."

For all of Nolan's faults, he makes up for it by being a great warrior.

"I take it you can't fly without magic?" I ask Knox.

Knox grimaces. "When the pain consumed our bodies, our wings instinctively retracted to protect them. You don't need magic to fly but you do need magic to access them."

I can't begin to imagine how the others feel right now. It was utter agony to have my magic ripped away from me, and that was only once. They've endured this for the past one hundred and fifty years. Every minute that passed meant another ounce of their magic had faded.

They have all lost so much already, and the fact that the king is responsible for this loss of magic makes guilt riddle my body. Not to mention none of them would be here if it weren't for me and the premonition.

Hazel may be safe in Ace's arms at this moment, but because of me, I put both of them in harm's way today. I continue to put the people I love in danger, and I can't seem to stop it.

"How did a human place wards around the lands?" Ace murmurs, breaking the silence.

The same thing I've been wondering. "I think the true question is who did it for him and how did they do it so quickly."

"Delilah's right. The soldier said the morning after the entrapment spell was broken, they were stationed around the lands. How did someone with magic place the wards so quickly? We only just got our powers back; they would have been weak at best," Axel says, a groove forming between his brows.

"No one witnessed anything suspicious, not to his knowledge," Nolan chimes in.

How did he do it, then? Who does he have working for him? Are they more powerful than Knox?

I suppose anyone is more powerful than Knox at this moment with his magic dormant. Perhaps that was the true reason for the wards. Maybe he knew all along that I was going to come with Knox and his court. Perhaps we are late to join a game the king has been playing for months.

"Are we surrounded?" Knox asks.

Axel looks past us to the tree line. "Not on this mountain

ridge. They're all dead now but the rest of the journey will be riddled with them."

"We use our strength then. Aurora and Zephlyn can still fly." Aurora doesn't possess magic, and even if she does, she doesn't need magic to summon her wings. "They can carry the satchels, Hazel, and myself." I look to Hazel, surprised to find no objection waiting there. The incident earlier must have frightened her more than she's leading on.

"And what do you suppose we do, Princess? Walk into trap-infested forests and be slaughtered?" Nolan rebukes.

Ignoring his tone, I look toward the twins and Knox. "We can't climb the mountains—they're too open and we'd be exposed to arrows—but we can snake through the forests. You can jump from treetop to treetop to avoid the soldiers on the ground. The forest lining the mountains is dense, so the trees are practically standing on top of one another. It wouldn't be a far leap and the king doesn't have an aerial legion." Turning back to Nolan, I stare him down. "You can use your strength to your advantage."

There is no other option, and the griffins can't carry everyone. The Fae men are too large and heavy. And if we learned anything from today, it's that the griffins should reserve as much energy as they possibly can.

"Any objections, Nolan?" Knox asks harshly.

Nolan grinds his jaw for a painful beat of silence before he shakes his head quickly.

"Very well." Knox clicks his tongue. "We leave now. We don't have time to waste."

"What about the location the mermaids gave you?" Ace asks.

"That's still the plan, but I'm not going to sit aside and do nothing to stop the atrocity the king is planning." That would make me as awful as him. "Whatever we do, though…I must stay hidden. We can't have him knowing I'm back in his lands."

Not now that he's marked me as a traitor. With all the soldiers now dead, my whereabouts are still unbeknownst to the king, and I will take any advantage I can use against him.

Knox slides his warm palm down my forearm, leaving a path of electricity burning beneath my skin. "Let's start climbing."

Chapter Eight

The passing two days were spent above the treetops, in the air on Aurora's back, eating the animals Nolan and Axel hunted. But the hours where I lay awake high within the treetops, with the night sky shining down upon me, were spent planning and calculating how to save the citizens of Sector One. Nothing has been able to cease my whirling thoughts, nor the striking truth that my thoughts and fears over these past years were correct.

I am, and was, nothing more to the king than a chess piece on his board game, viewed as an object to manipulate and control at his will.

I refuse for that to be my reality.

I am no longer his precious little doll he has control over. That man will *never* lay a finger on me again. And I'll be damned if he tries to ruin this glorious kingdom any further. I helped the Fae; I was a key component in saving them. It's not a feeble hope that I can save my people too.

Crouched along a thick branch high above the mountaintops, Knox passes me the raw fish he and Axel managed to catch through the passing streams. Nobody dares to light a fire, not wanting to give our location away to the soldiers that march beneath.

That was another pastime these last few days—gawking at the number of soldiers the king assigned to the forests. Every square inch of the mountains seems to be filled with black-and-gold-armored soldiers.

The color never fails to have acid burning my throat.

If eating raw fish is the price to pay for our silence and freedom, so be it.

I repeat that thought to myself a thousand times as my stomach rolls over the slimy food. The only ones who appear fine with it are Zephlyn, Aurora, and surprisingly, Nolan.

The sound of chewing pauses, the air growing thick with tension as leaves crunch and rattle below. Six pairs of Fae eyes snap to the forest floor as three soldiers stroll through the thick trees and bushes, careless, as if who and what they are hunting for is normal. Moonlight glints off the silver swords strapped to their hips.

My lip curls back, a snarl rising to the surface, tantalizing the seams of my lips and begging to escape. I hold my anger back as the three figures disappear out of view.

"Disgusting mutts," Nolan spits.

Aurora puffs, the air curling around my shoulder as she lies behind me on a thick branch. It's been a challenging feat finding trees to accommodate not only one griffin but two, along with camouflaging Zephlyn's white fur and the beacon that he is. He has had to give up hygiene, rolling around in mud puddles wherever we can find them to hide the fur coat.

Although, with the way his tongue lolled to the side as he squirmed in the brown muck, I'd say he didn't seem to mind the task.

My eyes snag on the tree the soldiers rounded, wishing more than anything to follow them and eavesdrop on the latest gossip. If any news of Sector One and their demise has reached their ears, whether they feel guilt over the lives about to be taken. But Knox ordered us not to take any risky moves, not with the lives of Sector One hanging in the balance.

Nolan notices my look and decides against better judgment to open his mouth. "Will you have what it takes? To kill when the time comes?"

But it isn't a taunt; it's a genuine question.

My eyes flare at the gall he has to ask such a thing.

"What type of question is that?" Axel spits.

Nolan shrugs, plopping a slice of fish in his mouth and swallowing with ease. "The kind that needs to be answered. If it's a no…" He points the blade in his hand at me, the silver glinting. "Which, by the look on her face I take is a no, I do not want her guarding my back when they strike."

My jaw clenches, grinding my teeth as if it's his bones.

"Stop provoking her simply because you cannot entertain yourself," Knox drawls. Despite the lack of shadows and mating bond to tell me so, I know it's an act, one that is trying to mask the wrath he feels at Nolan for how he speaks.

Nolan ignores his king, not heeding the violence promised in his gaze. Instead, he leans forward, his eyes imploring mine. "There will be bloodshed, Delilah, and when that moment comes—when it truly comes down to it—will you choose yourself, or will you allow others to decide your fate?"

Knox lunges, his hands lashing out until he has Nolan's neck in a death grip. He lifts the blond Fae until Nolan is at eye line. "Stand down!" Knox barks, spit flying as he seethes.

Growls and hisses rise. Hushed arguing ensues, quiet enough not to alert the soldiers below, but the violence and anger laced in their words are heard…to all but me.

As grateful as I am for Knox putting Nolan in his place, my ears won't stop ringing.

Such a moody Fae, and yet his words are true. I know they are because I've asked myself the same question. Will I be able to do it? Can I save myself at the expense of another life? Another beating heart?

I wish the twenty years of training could answer for me. I've trained in fighting rooms, not battlefields, and I fear that the path we have embarked on will lead us down the one of bloodshed.

Nolan may be rude and crass, but his words never hide the truth that others wish to ignore.

The only thing to silence their bickering is the rush of footfalls coming from the left. Everyone's mouths snap shut immediately as another set of soldiers, four this time, rush past. Instead of strolling as the others were, they are running.

Knox frowns, mirroring that of his court's displeasure.

We've watched their camps and their rotations. At this time, three soldiers scout their allocated perimeter before taking on the night watch.

These soldiers are not assigned to night watch.

"Perhaps someone torched their camp," Hazel offers meekly.

Knox shakes his head, his eyes boring into the trail below. "Two should stand on guard tonight."

"You think it's something to be concerned over?"

"Any change in their routine should be cause for concern," I answer softly.

And running certainly falls under that category.

Silence stretches along with time, punctuated by the calls of owls and the wings of bats, the calming rush of water flowing through the mountain streams.

We all continue to wait, seemingly holding our breaths, but nothing comes of the running soldiers.

"She's right," Knox murmurs.

Without warning Knox drops Nolan. He lands with a resounding thump at the base of the tree trunk. Knox ignoring his groans and grunts orders, "Take a walk and inspect it."

Nolan doesn't so much as look at any of us before he disappears into the cold night.

Hours later, despite Nolan coming back with no news and the court falling asleep, I can't help but stay awake, fearful that the screams and shouts of the soldiers will rise. The wind carrying the words that I dread most.

They found me.

At every minuscule sound, my head snaps to the ground, wondering if it's more soldiers. If they were running because they knew we were near. But they never come. Only sleep visits me as my heavy lids finally close.

Someone shakes my shoulders until my eyes jump open to find the depths of the ocean peering back at me.

Full lips move, parting to form words and yet all I hear is a buzzing, buzzing, buzzing-

"DELILAH!"

Gasping for air, sound rushes for me all at once as the fog gives way. My fight-or-flight reaction turned on within a blink.

Jumping to a standing position, I wipe the drool from my chin and search the forest below. "What? What is it? Is someone harmed?"

I find nothing and no one on the ground. Only the rush

and chaos of Knox's court moving about the trees as they quickly pack up what little supplies we have.

"They're gone."

I frown. "Who's gone?"

Knox runs a frustrated hand through his hair. "The soldiers, they're all gone."

"All of them?"

"Axel went on his morning scouting mission to find every single camp empty." A muscle ticks in his jaw, the only irritation he will allow to shine through. "Their fire pits are cold to the touch; they must have left hours ago."

Knox sends a seething glare in Nolan's direction and the Fae has the decency to flush with guilt.

I shake my head. *Did he even try to check on the soldiers?*

Axel stops packing to face me, his irritation clear in his pinched expression. "They moved out during their shift rotations. When I hadn't seen a group of soldiers for the morning shift, I inspected the camps and found they had disappeared."

"Why on gods would they—"

My thoughts cease, the words tumbling to a halt. There is only one reason they would leave, why they would desert their camps so precariously close to Sector One's borders.

I gasp. "No."

We were supposed to have two more days.

Jumping, I land on Aurora's thick branch and start shoving all the loose items into her satchel.

"Move! We need to hurry," I exclaim to no one in particular.

"Delilah, we don't know that anything has happened yet. It could—"

"I am not one to favor ifs, buts, or maybes," I hiss, cutting Hazel off. It's uncharacteristic of me to yell at her, but there's no doubt in my mind. "Those soldiers left in the middle of the night because they received orders to clear the forest."

Once everything is clear I waste no time attaching the satchels onto Zephlyn and Aurora's backs. My wide and frazzled eyes snap everyone to attention.

"Now go!" I scream, begging my words to carry the urgency I feel in my heart.

Nobody bothers to argue about saving the griffins' energy. Knox, Nolan, and I mount Aurora in one fell swoop, while the twins and Hazel ride Zephlyn.

The griffins don't need my orders. They shoot off, their bird-like feathers beating against the high winds above the treetops of the mountains.

The looming town center of Sector One comes into view as we crest over a mountain ridge.

Revealing the billowing smoke.

"Faster, Aurora, faster!" I plead; my voice frenzied.

Aurora tucks her chin, her chest vibrating with a purr as she begins to drop, tucking in her wings tightly. My thighs squeeze Aurora's sides, my fists clenching her fur so tightly the whites of my knuckles shine in the morning light. Zephlyn soars close behind on a current of wind. The cold morning air whips at my face and hair, dispelling any remaining drowsiness or fog.

Clouds of smoke curl in the air, rising to meet us and clinging to our fighting leathers, seemingly beckoning for us to join it on the ground. I gasp for fresh air only to sputter as the smoke fills my lungs.

Knox's large palms cling to my waist once it clears, giving us a view of Sector One's town.

Shock strikes me quickly and without mercy.

The ringing in my ears grows.

Aurora lands on the ground in one fluid motion, and in

the next, I'm jumping off her, ignoring the burning pain in my lungs.

I ignore it all because that pain is nothing compared to the harm being inflicted upon these citizens.

Nothing ever will.

Screams of terror and pleas of mercy pierce the morning sky. Soldiers adorning black and gold stalk the town of Sector One, dragging adults to their deaths and stealing children for war.

Chapter Nine

C hildren scream a bloodcurdling melody that pierces the tapestry of my heart.

With flushed, tear-stained cheeks, their heart's agony can be seen and heard for miles.

Their lungs may be small but the sound that pours from them is shockingly loud, so much so I must snap my hands over my ears. My heart drops at the pure undulated terror in their voices. The grief that their small hearts must feel. The innocence that is stolen so quickly. Their tiny hands reach for someone they'll never touch again. Their small legs kick with all their might against the king's soldiers as if they can wiggle free and run.

The older children have been rendered unconscious, syringes lying on the floor by their sleeping forms, their age and strength perhaps perceived as a threat.

The wails emanating from the stricken mothers will forever haunt me until the end of my days. The sound of women as their children are ripped from them is a death cry, the grief in the high note terrifying.

Thousands of the king's soldiers march through the town,

wrenching citizens from their homes like pieces of furniture. They must have already extracted those they deem worthy to keep alive, because what lies before me is pure chaos.

Soldiers light matches and throw the small kernel of fire into homes, belongings, stables, and any piece of furniture they can find. They aren't making the last moments of their lives easier, or less painful. They are taking a sledgehammer to their hearts while grinning ear to ear.

A man with his small child in his arms and his wife in his hand runs for the forest where we hide, their gazes wild and crazed with terror. They only get several feet before the parents drop to the ground, their bodies unmoving with arrows in their necks, courtesy of the soldiers stationed on the rooftops. The child is immediately crushed by its parents.

Everywhere I look breeds misery.

Women and men are separated on opposite sides of the town, the children huddled around the large well in the middle of the chaos. Forced to watch as parents' necks are sliced from ear to ear, snapped, or decapitated.

Crimson rains down on the streets, filling the cobblestone cracks. Metallic stuffs itself down my throat and nose, the smell of death and carnage burning my nostrils. Bile rises in earnest at the pile of heads I find the soldiers have stacked behind the children. The bodies lie separately, never to be laid to rest peacefully.

It takes painstaking moments to realize why the king would choose to slaughter the citizens individually instead of bombing. You may be able to run for shelter, but no one can escape the hands of his soldiers.

I stumble forward, emotions clogging my throat. These were the orders given not once but *twice*.

The rage that fills me isn't human; it isn't even Fae. Fury

isn't an accurate word to describe it. It's as if the burning depths of the underworld have ignited within me.

I have to rip myself away from the hands that hold me back.

Aurora stalks beside me as I march forward, into the center of the chaos, without a plan in mind and without a thought on how to stop it. All I know is that every step I take splatters blood on my boots and pants. That my body shakes with the restraint of holding back the rage bubbling beneath my skin. That the smell of their deaths clings to my hair.

I sink within myself, allowing the fire running through my veins to propel me forward.

The screams don't quiet, but the chatter and rumblings of the soldiers do as fear-filled gazes take in Aurora and the menacing growl rippling from her mouth. She drops, preparing to launch at the soldiers like the prey they are.

I know the moment Zephlyn and Knox's court come into their line of sight as well. I can practically smell the fear wafting off them. Especially as Knox comes to stand beside me, the vengeance rippling off him just as menacing as the griffins.

The humans may not know that Knox is a Fae king, but their instincts do. Eyes widen. Bodies shake and quiver as if warning them of the imminent danger that lurks before them.

"Who's in charge?" I bellow.

Laughter rings through the town.

I must be hallucinating, yet I know I'm not when Aurora's warning growl pierces through their thick skulls and snaps their mouths shut.

Taking a step forward, I allow them to see the fury shining within my ice blue eyes. Behind me, Knox and his court follow me into the pits of this hell.

Knox's hands glide to his hips, unsheathing the blades strapped to him in one fluid motion.

"I said. Who. Is. In. Charge."

A burly man steps forward, his gaze roaming us as if we're nothing but a speck of dirt on the bottom of his shoe. *How foolish.*

A sneer mars his face. "Who dares to ask?"

"Delilah Covington," I hiss, my name flying from my lips before I can stop it. Before I can think about the repercussions of uttering the name. "I suggest you kneel."

Gasps fly through the air, the cries and screams slowing to muffled sobs and whispers.

The only ounce of shock he allows to show is a slow blink. "Delightful. We've been looking for you." His stance is full of arrogance he shouldn't feel.

My brow quirks. "In the homes of these innocent civilians?"

The burly commander slides his gaze to the soldiers beside him. With a quick flick of his chin in my direction, soldiers move toward me. They only make it three steps.

Aurora roars and my own growl pierces the air. Knox flicks his wrist, throwing a dagger that lands an inch away from their toes.

The citizens emit a collective gasp. Some scream in terror, the sounds as potent as the smell of blood filling the once quiet coal mining town.

The shock that covers the soldiers' features isn't nearly as satisfying as it will be to watch them suffer for the heinous crimes they've inflicted today.

"Send your men after me. I dare you," I taunt.

The fire burning within me fuels a level of confidence I wouldn't otherwise feel. Especially as my name is whispered throughout the town.

Delilah Covington.
Delilah Covington.
Delilah Covington.

I would think it was a chant if not for the other word uttered along with it, filled with horror.

Fae.

Taking my eyes off the men for a moment, I crane my neck to Nolan and Axel, sliding my gaze to the archers along the rooftops. A slight dip of their chin is all the response I receive before they turn away, falling deep within the forest.

Pacing as if the conversation bores me, I wave my hands, trying to delay the soldiers and give us the precious seconds needed to get Nolan and Axel onto those rooftops. The utter confidence that oozes out of me would make even Harlow proud. "Let me take a guess at how the next few moments will go: I'll ask you politely to stop killing innocent citizens of Aloriah, and in return, you'll laugh in my face. Then you'll send your men after me, who will only end up dead."

I stop suddenly, pointing to Knox and his court. "I'm not sure if you remember, but Fae are much stronger than humans, and this isn't just any Fae." A genuine smile spreads across my face as I say, "This is Knox Holloway, King of Azalea and the Essence Court."

The commander's jaw ticks. "We don't acknowledge Fae kings." He spits the last two words as if they had personally cursed him.

Waves of fury roll off Knox. "You will wish you had in a moment."

His flippant tone and evident disgust make me clench my jaw so tightly I'm shocked a tooth doesn't chip. When I take a step forward, his men foolishly draw their swords and weapons. Some even dare point an arrow at Aurora and Zephlyn.

The violence promised in Knox's glare has the soldiers switching tactics and aiming their swords at him.

"Make a move against the princess and I will personally gut every single one of you," Knox says coolly. The ice in his voice is enough to freeze the spines of even the strongest of men.

Hazel and Ace's steps are silent, only heard by the Fae as they utilize the soldier's distraction to sneak toward the children. They're close, so close in fact a child weeps in relief, the little girl unable to hold back her tears.

The commander snaps his head to them. "Touch a child and you die."

Anger speaks for me. "I'd like to see you try and find that you are an utter failure of a man."

An infant crawls toward Hazel, the little one seeking comfort. Tears run down her small chubby cheeks.

Ace moves closer to Hazel as all eyes fall on her, and the worry I find in her gaze has me straightening, my hand reaching for the blade strapped to my hip.

Not a moment later, the child tries to stand, wobbling on her chubby legs until eventually falling forward. Hazel instinctively moves to catch the child before it face-plants.

A sinister smile spreads across the soldier's face. "I keep my promises, Princess."

Knox growls, viciously low, "And so do I."

He punctuates his words by throwing a blade, embedding it into the skull of an archer. In the next moment, he unsheathes the blade at his back.

A small whistle from the commander has metal and steel ringing throughout the courtyard. The soldiers take off into a run, aiming for Hazel and Ace, yet the commander only has eyes for me as he draws his blade.

But it isn't me the soldiers should fear, nor is it Ace or Hazel. It's the Fae's leaping from the rooftop behind them.

In one fluid motion, Axel lands in a crouch and rolls, the sword clutched in his hand swiping the nearest soldier. His Achilles heel is instantly shredded.

Hazel moves the baby girl in her arms behind her back to protect her as Ace draws his sword, joining his brother in combat. Zephlyn is the next to pounce, extended fangs and claws glinting in the early morning light.

Nolan cuts a path from whatever rooftop he jumped from. With the two swords in his hands, he cuts the king's soldiers in half with an ease that makes me rethink the continuous verbal jabs we throw at one another. It isn't until I see the determination in his gaze and the sneer marring his lips do I understand why he's such a powerful force to be reckoned with.

His swords swing in earnest now. Crimson blood drips from the steel only to join that of his next victim as he cuts his way through soldiers, creating a direct path to Knox—his king.

All I have ever heard from the Fae is bickering and disagreements, and yet when it comes down to it, Nolan is always right beside his king, guarding him with his life.

Knox moves to stand in front of me, but I sidestep him, my anger bubbling at the commander. He sneers at Knox as if he were a pest.

Unsheathing the dragon sword at my back, I flip it in my hand, relishing the feel of the hilt fitting perfectly in my palm. As if it was truly made for me. I bend my knees, waiting for his move.

"Any day now, Commander."

"Get rid of the dog and it will be a fair fight," he snarls.

I narrow my eyes, adrenaline propelling my legs forward.

"Like the fair fight you gave these innocent people? The fair fight you gave their children?" I thunder.

Vicious growls rumble behind me, the sounds of grown men screaming as Aurora rips into the small group of soldiers that attempted to sneak behind Knox and me.

"Fair fight?" I quip. "Your arrogance is going to get your men killed. I suggest you put an end to it before you're the last one standing and cornered by six Fae all wanting to spill your blood."

My body recoils at the humorless laugh that leaks between his thin lips. Especially as twenty more soldiers come to stand behind him.

The soldiers move, stretching on either side of the commander, attempting to surround us. But with every soldier that comes near, Aurora snaps her jaw, her teeth coming impossibly close to their flesh. The men closest to her squawk.

One foolishly lunges for Aurora's hind legs but she's faster, and she was expecting it—waiting for the move. Her mouth snaps over the soldier's head and she flings him. The man's body flails high in the sky as his head soars in the other direction.

Cries of outrage ring through the air as the soldiers charge for their fallen men.

The commander pounces, striking forward with his sword pointed at my heart. And while his loathing eyes stay squarely on mine, Knox lunges. His sword strikes against the hand aiming for my life.

The commander's sword drops with a string of curses and gushing blood. He takes a deep breath and then lets it all out in a piercing scream as he stares at his amputated hand lying before him.

Knox is already moving again, whirling until he's in front

of the soldiers focused on Aurora. This time, Knox doesn't go for their hands; he goes for their hearts and heads.

Aurora devours the left flank of soldiers, figuratively and literally.

A deafening cry rings out as Zephlyn whines in pain. The sound makes me whirl, my eyes widening when they connect with a large white ball of fur stained red. A flash of steel, embedded in the griffin's shoulder, glints off the morning rays.

Aurora's head snaps to the side, steam puffing from her snout before her golden eyes slide to mine, pleading.

"Go!" When she refuses to move, I scream once more. "GO!"

We aren't going to lose anyone because people are afraid to leave me to my own devices.

Two soldiers charge for me, their lips curled back with a snarl. They barely lift their swords before my arms whip out, rendering them unconscious with the hilt of my blades.

Knox and Aurora begin to cut a path to Axel and Ace, who are surrounded by dozens of men clambering to fight against one of the Fae and griffins, while I stay rooted, my eyes narrowed on who I truly want to take care of.

I don't wait for him to recover from the shock, or the bleeding hand. I lunge, sliding across the cobblestone as I strike out, the dragon pommel sword meeting nothing but air.

My smirk is ravenous as the commander moves how I want him to, sliding to the left to dodge my blade. Only, he cannot escape my Fae speed. I slide with him, wrapping my hands around his balding head as I bring it down upon my knee in one hard thrust.

The sickening crunch of bones breaking fills my heart with joy at the ounce of justice. His one hand snaps to his broken nose and he howls in pain. I spin, kicking the boot of my heel right into his stomach. He flies backward, rolling to a stop yards away.

He doesn't move when I come to stand above him, the tip of my blade pointing into his neck. The man's eyes burn with hatred at the sight of me, while mine narrow at the black and gold clinging to his skin, the blood that will never wash from his hands and the crimes that have tainted his soul.

I *beg* myself to pull the sword and slash his throat. Beg for Nolan's words to not ring true, for justice to overpower my hand. I beg myself to not think about the repercussions of taking a life.

But that's just it—I am not this man.

Knox calls my name, his voice sparing me from the decision that lies in my hands. The small reprieve of it is enough to raise the hairs on the back of my neck.

Only, the rise of my hair isn't from my mate's voice. It's from the soldiers at my back that I don't see but *feel*.

My sword is kicked from my hand as iron shackles are clamped around my wrists. The breath in my lungs expels in one fell swoop as four large hands dig their dirty nails into my skin. They yank me back, allowing the commander to stand.

He snarls and hisses in my face like a crazed animal while some of his men wrap bandages around his missing hand.

How is he still standing? The blood loss alone should have him on the ground.

"Despite my wishes, he wants you alive. You should thank him for it," he spits.

His words spur me on, my limbs thrashing. The soldiers holding me each claim a limb and whisk me into the air, carrying me as if I'm their prized possession and trophy. Panic spears through me.

"Traitor," a soldier sneers in my ear.

The triumph that is exchanged between joyous glances makes my stomach roll.

Thrashing against their blood-streaked hands, my wild gaze takes in the scene before me.

Axel and Ace fight against dozens of soldiers surrounding them and the children, all wanting to kill a Fae and prove their worth, despite their men lying dead at their feet. Hazel tries to calm the crying children over the sound of metal striking metal, yet I see her sword hand tremble.

Aurora bites the heads off any of those who dare to come near an injured Zephlyn. All the while, the citizens of Sector One watch, helpless to the fate of their innocent children.

The only reprieve I feel is when my eyes find Knox's cold, feral gaze, killing a path toward me while Nolan fights off the soldiers gunning for his back. Until the commander gathers his men and strikes from the side.

Knox is only open and vulnerable for a moment, yet that second costs him. The burly man lifts his mighty sword with the hand he has left and plunges the silver into Knox's side.

Knox's sapphire eyes snap to mine as I'm dragged away. They widen, shock infiltrating his gaze before his knees buckle, taking him out of my line of sight. Soldiers swallow him whole.

He simply vanishes.

Sound evades me, hollowing as if I'm running through a tunnel. My heart pounds rapidly in my ears when the commander makes his move toward Aurora, cornered and surrounded by far too many soldiers despite her size.

I thought I knew pain when Easton died. I thought I felt the weight of the world when the fate of the Fae race and magic rested in the palm of my hands. I thought I felt devastation when I learned the news of Sector Seven's bombing.

I was wrong.

Because the weight that settles over my heart when I can no longer find Knox, the image of a sword through his chest playing on a loop in my mind, is *unbearable*. And what happens next is purely instinctual.

Rage heightens my strength to an unimaginable level as I thrash, kicking and elbowing the hands holding me until I'm dropped onto the floor. Without missing a beat, I swipe the nearest sword strapped to the soldier's hip and bring it down upon the iron shackles at my wrists.

The soldiers scramble, latching their hands onto any part of me they can.

They try to drag me to my doom, but my heart takes over, and the fire running through my veins consumes me whole. It begins at my sternum, spreading throughout my body like a plague, until my skin begins to swelter. Perspiration drips down my neck. The soldiers holding me wince, practically juggling me as their hands sizzle against my burning flesh.

A guttural roar rips from the depths of my soul.

Grief tries to sweep me into its talons, only to spit me back out again as I burn it.

The soldiers finally let go, their hands incinerated.

The burn marks are a promise of death.

My steps are a war drum, my heavy boots splashing through the puddles of crimson blood as I eat up the distance to where I last saw Knox. I snatch the dragon sword from the ground and the metal heats in my hand, turning the once silver steel red as I allow the fire within me to shatter.

Only to rebuild me.

Fury strikes up and down my arms. Energy sizzles throughout my body, bubbling to a point of no return. Smashing on the walls of my skin, roaring for release.

The restraints around my chest loosen enough to allow

oxygen into my lungs once more as I find Knox clutching the side of his underarm, the blade inches from his heart.

Nolan fends off the attacks swinging for his king.

My mate, my mate.

Relief consumes me, threatening to bring me to the ground, but only for a moment.

"The mission has been compromised! Code black!" a soldier screams.

Soldiers start dragging children to the gallows.

A woman to my right wails, pleading for mercy as a four-year-old girl is dragged by her wrists to the podium. Her tiny chest moves rapidly, panic encasing her as the soldier places her head on the guillotine.

My feet move, propelling my legs to run as fast as I ever have, but it's not enough. The soldier pulls the lever and the silver drops.

Anger flies through my body as if soaring through the air until it reaches its peak, and I realize it isn't anger at all.

I explode with power.

Unending, world shattering *power*.

Golden light erupts, pouring from me in every direction. Moving faster than light itself, it spreads not only across Sector One but all of Aloriah, across untraveled seas and unmarked lands. Across the world.

My pure light shatters the flimsy wards placed over these lands.

Golden flames dance along the tips of my fingers, tendrils curling around my forearm. They travel down my body and engulf me until I'm nothing but a ball of golden flames.

Tipping my head back on a roar, wings explode from my back, stretching to their full length. The blade that was once rushing for the child is encased in golden power and instead embeds itself in the shoulder of the man who placed her innocent life there. And with only a look, the king's soldiers simply fall. Their bodies drop like dead weight as golden light spears their chests and stops their heart.

My golden magic enforces justice, taking it upon itself as if it's a living, breathing thing. Those marked by my burning skin are punished, their necks snapped in one swift moment. Through it all, it knows to leave the commander alive, who stands in the town center surrounded by his dead men, speechless.

Diving within myself, I come face-to-face with my magic smiling back at me, ready to play.

My knees nearly buckle with relief as a tendril of shadow slithers down the gate, caressing, as Knox makes himself known.

Hello, Angel.

My eyes close on their own accord, savoring the sound of his husky voice.

Do you want to handle him, or shall I?

I look over to Knox. His wounds are stitching together, his Fae healing power in full force.

Golden flames dance in my eyes as my gaze lands on the commander…running.

Mine.

With the flick of my wrist, golden tendrils rush for the burly man, wrapping around his ankles like the snare they captured Hazel in. The commander falls flat on his face, a high-pitched scream rushing from his lips, the fall undoubtedly breaking more bones.

I don't feel pity for the man as my power drags him back.

The soldiers that were lucky enough to survive my magic's wrath now run, no longer cocky or wanting to take on a Fae. Axel cuts off their airways and Ace sprouts vines from the sodden ground to wrap around their limbs and pin them to the crimson courtyard, their faces shoved into the blood they rejoiced in spilling. Nolan exacts his revenge with his bare hands, cutting through the soldiers' flesh and bone that the twins hold captive like sheets of paper.

Reaching my hand out, I send a tendril of golden magic for the mother whose wail spoke to my soul—to my power. The one that shattered the restraints on my magic and gave me the ability to break Aloriah's wards.

Her confines are snapped in an instant, and she immediately sprints for her baby girl beneath the guillotine. The mother wraps the child in her arms, weeping with relief instead of grief.

Hazel moves from citizen to citizen, that baby girl still held tightly in her arms as she cuts the ropes of those lucky enough to remain alive. We lost too many, and we may have been far too late as time worked against us, but we saved the remaining. And any life saved today is a life worth celebrating.

The sobs of relief as parents and loved ones are rejoined with their children is a beautiful melody in my ears, making up for the blood my power spilled at the hands of my anger.

I cannot believe all those lives, all those beating hearts, are just simply…gone.

Taking a deep breath, I face the commander. My power lifts him, dangling him upside down by his ankles. A gleeful sizzle comes from my sternum, my magic rejoicing in the revenge.

I cock my head, dragging out the well-deserved punishment.

Knox comes to stand beside me. His hard gaze narrows on the commander, the look searing the leathers from the man with tendrils of fire. The material burns from his body piece by piece until he's left in nothing but his under briefs.

"How do you wish to handle him?" Knox asks lazily as if we have all the time in the world.

The whimper that leaves his mouth has satisfaction coursing through my veins, though not nearly enough for the pain this man has caused.

"I would prefer him to suffer a slow death. To make him scream like he made the children do," I answer coldly. My steps are slow and precise as I move forward, letting the conviction of rage burn through my eyes. I lift the man higher until his face comes in line with mine. "However, I'll give you the courtesy you should have given those innocent people. You can either die, or you can live and relay a message for me."

"Message!" he screams.

My eyes shine. "Brilliant choice."

The man has the wits to pale. "Any other—"

Shadows strangle his mouth, cutting off the words. Knox's shadow fire dances along the commander's skin. The undeniable scent of burning flesh shoves itself down my nose.

It seems Knox is favoring fire and smoke. My lips spread into a grin; it complements golden power quite well.

"You will return to the capital and let the king know I have returned," I continue.

"W-what sh-should I tell him exactly?"

My smirk turns feline. "Tell the king that his dearest daughter is back and ready to claim her payment… *Retribution.*"

I step back, snapping my power away as I do, allowing the commander to fall on his back. As he gathers his trembling knees and arms beneath him, Knox continues singeing his clothing until he stands stark naked as the day he was born.

When all the commander does is stand there, ogling at both of us like a fish out of water, Knox snaps, "Run along. There's no use for you if you die with hyperthermia before you relay the message."

I don't bother watching as he runs for the forest, to the mountains he will have to climb. Instead, the moment my eyes lock on Knox, I fling myself into his arms, nestling my head into the crook of his neck. I rejoice in the feel of his strong arms wrapping around me and the way pinewood and ocean surround my senses.

Snaking a hand between us, I brush it over his healing skin, needing to feel the closed wound for myself, feel the ridges and bumps smooth out underneath my fingertips.

"That was too close," I say softly. I despise the images that infiltrate my mind, the moment Knox disappeared. The moment my heart thought I had lost him.

Now I have two graphic images of his death for my mind to assault me with.

Hazel joins us, her voice drawing our attention. "I thought you didn't want the king to know you were back?"

Knox snorts. "The golden light erupting throughout Aloriah was a message in itself."

I nod, a little crestfallen. Staying hidden isn't a possibility anymore. "The king saw my golden light the night he murdered Easton." Swallowing thickly past that memory, I force myself to go on. "He is many things, but he isn't stupid... He will know it was me."

He probably already sent out his hounds.

"And *how* did you do that?" Axel asks in awe, cocking his head as if he can study my power.

I shrug. "I thought it was anger I had felt building over the last three days. Turns out it was my magic."

Nolan claps Knox on the shoulder. "She might give you a run for your money on the title of most powerful Fae."

I cut off whatever cocky jab Knox was surely about to toss back. "We need to send them to safety," I say, looking at the citizens of Sector One both reuniting with loved ones and mourning over those whom we were too late to save.

"I don't think anywhere in the human lands is safe," Hazel says meekly.

Her eyes are haunted, and glassy, as if her mind has taken her far away. Considering the way, she's clutching the baby girl in her arms, she must be feeling immense pain.

How triggering it would have been for her, especially as the soldier dragged that little girl—

"Neither do I," I murmur, forcing my mind to change directions. "How hard would it be to get them to Azalea?"

Knox rubs the back of his neck, counting the number of people left. "The trek would be hard, but not impossible. The Water Court royals owe me a favor; they'll open their borders and allow them to pass through."

"It would take at least a month on foot," Axel chimes in.

"Couldn't Cardania spare boats?" Ace asks.

Knox's lips thin into a grim line. "I suppose I'll owe them a favor after all." Knox sighs deeply before meeting my eyes. "Leave it to me."

Without another word Knox takes off, Axel and Ace close on his heels as they whisper in hushed tones. Hazel assists me in helping those in need while Nolan starts hauling the soldiers' dead bodies away. Similarly to how they treated those they murdered, Nolan piles the bodies high, though keeps their heads and limbs together, a kindness those men didn't show the people of Aloriah.

Looking over the town's center, at the once bustling mining town, I'm shocked by the magnitude of destruction.

Burnt pieces of furniture lie charred on the ground, scattered throughout the square town. In the once bustling market square, now only trampled goods are sprawled in every direction, mingling with the debris of the stone buildings.

They'll never recover from this, nor will they be able to return to their homes.

The only thing that stands through it all is the old well that sits in the center, along with the gallows behind it. What the soldiers will always put first—death.

I can't help but replay the words Nolan spoke only nights ago, telling me the truth that those around me have avoided saying. There will be bloodshed, and, in the heat of the moment, it comes down to whether you choose yourself or if you allow others to choose your fate for you.

My magic chose for me.

Chapter Ten

The weight of what we witnessed today doesn't begin to compute until later in the evening. Hours after gathering supplies for the Sector One citizens' travels, we organize those who will ride the remaining horses from the sector and those who will go off first to meet and coordinate with Lenox and Harlow. The former who had apparently been annoying Harlow to no end when Knox's communication with the pair through telepathy was severed just hours after our departure, once we crossed the wards. Apparently, Harlow had to calm the nervous Fae several times, talking him out of searching for us.

My heart pinched when Knox relayed the mental messages he received. Lenox, out of them all, would not survive losing Knox, not only his king but his brother in every sense of the word. I can't imagine his mental and emotional distress after not hearing from us for close to four days.

Especially after my premonition.

It only took a moment for Knox to describe what happened, sending mental images and a handful of memories to Lenox and Harlow. Knox didn't convey what the half-breed witch said but it was enough to make Knox's lips twitch into a small smile.

After carefully crafting a letter, Knox handed it off to the local sector messenger, ordering the young man to give it directly to Lenox and to care for it with his life. Though the citizens were clearly grateful for our help, they were still skittish, as evident by the messenger's tremble and fear in the air. I couldn't blame them, especially not after the ordeal they just suffered.

As the messenger walked off, Knox grumbled under his breath about the headache Harlow would inflict since she couldn't receive the letter. He tried to play it off, but the tension that lined his shoulders made me question what it truly meant to be in debt to the royals of Cardania. The price Knox would ultimately have to pay.

It wasn't until Ace, the emissary of the Essence Court, whispered in my ear did I understand. Knox has never once in his reign owed anyone in the royal courts a favor, choosing to never place himself in a position where his kindness could be used against him.

It did strange things to my heart to know that Knox would do it to help my people.

It's been hours since we watched the last remaining three thousand people of Sector One take off through the mountains, moving in the direction of the Fae lands without us. Before they left, a few gave me tearful hugs and words of gratitude, which touched the bottom of my heart. It was a strong reminder that it's always worthwhile to seek out change if it gifts happiness.

We chose to rest for the night under the canopy of trees by the border that divides Sector One and Sector Four. Knox and his court sit around a small fire, courtesy of Knox's fire magic. We haven't encountered any other soldiers along the way, although we have heard tree branches and twigs snapping, along with footsteps scurrying in the other direction.

Other than that, utter silence greets our ears.

Even the pops of the logs are muted, the weight of the king's orders pressing heavily on our minds and hearts.

Devastation doesn't begin to express the suffering my people have been forced to endure day in and day out. To now turn around and be executed, sentenced to death for simply existing, is an abomination.

Bile churns in my stomach. Where does a man set forth a plan to turn children into orphans so he can create soldiers indebted to him for his own game? And *who* does he plan to fight against with this army? The Fae, now that their lands are accessible? Or is there a bigger plan in motion that none of us could ever dare dream of?

Clearly, that question is not just on my mind. When Knox's power was released, he was able to unshrink everything. Nolan was teary-eyed being reunited with his favorite blade. He now sharpens that sword with deadly intent. Ace's boot taps out a steady rhythm.

Near him, Zephlyn sleeps peacefully, his wound fully healed now—courtesy of Hazel. Though ever since Aurora hasn't left his side.

Nolan is the first to break the silence.

"How far until we reach—" He frowns, the cloth pausing in his hands as he cleans his blade. "Where are the mermaids sending us?"

My throat is raw and scratchy from the hours of unuse. "We should arrive tomorrow afternoon, before sundown. There's a waterfall at the edge of the western mountainside of Sector Four." I shrug, staring into the blazing fire, comparing its tendrils to my golden power. "That's all they told me."

Nolan's gaze narrows. "A waterfall," he says dubiously.

"Yes, a waterfall."

He throws his hands in the air. "We've already encountered one. How exactly do you think we're going to know which is the correct waterfall?" He scoffs. "Fucking mermaids and their stupid riddles."

I huff, exhausted by his voice already. "Were you born pessimistic or is it simply a personality trait you've chosen? Because if so, you chose poorly."

I should mind my manners, but I find I simply don't have the energy for it. Being forthcoming is far more pleasurable, especially as Nolan's head rears back with wide eyes full of shock.

Axel and Ace chuckle, Hazel's lips quiver, and Knox outright smirks as he stares down Nolan. "I agree, perhaps you could have a more hopeful view of the situation."

Nolan points the blade he was cleaning at me. "Her father has ordered his own people to be butchered like animals and the children sent to gods know where to fight in a war only he knows. Forgive me for being hesitant of the mermaids' words."

The truth of his statement not only sobers me, but all of us.

Knox's teeth grit, but he doesn't tell Nolan off.

"Do you have any idea what he could be planning?" Axel asks.

If only he knew I was asking myself the same question mere minutes before. "No. I sat in nearly every council meeting. *None* of this was discussed." Duke Harrison, the king's second, flashes through my mind. The burly duke with a heart as wicked as the king's. "But if anyone does, it's Duke Harrison."

Axel moves to grab a map of Aloriah, only to stop as I mumble, "Glued to the king's side."

I don't need to see the hopeless faces of Knox's court; I can feel the helplessness myself. Shaking my head in frustration I stand, going for a walk to clear my mind.

I wander aimlessly through the dense forest before I stop and lean against a large oak tree. Tipping my head back to the sky, I allow the stars and night air to calm me, to soothe the tightness in my chest.

It isn't long before I have company.

"Angel."

A rush of air leaves me as Knox's husky drawl races down my spine.

The heat of his body warms my cold skin. The moment his fingertips drag down my cheeks my eyes snap open, finding his sparkling down at mine with a ferocity that steals my breath.

Running through my garden, to the bridge forged between our minds, I find his soul standing there, waiting for me, surrounded by the flowers we planted out of the care for one another.

I run to him, throwing my arms around his middle as he wraps his own around me.

Oh, how I missed this. How I missed *us*.

It's a magical thing to feel one another, to hear their thoughts, and to have such an extraordinary bond between two souls.

"Care to tell me what you're thinking?"

I grin. "Why should I waste words on what you already know?"

"Sometimes it helps to say it out loud."

I step back, needing space to arrange the whirlwind of

Heir of Broken Kingdom 117

thoughts consuming my mind. When Knox is near it's hard to concentrate, even harder when he's touching me.

It's a shock to see him so disheveled, even while training and running through the mountains and forests of the Essence court, Knox looked pristine, not a hair out of place. It's odd to see him covered in filth.

It's almost riveting to see.

My smile fades as I say, "I'm thinking about how I've dragged your court into my mess, one that might likely kill us all."

"You didn't drag us. Every single one of them—including Nolan, which I feel I may need to remind him—stepped forward and offered their assistance. We are here by choice, Angel, and we are not going to die." He steps forward, struggling with being near and not touching my skin. "What I want to know is how."

I frown. "How what?"

He licks his lips after they part on a deep exhale. "How did you break it?"

Panic. It squeezes my chest before I bore into his depths, and it relinquishes its control. It can never stay around long when Knox is nearby.

"I don't know," I answer simply.

His head cocks. "You didn't feel it building?"

"It felt like anger. I thought it was just the hatred I felt for the king."

"Perhaps it was. You have always had—" He stops himself.

"It's okay, Knox. If anyone is aware of my emotional reactions fueling my power, it's me." I swallow thickly. "I need to get that under control, don't I?"

All of Hazel's hard work in those first few days I entered

the Fae lands all flew out the window today. At least my emotional explosion saved us all, rather than doomed us.

His lip twitches, a single dimple appearing as he tries to hold his smile back. "That would be a stark yes. I don't think any of us feel like having our heartbeats stolen by your beautiful golden swirls."

The men simply dropped.

I shake my head as the image of it filters through my mind. "I didn't mean to do that," I whisper. "I never chose that. I didn't even control it; my magic did."

Can I even say I took a life? It may have been my magic, but it certainly was never my intention. Although I suppose that's a sorry excuse for not wanting the guilt upon my shoulders.

Because that's all my words are—denial.

My magic is the reason those men aren't breathing…why their hearts no longer beat. The guilt most certainly lies atop my shoulders. Except, I do not have the luxury of crumbling beneath what that means.

Knox frowns. "You weren't in control of your power?"

"No, my magic chose for me." I loosen a deep sigh. "It chose to save my life and that little girl."

"Delilah…" His mouth hangs open as he chooses his next words carefully. "Magic doesn't work that way." When all I do is stare, he goes on, his eyes searching mine. He reaches out, his fingertips skimming my arms. "*We* control magic. It should never control us, and it certainly shouldn't have a mind of its own."

"Do you not have a connection with yours?"

"Of course I do, it's just…a far different connection."

It puzzles him. I can see it written across his face.

"Should I be afraid?"

Both dimples appear as a gentle smile spreads across his

face. "No, Angel, just because your magic is different doesn't mean you should be afraid of it. Abnormalities are never something to fear. Instead, I believe they are to be cherished."

I lay my palm on his cheek, savoring the sight of his thick eyelashes fluttering closed as he nestles further into my touch. "You are a beautiful man, Knox Holloway."

I can almost feel his soul sighing at the words.

Knox tilts his head, his eyes straying to the soft glow of the fire. "We need to get back," he murmurs, a deep frown marring his face.

I chuckle. "Don't look so detested at the idea of sleep."

I know I'm certainly exhausted, although it's more so my body begging for rest. My mind, on the other hand, remains restless.

Knox's eyes flit between the camp behind me and my lips. Whatever thoughts drift through his mind relinquish into nothing but dust as he leans forward and places his lips against mine.

We both sigh into the kiss, as if we have been starved of each other's touch.

Home, my body screams.

Endless emotions from Knox's heart pour down the bond. Care, tenderness, and pure undulated need.

His tongue slips into my mouth, silky and smooth as it begins to—

A rough cough behind us jolts us apart.

"Not to disturb you, but if you two are going to make out, I'd rather you do it closer to the camp," Axel says sheepishly. "Better to be safe than sorry."

My eyes widen with embarrassment and my cheeks burn. My head falls into Knox's chest, though I can't help but giggle.

I can practically hear the smirk in Knox's voice as he drawls, "We'll be there in a moment."

I don't pull back until I hear Axel's voice join the others.

Gasping, I cover my mouth with my hand. "That was mortifying!"

Sliding his hand into mine, Knox pulls me along, practically vibrating as he gloats, "That was enjoyable. We should do it again. Seeing you blush like a mad man might be my favorite way to pass the time."

I whack his shoulder as we round the trees and join the others.

"I'm taking the first shift," Axel says as if he didn't just catch us making out in the forest.

Knox dips his head. "Note if any soldiers resume schedules."

"I'll take the next," Nolan grumbles.

I nestle next to Knox on the ground. Though the satchel full of clothing is meant to act as a pillow, nothing can salvage the pinecones and sticks digging into my back. If Knox can travel with shrunken items, why did no one think to bring rollaway mats?

Knox's deep breathing floats to me instantly, his face soft as sleep pulls him under. The return of magic to all of us demands sleep, mine, especially after my outburst, but my mind won't stop spinning an endless web of thoughts.

I lift my head, my eyes connecting with a shade of green that mirrors the leaves. I slowly pull myself up and out of Knox's embrace and lean against the tree at my back.

"Can't sleep?" Axel whispers.

I shake my head.

His eyes bore into mine, and I can see it written in their depths that he knows why.

"I'm sorry, Delilah. I can't imagine how you're feeling."

For what? The lives my power claimed, or the fact the king will know I am here?

But Axel can imagine how I'm feeling, and he is, it's why so much sadness floods his gaze. But sometimes denial feels like an offered glass of water in the desert.

"I'm sorry I dragged you all into this."

Axel shrugs. "There will always be battles and wars to fight, although this one in particular feels like one worthy to conquer." His mouth twists with a grimace. "My imagination didn't do him justice to how sadistic he is."

"Even I was shocked at what we saw today. Anyone would be."

"Except the soldiers." He searches the forest as if someone might overhear before barely whispering, "Why are the soldiers doing it? Loyalty is one thing—I would hand over my life for Knox—but I would never carry out what the king is ordering. Your father's army… It's another thing entirely."

I flinch at the word *father*, though the apology is already in his eyes at the slip.

"What Nolan said the other night is true. In the human lands, it's either you or them, and the soldiers will do anything to save themselves."

I never truly understood it until today, when it came down to either them or me. Perhaps that's it—the soldiers are fighting for their lives by taking them.

Axel looks away. "I don't think so," he mutters

His mind seems to take him far away.

"Axel," I whisper, breaking whatever train of thought his mind had dragged him down. "About what happened at the Tree of Life." His mask cracks, a sliver of pain flashing across his face before he shuts it down. And that's when I know exactly what has the second-in-command acting withdrawn day in and day out.

"Nobody is responsible for what happened besides Emmalyn."

Although apparently, even she is not to blame, simply a puppet.

A sad smile ghosts his face. "It's kind of you to try and appease my guilt but it's a waste of your time."

"No, it's not. Your guilt is misplaced and if I have to shout that into your ear every night then I will." My eyes steel, letting him see just how stubborn I'm willing to be.

But the longer the silence stretches, the more my confidence slips and so does his mask. It's as if the emotions raging beneath his surface are clamoring to the forefront and he's scrambling to shove them down. He cannot hide the misguided belief anymore.

"Explain it to me then," I whisper.

He blows out a shaky breath. "I-I—" He clears his throat, looking away. "I get to people too late." The sentence is a garble of words that he rushes out.

I lick my suddenly dry lips, surprised he answered my question at all. "Besides me, which I would like to state that you were never meant to be at the tree, who have you not been able to save?"

When Axel lifts his head, silver glints in his eyes, pooling faster than he can blink away. "My mother liked to play games with me." His voice cracks before he continues. "She knew I wanted to be a warrior, to train at the island…so she used it against me. She used to say that every good warrior needed to be fast and think quickly in situations so she'd—" He stops abruptly. His chin quivers, forcing him to clench his jaw. "The day she died was a test. She wanted to see if I could get to her fast enough and save her from the pills she ingested." Barely above a breath, he whispers, "I was too late."

I don't care who I wake up. I lunge for Axel, squeezing him in a hug. I wish more than anything I could comfort the child who was abused and the man who was too late to save his wicked mother.

His arms are slow to move around me at first but then his hold tightens, as if I'm a raft he found in the endless ocean.

"Axel, I—" My voice cuts off. No words I utter will ever be able to fix the damage she inflicted. "I am so sorry," is what I manage to whisper. "You were never meant to save her, Axel. Someone who toys with a child like that...she knew how many pills to take to end her life. Her choice should not lie on your conscious."

A lone tear falls down his cheek. "I've never told anyone that. Ace believes she overdosed on drugs, not because of a test I failed."

My heart cracks, pinching painfully. "Thank you for entrusting me with your truth."

He clears his throat. "What do you think we'll find tomorrow?"

The change in subject is abrupt, but I take the hint and allow it. I pull back, looking up to the night sky as if the stars will answer the question for me. "I have no idea."

Whispers spread throughout the mountains. Throughout the sectors. Throughout the king's army. Rumblings of the six Fae and two griffins who stalk the human lands and the carnage they leave in their wake.

Despite the king's original orders to capture any Fae, those we see with our Fae sight run in the opposite direction out of fear, not once aiming their arrows at us. The fact that they flee brings us a slight comfort, though Knox keeps Nolan at the back, the warrior on high alert and ready for any surprise attack.

I keep my footsteps light as I crouch behind Knox, following his lead through the thick, tall strands of grass. But I suppose it wouldn't matter even if they were heavy—the waterfall to our right drowns out every sound in the vicinity.

Knox stops abruptly as a small, one-story cottage comes into view, smoke puffing from the chimney. It's obviously well taken care of, the surrounding forest maintained as if a personal garden. In response, the trees seem to lean toward the home, protecting it and hiding the chimney stone and its tendrils of smoke.

If not for my Fae eyesight, I never would have seen it.

Is this what the mermaids have led us toward?

I had assumed that following their trail would send us toward something demonic, yet there's not an ounce of the corrupt magic here.

There's no ill feeling, no slithering of ice down my spine and there's certainly no horrid odor that I've come to expect with those that are demonic.

If anything, it's…peaceful.

I didn't know such a thing existed in the human lands.

The mermaids said to continue until we reached the waterfall, and this is the only one we've come across since that first unfortunate day in the mountains. If it weren't for the high altitude and the number of hours spent trekking, I would have thought to continue until we encountered a waterfall inhabited by creatures with dark magic.

With the setting sun, the glow of a fire begins to stream through the glass windows. It also highlights a shadow moving throughout the cabin.

Beside me, Aurora lowers her head into the bush, her raven coat blending into the shadows.

Squinting, I let my Fae sight overpower me, zoning in on the details of the cottage. The splinters, lines, and divots in the wood. The floral curtains, its finery and thread count fluttering in the wind. Yet it isn't enough; I still can't see *who* is inside.

They hide carefully behind walls and objects as they flit from room to room, lighting candles along the windowsills.

I hold my breath, the others seeming to do the same as the front door squeaks open, a shadow falling over the small veranda.

My heart drops.

It can't be.

Ignoring the court's protests, I stand on wobbly legs, my knees threatening to buckle with every step I take.

Knox and Aurora don't try to hold me back. They feel the recognition within my heart and the emotions flooding the chambers.

Leaves rustle beneath my boots, making the person lift their head to mine.

Their mouth drops open. Shock twists their features.

I *hear* the inhale of air that gets lodged in their throat.

My body freezes, only for a moment—for a second—and then I'm running.

A whimper tumbles from my lips as I throw myself into their awaiting arms.

They sigh in relief. "Delilah."

"Annie," I croak.

Chapter Eleven

The weight of what I've endured these past few months pours out of me with abandon. I couldn't possibly hold my tears at bay even if I tried. Not with her. The relief of seeing her alive and unharmed has my knees buckling, taking us to the forest floor.

My eyes hook on her signature white bow. As if seeing it confirms the woman before me is real and not a figment of my imagination.

Her delicate fingers run down my chocolate brown hair. "It's okay now, dear. I'm here."

Her honey smooth voice does nothing to stop the tears from flowing. I hadn't realized how much I longed for her comfort and care.

My arms shake as I hold her out before me, searching every inch of her for any signs of pain that *he* could have inflicted.

It isn't until Annie lays her hand on my cheek, forcing my wild gaze to snap to her gold-ringed eyes—akin to Aurora's—do I pause my search.

"I'm okay, Delilah. I promise."

I shake my head, knowing in my heart that what I'm about to tell her will destroy her. That if she didn't feel pain before, she will now. My chin wobbles, my voice shaking as I whisper, "Easton is—" I swallow. Despite the time that has lapsed that word is still stuck in my throat.

Dead.

Annie's eyes soften, tears pooling instantly. "I know, dear."

"W-what? How?"

I don't hear Annie's answer, I only see her mouth move. Like my head has been dunked underwater.

Just a simple sentence, and yet it was detrimental.

Because if Annie knows…it confirms it all. That it's real. Easton is truly gone, and he is never coming back.

Easton is dead.

Something I had known for months, something I witnessed myself, and yet there was still a part of my heart that had clung to hope. I feel that piece break as the tears fall once more.

"It happened so quickly. I tried to stop it; I tried to stop *him*!" I rush on. Talking as quickly as I can as Annie blurs before me. My next words are muffled by hiccups as my crying turns hysterical. "I finally stood up to him…and he killed Easton for it."

It's my fault.

Annie pulls me into her. "You have always taken on the ownership of his actions, and that ends now. Easton wouldn't want you to blame yourself. I may not know exactly what occurred out there…but I know it wasn't your doing, Delilah."

"But—"

"No, dear. The man who sits atop a throne of malice is to blame. Not you."

Even with the conviction in her words, I will forever blame myself. I was the reason he was there in the first place. I put a target over his head the moment I allowed him to crawl through those bushes when we were children and kept it there as I let him into my heart day in and day out.

I should have protected him better. I should have pushed him away. Instead, I was selfish. I couldn't bear to lose his friendship, the companionship he brought me, and yet in doing so—in holding on tighter—he was ripped away from me.

Annie opens her mouth to speak, only for a snapping twig to cut her off as Knox's court makes themselves known behind me. The sight has Annie visibly paling, her hands quivering as she covers her mouth.

Despite the shockingly large Fae males, I know it's not them that has Annie stumbling backward. It's Aurora and Zephlyn, standing to their full height and stalking forward.

It's the revelation of not only Fae but also Griffins.

Aurora cocks her head, studying the woman beside me. Annie grabs my arm instinctively and tries to usher me behind her, those fierce protective instincts kicking in.

With so many things brimming on the tip of my tongue, stories, and ugly truths that need to be told, I don't know where to start… I don't know how to explain it all to her. So instead, I stand, pulling away from Annie's grasp, and walk to meet Aurora halfway.

Out of all the people who have come through my life, Annie and Easton were the two to accept me with open arms. Yet there is nothing I can do to stop the trembling in my fingers as I tuck my hair behind my ears and let Annie discover the truth I have been trying to wrap my head around since the moment I stumbled into Hazel's bathroom and saw my new features.

I hold my breath as Annie loosens hers.

Disbelief flashes across her eyes first before they roam, scanning every inch of my body before flicking towards the others. Her eyes widen with every similarity she finds, but when her gaze comes back to mine, I don't find disgust, hatred, or fear.

Instead, she simply murmurs, "It's impossible."

My lips spread into a smile as I bear my canines. Then golden light, matching that of the setting sun, twirls around my palm before encasing my forearm in tendrils of flame.

Annie's eyes grow impossibly wide as she stumbles forward, her arms outstretched to grab me as if her instincts are trying to save me from myself. She swallows thickly, awe coating her words. "It seems I'm not the only one with a story to share."

The golden magic disappears just as quickly as it formed. "Indeed, there's a lot to catch up on."

I *feel* him before I smell his pinewood or hear his light footsteps. The indescribable pull that's between us sparks, our bond singing its praises at being alive and free once more.

Knox places his palm on my lower back, his touch electric.

Turning to Knox, I try to see him as Annie does, trying to see him for the first time and ignoring the teasing in my mind that reminds me I visit that memory daily. The way he leaned against the tree, his cocky smirk, his husky teasing. The devastating beauty that is Knox.

Despite where my mind and heart want to take me, I see the strength in which he carries himself, the regal posture and confidence that oozes from it. How self-assured he is in every move he makes. The way his fighting leathers highlight the decades' worth of training. The swords strapped to his waist look like mere accessories on the lethal warrior poised to strike.

I adore it all and yet that isn't what knocks the breath from me. Those sapphire eyes glint with mischief as they connect with mine. His knowing smirk grazes my skin as he catches me ogling him.

His jaw is peppered with stubble, adding to his dark mystery. His raven hair is tousled from his fingers running through the strands constantly, a nervous tick of his that only adds to his appeal.

His strong jawline softens as I smile up at him. My voice is husky as I say, "Annie, this is Knox Holloway, King of Azalea and the Essence Court."

Annie stumbles over her words before bowing deeply. "Your Majesty, it's an honor."

"There's no need for that, Annie. If anything, I should be bowing to you, the woman who raised Delilah." Knox dips his head. "You did an impeccable job."

Annie's cheeks aren't the only ones that flush crimson. A glassy sheen covers her eyes. "Thank you."

"Knox is my mate!" I blurt.

Aurora puffs air beside me as if chuckling at my nervousness.

I can't help it. Knox is right. When my mother became…distant, Annie took over. She was a mother to me in every sense of the word and her approval means everything to me. I don't know how I'd feel if she didn't approve of who I am becoming, alongside the company I keep.

It may make me childish but with the few loved ones I

have left from my old life, it means a great deal to me to be able to have Annie in my current life.

"So, you're truly a—"

"Fae," I finish for her. "Apparently."

Her head tilts as she glances toward Knox. "And he is your mate?" she asks, perplexed.

My tongue clicks.

Of course.

I mustn't forget that Annie needs to learn everything I had to about the Fae and their magical world. Mates included.

"Every Fae has a mate, a bond that connects their souls, hearts, and minds." My cheeks flush. "Some are rare enough to have a soul pair with animals, which is platonic, but the…" I clear my suddenly dry throat. "The Fae mating bond is a romantic connection…your true love and partner in life."

It's the first time I've said the word *love* out loud regarding Knox and the mating bond, and the word has fear striking my heart.

With Knox standing beside me, his heat radiating against my skin, the bond between us grows hot. It burns my entire face, turning it an ugly shade of red.

Aurora lowers her head to nudge it against my shoulder. I smile up at her, thankful for the change of topic as I say, "This is Aurora, my soul pair."

"You have a rare bond?"

"Rare everything," Nolan mutters under his breath.

I don't miss the confusion that fills Annie's eyes. There's a lot to explain to her.

I gesture for everyone to step forward. "This is Knox's court and my friends."

I pointedly look at Hazel, who is a spitting image of Annie. No wonder I confused her for Annie when I awoke that first day she found me.

Hazel steps forward, a tentative smile spreading across her rosy cheeks. "My name's Hazel. The mermaids brought Delilah to me."

Annie's brows jump high, her eyes sparking with excitement.

"Nolan, Knox's army commander," he says gruffly, trying to move along the introductions.

Axel dips his head, his voice soft. "I'm Knox's second-in-command, Axel." He slides his forest-green eyes to me. "And Delilah's friend."

Warmth rushes through my heart at the sentiment.

Ace is last and perhaps that was his own doing because no one misses the way grief consumes Annie, crumbling her features as he steps forward. *Easton's doppelgänger.*

The twins may be identical but the tattoos, long black hair, and the way Axel carries himself differentiates himself from Ace, making the comparison between him and Easton astronomical.

Annie doesn't move as tears roll freely down her cheeks, seeming to forget the rest of their presence. Her lips wobble with a strained smile.

Easton was like a son to her; she would have felt the grief just as deeply as I had…perhaps more so. How would it feel to raise a child, only to outlive them and watch them die?

He swallows thickly, his voice barely above a whisper. "I'm Ace. It's nice to… I'm sorry for your loss." He quickly steps away after his stumbling words, as if it physically pangs him to harm her.

"Thank you," Annie says, her voice cracking. Ace tries to hide behind his brother, but Annie's eyes never leave his face, taking in every intricate detail and cataloging the differences.

She won't find many.

Knox is the one to break the tense silence. "If you don't

mind, we've been traveling for a long time. We'd love to sit somewhere that isn't the forest floor."

Annie's eyes snap from Ace to Knox, a sheepish smile curving her lips. "Where are my manners? Of course!" She begins backing away to the cottage. "Come in, I hope you don't mind—" She stops abruptly, staring at the log cottage before turning back with a grimace.

Within an instant, I know my heart is about to hurt.

"There's something you must know first, Delilah."

Worry clutches my heart like a vise. "What is it?"

Annie wrings her hands. "Perhaps it's easier if I show you."

Knox and Aurora never leave my side as Annie beckons me to follow her. My two protectors, willing to fight any battle that threatens my heart.

Walking around the side of the cottage, we're met with a large wooden fence that appears to stretch on for miles into the shadows of the dense forest.

My footsteps pause and at first, I question whether I'm hallucinating.

But as two shadowed figures break through the tree line, running side by side in sync, their excited squeals rushing through my ears, I know I'm not.

Elation fills my chest instead of oxygen as I gasp.

Creseda and Henry gallop as fast as the wind will take them. Creseda throws her head back, squealing in delight.

The last time I saw Creseda was when Easton and I took off in the carriage. I peered back at her, our eyes never leaving each other's until the carriage had taken us deep within the forest.

I swore to her that we would reunite. At least I didn't break that vow.

Easton's loss becomes a tangible thing as I stare at the remnants of our old life. Annie, Creseda, and Henry.

My hand visibly trembles as I reach out and lay my palm against her snout.

Creseda's lips tickle my neck as she nickers. The soft sound sends a pang through my heart. I wonder what they think happened. I wonder if Henry blames me. Considering we left them alone at the palace, that I left with Easton only to return without him. I wonder if Henry's roving eyes are searching for him…searching for a man who will never sit atop him again.

I wouldn't blame Henry or Annie if they lost their faith in me. I lost it within myself the moment the king dragged his blade across Easton's neck.

And through all the suffering and guilt consuming me, all I can think of is how he kept his promise to me, even in the afterlife.

The moment he had asked if I trusted him, I said yes without hesitation, without even thinking…because I didn't need to. Easton had grinned, vowing to keep Creseda safe. He kept his promise, and yet I couldn't fulfill mine. I trusted Easton with my life, and he trusted his with me.

That was his downfall.

Annie's delicate arms wrap around me, enveloping me in her signature rosemary scent, and we mourn together. Over the loss we will forever carry in our hearts. The memories we will cherish, and the name we will never forget.

The love he gave us.

"There's something else you need to see, Delilah," Annie whispers between patting the two horses.

Knox comes to me the moment I turn around, having given Annie and me the needed space and time. Yet he is not far; he never truly is. Knox will always be there to put the pieces of my heart back together, no matter how many times it shatters.

But as Easton's words float through my mind, the memory of the days before his passing, I snap my gaze to the cottage and blink rapidly, the answers to many questions begin to settle in my bones.

The truth that lies in Annie's eyes.

"It was his—yours, technically. It was his gift to you." Her eyes grow impossibly soft, trying to be as delicate as she can, as she whispers, "For when you were ready to leave the palace."

The confession breaks me.

It's a quiet breaking. I don't wail or scream for the loss I feel ripping me apart. My features barely move an inch. Instead, it happens internally, my soul screaming, my heart shredding into two at the one-story cottage staring back at me.

An intricate part of me dies before I even step foot inside.

You wouldn't know there was a death within me. I simply walk inside with my head held high but a war rages within me, and the only one who can feel it besides myself is Knox.

My emotions pummel him, yet he allows it, opening that door in his mind and shouldering the burden no one asked him to feel. He stands on the other side of the bridge, taking my pain and soothing it.

Trying to take it all away before it kills me from the inside out.

He trails behind me, his hand always touching me as I walk from room to room. Easton knew me well. The full bookcases hold the titles of my favorite books. The large tub overlooks the quiet forest. The cozy fireplaces in every room to scare away the winter blues. The endless pots and pans that fill the kitchen and the sword racks.

Although it's not just my personality that Easton filled the rooms with, it's his. The dream he envisioned for us, the life he wished to create.

For a moment I think I'm screaming, but my mouth isn't moving.

I find a kitchen cupboard filled to the brim with chocolate. Stationary ink sits neatly at a table before a large window in the living room—a dream of Easton's to have a sanctuary that would fill his imaginative mind with endless stories to write.

The untouched bedroom at the far end of the cottage sits with a thick coat of dust. Of course, Easton would claim the room closest to the stables, to be close to his deep love—Henry.

Closing my eyes, I take deep breaths as I allow my mind to wander—to imagine a life with him still in it. The life Easton not only pleaded with me every day for but the one he *deserved*.

I imagine the cottage brimming with his deep laughter, the way his eyes would have gleamed in the sunlight streaming through the windows. The way he would have sat at that stationary desk and written every morning, his brows furrowed deeply as he concentrated. The way he would have enjoyed the routine of mundane things—cleaning, cooking, and even the caretaking of the garden and stables.

Easton wanted nothing more in life than to have the freedom to choose his days.

And now, he will never have that choice.

I feel the protest in the rhythmic beats of my chest.

I fight against the lump in my throat as I force myself to say my next words.

"Where is he?" I whisper the question I have been too afraid to ask. "Did his mother bury him on their estate?"

Easton rarely saw his mother. She was sequestered in his father's home for the majority of her days, but when she was able to see her only son, she bestowed love upon him.

Unfortunately, love from one parent does not erase the horrible acts of the other. But I have no doubt she would have wanted Easton buried on their property.

When I'm only greeted with silence, I turn to Annie.

Her expression is caged. She leans against the wooden table in the kitchen, as if needing the strength.

My brows furrow, panic settling in. "Where is he?"

Knox steps in, partially blocking me from Annie. "Perhaps that's enough information for one day," he says as if picking up on something I cannot see.

I move around him. "No! I want to know where he is." I march toward Annie. "Where was he laid to rest?"

I need to have my goodbye.

Annie's eyes flutter closed. I expect tears, but when she opens them again, I'm shocked to find they're full of hatred —malevolence.

"He wasn't."

I blink. "Of course he was. Perhaps his father took—"

"Your father keeps his head as a trophy. A warning to all in the palace and capital of what is done to traitors." Disgust and hatred fill her voice. "He has him poised on a spike next to his throne."

Knox's court stills as silence descends.

My mind falls quiet—the calm before the storm.

Until it isn't quiet anymore.

I explode, a surge of power rippling through me.

Golden flames blast from within me, scattering for the wooden cottage. Within a second, air wraps around me, containing the power in a bubble.

I scream, the sound a vicious melody in the air as I kick and rage against the invisible shield, but it never buckles.

He kept his head as a trophy.

He kept his head as a *trophy*.

He kept his head as a trophy.

Golden flames consume me.

Chapter Twelve

I've often wondered what I look like during dissociation.

Whether my eyes change, if my expression changes…if *I* change. But I've never questioned what happens *after*. What happens when I come to? When my mind decides it's safe for my heart to return?

Often times when I come to, I can picture the moment it happened. The moment my feelings overwhelmed me, the moment that made my brain shut down, forcing my heart to abandon me.

I can remember the *before*, and yet when I try to go back and look at the memory of *during* and *after,* it's blank. It may be draining, and parts of my life are full of endless black holes, but I'm grateful. Thankful that my brain wiped whatever hurt from my memory. As if what I witnessed, felt, smelt, and heard was never filed correctly.

Do you want to know what happens after?

I have to remember how to be human again—or, should I say, Fae.

I'm no longer standing in the kitchen with golden flames

engulfing me. Instead, I'm lying in a comfortable bed with pinewood and ocean surrounding my senses. Knox's body heat radiates warmth into my chilled bones as he holds me from behind. An iridescent black wing draped over me, blocking the afternoon sun's rays from blinding me.

"Angel?"

His voice is gruff and uncertain as if I've awakened many times before.

I roll over to face him, taking in his beauty. Relief washes over his features.

Dark circles ring his eyes and his tousled hair, which he's surely been brushing his fingers through is proof he barely slept last night.

Or should I say nights?

"How long was I out?" I ask, my throat raw.

Knox leans forward and plants a gentle kiss on my forehead. "That doesn't matter. You're here now."

I close my eyes again as he brushes his fingers through my hair. The connection between us amplifies, the bond tugging and crackling beneath the surface of every touch, every breath, and every look.

"Was it a dream?"

"No, Angel," he says gently, his warm breath whispering across my skin.

Despite knowing the answer, another knife lodges itself into my heart.

The king is keeping Easton's head as a trophy, using him to make a point, to send a message.

Bile rushes for my throat, but it only manifests as a dry heave. My empty stomach violently grumbles, reminding my body of the comatose state I've apparently been in.

"Do you want me to get you something to eat?" Knox asks, already halfway to the door.

I shake my head, ignoring the pang my stomach sends as a protest. Instead, I turn to the window, watching as the sun shines between the leaves in the canopy of trees. How the light flutters through to the mossy forest floor like a lover's gentle brush.

"I want to go for a walk."

I need to get out of this cabin and its constant reminder of what I have lost.

Knox doesn't coddle me or refuse. He simply holds his hand out and helps me stand.

Leaving the room, I don't dare let my gaze wander to the kitchen or sitting area where I hear the soft rumblings of voices. I don't want to see the worried glances or pitiful expressions of my friends. I especially don't want to see Annie's gaze—afraid of what I might find there.

That's the thing with family, especially with ones you've created and found—they're the people you most don't want to disappoint.

My heart also wasn't the only thing to return to me. With it came the emotional war that sent my mind spiraling and magic exploding. It's still very much raging inside of me.

How awful, to have a body and mind that work against you.

But when my feet step outside and I round the cottage corner to find Creseda and Henry standing side by side, the voices in my mind quiet into a small mumble.

I barely said hello to them yesterday, not a greeting they both greatly deserve.

Laying a trembling hand on Creseda's snout, I find I can't speak, but no words are needed. They've never been needed with her. *Same with Easton.*

Dropping my head, Creseda does the same, meeting me in the middle. My forehead comes to rest against her snout as I stroke her with my hand. Her hairs tickle my palm, while the steady beat of her heart and her breath puffing across my face lull me.

I continue patting her as Henry moves beside me, joining us in this special moment.

Pushing past the lump in my throat, I turn my heavy gaze to Henry. "I'm so sorry."

I wish I had Hazel's ability to hear Henry for myself. To know what he truly thinks and feels. To carry the weight of his grief in my heart.

But I don't, and if there is anything I have learned over the past few months it is that grief is a battle meant to be climbed by the one carrying it.

Lifting my head, my gaze locks on piercing golden eyes.

Aurora and Zephlyn lie across the other side of the stable fence. A respectful distance is kept between the griffins and horses as if the creatures came to a mutual agreement to share the space.

I could swear her eyes ask me if I'm all right.

The corner of my lip lifts, my first attempt at a smile in… I lost count and track of time, but I know it's been a while. I dip my head before I turn away, the creatures eliciting too many emotions that I don't particularly want to feel.

That's what the walk was intended for—to get away. And as I stare at the stable fence that runs deep within the forest, at the care of everything within the surrounding area, the evidence of Easton's attention to detail—I rip my eyes away as they begin to burn with unshed tears.

Knox wraps his arm around my shoulder. "Come on, Angel, walk with me."

Always knowing exactly what I need and when Knox leads me away from the cottage, our steps grow lighter with every inch of space put between us and Easton's dream.

My lungs fill with air for what feels like the first time in days. The golden rays of sunshine tease my skin.

"Do you want to talk about it?"

"Not particularly."

Knox sighs. "You can't continue bottling things up."

My lips pucker. "Yes, I can."

Knox stops abruptly, turning me to face him. It frightens me how grave his features are.

"No, you can't. Not after what nearly happened."

I swallow, shame coating my tongue. "It was just a small episode—"

"Your magic almost consumed you."

His chest heaves, as if the danger is in front of him again.

I suppose it is. *I am the problem.*

But I can't tell him that I fear if I allow myself to feel everything brewing within me, it will consume me entirely. That it won't be my magic that he has to worry about devouring me but my heart.

I cannot give these emotions an inch because they will run red until there's no more blood left within me.

I shake my head, ignoring the worry that fills Knox's gaze. I can't have this be another thing we need to be concerned about, not with the weight of Aloriah and its civilization hanging in the balance.

Knox needs to be able to focus on himself, not be looking at me when his enemy is at his back. He needs to perform at his best, not be distracted and full of worry every time I use my magic. Especially not when every time I close my eyes, I see Knox's head dangling from the mouth of a demonic dragon. And it may be foolish, Knox can walk into my well of power whenever he pleases, but I know he won't without my consent.

So, I lie—no matter how sour it tastes, and pray he can't

feel it through the bond.

"It was just a horribly intense episode. I don't think you can blame me with the news I received."

I send a trickle of warmth down the bond, hoping it overpowers the lie. It's hard to keep things from your bonded one. The link is like no other I have felt, fusing together the very things that make us who we are. As if we truly are one.

His eyes soften. "I never blame you, Angel."

Taking a deep breath, I let the tension in our bond simmer, letting the fear within me build, brimming to the surface of my skin until it propels my next words. Because fear and courage are one and the same to me. One is just more heroic.

"I don't think we will ever win if we play his game. Our minds are not wicked and corrupt like his." Knox opens his mouth, but I rush on before he can speak. "I have too much anger in me to allow things to continue how they are, but things will not change by playing his game. It will be won by making our own."

Pride sparks in his eyes. "Now you're thinking like a warrior."

My cheeks tint pink. Clearing my throat, my mind drifts toward a thought that washes away my blush within seconds. "Now that the king has marked me a traitor, I suppose he no longer sees me as his heir."

A growl slips from his mouth. "He won't be on the throne long enough to make that decision for you."

My lips twitch, a smile threatening to bloom. "If everything goes well, yes, but until then…you won't like what I'm about to say."

"I'll listen regardless. With you, I always will."

He won't be saying that in a moment.

"No one can know we are mates."

Any semblance of control that was on Knox's features

vanishes entirely.

"No." That one syllable is as vicious as a whip.

"Knox, don't be—"

"I will not hide what we are to each other," he snarls.

My eyes soften. "I am not hiding—I am protecting. He has already eliminated one of my weaknesses." I swallow thickly, his name stuck in my throat. "Annie is nowhere near him, and I pray it stays that way. But mark my words, Knox, he will use any and every chance he can to destroy me when I go against him, and if he finds out that I have a mate... So help the forgotten gods, there will be nothing to stop him from coming after you to ruin me."

His gaze flicks back and forth, searching for what, I'm not sure.

That devilish smirk returns, along with the cocky glint in his eyes. "I can handle myself. You know they call me the most powerful Fae in all our lands, right?"

Ignoring his teasing tone, I wet my dry lips as my throat constricts around the unbearable truth, the one that has been haunting me since the premonition.

"I will not be able to handle it if he takes you away from me." My voice cracks. "Not you, Knox... I cannot lose you."

Knox wears his vulnerability and emotions in his eyes as he opens the door to his heart and lets it beat for me. I can feel the resistance on his side of the bridge, the bond practically screaming for him not to agree. His body visibly shudders as he relents.

"I will be whoever you need me to be, Angel." He rests his forehead against mine. "Whatever will get you through this." He loses a quick breath, a small groan tumbling from him. "How exactly am I meant to not touch you in front of others, though?"

"You must restrain yourself, Mr. Holloway."

His eyes fly open, a brow quirking. "Oh and do tell how we can do that when the bond pulls until our skin burns because it has been starved from affection."

"Is that a real thing?" I rasp.

Knox licks his bottom lip slowly. "Yes."

The liquid heat that pools in his sapphire eyes makes it difficult to discern whether he's telling the truth or teasing. But as I stare longer, my lips lift into an impish smile, and I find that I do not care.

Not in this precious moment of freedom he has created for me.

My heart beats rapidly, my breath quickening along with it. Knox's gaze flits from my eyes to my lips. My cheeks grow warm as I bite my lower lip, wishing more than anything that it was Knox's teeth grazing the soft skin instead of my own.

Knox's eyes flare.

Careful what you wish for, Angel.

"It could be fun," I say, surprised to hear how sultry my voice is.

"What could be?" Knox asks, his eyes never leaving my lips.

I lean forward, gently placing my palm on his chest and salivating as his body shudders from the simple touch. "Drawing out the pleasure we both so deeply yearn for." Desire pools between my legs at Knox's shaky breath. "Delayed gratification."

Our gazes are electric when they connect. As if lightning is jumping between us, a current of energy crafted by the intense bond.

It tugs, tightening to the point it feels like it's going to snap at any moment until we lean forward, our bodies coming to touch.

Our skin sings its praises, the bond sighing in relief.

What is your body begging for, Angel?

His intoxicating voice sends a shiver down my spine. Tipping my head back, I gaze into those sparkling sapphire eyes. Glee fills me at the heat I find sizzling in their depths.

We pause, waiting to see who will break first, who will be the one to make the first move. It's drawn out so long that my body begins to scream, heat tingling through the veins.

Knox lifts his hand ever so slowly, his resolve slipping, and as his fingertip finally grazes the underside of my jaw, I whimper. Leaning further into his touch, he trails his fingers up and down my neck, brushing over my collarbones.

My breathing turns shallow as he lowers, his lips a hair's breadth away from mine, his hot puffs of air drifting over my mouth. A tease of the heat that's to come.

"Answer me, Angel," Knox whispers.

I can't for the life of me remember what it is I'm supposed to answer.

"W-what was the question?" I stutter.

My clit pulses in response to his dark chuckle.

"Tell me what your body needs."

You.

The thought is instant as if I ingested a truth serum. But the answer mind to mind doesn't satisfy him.

His fingers trail over my collarbone, but instead of stopping and rounding back up my neck, he descends lower, taking my breath with him as his fingers graze over the mounds of my heavy breasts.

Let me hear the words, Angel.

His large palm comes to rest on my rib cage, his thumb brushing back and forth, dangerously close to where I want it. So much so my back arches involuntarily.

"I need you inside of me, Knox."

Need, not want. There's a difference.

And Knox knows that.

My eyes roll into the back of my head as he smashes his lips to mine. The kiss is hungry and urgent, devouring. I give it right back to him, feeding the insatiable need that surges through my body, demanding *more, more, more*.

Our groans fill each other's mouths as I slide my tongue against his, the warmth sending a lightning bolt through my heart.

I sink my hand into his hair. The silky raven strands glide between my fingertips and I use the strands to pull him closer.

Knox's self-control snaps with the movement.

His hands slide down my back, over the swell of my ass, until they rest on my thighs. He hauls me up and wraps my legs around his waist. Excitement fills me as he begins to walk, every step and thud of his boots sending a wave of desire through me. Until he stops, pinning me against a large tree trunk, and the weight of him against my front has wetness trickling down my thighs.

The moment his large cock brushes against my center, lining up perfectly through our clothing, we moan, the sounds in sync with one another.

My hips swivel of their own accord, seeking the friction I so desperately need.

Knox rips his mouth away from mine, his canines flaring before he scrapes them down my neck, eliciting a full-body shudder. The sensation makes me gyrate against him.

"Want something, Angel?" Knox teases.

With my hand still in his hair I yank his head back hard. Pleasure fills me to find him just as undone as I am—his chest heaving, his cock throbbing beneath his pants. His heavy-lidded gaze sears me with such heat I gulp.

"I already asked for what I want. Don't make me beg."

Knox's eyes blaze. "I'm just giving you a prelude of what's to come, Angel. After all, I'm no longer able to touch you in front of others, correct?"

My breathing stutters. "Y-yes, but there's no one around."

He shrugs. "Call it a practice run. I wouldn't want my *mate* to be surprised."

Knox smirks, the gesture turning predatory as he frees one of his hands, balancing me against the tree with the other he pins me with his hips to the bark. He lifts the flimsy white material of my shirt, dragging it over my head until my breasts spill free. Crisp air strokes the hard pebbles, Knox's magic caressing until goosebumps line the creamy skin.

When his large palm cups my breast, his thumb brushing back and forth over the sensitive bud, a moan tumbles from my lips. A quick pinch has my hips bucking, the pain sending a jolt between my thighs.

"Knox," I plead.

"Beg."

I snap my eyes open at the demand but shake my head before I think. Perhaps I'm a masochist and enjoy the sexual torture, or perhaps I want to make this last as long as possible. Either way, the feral growl of need that leaves his mouth is enough to make me squirm against his large length and whimper.

Knox lowers his head, his body trembling with the restraint of holding himself back, and captures my right nipple between his canines, his fingers gliding to tweak the other. His tongue rolls effortlessly over the tight bud as my chest rises and falls. I cling to him, my clit pulsing with a heavy ache.

Knox moves to the other nipple, licking and sucking in earnest as his free hand travels down my body before dipping into my fighting leathers. I hold my breath, praying and hoping for his touch.

My prayers are answered.

He sinks his fingers inside me, gliding in and out easily in the wetness there. His breath hitches. "You're so wet, Angel." His thumb brushes my clit in earnest as he begins to pump his fingers. The moans that fall from my lips are breathless, making my head spin.

His fingers crook inside me, brushing the spot only he can find, and at the same time, he clamps down on my nipple, sending unending waves of pleasure through my body. Every nerve ending alights at the pressure climbing inside of me with every pump of his fingers. Words fail me until all I am is a squirming mess in his arms, pleading for him to never stop as I chant his name like a prayer.

My body begins to tense, my toes curling and eyes squeezing shut—only for Knox to rip his fingers away.

I snap my eyes open. A satisfied smirk plays across his lips as he puts his fingers in his mouth and sucks, though his eyes are also dazed and heavy.

My hips rock, seeking the friction they had moments before.

"Knox," I growl.

"I'm sorry, Angel. Do you want something?" he drawls, the epitome of arrogance.

I practically throw my body at him as I lean forward, capturing his bottom lip between my teeth. Knox's hips betray him, rocking ever so slightly into my center, unable to hide the heat between us. The passion. The raw desire.

A low groan escapes him as I meet him movement for movement, our hips grinding against each other, his length growing impossibly hard.

The friction becomes my undoing.

"Knox," I plead.

"Say it," he hisses as if begging to put us out of our misery.

With pleasure. "Please, Knox, I need you inside of me."

Knox smashes his lips to mine and spins us, laying me on the forest floor before yanking my pants down with such force, he pulls my body with them. His wild eyes feverishly scan every inch of my skin that he reveals, his hands roaming with them as if he can't get enough.

My pants fly behind him. My shirt follows a second behind, leaving me bare against the forest floor.

His hands work quickly against his own pants, ripping them off in one tug. Without warning, he enters me in one deep, long stroke that has me screaming in ecstasy.

His large length stretches me, my body accommodating to what it wants most.

Knox throws his head back, the veins pulsing in his neck as he lets out a low groan, seating himself fully inside of me and hovering there. His body shudders as he pulls back only to slam in again.

I wrap my legs around his waist, struggling to rip off his linen shirt. In desperation, I pull, buttons flying off in all directions. But I don't care as I run my hands down his chest, soaking up the feverish heat of his smooth skin as his pace begins to pick up.

Knox lowers his head, his tongue darting out to lick a path up my neck and to the shell of my ear. His hot panting makes me shiver.

"I need more, I need more, I need more."

In the next second, Knox slips out of me, my cry of protest dying as he flips me onto my knees and places my hands on the tree in front of me. His knees knock into mine and he guides his length into me from behind.

My mouth drops open at the intrusion only for my hips to instinctively push back. Our groans join one another as he buries himself to the hilt, filling me and falling deeper than ever before. He pulls out slowly, only to thrust back in hard and fast.

The pace steals my breath. I cling to the bark with such force handfuls of it crumble and break in the palm of my hand. The tree trunk groans as it's pushed forward by the sheer might of our movements, its roots practically clinging for life.

Thank the gods we're in the human lands and I don't have to worry about the tree coming to life.

He wraps my hair around his palm and yanks my head back, his warm breath tickling my neck. Then his other hand begins to explore.

His fingers wrap around my neck, squeezing gently for a second before sliding down my body. His hand glides over my large breasts, his fingers rubbing circles around the buds. My nerves spark, sending tingles racing through my clit.

"Fuck, Angel, nothing has ever felt so perfect."

My hips rush back, meeting him thrust for thrust, making a deep growl fill my ear. Our breaths mingle, falling in sync with one another as we run for the cliff of ecstasy. Building the mountain higher and higher. And as Knox's fingers leave my breasts, sliding down to the sensitive flesh of my clit, my hips buck wildly, my knees beginning to quiver.

I scream, begging him to pick up his relentless pace. The tip of his enlarged cock brushes the sensitive spot inside me while his fingers play me like I'm his favorite game.

"You're so beautiful wrapped around my cock. So perfectly made for me, like you were sent to me."

His filthy beautiful words fill my body with such desire and passion I feel like I'm on fire. My body burns hot, sweat sliding down my neck. I bring my arms behind me, around his neck, and tip my head back to meet his mouth. His tongue slides in and fucks me as relentlessly as his hips.

He leans forward ever so slightly and my mouth pops open on a gasp as the bark brushes my nipples, sending a wave of shock and fire through my veins.

"Yes, yes!" I scream.

With every nerve sparking from Knox and his touch, my nipples grazing the tree, my clit being stroked, and his pulsing velvet-wrapped steel entering me with abandon, my desire builds to a point of no return.

"That's it, Angel, squeeze my cock."

His words spur me on as I feel my body about to break, willing to fall apart in his arms.

"Make me come, Knox, make me come!"

Knox pushes me further into the tree, sending a welcome rush of tender pain through my hard and heavy breasts, right as his fingers pinch my buzzing clit hard and his canines sink into my neck.

I fall apart with a sharp cry.

His name falls from my lips like a chant and an answered prayer as I convulse around him.

"Come with me, Knox," I cry.

The sound of his name on my lips is his ruin.

Knox growls in my ear as he shatters. Wrapping his arms around me, Knox clings to my body as it threatens to soar, flying high through the clouds with the intensity of the pleasure.

I milk him for everything he has, my walls pulsing around his hard length as he twitches inside of me.

"My beautiful angel," he whispers in my ear, planting a gentle kiss on my lips.

Chapter Thirteen

Nightfall has descended by the time Knox and I approach the cottage, walking hand in hand. The bond between our two souls sizzles with elation. The bridge between our minds is full of life, flowers sprouting in all directions, blooming with joy and radiance. The river that rushes under the bridge flows at a steady rate as if the care and tenderness we feel for one another determines its current.

Creseda's whines pull my gaze away from Knox, from the sizzling eye contact and knowing smirk playing on his lips. Despite the darkness and dropping temperature, everyone is standing outside, huddled around Creseda, Henry, Aurora, and Zephlyn.

Annie spots us first, a tentative kindness sparkling in her eyes. A soft smile spreads across her lips.

Annie knows how I feel after those long stretches of time when my emotions pummel me. How difficult it is to come back.

My cheeks flush despite the fact that Annie has seen what my mind can do, what it's capable of. But this time is different. This episode contained magic, and I can't stop the looming worry that overtakes my chest.

The last thing I ever want to do is harm anyone—to harm the people I love. And yet I exploded, despite my best intentions. I had no control over my magic, my body, or my reaction and that's simply unacceptable. Something to be feared.

Though I ignored Knox's concerns about my magic and its untimely lack of control, I am fully aware of the change within me. I can feel it growing, my well expanding, day in and day out, so fast that I can't control it, and I'm afraid my foothold on my magic is slipping.

What would happen to me if it took over completely? If it turned from a partnership to domination? Would I be lost forever like my vision, simply floating in the endless black pit of the universe?

I hope I never discover the answer to that.

As we approach, I search Annie's gaze for any sign that I frightened her, that this new version of myself is too much for her to handle.

The only thing I find is love and adoration.

My lungs are able to function and breathe freely once more. "What's all of this? A welcoming party?" I joke, but it doesn't hit its mark. Instead, the others disperse, their bags littering the cottage's small veranda.

Annie steps forward, clutching my hand in hers. "How are you feeling? Do you feel well rested?"

I shrug, watching as the others start to pack up. "I feel fine, more embarrassed than anything." I shake my head. "That doesn't matter, what is everyone doing? Where are they going?"

Annie's gaze flicks to Knox, there and back in an instant. "There's a friend of mine I want you to meet. She's in Sector Four's town center."

"We can't go into town; his men will spot me from a mile away," I object. "We only got here in one piece because the Sector One army knew what I did and feared me. Sector Four will want my head on a platter." Dread coils in my stomach. "What if the remaining soldiers in Sector One team up and tell them and they come for us?"

Knox cuts in. "If they knew anything about you being in these mountains, they would have come days ago."

Days.

How long was I out for?

"How would I get past the soldiers?" I ask, not wanting to know the answer to my original question.

Knox shrugs. "Glamours."

I've never used a glamour before, never seen one beyond the workings of the in-between. However, that was on a much larger scale, one that made not only the people within it disappear but the buildings themselves.

"Glamours and wards can do far more things than just conceal."

"Like keep magic out?" I ask, referring to the wards placed around the human lands.

Knox nods. "Wards can do and be anything. They can even be concealed from magic itself. Some wards stop magic from entering spaces, others will alert the creator when magic is being used. Wards depend entirely on the magic wielder's intention."

"Like a spell?"

"Exactly. There are hundreds—thousands—of countless wards that can be created."

I wonder if I possess the ability to wield one. Considering I can disappear by thought and the will of my magic alone, my hope is high.

"How long will it take to arrive?"

"It's a two-day journey," Annie says. "If everything goes right, we've planned to arrive at nightfall. If the glamour fails for whatever reason, no one will even be able to get a good look at you."

I can't believe I'm sneaking around the sectors within a kingdom I'm the rightful heir of. He has me acting like an escaped prisoner, not the princess trying to save her own people.

I suppose I am a prisoner, though. I was never allowed to leave the palace grounds on my own merit, let alone the capital. The tree house was my only salvation, though even that was located on the outskirts of the palace estate. I was a twenty-two-year-old woman being dressed like a doll, moved like a puppet, and fed a spoonful of words to spew to others.

I dip my head as if the movement can shake the thoughts. "Very well. Have I met this friend of yours before?"

Chuckles pour from the cottage, and the flickering candlelight shimmering through the windows is extinguished one by one as shadows move from room to room.

I didn't get time to explore it. What Easton created for us…I barely even looked.

"We'll come back, Angel," Knox whispers in my ear, reading my mind.

Will we even have that possibility? The doubt burrows into the beautiful garden I'd built for myself, sinking its roots in deep.

Axel and Nolan barrel out of the cottage, Ace and Hazel close on their heels.

"Ready?" Nolan drawls.

Creseda and Aurora are both saddled, satchels strapped and ready. I leave Knox to speak with the others. Annie follows me to the two raven-black animals, standing poised as if ready to ride into battle.

I suppose we are, in the grand scheme of things.

Standing between the two, I pat them simultaneously while Annie feeds Henry carrots.

"We will make him pay for the pain he has inflicted, Delilah."

The words alone would have shocked me if it weren't for the sheer conviction ringing in her voice, and the hatred in her eyes. I nod, hoping and praying with everything in me that our attempts won't be futile.

Everyone has tried to overthrow him, and they not only have failed miserably but they have ended up dead. But with our fate looking as bleak as it is, I suppose it doesn't matter. Either way, I'm predicted to die trying to save other's lives.

A worthy cause, if you ask me.

I feel horrid but I have nothing to say back to Annie. Nothing comforting to share, no vows or promises to utter. Not an ounce of motivation to spread. Because the last time I promised anything, I failed. I lost Easton and she lost her son because of those failures.

I'm not willing to fail her again.

"We'll leave when you're ready," she whispers after the long stretch of silence.

Again, all I can do is nod.

She said it wasn't my fault, but I know, somewhere in her heart, she must partially blame me for his death. How could she not?

I certainly do.

"I want to ride Creseda first. We have a lot to catch up on," I say to no one in particular. Aurora's gaze pins me to the spot as if she heard every single awful thought that just passed through my mind.

Ignoring the way she seems to read into my very soul, I

turn away and mount Creseda. I don't look at her as I ask, "Is that all right with you?"

A large furry lion head brushes against my shoulder, a small purr filling the space as she gives the one thing I can't seem to give myself—acceptance.

"Thank you," I whisper.

Muscle memory kicks in when I mount Creseda. When I was a human, it took a great deal of effort and strength to keep myself upright and balanced, and years of riding to make me feel comfortable. My muscles would cramp, and my legs would become stiff over time, along with my lower back. Now it feels as if I'm lounging in a chair with the enhancement of my muscles and renowned strength sizzling through my limbs.

My lips twitch when Creseda nickers in joy. Yet the smile never fully blooms, because there's one thought I can't seem to shake as I stare at Henry across from us, without his rider.

It should be my head on that spike, not Easton's.

I freeze when indignant fury rolls across the field. When I lift my head, I meet a pair of burning sapphire eyes that see far too much.

I rip my gaze away.

My emotional burdens don't have to continue being his to take care—

Yes, they do, and if you continue to speak nonsense like that, I will suggest the others go on while you stay back and rest. Because clearly, you aren't in your right mind.

My eyes turn to slits. *I am not a child you can boss around.*

Let me in to take care of you and I wouldn't have to treat you as such. His brow quirks, daring me to protest the truth. *As one,* he says simply, as if that explains it all.

The sincerity and tenderness in his voice have my resolve crumbling, as it always does with him.

As one, I repeat.

"If you two are done mind fucking, some of us would like to leave," Nolan drawls.

My eyes roll. "You simply have a way with words, Nolan."

Ignoring my jab, he roves a hand around the group. "I would also like to state for the record that I am not in agreement with this little sidestep down memory lane. Have we all just forgotten about the death sentence hanging over our heads?"

Axel's jaw tenses before he retorts, "No, we are following the mermaid's wishes, who unlike you, Nolan, do possess the ability to see."

"Clearly not well," Nolan mutters, throwing his arms up in exasperation. "I don't *see* any demons, do you?"

My jaw clenches. "They wanted me to find Annie for a reason, Nolan. Their visions work in unique ways. I mean, look at the soul eater! The only reason they sent me on that horrid mission was to find Knox."

"Okay, Princess," he spits. "Who do you think we're going to find on this excursion? Dear old Father with parchment signing the kingdom over to you? Good for you, you will inherit a kingdom only to die because you were too selfish to—"

Shadows slam into Nolan's mouth. Another shadowed hand wraps around his neck and lifts him. Knox marches up to the blond Fae, fury pulsing off him in waves as he whispers so quietly in Nolan's ear none of us hear, but whatever it is, it's enough to make the Fae pale.

"If I must listen to your voice snap ludicrous statements one more time, I don't care who you work for. I will make you *bleed*," I hiss once Knox is done reprimanding him. "You are in my lands, Nolan. Traitor or not, I possess the last name Covington and I will not hear another word of disagreement from your mouth."

Tugging on Creseda's reins, I leave them all behind with their mouths hanging open. However, when Henry trots up beside me with Annie atop him, I can't help but notice the corner of her lips twitching.

"Spit it out. You think I'm an awful person."

She shrugs, finally letting that smile bloom. "No, I just never knew you had it in you."

A snort from behind startles me as Knox appears beside me atop Aurora. "Have you seen what she's like in the mornings?"

I gasp. "I am not grumpy in the mornings, Knox!"

"Yes, you are," Annie and Knox sing in unison.

The pair look toward one another, a conspiratorial glance passing between them at the dirt they realize the other can share. I, however, sit between the two, huffing as they use me for banter.

After losing our magic and our belongings, we've learned our lesson and decided to strap our respective satchels to the animals where we can without burdening them.

Thankfully for us, we have a Fae that can communicate with animals, and oh, how I wish I could hear their voices and responses.

Especially as I watch Annie ride Henry. I wonder how he feels to have someone who isn't Easton ride him. Though out of everyone, I'm glad it's Annie. I don't think my brain could handle seeing someone else from outside the palace, as if mixing the two worlds would be far too painful.

I clear my throat. "When did you leave the palace?"

Perhaps not the best topic to take my mind off the whirlwind of emotions running havoc through my body, but I must know. The unanswered questions are beginning to drive me insane.

Annie's eyes sadden. "The moment the whispers spread of the king returning without an army and instead Easton's head."

My eyes close, trying to shut out the truth. "How did you know about the cottage?"

"I was planning to go there that weekend to take Creseda and Henry. That's what Easton spoke with me about the morning you came to say goodbye. I just simply never returned once I arrived."

We fall into a silence filled with the weight of immense grief.

"How did you fill your time at the cottage?" I ask, scrambling for safer ground.

Annie's cheeks flush. "I've actually been tinkering with herbs and spices to create tonics."

"That's amazing, Annie!"

A surge of happiness fills my lungs that she still has a love for medicine. Especially after she confessed to me in the days before I left the palace that her love for medicine was dwindling, due to the reason *why* she treated people, especially me.

She shrugs. "I plan to create supplies for the sectors I can reach."

"Are their supplies low?"

A dark look crosses her features, and I'm not the only one who feels the shift within her. Knox pulls back, slowing until he's riding beside me. Aurora's golden eyes flit from me to the forest ahead.

"He cut off supplies…to *weed* out the weak," she says tightly.

I shouldn't be shocked at this point. The king's actions will always be heinous.

"Who is the friend we're to meet?" Knox asks, quickly changing the subject as my knuckles turn white around Creseda's reins.

Annie shakes her head, tapping her ears. "The forest is alive, and you all should be aware of that over the next two days. Anything said here will always make it back to the king." Annie juts her chin forward. "You will know who they are soon enough, and if I were you, I wouldn't be calling anyone by their names. We don't need our cover blown."

How she speaks of the forest, it's as if it's filled with magic, the tree's branches whispering the words of travelers to one another. But there is no magic in the human lands.

The king just has spies *everywhere*.

Knox places a silencing shield around Annie and me, as I tell her the endless stories from my time in the Fae lands.

Knox sits atop Aurora—reluctantly, I might add. I don't know whether she will ever get over her fear of men, but I am so proud of her for slowly building a connection with Knox.

Ace and Hazel ride Zephlyn, while Nolan and Axel drew the short straw and walk beside us all.

Annie looks just as perplexed to be riding Henry as I was to see her on him. I wish these moments weren't so painful. That the things that used to be so mundane and normal hadn't turned into an act of grief-stricken responses.

I suppose life will never be some semblance of what it used to be.

I don't know whether to be grateful or fearful for that.

Chapter Fourteen

After riding through the outskirts of Sector Four's forest for two days, we begin to breach the heart of the sector's wilderness during nightfall. Zigzagging up and down the mountains wasn't ideal—the thousand cuts on my exposed skin can attest to that—but it was worth it to arrive under the cover of nightfall as originally planned.

However, not calling anyone by their first name during the journey was a challenge, trying to lose the muscle memory of our tongues. But at least we never heard whispers about the traitor princess traveling with five Fae and two griffins from the other rogue travelers we came across. Thanks to Knox's glamours, where we see Aurora and Zephlyn in their natural form, any of those who had passed us would have seen two horses instead.

Magic is a glorious thing to behold.

After experiencing the wonders of what magic created in the Fae lands, trekking through the human lands of Aloriah's forests felt…bland. As if an intricate part of the land is missing, a piece of its soul and heart.

I wonder if, long ago, magic used to be present here. If the land is bleak and sad because it has experienced the joy and wonder of what magic can offer.

Perhaps its magic can be restored once the king is dethroned.

"Were there ever rumors of magic residing in the human lands?" I ask Hazel beside me.

Hazel seems perplexed, her lips pinching as she frowns. "Not that I'm aware of, although, before these past few months, my social life was lacking."

I mentally chastise myself, trying to move away from the reminder of Luna. "But growing up, were you ever told stories about the human lands?"

Hazel mulls over the question. "My parents weren't the type to tell bedtime stories, but I do remember the children singing a song that mentioned the human lands."

My eyebrows rise. "What was it?"

At seeing my excitement, Hazel waves away the notion. "I'm sure it was just a lullaby of sorts."

"Are you talking of the guardian spirit song?" Ace asks, chiming in.

"Oh, yes. It mentions the human lands once sprouting with divine life force." Hazel turns to me, her voice taking on a graceful tone. "*Whispers in the breeze, of the songs they used to sing, the tales of the lands who once used to see—*"

Aurora halts suddenly, making my thoughts vanish.

The warning growl that rumbles from her jaw sends a chill down my spine.

Knox is next to me in a heartbeat, his protection shield snapping around me, Creseda, Aurora, Annie, and Henry. The others shield themselves too.

At first, I don't see it.

The soft glow of village fires burns ahead, plumes of smoke rising into the sky. Yet the longer I stare the smaller the fires become, and I realize we aren't looking at fires burning in townsfolks' homes.

Those are the flames of soldiers.

"Knox," I breathe.

His name is barely out of my mouth before a trample of hooves fills the otherwise silent night. The ground reverberates beneath me as horses surround us from all directions.

Thousands upon thousands of soldiers, lined and armed to the teeth, pour in, a wall of men keeping us out of Sector Four. The rest of the king's army rides up behind us, trapping us between two masses of soldiers.

Ready to defend their post and act out their orders.

I steal a glance at Knox, praying to find the cocky, boastful glint in his eyes, the look of a warrior ready to play. Except all I find is terror.

Knox lifts me off Creseda, only to shove me toward Aurora. "Run! I'll teleport us all along beside you, but you need to go—"

"That won't be necessary, Princess."

My eyes widen at the soldier appearing through the shadows of the forest. Dozens of men stand behind him atop their horses as he stalks forward with a confidence that shocks me. Not because it fears me, but because I know that voice and its owner. And I've never seen him with a speck of it.

"Hello, Delilah. I'd say it's a pleasure to see you again, but…" His gaze roams the Fae surrounding me. "I don't think the situation calls for it."

"Phillip. I can say the same thing to you, but it was never really a pleasure, was it?"

Phillip, the scraggily middle-aged man with gray peppered hair, sat across from me in council meetings, always squeamish and shy. His fear was a potent thing in the air as the king babbled off his orders.

A soldier moves for Knox, though shadow fire flings him back, melting his black and gold uniform.

Narrowing my eyes, I make golden power fly for them all, only for an iron arrow to whiz through it, dissipating the magic before my very eyes.

Knox stands protectively in front of me as shadows blast, rising above him and then slithering across the forest floor, flying for the men who surround us. But then they suddenly drop, and Knox's eyes widen at the metal grazing his skin.

I see that the king has prepared for the Fae, using our one and only weakness against us—iron.

Another arrow lays against my neck.

This feels all too similar to Sector One, how their hands grabbed me in all directions and Knox went down—

I force the panicked thoughts out of my head.

Phillip smiles down at me as another iron-tipped arrow points at me, along with two more being added to each Fae. I know all he sees is money and power as he gazes at me, the capture that will make his career.

This is not the Phillip I remember. Which one is the real Phillip? Which one is a mask, or are they both identities created to hide behind?

"Put an extra arrow to each of these abomination's necks. We don't need a repeat of Sector One," Phillip orders.

The whispers of what happened in Sector One have reached them, and I have a feeling they won't make the same mistake.

"Where's the griffins?"

No one utters a word. Soldiers look at each other with quizzical expressions. Some are wise enough to possess fear in their eyes.

"There is enough iron to go around and enough men to pin you down. Now where are the griffins?" he bellows.

Knox drops the glamours.

The two horses that stood in front of us transform into large griffins, roaring as moonlight glints off their impeccably sharp canines. The soldiers standing there with arrows poised stumble backward, shrieking in fear.

Knox goes to move, using their moment of fear as a distraction, only for four iron arrows to slice his neck. Crimson blood drips down his tan skin.

"*No!*" I scream.

The soldiers regain their footing, large blades unsheathing from their backs. Despite the tremble in their arms, they hold their ground.

"Back down," I whisper.

Aurora puts the fangs away, despite the anger clouding her eyes.

I will not watch another drop of blood be spilled. We are outnumbered, especially with the iron. I'm not sure we would even be able to teleport in time without getting an iron arrow embedded in a vital organ.

"Bring them to the town center," Phillip demands.

A jolt of electricity strikes through my body, stunning me.

Did the king change his order? The soldiers in Sector One said he wanted me alive, but the town center hold the gallows and whipping posts.

Ten guards flank each of us. The horses surrounding Aurora and Zephlyn give them a wide berth as they both growl and hiss at the men stationed atop them who hold blades against their magnificent wings.

Knox's eyes roam the forest wildly, looking for any chance of escape, any pitfalls that the soldiers didn't consider. With each passing second, I know there isn't one.

How did the king know to supply his men with arrows tipped in iron? He couldn't possibly have had them made and sent to each army base in time. Not with Sector Seven, who created the king's armory, now gone.

He may have evacuated and kidnapped who he deemed important, but it surely couldn't have been hundreds of people. He would have needed at least a thousand men working on these weapons.

How did any of this come to fruition so quickly?

In the last stretch of forest before Sector Four's town, my stomach turns queasy. I wipe my clammy hands against my pants, but my sudden movements draw the guards' attention, and the iron-tipped arrows dig deeper into my skin.

Knox hisses like a feral lion at the sight.

Everyone falls silent; the soldiers don't utter a word. Then there's a loud crash. Metal grating against metal. The line of soldiers guarding Sector Four's entrance move like a gate to allow us through, shields and swords shifting with the movement, and I can't help but compare them to farmers as they herd us like cattle.

The line of soldiers' faces is grim, stoic even. Not a single muscle twitches as we finally embark into the town center of Sector Four. Not one of them reacts to our Fae features or the griffins, the creatures they had been told were extinct.

How strange.

We walk down a large strip of dirt with fields of crops growing on either side for miles. It takes several minutes to reach a large wooden fence. It's a simple design, carved purely for necessity as opposed to beauty.

That's another difference between the Fae cities and the

sectors of Aloriah. The Fae love the arts. Vibrant buildings are painted and designed to represent their home, their element. Whereas the sectors…I don't ever remember seeing anything built for creativity.

The soldiers standing before the carved fence don't bat an eye as we pass them.

Sector Four overseas grains production. When did their soldiers begin guarding the perimeter to keep people out?

Perhaps it's to keep people in.

Knox's assumption sends a wave of horror through me.

Creseda tries to dig her hooves into the muddy ground, throwing back her head in protest as she no doubt understands the soldiers are not walking us to our accommodation but to our deaths. A whip cracks through the air like thunder, catapulting Creseda forward with a whine.

Fire erupts down my arm, flying through the air before any of the soldiers around us can move. It surges for the soldier holding the whip, burning the leather to a crisp and singeing his fingers.

I don't feel an ounce of pity as he screams.

My canines flare on a hiss. "If you so much as go near her, I'll do more than just burn your hand."

Three iron-tipped spikes point to my neck, the cool metal kissing my skin.

Phillip canters over. "There, there, Princess. That language isn't needed."

"Princess or traitor, Phillip? Which one is it?"

Our eyes clash, mine a depthless pit of fire, his cold as ice.

The brief pause allows me to check in on the rest of Knox's court. Hazel and Ace are huddled beside each other, Ace's arm wrapped protectively around her. Annie is surprisingly calm, her face guarded to give away nothing as she remains in Henry's saddle. Only four soldiers surround her, not deeming the only human among us a threat. Axel walks behind them, murderous eyes never leaving his twin and Hazel. His lips are curled back on a low growl, pure rage rolling off him in waves. Even the horses surrounding him are giving him the widest berth they can, feeling the demise promised in Axel's energy.

Nolan is no different. Despite the ten iron arrows aimed at his jugular, he strolls through the sector with a grin plastered to his lips as if death and the dark forgotten gods hovering over our shoulders aren't waiting to claim us.

The sight of Nolan almost makes my lips twitch—*almost*.

Boots begin to stomp once more, and I swallow thickly as I watch the soldiers around Knox poke and prod him with their arrows to get him to move forward. But he stays rooted to the spot, eyes never wavering from me…waiting.

I nod reluctantly and the sorrow in his depths as he steps away will haunt me.

I'm grateful for nightfall. If we were to be escorted through the town center during daylight, it would have been a spectacle—a parade.

I suppose it doesn't matter considering Phillip is walking straight to where I guessed he would: the gallows. He guides his horse to the center.

But to my surprise, Phillip doesn't stop at the gallows. He keeps going, aiming straight for a three-story stone building behind it. Soldiers line the perimeter, hands resting on the hilts of their swords.

Phillip raises his right hand, his fingers clenched in a fist, and within a second everyone halts, plunging us into a deafening silence.

Dread burrows deep within my heart, speeding up the rhythmic beat until it's an incessant pounding against my ears. Panic clutches me in its talons once more. Knox's magic slithers through my mind, trying to soothe the burning sensation growing behind my eyes. But with the nooses fluttering in the wind behind my back, nothing can stop the fear.

My breath lodges in my throat as the front door of the stone building opens and six soldiers pour out. Their impassive features never break as they take formation in front of Phillip. With a flick of his fingers, the soldiers surrounding me move forward, ushering me along with them.

As I pass Creseda and Aurora, their bodies buzz with anticipation and nerves. They stare at me with such fear I have to avert my gaze, not wanting to look them in the eyes as I'm killed.

Because this is no ordinary stroll. No, these steps will lead me to my death. The gallows are far too nice for the traitor who killed thousands of soldiers without moving an inch.

Blood must be spilled.

Taking my first step, grunts and groans erupt behind me. Craning my neck, I find Knox thrashing against ten soldiers, all armed to the teeth with iron shackles, collars, arrows, and blades that slice him with each movement.

He doesn't care that he's bleeding. I don't think he even notices it. All he is focused on is me.

Where our mental bridge is usually calm, the water below a steady current, treacherous winds and stormy currents now thrash against the shores. The tumultuous weather matching the rage coursing through Knox.

A shiver wracks my body as Phillip holds up his hand when I reach the open door. The soldiers guarding it straighten as they stand to attention.

"Kneel."

My eyes snap to Phillip.

The councilmen I knew wouldn't have the guts to speak to me in such a manner. Nor would he have the guts to unsheathe his blade and kill me on sight.

I do as he says, my knees reluctantly falling to the cobblestone.

My eyes pierce his, never wavering. If he is going to kill me, I will not let him forget my eyes. He should reap the consequences of watching the fire extinguish from them.

Sobs break out behind me, a commotion of screams and growls as Knox fights them again. The second he's free of the iron touching his skin, shadow magic spreads for me, covering everyone in the vicinity.

"Stop it, Phillip!" Annie calls as darkness consumes them.

"Iron now!" Phillip demands.

And before the shadows can reach me, the tendrils stretching for my fingertips, iron shackles are slapped around Knox's wrists, ankles, and neck. The shadows vanish.

His eyes widen. Not only does his magic recede, but the bond on his side grows quiet, muffled by the iron.

The fury and indignation that burns in my eyes dies quickly as a small figure, smaller than even Hazel, emerges from the building.

It's a woman, dressed in a black and gold soldier's uniform, tailored to fit her tiny frame.

I don't have to question her superiority or rank in the army, not with the way Phillip bows his head and the soldiers stand just an extra bit taller. *Their commander.* Scars mar her beautiful chocolate skin, though one stands stark across her face.

The scar starts at the right side of her forehead, tracking down over her brow and crossing over her light brown eye.

The scar then explodes into different lines as if it were a lightning bolt.

Her face is all strong lines. Deep cheekbones, cut jawline, precise eyebrows. Only the full soft lips and long curly hair contradict the sharpness of her features.

Her light brown eyes are cold and full of age. A type of tiredness that comes from weathering through storms darker than most, seeing things others could barely endure and yet still coming out on the other side.

Every step the woman takes is calculated, measured, and emanates strength. The moment her gaze collides with mine, oxygen evades me. The woman stares at me as if she can see all the way to my soul and beyond. As she comes closer, the soldiers surrounding me bow—low and deep.

I don't dare turn around to see the look on Knox's face. I conjure up the last moment I saw him smiling freely, our private moment in the forest before we left two days ago. The radiant joy that spread across his cheeks. I will go out with this image being the last thing I remember, not Knox's gaze stricken with grief.

After all, this is what this is, isn't it? An execution of the princess who betrayed her crown. The death of the heir who was marked as a traitor.

I prepare myself, locking my muscles in place and gritting my teeth, refusing to show her an ounce of fear. Preparing for the command that will end my life.

Instead...the woman smiles.

Not a fake smile, or one full of glee or triumph at my downfall, but a warm and caring smile.

It shocks me to my core when the woman sighs in relief. *Relief.* "I've been waiting for you, Delilah."

Before I have time to process her words she turns to Phillip, their interaction friendly. "Bring them all inside, but leave the griffins and horses until we return," she commands. "And for the love of gods, remove the iron shackles."

Hands slide under my arms, lifting me to my feet. A low hiss escapes Knox's lips as they touch me. The soldiers drop my arms as if I had burned them as they now face a Knox not restrained by iron.

His mouth opens, but before his fear can overtake logic, I take a play from his book.

A shadowed hand made of glistening gold smacks over his mouth, silencing him.

His sapphire eyes grow impossibly wide.

Do not let them know we are each other's weakness.

Knox's gaze sears into the back of my head. His voice holding a hint of pain.

We are not each other's weakness; we are each other's strength.

I coax a tendril of my magic down his spine, comforting and apologetic, as I walk forward to the front door of the stone building.

We spoke about this, Knox. I would bow to demons themselves if it meant I could save you from harm. They mustn't use us against one another.

I would hand myself over to the king for Knox—and that is precisely why no one must know Knox is my mate.

My words must pacify Knox because shadows twirl around my garden, joyful and full of tenderness. And he doesn't bite the head off the soldier who touched me as he walks past him to join me.

The guards never lower their iron-tipped arrows as they escort us into the stone building, but they do take a step back, giving us a small reprieve from the cold metal.

Hazel and Ace walk in first, Axel glaring daggers at the soldiers surrounding them, while Nolan simply struts inside the building. Annie shows not an ounce of fear, though she hadn't even appeared fearful with the soldiers surrounding us. Knox is behind me, not letting me be last, and left alone with thousands of soldiers.

Before I enter, a large raven-black paw steps on my foot, blocking me from entering the building. A foolish soldier lifts his blade to Aurora.

My head snaps to the side. "Do not move another inch if you value your life."

Aurora growls at the young man when he doesn't move. Knox slides his hands into his pockets. "I suggest you lower it unless you want to be gutted," he drawls.

The soldier's mask finally cracks, fear shining in his eyes. He is no match for the griffin that towers over him. He tentatively steps aside, his Adam's apple bobbing on a rather large gulp.

Turning back to Aurora, I lay my palm on her chest. "I will call you if I need you. You and Zephlyn can guard the soldiers." I lean forward, lowering my voice to a whisper. "From themselves."

I'm aware the joke holds no humor, not with how we were unable to fight against them seconds before, but it works. Aurora takes a step back, and the two griffins unfurl their wings, flapping until they perch on a roof across the courtyard with a perfect view.

A handful of soldiers pale at the sight.

A protection shield snaps around Knox and me as we enter the building, our strides long and fast as we work to catch up with the others down the long hall.

The building is quaint and simple. No decorations adorn the walls, and the rooms are packed with only necessities. As if whoever resides here is prepared to leave at a moment's notice.

I would bet it's their headquarters.

But why is the army so strong in Sector Four? They have more than three times the numbers and manpower than the average sector army base.

What war is the king preparing for that not only requires such a strong army unit on the outskirts of the sectors, but one that has the need for children?

The commander never turns back to check that we're following her, and neither do the four soldiers flanking her. Phillip marches beside her, towering over her small figure. None of them speak, presumably because of the Fae ears trailing them.

Turning the corner, we enter a large room. A dining table that could seat twenty sits in the center, while a roaring fire at the back of the room makes the temperature sweltering.

The woman takes her position at the head of the table, the glow of the fireplace lighting her back. Phillip stands to her right. None of us move to sit and my brows furrow as the soldiers shut the door behind me, leaving the commander and Phillip alone in a room full of six Fae.

Perhaps the commander has a death wish.

The instant the door shuts, Annie propels forward. I move to stop her, yet I pause at the happiness in the commander's eyes.

"It's been far too long, Ordelia," Annie gushes.

"Far too long!" the commander says, her voice solemn.

My jaw falls open when they embrace. The pair giggle in each other's arms.

"Care to explain what the fuck is going on?" Nolan snaps.

I don't reprimand him, and neither does Knox. We're all wondering the same thing.

Especially me, who was kneeling no more than five

minutes ago, waiting for a sword to slash my neck and bring an early death.

Annie turns to face us. Her features twinkle with amusement as she says, "This is Ordelia, commander of the king's Sector Four army, and the leader of the rebellion."

Chapter Fifteen

Shock thunders through me so viciously that I stumble backward until Knox's black shadowed hands steady me. Only for utter disbelief to sear through me again when Phillip moves forward, a gentle smile stretching across his cheeks as his fingers link with Ordelia's.

Lovers.

I don't know what to ask first. Thoughts crash together, only to disappear as another flies through.

Nolan grins like a cat. He crosses his arms over his chest. "Well, well, I certainly didn't foresee *this*."

Ignoring Nolan, I shake my head as I finally land on the most important question. "How?"

"We have a lot to discuss, Delilah. Why don't you take a seat?"

The softness in Phillip's voice jars me. Another version, another mask. A fearful councilman, a cold and indifferent leader, and a soft-spoken man.

Phillip assesses me, and he dips his head in apology. "Sorry, Delilah. The forests are full of eyes and ears."

Exactly what Annie said.

I don't respond, because what can I say? *Thank you for holding several arrows to my neck and making me believe you were walking me to my death?*

We need to hear their story, Knox encourages.

I don't disagree, it's just jarring. I feel like there are daily revelations knocking me off balance, and as soon as I find my footing, another one slams into me.

I take a seat at the far end of the table, my gaze never wavering from the three standing across from me, their eyes open and…hopeful. I pray I won't be like the king and rip their hope away, but trust is earned, and stories should be taken at face value. Especially from the man who can wear a mask as easily as a piece of clothing.

Despite Knox and I keeping the pretense of not being romantically involved, he takes a seat beside me. It's one thing to not show affection—it's another to be separated.

His fingers graze my leg under the table, sending electricity through every fiber of my body. His touch is magnetic, drawing my legs closer to his until our knees brush.

Under the wooden table, there is love and tenderness. Above it sits a cruel and stoic Fae king with his arms crossed over his chest.

Chairs scrape backward, dragging my attention away from Knox's enthralling presence. Ace takes a seat to my right with Hazel, Axel also not far from his twin, while Nolan doesn't budge.

He stands behind his king, his menacing scowl not budging an inch.

As the humans take a seat across from us, I don't miss the divide, one half of the table containing Fae and the other humans. I also don't miss the fact that Annie sits beside Ordelia.

"Start at the beginning," I say.

Knox snaps a silencing shield around the room without so much as blinking. Ordelia and Phillip don't react, but humans wouldn't be able to detect the subtle shift in energy.

Ordelia starts speaking as if nothing changed. "My family was brutally murdered in the first hangings nineteen years ago—the first wave of fear the king induced. Three, beautiful young girls and my husband." Her brows flick up, as if in defiance and a taunt to challenge her. "They were all innocent. Simply at the wrong place at the wrong time."

Ordelia's words—her story—settle into my heart like a boulder.

Those around me have always wondered why I take accountability, why I feel the guilt for the king. His spilled blood isn't my doing, but if no one soaks it up, it will linger, festering into every crack and crevice.

Someone must clean it up.

"The grieving widows and childless parents joined that night to comfort each other. Soon, anger spread throughout the meeting. Rage of a parent, rage of a loved one, and rage of the injustice of it all." Ordelia swallows, her eyes growing glassy. "I was a soldier moving up in the ranks, and the people were shocked my family was taken from me considering my allegiance. Not to mention the vows the king promises when you join his cause, safety for ourselves and for our family. He destroyed them without a second thought," she spits. "Fifteen years of service meant nothing in the moment where it should have counted the most."

Ordelia's voice grows quiet, the fire crackling behind her. "I had nothing to lose after that. I was completely engulfed by rage. It was either I let it kill me or I kill them." Her chin raises. "I chose myself."

The words are so similar to that of Nolan's when he challenged me in the mountains. He asked me if I would be able to choose myself when the time came to it.

Ordelia chose to save herself, and by doing so, she saved others in creating the rebellion.

Phillip rests his hand over hers, his lips thinned into a sad smile. When he speaks, he doesn't take his eyes off hers. "My sister, nieces, and nephews were murdered. Again, even on the council, my rank meant nothing. I joined the rebellion, trading insider secrets and movements of the king whenever I could. I met Ordelia on my seventh run of information and never looked back."

Annie nods, backing up his story. "I was treating Phillip in the palace's infirmary after an incident. He wasn't lucid, speaking nonsense about rebels and muttering the name Ordelia repeatedly. I chose to follow him out of the palace grounds once he was better and caught the two. I joined the rebellion that night and pledged my allegiance to the movement." Her eyes grow heavy, a million emotions flitting in their depths. "It was an easy choice. Yes, because of what he is doing to the citizens, but…" She swallows thickly before locking her gaze on mine. "For you, to feel as if I had a semblance of control in stopping the pain you were forced to endure every day."

Silver swells in my eyes, a lump of emotion rising along with it so quickly that I clear my throat and clench my teeth.

We can talk later, without everyone else watching.

Instead, I ask the easiest question on the tip of my tongue. "You were a rebel when I was freeing the prisoners?"

"Who do you think distracted the new guards on shift during the weeknight?" Annie quirks a brow, a knowing smirk playing across her lips. "They were late the same day of the week for a reason."

"Why did you never tell me?" I can't keep the hurt from my voice.

Pain twists her features as her eyes flick to Ace, there and back in an instant. "I wanted to keep you and Easton safe."

I slam my fists against the door in my mind, the one that contains the heavy grief of Easton. I keep it closed and instead turn to Phillip. "How did he never suspect you? He has spies everywhere."

"People underestimate a coward's ability," he says simply with a shrug.

I narrow my gaze. "Was the whole act, then, really necessary?"

His shoulders slump with the inklings of guilt, though I can't tell for sure.

"I apologize from the bottom of my heart for doing that to you. I wasn't lying before, the mountains are crawling with your father's spies." He turns to Ordelia with a grimace. "We also thought you wouldn't come willingly to talk to me, and after seeing your face in the forest when you saw me, I knew my assumptions were correct."

"King."

"I'm sorry, what?"

"King," I repeat, lifting my chin. "You said my father—it's king. If I am to continue speaking with you, you must be made aware that I will never willingly accept nor acknowledge that vile monstrosity as a father."

Multiple brows jump high around the room. Nolan outright laughs into his fist, trying to conceal it as a cough.

Phillip dips his chin. "My mistake…the king."

"Thank you," I mutter, squirming in my seat at the tension I created.

Can their stories be trusted?

Knox doesn't move an inch as he replies, *According to their vivid memories, yes.*

Phillip continues as if the moment never occurred. "The king would also know of you and your companions by now. Especially after the incident in Sector One. If his spies saw us opening our gates willingly, our cover would have been blown."

"The soldiers along the border are not with the movement. They are loyal to a fault to the king. I had to post them as far away from the town center as possible," Ordelia explains. "The show was just as much for them as well."

Maybe that's why they hadn't been surprised to see us or the griffins. Had they been expecting us? But the sight of the griffins would scare even the bravest of men…

"Apologies for that as well, and for your horse. To be honest, I was too busy making sure none of you killed my men." Philip clears his throat. "And who might your companions be?"

My lips twitch, a small understanding smile playing on my lips as I wave my hand to the Fae beside me. "This is Knox Holloway, King of Azalea and his court. As well as Axel, Ace, Nolan, and Hazel."

I don't mention that Hazel isn't officially a part of his court, nor the intricacies of whose mate is whose. Allies or not, I'm not giving anyone ammunition on how to destroy a Fae.

"Knox has kindly offered his services and court in exchange for the assistance and help I offered in freeing their race," I explain. Quizzical looks pass between the court and Annie. I thought I had more time to explain our idea of hiding that we're mates for Knox's safety, but I'll fill them in later.

Or rather, I'll fill Annie in later this evening. Because by the subtle jumps and raised brows, Knox just spoke into his court's minds and told them why we aren't declaring we're mates.

Surprise has Ordelia and Phillips's jaws opening. Horror flashes across Phillip's green eyes as he comes to terms with whose neck he held several arrows to, and the court he threatened.

It may be cruel, but their utter surprise sends a jolt of elation through my bones. I tuck my hair behind my ears, golden flames alighting in my eyes, as I reveal to them that no humans sit amongst the Fae at this side of the table.

Phillip coughs. "We heard about Sector One. I think everyone saw it and felt it, too, but seeing…" He waves his hand in my direction.

Ordelia smacks his arm. "What he's trying to say is seeing your transformation and abilities in person is different from hearing about it."

I lean forward, placing my arms on the table as I make golden flames twirl around my forearms. The pair yelp, flying back into their seats. "I would assume it's a delightful shock?"

Knox's face remains impassive and stoic, but his deep rumbling laughter floats down the bridge in my mind.

After having my fun, I make the flames disappear with a single thought. "Speaking of magic, how did he create the wards so quickly? And more importantly, *who* created them?"

Phillips's lips flatten into a tight line and he glances at Ordelia. "We didn't know before now whether it was true or not. You've just confirmed it."

"Those who were sent into the mountains to guard the border had an inclination they were there, but the rest of us were left clueless," Ordelia says.

"You didn't hear anything in the palace?" I ask Phillip. Just thinking about that cold place makes me shudder.

Phillip shakes his head. "I was sent to each sector to collect information on rebel movements and numbers, and that was weeks ago. I've been delaying my trip back for some time now."

Knox speaks for the first time since entering the room, allowing me the space to lead the conversation. "Do you have any other informants inside the palace walls?"

"Unfortunately, no. We got lucky with Phillip. The others are loyal, despite what's been done to their loved ones."

I frown. "Others in the palace have lost loved ones?"

"Yes, many."

"Why on Mother Gaia's world would they stay loyal to him?"

Ordelia sighs. "That's a question we ask ourselves every day."

Axel cocks his head, the gears turning in his mind. "Have they always been this loyal or did it begin with the deaths?"

Phillip helplessly shrugs, splaying his hands in front of him as if to show he can offer nothing. "We don't know. It was a gradual loyalty, one that no one noticed until it was too late."

"It was one of the things Phillip and I were looking into before we left the palace," Annie cuts in.

Axel's gaze flicks to Knox for a moment, a silent conversation passing through their eyes.

As they talk, my gaze drifts back to Phillip.

There was no one kind in the palace besides Annie and Easton. If there was, they would have tried to help me. They wouldn't have watched me suffer every day.

Right?

I don't know what's worse—believing he was loyal to a sadistic king like all the others, or knowing he was part of the rebellion and watched the king beat an innocent little girl every day and did nothing to stop it.

I swallow thickly and clear my swirling thoughts. "Before you left, what was the king planning? Were you involved in the meetings regarding the children?"

If memory serves me, Phillip was in the meeting the day the king ordered his army to Sector Seven. Little did we know the king's true plan was to bomb and kill eleven thousand innocent lives.

Phillip's eyes grow heavy as if the question weighs on him physically. "No one but Duke Harrison knew. We've only just figured out that he has been keeping the children in a complex in the mountains along the border of the capital, but the king would have had to begin building it years before Sector Seven."

How long has the king been planning this? How calculated must one be to orchestrate it?

Knox's expression turns quizzical. "What type of complex?"

"From the murmurings that have reached my border, we should be calling it a fortress instead," Ordelia scowls.

Phillip shakes his head in astonishment. "No men outside of those hand selected by the king have been able to penetrate its walls."

"How many children has he stolen?" Hazel asks quietly.

My heart stops beating. Hazel would feel the rage of a mother at the news. She knows how it feels to have a child ripped away, stolen from you.

Ordelia softens at the sadness and grief overtaking Hazel's entire being. "We don't have the exact number, but we estimate six thousand."

My brows pinch. Sector Seven had roughly two thousand

children, not over double the amount. "Were there more sectors bombed?"

The trio turns toward each other, a silent conversation in their eyes before Annie fixes me with a wary grimace. "I didn't want to overwhelm you with information…"

My back straightens. "What happened?"

What could be as horrific as the king placing Easton's head on a spike next to the throne? What could be worse than the king making children orphans to create soldiers?

I stare at all three of them, waiting for someone to answer the question.

Ordelia, surprisingly, is the one to break the news. Taking a sledgehammer to my heart. "Sector Seven was only the beginning."

I frown. "I know. Sector One was next, but we intervened."

Ordelia takes a steadying breath. "A week after you left, the king bombed Sector Six. To the citizens of Aloriah, they think there were no survivors. However, he evacuated the children and those he needed from the fishing sector."

For over twenty years my heart has been catapulted into the air, fear making it soar to new heights every time it flies, only to plummet, dropping to the ground and splattering into a million pieces.

And every time, I have to glue the pieces back together. After painstakingly tending to the wounds, it is ripped from my hands and thrown again.

Up and down.

Up and down.

Up and down.

Similarly to my heartbeat, it's just as erratic and uncontrollable.

It feels unstable, it feels uneasy, and I can't help but think to myself, *Do I have to do this again?*

My heart is tired. A Fae is meant to live for hundreds—thousands—of years. And yet I am barely twenty-three and my heart is already on its hands and knees crawling, begging for mercy from life to leave it alone.

It never does, though. Not long enough to recover.

The room holds its breath. No one will say it but they're all waiting for me to explode, and I feel it, bubbling beneath the surface. My golden magic screaming to be released. Instead, I lift my chin and ask, "Do you have a plan to stop it? To free the children from the complex?"

Surprise.

It ripples throughout the room, making the hairs on my arm rise.

I may not be able to save the people of Sectors Six or Seven. But I will do everything in my power to save those children.

Ordelia glances at Phillip. "We have an idea, yes."

Time slows, impossibly so to the point that as I watch Ordelia blink in slow motion, I push away from the table, my chair scraping against the stone floor.

A familiar calmness washes over me, light and soothing as a soft feather, and then I suddenly know what to do.

That ethereal voice whispers in my ear, and it feels like home.

Help them.

Choose them.

Fight for them.

The voice is just as I remember it in Hazel's cabin. Eerie, and yet the sense of tranquility that washes over me from its sound is uncanny.

I cherish its warmth before time resumes. I blink everyone back into focus.

This is why the mermaids led me to Annie, to Sector Four, I whisper down the bridge to Knox.

"Let us help. Use us—we have abilities that could help change the trajectory of those children's lives."

I can feel the air shift on this side of the table. The ripple of energy slams into me, as if their emotions are an invisible blast.

They believe it's a detour from our original plan. But if there is one thing I believe in, it's fate. As broken as mine has been, everything happens for a reason.

That ethereal voice led me to Knox and his court. The mermaids sent me to Annie's cottage for a reason. It did not fail me before, and it will not fail me now.

Knox straightens, moving not as the mate I cherish but as king of Azalea. "My court offers our services, services that you will not foolishly deny."

Knox's tone leaves no room for argument. His court *will* be an ally to the rebellion movement.

A spark of an idea comes to mind, and I blurt, "Tell him I died."

Annie's eyes widen. "What?"

"We need the upper hand against the king. He is always ten steps ahead, so tell him you murdered me on sight for being a traitor. The bastard won't care."

Sounds cease to exist, only that of the crackling fire pop throughout the room.

"He marked me as a traitor, tell him I betrayed. Tell him I started swinging and began killing. Tell him that there was no other choice but to put me down."

Phillip blubbers as his face turns ashen. "Ah, y-yes, I suppose…That will give us the upper hand indeed."

"Delilah, your death will create a butterfly effect that you will not be able to stop once started," Annie explains as if I am still a little girl cowering under the table.

I look her dead in the eyes. "Good. Give them something to rebel against."

"No, I don't think you understand. It will—"

"I understand exactly what my death will symbolize and do to the people. They need to feel the burning hatred they have been repressing." I turn back to Ordelia, the one in charge of the rebellion. "Tell him I died."

She thinks for a moment, but reluctantly nods. "We will tell him you had to be executed for sanctioning an attack on our army."

Phillip is momentarily stunned by Ordelia's words before he mumbles, "I'll send our messenger at first light."

Axel's brows furrow deeply. "Should we be concerned that there will be a retaliation to 'killing' Delilah?"

"Yes, but not as much as the payoff will be at having a secret weapon," Knox murmurs.

I dip my chin before summoning the courage to ask, "And what of my mother?" I couldn't find the strength to ask Annie during the two-day trek, but now I need to face the fear. My death will inevitably come back on her. "What has become of her?"

Annie visibly recoils as she lowers her eyes, adverting my gaze. Ashamed.

Ordelia answers the question. "Your mother hasn't been seen since the night you left."

They must take my silence for acceptance because they continue to speak as if the well-being of my mother isn't important.

"How many men do you have at your disposal?" Ace asks.

"Six thousand," Phillip says proudly.

"What do you mean she hasn't been seen?" I blurt, panic beginning to rise despite my best efforts to tame it.

Knox's fingers find mine under the table, squeezing gently as he sits stoically at the table.

The king is punishing me.

It's a punishment my mother and I know well. Hurt the ones we love most in retaliation for our 'wrongdoings.' Sometimes he would make me watch him beat her because of how much he knew it hurt me to see her in pain. He made me think I had inflicted the beating.

"No one has seen or heard from your mother," Annie repeats, full of sorrow.

"Perhaps he took her to the complex?" Nolan suggests. His green eyes are slightly wild, and my heart catches. If anyone knows how it feels to have missing family members, it would be him.

Knox's knee brushes mine, his magic whispering through my mind. The only way he can comfort me in front of others.

"He wouldn't take her there. The one thing he cherishes most in this world is control. He wouldn't let another person oversee her," I explain.

The look that crosses everyone in the room is the look I have despised for years—pity.

I turn to Knox, relief flooding my chest when I find his gaze free of pity and full of understanding. I'm grateful for him and his open mind. For the patience he has with me to listen to every thought I have, regardless of how panicked it may be.

Don't look at me like that, Angel. I'm just another king, remember?

Right. Except, I can do nothing about the blush that creeps over my cheeks at his flirty tone.

I clear my throat. "She's still inside the palace. He would never relinquish control over her," I reiterate.

Phillip leans back in his seat and barks a laugh, yet the sound holds no humor. "What do you propose, that we walk into the palace and take her?"

"Yes."

"Delilah, it would be a suicide mission," Ordelia argues.

"We have to travel near the capital anyway to get to the complex. I'm not passing by the palace without saving her. She would be just as tortured as the children…if not more." I flick my attention between Phillip and Ordelia. "I'm not asking you to join me, simply wait for me." I lean forward. "But I will say, this is your *queen* we are talking about."

My mother may not be lucid, but she has done no wrong and brought no harm to anyone. She's the most innocent woman in that palace and I'll be damned if I leave her there to wither into nothing.

They wince and I know I've hit a nerve, so I push further. "Please. The torture he would be inflicting upon her is beyond what your imagination is capable of conjuring." My eyes flick to Phillip and I can't help the accusatory glint they take on. "You know exactly what he will do."

The scars that pepper my back are proof of that fact.

Ordelia sighs and pinches the bridge of her nose. "Perhaps this could work as the distraction we need."

The relief that washes through me makes me slump in my chair. "What do you propose?"

Tendrils of shadow magic slither down my spine, beneath my fighting leathers. Sending my own magic down the bridge between our minds, it dances to the song of joy and relief as our magic meets halfway.

Phillip moves to the cabinets in the corner of the room, collecting rolled-up parchment and placing them on the table before us. Everybody leans in as he rolls out a map of Aloriah. It's odd to see the second half of the map vacant after traveling through the bustling Fae lands for months. It's as if the Fae were wiped away, along with its history.

Not one of the Fae surrounding me misses the detail. Their brows pinch in confusion at being forgotten. Yet it wasn't from a lack of memory, it was forced, purposeful negligence by the ruling king of that time. The beliefs then were passed down in generations.

I look around my friends—my family—and my heart catches in pain for them. That anyone could have forgotten and accepted the loss of such beautiful people is a mystery to me.

Axel, Nolan, and Ace move into their respective positions. Nolan's gaze assesses the map as the commander of Knox's armies, while Axel, the cunning second, analyzes the opportunities others may miss. Ace's smile turns bright, his posture easy and open as he talks with Phillip about the information he last gathered in the palace, effortlessly slipping into the role of emissary.

I once said it was the perfect title for him because he is so loveable it would be hard to hold anger against him, and now seeing him in action, I know I was right all along.

Axel may have been the twin who protected Ace, but he never notices all the ways in which Ace protects him. How he can calm anyone in a room, make them feel at ease and comfortable enough to spill their troubles. Ace is able to diffuse situations before they arise. And in that way, they both protect each other with how they learned to survive their abuse.

Phillip points to the mountain peaks in the center of Sector Six, Seven, and the capital. Where the complex lies, full of thousands of children being trained into mindless soldiers.

"What's left of Sector Six and Seven?" Nolan asks.

Ordelia grimaces. "Nothing."

Axel leans back, crossing his arms over his chest. "Do the king's men patrol the area?"

"No, it's been deserted since the bombings."

He considers that. "It will take longer but I suggest we travel through the sectors and come up from behind," Axel murmurs, pointing to the traveled path.

Ace leans in and takes a look at the map. "Are there still citizens in Sector Five?" he asks.

Annie watches him closely as he speaks. From my own experience, I assume she's also tracking his mannerisms, trying to remind herself that it isn't Easton.

Phillip rubs his chin, his lips flattening. "Yes, his largest army is stationed there, protecting the mountain wall that separates the capital."

"We'll send half our troops to scout ahead," Ordelia says, her eyes glued to the map. "We have to travel through the lake. It's the only diplomatic area."

"No guards are stationed around it?" Nolan asks, his brows flicking up in surprise.

"No, the king uses his armies to protect himself from any threats, from his own citizens, and…" She dips her chin toward the Fae. "Outside forces."

"We'd need a boat," Phillip declares to no one in particular. "Though transportation for an army this size could be difficult without raising suspicion."

"Not necessarily," I mutter. "I could freeze the lake."

I lift my hand, letting a handful of water float above my palm. It twists this way and that, confirming into a butterfly, an arrow, and a dagger at the demand of my thoughts.

With one more, the water dagger freezes in my palm. The ice sculpture explodes into a thousand shards of ice, flying throughout the room.

Nolan claps slowly.

Darkness wraps around Nolan's hands, Knox's jaw clenching as his magic squeezes Nolan's hands until they turn bone white.

Sending a trickle of calm down our bond, I breathe a sigh of relief as his shoulders loosen, along with the magic capturing Nolan.

"It's indeed marvelous what you can do, Delilah, and that's one way to get to the complex, yet I don't see how you'll get into the palace," Phillip chimes in.

My mind whirls, churning and ruminating. Doing what it does best, I allow my anxiety to take over and run through every situation, to see the pitfalls others may not, and create imaginative plans that are so crazy they just may work in our favor.

"What if we set off a distraction in the northern lands of the capital?" I ask, pointing to the forest that lies on the border. "If we create a situation large enough, he will send out most of his men from the palace. Knox's court and I could fly onto the grounds without as many watchful eyes."

"But then what? The king and the rest of his men would see you coming."

I lock my eyes on Ordelia and Phillip. "I have invisibility magic. I'd be able to walk right through the front doors."

Phillip blanches. "Impossible."

Diving into the golden magic well within myself, I let it become me. My body tingles, veins thrumming with magic as I simply disappear. Annie's face turns a sickly shade of green as Ordelia and Phillip fall backward.

It doesn't take much to return to my body, to restore my

being. I'm surprised it feels so easy. Only weeks earlier, I had to consciously choose to return to my original state, but now—

Panic, quick and fierce, claws up my throat when I struggle to put the lid on my magic. I grapple with the power to contain it at all, fighting against an intricate part within myself to control it.

I swallow through the slither of fear still lingering as perspiration rolls down my neck. I lock every ounce of the emotion away, wiping the surprise from my face as I quickly take in everyone around me. Not one of them looks concerned, but my relief is short-lived when Knox frowns at me down the mental bridge.

Lifting my chin, I ignore the unsettling feeling sinking into my heart.

"I don't want to further risk any more lives. Especially for a mission that, as you said before, is suicide. We need your men to help rescue the children."

"They're also our secret weapon. The king doesn't know some of his own men have turned against him," Nolan chimes in with a lethal grin. "He won't see the hit coming."

Axel juts his chin in my direction. "Let's also not forget that in a few days' time when messengers reach the king, he will believe she's dead."

"We can't count on him believing it; he's a paranoid man. He will want to see my body but, in the meantime, I agree, Ordelia's men are our secret weapon." I lean back. "I must, however, ask to use a handful of your men to create the distraction."

Ordelia muses over my words, her gaze focused on the mountains bordering the capital on the map. "It would also work in moving some of the soldiers away from the complex."

"We can escort you and your men to Sector Seven safely and then fly to the palace," Knox offers.

Ordelia dips her head. "Thank you."

Phillip cuts in, stealing a nervous glance my way before speaking. "We also need to take into account the possibility of the king avenging what took place in Sector One."

Ordelia nods. "You could be walking into a trap. He could be waiting for you to free your mother."

Ordelia's words slice right through my heart, flying into the pile of anxious thoughts.

"We'll prepare for that," Knox answers for me. "Just see to it that your men create a large enough distraction to move a thousand soldiers toward that forest."

"What about the complex? What's your plan of attack?" Axel asks, his focus on the circle Phillip drew in the forest-covered mountains.

Ordelia straightens, her eyes steeling. "We would kindly ask to command the room to discuss those plans."

Knox's shoulders stiffen as he rises to his full height. "You don't trust the ability of my court?"

"With all due respect, Your Highness, the mission is on a need-to-know basis. Even my own men are not aware of it." Ordelia's gaze is strong and unyielding, yet the small quiver in her lip gives way to the fear of facing down a Fae king.

Allow them this ounce of control, I whisper soothingly.

Humor dances down the bridge—at what, I'm unsure—especially as he stands stoically at my side, not breaking eye contact with the two humans.

Tension crackles around the room.

"Ordelia has been orchestrating rebellion movements for years undetected," I interject before it gets too out of control. "Clearly, it's worked, considering she's standing here as the commander of one of his armies."

"My court and I work as a team. I'm not hiding information from them, especially plans that put their lives in danger," Knox argues.

Knox, I growl down the bridge, a plea and a warning. *We could benefit from their numbers and spies.*

A dark chuckle fills my mind as shadows fall around me. The sound and essence of his magic send a shiver down my spine.

I'm playing my part, Angel.

The teasing tone is a stark difference compared to the moody Fae beside me, the king who demands respect and equality among his court. It may be unfair of me to ask Knox to follow their demands, but we need them and their trust, otherwise we will all fall through the webs the king has weaved.

"You may tell them what they need to know in regard to their respective duties. Anything beyond that is confidential." Ordelia swallows thickly, her left eye twitching and giving way to her worry.

A muscle ticks in Knox's jaw. Shadows spread out behind him, devouring his back. They're wise enough to show their fear, to know their vulnerabilities and to acknowledge that this is a partnership and not a favor we are begging for.

While their focus remains on Knox, a shadowed hand brushes down my cheek, ever so softly caressing the creamy skin. It's only for a moment, unnoticeable, but Knox's shadows keep growing, spreading so far they begin to swallow me whole.

And then it becomes apparent what this show is truly about.

Every inch of skin the shadows touch tingles with the burning passion of a lover's caress, teasing, until the shadows suddenly snap back.

"As you wish," Knox pushes out, as if muttering the words frustrates him to no end.

Knox's court leaves the room one by one without another word. Annie brushes my forearm as she gives me an apologetic smile. Ace is the last to leave, his brows furrowing in concern as he flits his attention between Knox and me. A moment passes between the two Fae men, and whatever Ace finds in Knox's features is enough to settle his concerns. The heavy double wooden doors slam shut behind him.

Knox's silencing shield covers the perimeter of the room as Knox and I face Ordelia and Phillip. They waste no time launching into their current plans to free over six thousand children from the complex.

Chapter Sixteen

Ordelia and Phillip excuse themselves once they show us to our rooms, after informing us that Annie will be staying with them in their wing.

I take it there's a lot for the friends to catch up on.

Neither Knox nor I reach for the door handle until the pair has rounded the corner and their quiet whispers have disappeared.

Axel jumps to his feet the moment the door closes behind us. "What's the plan?"

"How many soldiers are they sending?" Ace blurts over his twin.

The dip between Hazel's brow creases. "Are you truly going to keep the plan from us?"

Nolan scoffs. "Don't be ridiculous. Knox hasn't kept war movements from us before."

More like chess movements.

They only quiet a moment, long enough to hear Knox say, "I also don't break my promises, and I vowed to keep their plans a secret."

What Knox isn't telling them is that the moment those

doors shut, Ordelia begged—*pleaded*—with the Fae king to vow to keep their plans a secret. Too much was riding on the complex mission, months of organization, and tactful movements on her part. Far too many people's lives were at stake and those children... Her eyes had welled with tears. Those children are entirely innocent and the future of this kingdom; the king cannot turn them into soldiers.

I wouldn't have been surprised if she got on her knees, but Knox stopped her before it could go too far. Knox understood more than she knew. He would do anything for his people, and that's what Ordelia has done for hers.

"*You did what?*" Nolan barks.

Knox's eyes narrow on the warrior. "You will be given orders, and I will tell you what you need to know. Beyond that, you are not privy to the information. As your king and fellow family member, I would expect a level of trust."

The ice in Knox's voice makes me grimace, directly rivaled by the pure heat and rage that contorts Nolan's face.

My muscles lock into a defensive position as I prepare myself for the explosion of anger I have come to expect from Nolan.

"Since when do we operate like that?" he spits through gritted teeth.

I don't miss the moment his eyes flick to mine. There and gone in an instant.

What more do I have to do to prove my loyalty to Knox and his court?

Nothing, Knox growls in my mind.

"Why are we even aiding in this mission when we came here for our own?" His green eyes bore into me. "Or was this all a ploy to get us here? I find it rather a coincidence that the supposed coordinates from the mermaids sent us to Annie's cottage." His head cocks, a predator closing in on its prey. "Why did they send us here, Delilah?"

"I don't know!" I scream. "How dare you continue to question me when all I have done is save your sorry ass of a life!"

His eyes flare and he takes a menacing step forward, only to be flung backward by dark shadows racing for his throat. His body smashes into the wall.

Nolan struggles against the hold until Knox steps forward, his presence demanding attention, and Nolan's gaze snaps to his.

"We are here to aid in the rebellion. We will not storm into their lands—Delilah's kingdom, may I remind you—and start ordering them around like children. *That* is not how we operate," Knox spits. "And if you continue to question my leadership and commands, I will send you back to Azalea, stripped of your title." Knox drops him without warning.

Nolan crumbles to the ground, gasping for air, but he doesn't glare at Knox. As if the stunt calmed him instead of fueling his anger.

"Let Nolan serve as a reminder for all of you." Knox lets the words hang in the air, his gaze roaming his court. "Yes, we have strayed from the path *we* intended, but I do not doubt for one moment that this isn't where we were always meant to be."

Nolan grazes his top teeth with his tongue, his clenched fists shaking. Yet despite it all, he dips his head in surrender.

I should open my mouth and explain the ethereal voice. I should tell Knox and allow him into my mind, letting him share the memory with everyone in the room. To reassure them that this is indeed the correct path. But when I try, betrayal floods me.

Deep and utter gut-wrenching betrayal, so vicious it snaps my jaw shut.

My magic, my *soul*, does not want to share this information with anyone in the room.

But why?

"Where else would you like us to go?" Hazel asks softly.

Ace tenses as Nolan slides his gaze to the small Fae.

Hazel doesn't back down at Nolan's withering glare. "Where else would you like us to go?" she repeats. "What leads do we have to follow?"

Nolan opens his mouth, only to snap it closed.

Hazel's brow quirks. "You need to start trusting the journey the mermaids have led us on."

"Can Ordelia and Phillip be trusted?" Axel asks, returning the conversation to the rebels.

"I hope so," Knox answers honestly. "Their men and their informants would be a great asset. Moving forward, we all need to be cautious and on high alert, but I'm not asking you to trust them…I'm asking you to trust me."

"How would they benefit from going against us?" Hazel asks.

"Wealth, power, infiltration to the capital, a debt owed to the king," Ace grumbles, ticking off the reasons on his fingers. "Shall I go on?"

I shake my head. "Annie would never put me in harm's way. If she trusts Ordelia, I do too. Phillip, on the other hand… The man wears far too many masks for my liking."

"Ordelia could be too, with Annie none the wiser," Ace says.

"Let's not get caught up in the what ifs right now," Hazel says, placing a hand on her mate's arm. "When do we leave?"

"In two days. It allows Ordelia to gather her trusted men, and for us to fully replenish our energy and magic."

The second Knox acknowledges the exhaustion burning through us, our adrenaline vanishes, swept into the full extent of our fatigue from the past forty-eight hours with no rest.

"How gracious of them," Nolan grumbles. But despite his characteristically predictable comment, he trudges away to the nearest cot.

Ace rubs the back of his neck as he yawns deeply. "I'm going to go sort out a place for Zephlyn to sleep and make sure he hasn't eaten anybody."

"I'll come with you," I offer.

Knox moves to follow, but Ace flashes him a quick smile. "It's okay, Knox, I got her. I won't let anything happen."

At first, I think Knox is about to bark orders at him, but then the tightness of the bond relinquishes, and Knox dips his head with a weary grimace.

Ace stops me before we leave. "The king needs to believe you're dead, so wear your hood. We don't need whispers spreading about the princess with pointy ears."

"Good idea." I wrap the material around my shoulders and place the heavy cloak over my head.

And so, the Black Hood returns to Aloriah.

Chapter Seventeen

I t's a miracle that the stables are not only empty but large enough to comfortably house the two griffins and horses. Not to mention there's a back door that leads straight into the building, allowing me to remain hidden from the citizens of Sector Four for the remainder of our stay.

While Creseda and Henry munch on the bucket of carrots we laid out for them, Zephlyn and Aurora purr away over the chopped lamb meat as Ace and I brush down their coats. The stench emanating from Zephlyn makes me scrunch my nose every time I get a waft. The mud layered in his coat will take days to clean.

"What information did you glean from Phillip?" I ask, breaking the comfortable silence we were working in.

He shrugs. "Not much more than he already told you. His main concern during his time in the palace was if anyone else was like him."

"What do you mean?"

"If they were also pretending just to survive, or if they were truly loyal to the king."

I'm ashamed to admit that I never thought of it like that.

That Phillip's masks were a shield to him, a survival technique. I still don't fully trust him, not with a man who can lie undetected, but it does make me open to questioning his true motives.

Although I don't think I can ever forgive anyone for turning their heads to the king's abuse. How can I, when I sobbed into my pillow every night praying to the forgotten gods to save me?

Ace notices the storm clouds that roil in my eyes.

"It doesn't take away from the fact that no one helped you," he says gently.

I clear my throat, stepping away physically as if I can do so emotionally too.

"No point dwelling on the possibilities of the past."

Ace lays a gentle hand on my arm. "I'm sorry that you had to endure that. It should never happen to anyone."

I lift my gaze, only to have the wind knocked out of me. I could have sworn for a moment Easton and his pine-green eyes were looking back at me.

I take a shuddering breath to clear my mind and refocus on Ace. "No, it certainly shouldn't."

We both go back to tending our griffins, and by the subtle glances between our respective soul pairs and each other, it makes me watch Ace more carefully. Like the way his eyes are slightly pinched, his lips tightening with every passing second—as if trying to get a handle on something wrangling to get out.

"It's not fair," I say, hoping to guide the conversation in the direction Ace desperately needs.

"What's not?"

"That the ones who deeply hurt you always get away with it. That they're never brought to justice." I shake my head, anger bubbling to the surface as the door cracks open. "The fact that they will never take accountability, or that you'll never hear them apologize. Because you know, deep down, they're not truly sorry."

My chest heaves as the words pour from me.

"Being an immortal with no closure is a hard thing to face," he whispers, as if scared to utter the words.

"Gods, I never thought about that."

He laughs but it holds no humor. "I certainly have. I think what's cruel is how your own mind works against you, torturing you with memories you want to forget and the hurt that nearly destroyed you."

I blink, surprising myself with the words I say next. "I've started to look at it as a blessing."

His head snaps up. "Why on Mother Gaia's world would you want that?"

"Because then I will never forget, and if you never forget, you will never allow them or anyone to do that to you again." I shrug. "I can't control the memories, so I may as well learn from them."

"What? To never trust a soul? Because if you can't trust the person who is meant to love you unconditionally, then who can you trust?"

I frown. I never knew Ace thought like this. His thoughts sound eerily similar to mine.

At least, I believed it months ago, though I know deep down I still do. I may have kept people away for their own safety, but it was for mine too. It took everything within me to be strong enough to let Knox in. And even more to come to know his court.

Especially after the loss of Easton.

"You trust Hazel and Zephlyn," I counter.

I bring it up because I know what the bond feels like, the

utter trust you have within the connection. Perhaps that trust is built upon how much you trust yourself.

Ace shakes his head. "It's not the same. Without the bond binding us, I sometimes—" He stops abruptly. "It's a horrible thought and a horrible thing to say. Ignore me."

"Whatever you tell me, I won't judge, Ace. I've had horrible thoughts myself." I sigh. "I believe it's a consequence of being raised by a horrible person. I also think it's natural. The brain has so many vast emotions, and we came to this world to experience them all...the good and the bad."

He swallows thickly, the sound audible as his Adam's apple bobs. He gives an apologetic smile to Zephlyn before turning to me. "Sometimes I wonder if I would fully trust them without the bond—whether the trust is there because of it, or because of who they are."

"That's not a horrible thing to question. Self-exploration isn't shameful, Ace. It's part of the human—sorry, Fae—condition."

He chuckles. "Still getting used to it?"

I don't call him out on the subject change. Instead, I start packing up the grooming equipment one of Ordelia's men gave us. "Honestly, I think it will take a few years for my mind to fully wrap around this new reality." *The body I was forced into.*

His hand hovers between us after he passes me his brush. "Do you ever miss it?" he whispers.

"Being human?"

Ace nods with an open expression.

I ponder on the question, one that no one including myself has asked.

Do I miss being human? Do I miss how long it took to heal after the king pummeled me within an inch of my life?

No. Do I miss the way I felt weak against him regardless of how many hours I spent training? No.

Ace was vulnerable with me, so the least I could do is share this small part of myself.

"No, but I don't like how foreign I feel in my own skin."

He chews on his lips. "I guess the only thing I could compare it to is the moment magic was returned to us. We were all born with it, but that moment felt so…odd. As if my body was utterly out of control." The small, understanding smile he gives me is sad. "I hope that feeling goes away for you soon."

"Me too," I answer solemnly.

Everyone has already claimed a respective cot by the time we return. Knox sits up on his elbows when the door opens. He's created a double bed for us by pushing two cots together.

Puzzled at what put the heated look I find lingering in his sapphire eyes, my cheeks burn as he sends a memory into my mind, the one of our first kiss. When I finally let down my walls for him after endless days of teasing. Knox had finally pushed me to the point of no return when he was teaching me how to fly. When his lips were finally upon mine, I felt as if I was going to combust right there on the spot and then—

We were rudely interrupted, he growls.

My breath escapes in a rush before I hurry over to the makeshift double bed he's created. My skin tingles at finally being able to touch him without fear lingering in the back of my heart. Except, in this common room, there's no privacy.

"Where's Hazel?" I ask. She's also made a double bed, though it's empty save for Ace.

"Bathroom," Nolan grunts, not lifting his eyes from

cleaning his nails with a blade. Both he and Axel lie in their respective beds across from us, clearly wanting as much space from the mated Fae's as possible.

I snort at the sight of them all. It's wildly different accommodations from the luxury of the palace where I'm used to seeing them, but—

"You all barely fit." Their feet dangle off the cots, their Fae builds not made for human-size beds.

"You don't fit either," Axel points out.

My brows rise to find that my feet are indeed dangling off the bed as well. Another thing to grow accustomed to.

Knox's eyes glint. "The less space between us, the better, in my opinion."

"Knox is already going insane not being able to touch you," Axel teases, his eyes dipping to Knox's hand caressing my leg.

Axel has just confirmed that Knox updated them on our plan earlier, but I nip their jokes in the bud. "We are not discussing this."

Ace throws himself backward on the bed, his arms splaying out beside him. "Oh, come on! Axel never jokes with us. It's always work with him," the twin whines.

"This is true. You wouldn't want to deprive the man of humor now, would you, Angel?" Knox drawls.

I narrow my eyes. "I think you're all forgetting I have magic now. I can quite literally force you to keep quiet."

Ace has the decency to widen his eyes. "Back to work," he mutters.

Hmph.

Hazel barrels into the room, taking a seat beside Ace. "What did I miss?"

"Absolutely nothing," I blurt before one of the men starts. "We were discussing how to get me onto the palace grounds."

A look passes between Axel and Knox.

It's fast, so quick I question if it even happened at all. "What?" I demand.

"Nothing," Axel says quickly.

I turn to Knox, my lip curling. "Don't lie to me."

Knox sighs. "We're wondering if the king has someone doing his bidding through magic."

A quick snort escapes me. The king detests magic; he would rather cut off his own hands than have anything to do with it.

"You think the king is behind the magic wards?" I ask, entertaining the idea. "Why then send his army to the border to stop Fae from entering?"

"It's more than just the wards," Knox says gently.

"His army is loyal to a fault, regardless of what's done to their loved ones and family. That's absolutely—"

"Unheard of," Axel cuts Knox off with a grimace.

Nolan drags himself forward. "You think he's controlling them?"

My stomach drops.

"That's impossible," I say, shaking my head. "Ludicrous. His men were loyal before the entrapment spell was broken." My next protest gets stuck in my throat. They all seem to realize it the second I do, unable to hide their grim expressions. I snap my head to Knox. "That would mean he had someone with magic before I left…before my powers…" My eyes widen.

A spell.

The golden eruption of magic…could it have been from breaking a spell?

All my life, my memories, my identity—my being.

Was it all part of some elaborate spell?

Was that why I could never fight back? He had someone

performing magic against me, to control me?

Is that why he detests magic so much? Is that why he loathes *me*?

"No, it's not possible," I wheeze, gasping for oxygen that never comes.

A spell.

It was all a spell.

Panic makes my body begin to tingle and float, my heart leaving me once more. I can barely feel my body as I stand.

Ace's soft voice says my name like a question of hope. "Delilah?"

Bile rushes up my throat, making me swallow repeatedly until the ball subsides. Figures lurch for me as I sway but I shoot my hands out, golden fire erupting along my forearms.

"Don't touch me!"

Angel.

I see Knox in my mind, running around my garden in search of me, his flames and shadows roaming every inch. But I have floated far, far away.

Is this what I am now? A spell?

Is my body even my own?

How do I know that this is who I truly am?

Thought after thought pummels me, each one as horrid as the last.

Is any of this real?

How will I ever know what the truth is? How will I know if I'm my true self?

"I need a minute," I rasp.

Knox's search in my mind grows with intensity, the panic that consumes him visible, dimming his soul.

I can't do this again; I can't dissociate for days. People need me—my *mother* needs me.

I gasp as the word slams into my mind, tugging a piece of my heart back.

When Knox's arms wrap around me, I allow him to scoop me into his chest. I don't protest when he kicks the door open, or when his beautiful black wings expand, and we take off into the night sky.

I lay my heavy head against his chest, his heartbeat the only sound that keeps my body tethered to this world.

Chapter Eighteen

"You are Delilah Covington, and you, my Angel, will forever hold the power and strength in your heart to decide—to *choose*—who you want to be," Knox soothes.

Tears fall freely down my cheeks. Not from pain, but grief—over the loss of who I thought I was, and the person I will never be.

My mind struggles to come to terms with my identity. That I'll far outlive a human life expectancy, to hundreds, perhaps thousands, of years. That the enhanced power inside me is already threatening to consume me from the inside out. That the strength of my body makes me feel like a foreigner in my own skin.

And then there's the human side of me, the life that was never human, the lie that I was made to believe for over twenty-two years.

I don't know who I am, let alone who I *was*. The questions that continue to pile on with each day will continue to grow until it becomes so large it suffocates me.

If I was never human…

Fix the thought, adjust to the truth.

I was never human.

Was that why I never truly fit in? Why I dreamt of the Fae all my life and was drawn to the mythical stories? More specifically, why I was drawn to the in-between where the Fae were hidden?

Was that why the king detests magic? Was that why my father never loved me?

The last question makes my mind silent enough I hear my heart beating through my ears.

Was that why my father never loved me?

The questions about my lineage open a hole in my heart so large I have to slam the door shut, lock it, and throw away the key.

The possibility that the king ordered a spell to be placed upon me…to trap me within a shell of a human body…

Knox's rough hands glide across my cheek before gently lifting my head to him. "Delilah, did you hear me?"

I dip my head as if the beautiful words he spoke made a dent against the fear, but they didn't.

Swallowing through the agony ripping me apart, I breathe in deeply and force my emotions down. I cast out a net to bring my heart back into my body.

Dissociation is an odd thing. It's alive, and yet makes you feel like you're not.

"Where are we?"

Knox's eyes pinch. "On top of the highest building I could find."

"What if someone sees us? What about the spies?"

Knox maneuvers my body until my back is against his chest. "I used some of your invisibility."

My head rears back until it lays against his chest. "You can do that?"

Peering down at my hands, I marvel at the fact that whoever is using the invisibility can choose to still see themselves.

"You can too. However, it was easier using yours because when you…" Knox clears his throat. "When you disappear, your magic overtakes your mind, as if shielding it while you're away. I simply walked across the bridge and took a handful."

My chest warms. They say magic is a part of you, but it feels like we're more of a team. That sometimes, it has a mind of its own and it chooses to protect me. It wouldn't be the first time.

Then Ace's words rush to the forefront of my mind, and I think about how utterly devastating it is that my own mind works against me to the point that my heart no longer feels safe with it.

"Do you think I'll always be damaged?"

Knox's body stiffens, freezing beneath me. "Delilah, you aren't broken."

"Why do I feel like I need to be fixed then?"

Gentle lips brush across my neck. "People are perfectly imperfect. Flaws are a part of what makes us who we are."

"I don't want flaws." Indignation flares in my chest. "I don't want scars—physical or emotional. I hate them. I hate that they make me feel weak and broken and…*ugly*." My chin wobbles. "They make me feel so ugly, like I'm the Tree of Life and the inside of my heart is rotten."

Knox pulls away, only to move in front of me. I expect to find his eyes soft but they're as hard as steel as he pins me to the spot. "*You* are not ugly. Your *scars* are not ugly." He takes my hand in his and squeezes. "You are *strong*. Let your scars be a reminder of that, of all you have overcome. Let them remind you in your darkest of days that this is not the end.

That you will make it out the other side, with a new *scar* that proves your journey and bravery."

Knox's voice lowers and thickens. "Your imperfections are beautiful, Delilah. They show not only me, but all those who cross your path, that scars are powerful."

Tears flow down my face for another reason entirely.

Love.

Love pours out of me with abandon. Love for the man on his knees in front of me, gluing back together the pieces of my heart with one beautiful word at a time.

Without anything to say, without words strong enough to express my feelings, I lean forward and capture his mouth. It isn't hungry or devouring. Instead, it's a soft, gentle kiss, for everything he has ever done for me. It's a kiss to prove with actions how much I care, and the love that beats a wild melody in my heart for him.

In the air once more in Knox's arms, I whisper what I fear most.

"My magic is slipping away from me. It won't stop growing and I'm afraid I won't be able to control it for much longer."

Surprise sparks across Knox's face. "What do you mean it's growing?"

"My well—it keeps growing, expanding. *Deepening.*" I take a shuddering breath. "I haven't been able to reach the bottom yet."

Knox drops from the sky, plummeting to the ground before landing behind Ordelia's stone building, where no man or soldier can see. The heavy breathing of the sleeping griffins and horses fills the otherwise silent night.

Heir of Broken Kingdom

Knox places me down gently, despite the tremble of his hands.

"Can I see?" he asks.

I nod, opening the gate in my heart and allow him to enter.

It's an odd feeling, stranger than when Emory slithered up against me and felt my power. It's as if Knox becomes me, transforming to acquaint himself with the golden iridescent magic. He runs his fingers along it before plunging them into the well, to get a taste for what I feel every time I dive into my magic.

His magic swirls around the top of the well, creating a wall of sparkling thick shadows before his shadowed figure dives into it.

I gasp as he enters, not because it feels foreign or intrusive, but because of how it makes me feel complete—whole.

Knox isn't in there long. He barely lasts a few seconds before he's gasping for air in front of me, ripping his shadows out of the glittering golden pool and clutching his chest. His features twist in agony.

"It's impossible," he chokes out.

I wring my hands as I move toward him. "Knox, you're scaring me."

His eyes snap to me. He holds my gaze for a moment before lowering it to my chest, to my sternum. As if the force of my magic pulls him there.

"I'm sorry," he stutters. "It's just—it's, well—I don't—" Knox gulps, trying to grapple with his emotions and words. "When you entered the Fae lands, you didn't possess all of your magic."

"That's not true. I didn't have the poison injected into me, so it was never limited."

"Yes, it was." His words are breathless as he moves

closer. "Delilah, your magic is growing every day because you're coming into your power. This is nowhere near the extent of your full magic—it's…phenomenal. I've never met anyone with such power."

My eyes widen as the most powerful Fae in all the courts whispers this to me. As if his magic pales in comparison.

With my heart in my throat, I ask, "How?"

"It was held back, sleeping for over twenty years. It's still waking up, Delilah."

Except, he doesn't say that with awe. A hint of terror coats his words.

"What aren't you telling me?"

He shakes his head in bewilderment. "You're young, Delilah. A Fae's magic doesn't fully awaken until they reach their late twenties." Knox lets out a string of curses under his breath. "I can't believe I didn't think of this sooner."

"I have years of magic growth to come?" My chest squeezes impossibly tight as my breathing becomes labored. "But it's already too much."

Knox continues to stare at me in utter disbelief. I've never seen such shock pass through another person until now.

I fear the answer, but force myself to ask, "Is it not similar to your well of power?"

Knox grimaces. "It's beginning to surpass my own."

My throat turns as dry as a desert. "Who before me has had as much power as this?" I pray to the forgotten gods that someone has dealt with this before and can help me—

"No one."

Knox whispers the answer I dreaded with such horror and fear in his eyes that my heart plummets.

"There must be someone with this amount of power!" I argue. "I can't possibly be the first."

"Not with divine magic. Those with black magic, sure.

That's why they were so dangerous. But divine…Mother Gaia believes in balance and harmony. If you have too much —" Knox slams his mouth shut.

"If I have too much…what?"

Knox slices his hand through the air. "Nothing. I will train you to control it. You will be fine."

I choose to believe him and the uncharacteristically shaky voice because my mind simply cannot handle any more pressure. Before my mind can read into it too much, I do what I do best.

I push.

Shove it all away into a box and throw it into the dark vortex of my mind.

"I'm sure it's a mistake and Aurora just funneled power to me in her sleep," I say. "Either way, training will be an easy feat." I walk away, heading back toward our room. "I'm exhausted, let's go to bed."

I don't check to see if he's following me; the shadows trailing my heels tell me he is. The searing hole in my head also tells me his narrowed gaze is still upon me.

We slide into bed without uttering another word, but the questions bouncing around my head keep me up for hours.

Chapter Nineteen

Eventually, the emotional and physical exhaustion dragged me into a sleep so deep that when I awake it takes me several minutes to gather my bearings on where and who I am.

With my limbs cramping, I stretch the strained muscles, feeling them become alive from the deep rest. Renewed energy sizzles through my bones, my magic singing its praises at being awake.

It feels far more alive than it did before I fell asleep. It's bubbling to the surface, screaming to be let out, stretching and pulling with such force it has my heart dropping.

How much has it grown overnight?

Searching the endless empty halls for a familiar face, silence trails behind me until I move closer to the front of the building. The black hood concealing my features also hides my surprise as I step outside and join three thousand soldiers.

A crowd of voices, boots marching, and the hooves of horses stomping blends into a cacophony of noise. The soldiers move about, saddling up horses, filling wagons, and preparing personal satchels.

Ordelia's camp is a finely tuned operation.

My eyes land on Creseda and Henry, saddled side by side with fresh supplies bursting from the satchel seams. Annie and Ordelia are huddled together between the two horses, whispering to one another, while Phillip feeds the animals carrots.

With Knox, his court, and the griffins nowhere in sight, I stride forward, the corners of my lips twitching as Creseda and Henry throw their heads back, nickering.

Relief shines in Annie's eyes when she spots me. "I was beginning to fear you'd slipped into a coma!"

"It feels like it sometimes. Magic requires a lot of sleep." I dip my head in greeting at Ordelia before perusing the area. "Speaking of magic, where are the others?"

"They've flown ahead to scout the day's trek and check on how the first legion of soldiers are doing. They should be back in any minute," Ordelia explains.

I try not to let my disappointment show. Why wouldn't they wake me?

I tried. You were snoring like the dead.

The deep timbre of his voice elicits an involuntary smile on my face, but at Annie's quizzical look, I wipe it away instantly.

An electric current runs through my skin, raising the hairs on the back of my neck. I turn to the source pulling at my nerve endings. Knox is already there behind me.

He stands poised, not as the king of Azalea but as a warrior.

Dressed impeccably in black fighting leathers, covered head to toe in weapons, his form is enough to scare the soldiers into taking several steps backward. Rightfully so.

His magic slithers down the bond between us, a flicker of

surprise striking the bridge as it passes what can only be described as a bubbling cauldron of magic.

No wonder you were out for two days. Gods, it's grown so much.

I was out for two days?

Magic will force your body to rest as it grows.

What did you tell the others?

That you were exhausted from….something other than magic.

Knox strides toward me with heat sizzling in his eyes. He has the look of a man who knows exactly what he wants, and he's moments away from getting it. The bond tugs impossibly tight. My lips part, my chest heaving from the heat thrumming through my blood.

I have to shake myself. *Secret, remember?*

Knox's strides slow before a wall slams over his eyes. That sliver of vulnerability and want that was beautifully shining a moment before is gone, wiped away within a second.

This already feels like torture.

No, that's what we're avoiding by remaining private, I remind him.

I don't let him see just how much it's affecting me; I wouldn't want to give him the satisfaction. Yet by the small devilish smirk playing on his lips, he already knows. My heart is beating so furiously I could have sworn it was trying to kick me for not embracing him.

Silence falls over the camp like a thick blanket, instantly making my back straighten.

Aurora and Zephlyn round the corner, the twins leading them. Every soldier within the path of their large lion bodies and bird-like wings cowers away. Their chests puff up and their hackles rise as a thousand eyes watch the creatures' every move with various expressions of awe, horror, and fear.

Creseda and Henry break the silence with their joyous nickering at seeing them. It warms my heart that the animals have bonded.

Relief slams into me when Aurora's eyes connect with mine, her emotions pummeling me after the long separation. The poor thing must have been out of her mind not being able to see me.

Knox walks past me to report to Ordelia. I ignore the contact my body begs from him, an incessant buzzing that can't be tamed until his skin touches mine.

I take deep, measured breaths through my nose. *This is going to be difficult.*

Tell me about it, he growls.

I bite back the grin threatening to escape and drop back toward the twins. My eyes soften as Ace reaches behind him and links his fingers with Hazel. I suppose Knox and I aren't the only ones that always feel the need to be touching.

"We're all clear to move out today. We found none of the king's soldiers," he says.

"According to your men in front, the nearest moving soldiers are located east of Sector Five," Axel chimes in, standing behind Knox.

Phillip dips his head. "Thank you, Holloway. Your efforts are appreciated."

"Please, call me Knox."

A grateful smile plays on Ordelia's lips. "Thank you, Knox. We'll move out in twenty minutes, so ready yourself and your court. We have a long journey ahead of us."

No sooner are the orders given do the tears fall. The sound of weeping women, children, family, and friends saying goodbye to their loved ones.

An immense amount of pressure is upon us. Thousands of lives rest in the balance and not just those of the soldiers but everyone here. I pray to the forgotten gods, whichever one may listen, that I don't make things worse.

With the newfound energy and strength coursing through my bones and muscles, I help Annie up on Creseda. She feels like she weighs nothing but a bag of cloth.

"Oh," she says, surprised. "Thank you, dear."

I pat Creseda's snout, a part of me sad that I won't be riding her as much.

I settle atop Aurora and take up the position in front. Her predatory gaze assesses any who come near with a perusal that promises violence if they make a wrong move.

Despite her incessant mistrust of humans, her protection warms my heart.

Dragons may bring the force and magic, but the griffins' burning loyalty is the true heart of the aerial legion.

"What other gifts do you possess?" Annie asks. She whispers the question as if one of the many rumors spreading throughout the rebels isn't about how the princess of Aloriah has elongated, pointy ears.

I just pray none of them will go against Ordelia's orders and tell anyone outside of their station that I'm still alive. The king cannot hear about me riding amongst his army.

Knox must have the same thought because no sooner does the question leave her lips, a silencing shield snaps around us, his power caressing my back beneath my clothes in a comforting touch.

I pull my hood down a little further.

"I surprisingly possess the majority of them. Water, fire, earth, air, and of course the enhanced senses of a Fae."

"Is there anything more than the elemental power? I know you mentioned invisibility."

"There are special gifts within the elemental system. For instance, some earth Fae are gifted healers and others have the ability to shapeshift."

A spark of delight fills her eyes. "Is it wonderful?" she asks wistfully.

"Yes, very much so," I find myself saying, despite my previous conversation with Knox. My lips tug into a wide smile. No matter the worries that come with my magic, I am grateful beyond words for my abilities.

"What's the golden power?"

"I would also love an answer to that," I mutter under my breath.

Annie's questions die on her tongue when Phillip approaches, soldiers pulling along three horses as large as Creseda behind him. "These are yours, courtesy of Ordelia. We don't want you and your men to waste their energy on something as mundane as walking."

Knox steps forward to accept the horses. "Thank you, Phillip, that's very gracious of Ordelia."

Some of the soldiers' legs quiver as they near the group of Fae and griffins. A far difference in these men's attitudes to those who held iron-tipped arrows to our necks.

Knox softens the hard edges of his features, offering a kind and tentative smile to them.

It's hard to believe Fae and humans used to coexist or help each other like Knox is today. It'll take time to trust each other again, but perhaps one day we can live together in peace once more. It makes me think of how the Sector One citizens are faring right now as they travel through the Fae lands, and what they must think of all the creatures.

Ordelia and her closest soldiers stand to attention in the middle of the army. Annie tightens her hold on the reins as we begin to move, descending into our long three-week journey to Sector Seven.

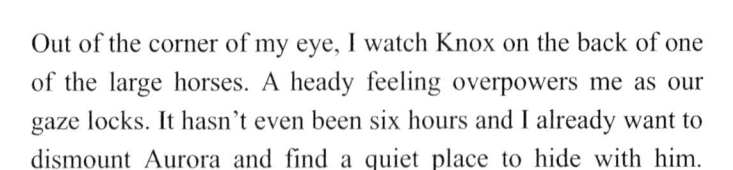

Out of the corner of my eye, I watch Knox on the back of one of the large horses. A heady feeling overpowers me as our gaze locks. It hasn't even been six hours and I already want to dismount Aurora and find a quiet place to hide with him. Perhaps within the trees again.

Knox's teeth graze over his bottom lip and the smoldering look he gives me momentarily disarms me.

A single dimple appears, the corner of his mouth lifting as he watches me unravel at the mere sight of him. His mouth tilts in amusement, and with that, I have the overwhelming urge to throw something at his head.

We're not very inconspicuous, I say, surprised to find my voice breathy and sultry.

His answering response is a wave of need down the bridge, slamming into me so hard I tighten my hold on Aurora.

I narrow my eyes. *Two can play at this game, Holloway.*

My own wave flows down the bridge, along with snippets of my favorite memories. In the bathroom, the bed, the garden, the forest…

A vicious growl tumbles from him out loud. A few soldiers edge farther away from him.

"Feeling a bit tense, are we?" I tease. My eyes glow with mirth.

No sooner does his mask slip does he have it under control once more, slamming those walls over his eyes.

Perhaps we play a game, Angel.

Heir of Broken Kingdom

The teasing tone doesn't fool me. I can hear the arrogance beneath, but I bite. *What do you have in mind?*

Regardless of what it is, I need something to make the time pass. No one warned me how dull and boring this would be, and three weeks is a long time to travel staring at trees, mountains, and endless fields.

The views aren't always bad, I suppose. My eyes wander to Knox's arms. The exposed skin is slick with sweat from the burning midday sun. The veins have protruded, and the muscles bulge from the grip on his reins as if his mind cannot stop picturing his hands wrapped around another thing entirely.

Whoever breaks first...wins.

An anticipatory hum rushes through my blood. *The first to break in...?*

Need, Angel. Pure, unadulterated need.

My body grows taut, the alluring tease of his gravelly voice making my blood boil. Goosebumps line my skin as a shiver runs down my spine. His eyes—I can always feel when they're on me.

Is teasing allowed?

Oh, it's not only allowed but encouraged, Angel.

With a sultry glance, Knox's eyes turn molten at my answer.

You're on, Holloway.

Ace comes up beside me on Zephlyn, with Hazel's arms wrapped around him. "Would you like some water, Delilah?"

"No, but perhaps offer some to Knox. He's beginning to drool."

Once night descends, we set up camp in the dense woods. Knox places a ward around the campfires, hiding not only the chatter of soldiers and their animals but the fire's scent and smoke from anyone who walks past.

Knox sets up his tent, declining the offered help of fear-filled soldiers. At least they're trying. After caring and tending to Aurora and Creseda, I trail to my tent, smiling to myself when I see Knox has set up his beside mine.

I only enter my tent for a moment, long enough to make myself invisible before leaving, before I leave and slip into Knox's. My smile turns saccharine as I sit on his makeshift cot, crossing one leg over the other.

My fighting leathers were the first thing I shed when I dismounted Aurora. Now that only leaves me in thin white cotton shorts.

When Knox comes back, I hold off on revealing myself, graciously allowing my eyes to roam his body as he begins to undress, peeling off the skintight leathers.

I give myself a moment to soak it up, the glorious sight that is Knox Holloway, King of Azalea and the Essence Court. The king that captured my heart and cradled it next to his own.

I click my tongue as he turns toward me, my invisibility vanishing. I expect a hiss or a jump, perhaps even a dagger or two thrown. Instead, all I receive is a grin as Knox trails his hand down his lower abdominals…to his pants.

"Like what you see, Angel?" he drawls.

I smirk. "Of course."

"Ready to give in?" he asks, pulling the pants off until he's left in nothing but boxers.

I let my weight slowly sink into the bed, my hands gliding backward as I bring my knees higher. My back arches and my chest rises as I tip my head back.

"No…are you?"

He leans against the pole in the middle of the tent, crossing his arms over his chest. "No, barely feel affected."

I roll my eyes as I drop my weight fully to the cot. "Neither do I," I lie.

Knox moves across the room faster than I can blink, a gentle hand wrapping around my throat. His body covers mine. "That's not what I felt earlier."

I lift my knee higher, a devilish grin spreading on my face. "That's not what I'm *feeling* either," I tease, brushing my knee against the hardened length.

He drops his face to mine, his lips a hair's breadth away. "Give in," he growls.

I lift my chin, enough so our lips graze, a spark igniting between us. "Never."

His tongue darts out, sliding against my bottom lip. "If memory serves me, Angel, that intoxicating feeling that overcame you earlier was want…lust…. need," he drawls huskily. His fingers move to my thighs. "And…what was that other thing?"

Before he can utter the word, I wrap my legs around his waist and roll him to the cot. I copy his earlier movements, wrapping my hand around his neck and gently squeezing. I drop my face beside him, letting my hot breath fan over his ear.

A rush of delight runs through me as he shudders.

"Perhaps you're the one who needs training and not me… considering how easily I can disarm you."

Competitive delight swims in his sapphire eyes. "Perhaps," he muses.

Boots stomp, rustling the twigs and fallen pinecones outside. I make myself invisible just as Ace strolls into the tent.

"They're telling stories around the fire and eating dinner. Are you coming?" he asks.

Knox stands, rummaging through his pack for fresh clothing. "I'll join you in a moment."

"I'll see you soon, Delilah," he throws over his shoulder in a singsong voice as he leaves.

I gasp, my eyes connecting with Knox's when I reappear. A surprise cackle bursts free from Knox. He tips his head back with laughter, and the sound is music to my ears. I join him, my smile infectious seeing him for once without the weight of the world on his shoulders.

Knox and I may be playing the role of platonic friends, but that doesn't mean I cannot be cordial. At least, that's how I rationalize sitting next to Knox around the campfire, squished between his strong, warrior frame and Hazel.

The soldiers have dug out a hole for the large firepit and placed fallen logs around it. Ordelia and Phillip sit perpendicular to me, their faces blurry through the fire, courtesy of Knox.

Considering no one knows what my golden power truly is, I've kept it at a minimum, only using it when no leering eyes are around and only to relieve the pressure I feel building throughout the day. Especially in the morning, after a full night's sleep, the magic practically bangs on my chest.

Even now, jealousy sizzles in my well of power as Hazel plays and toys with her magic for all to see. Her hands rise, building a beautiful green stem for a flower to flourish. I swallow the gasp as she kills it, making it turn black and rotten.

Then slowly, painstakingly so, she begins to revive the

plant, making the blackened daisy turn to pure white once more. The soldiers who were watching, men and the few females, clap at her performance.

That was one of the first things Axel noticed, how limited the female numbers are in the king's armies. I explained the barbaric notions of the king and how difficult the challenges are made for females who wish to join the ranks. The majority of the men here would fail miserably at the tests they put the females through. It's a miracle how many females are here now, along with Ordelia, a shining beacon of hope to females sitting as the army's commander.

Ordelia clears her throat. "Those who have been with me from the beginning know this one, but those of you that are new…I hope this story blossoms courage in your heart as it did for mine."

Ordelia's eyes pierce mine as if she's only telling the story with the intention of me hearing it.

"At the beginning of the rebellion, people were in a trance of grief, one so tumultuous and deep you couldn't pull them out. I almost fell into a hole of darkness myself, but the sheer will of my stubbornness kept me afloat. And so did my anger.

"There were rumors of a group of soldiers, more like a pack of animals, that would sneak into the homes of the widows." She swallows thickly as her eyes take on a glassy sheen. "They fed off the sorrow of the people and took what they wanted. They were entitled pricks who thought they owned the women of the sector."

Her index finger reaches up and traces the scar along her face. "They may have marked me, but their wicked hearts stopped beating that night. And I cherish the scar for what it is, a reminder of my strength and ability to make a change in this horrid world."

Her words pierce my heart, my soul, and my scars.

Because maybe I'm not tarnished and damaged. Maybe I'm not a victim at all.

Perhaps I'm a survivor.

Story after story is told, whispers of the horror they've faced, but when the Fae begin to share their own legends, stories created before even the ancestors of the humans, commotion in the camp, grounds to a halt. Everyone finds a seat to perch atop, and for those that cannot, the Fae use their magic to spread their words.

The warrior, who has likely heard thousands of stories among his commanding soldiers' camps, sits forward, a gleam in his hazel eyes that I have never seen before, and for the first time since stumbling through the wards of the Fae lands and into Knox's home, I watch Nolan become exhilarated as he launches into his favorite telling of the twisted family.

"At the beginning of time in Aloriah, before the Fae courts were forged and the lands were divided, there was a handmaiden." Nolan's gaze roams the men around the fire. "She was a beautiful handmaiden, and despite being born into the lower class, she was sought after. Those around her wished upon the stars for her beauty. Yet after years of men's unwanted affection, and women taking out their jealousy on the handmaiden for their husbands' wandering eyes, she had grown tired. For the people only cared and saw her for one thing—beauty."

The soldiers hush to a whisper as Nolan pauses for dramatic effect.

"The handmaiden sought out a witch, a powerful one at that. Some say the most high-powered witch to walk this world. They could turn a friend to foe, a frog to a prince, change the trajectory of your life, grant your deepest desire, and…turn a handmaiden into a faerie."

The soldiers' small inhale of breath isn't lost on the Fae hearing.

"She requested one thing: power. An ungodly power that would make the men turn away and the women think twice before coming after her. The witch laughed in her face and asked, 'Is that all?' The handmaiden was perplexed; she was asking for such dangers, after all. It was believed to be a fearful thing to possess such abilities and power, and at the one thing she had been dreaming of all her life—to be seen past her beauty—the witch simply laughed in her face and asked for a copper.

"So, the handmaiden changed her answer. She asked for a rare power that the masses didn't have, one the Fae race had not dealt with. And the witch granted her wish, just not in the way she thought."

I lean forward on the edge of the log, subconsciously leaning into Knox's side as I await Nolan's next words.

"The handmaiden awoke as a Fae, but that wasn't it. The crimson blood that pumped through her veins was no more. Instead, it ran black, a putrid smell lingering beneath her skin. Because it was not divine magic that was granted, it was black. As dark as her soul had turned when the witch spun her a web of lies and deceit. The handmaiden was granted her wish, though. She could conjure anything, from this world or another, and she fell in love with the power she held in her hands.

"But it came with a price. For every dark spell she cast, she exchanged the soul of an unborn child. And so, what started as a plea for help, an answer to humanity's vanity, became a deep hunger for power the handmaiden could not escape. So much so that the dark magic plagued her lineage for centuries until it finally came full circle.

"The last of the children to be born of sacrifice had

souls only partly plagued with black magic. Divine magic had grown in their lineage, enough so that they could reclaim their soul. Yet despite most of their souls being divine, that sliver of dark magic intrigued them. The curiosity and fascination with the dark cost them. The children were banished, for fear of their dark ancient magic taking over once more."

Nolan's story trails off on an eerie tone. No one utters a word, crickets filling in the silence. Axel whistles, breaking the tension that grew with every word over the blistering fire.

"That's one way to make the humans trust us," Axel jokes. And it's so out of character for him that it pulls a chuckle from me, albeit a nervous one.

"On that *glorious* note, who wants another round?" Lucca, Ordelia's second-in-command asks as he winds his way around the fire with mugs. I haven't seen him much while traveling, but the times I have, he was talking with the Fae and asking them questions, one of the few who has.

Even now, he fearlessly approaches and places a mug in my hand and Knox's, while Marcus, his companion, does the same for the rest of Knox's court. Chocolate stuffs itself down my throat, the scent a familiar and comforting aroma, and I decide I've already taken a shine to him.

He can't possibly know what it means to me, but when I look up to thank him, he winks at me, the campfire glow dancing along his chocolate skin. "Alcohol isn't the only thing to keep you warm on nights like these."

Knox returns his easy smile with one of his own. "It's perfect, Lucca."

Lucca and Marcus take a seat on Ordelia's log, settling in for another story. The two nestle closer until their shoulders connect and they link their fingers together.

Knox takes up the task. He doesn't wait to see if others

have a story to share, because the second he leans forward, his dark rumbling voice commands everyone in the vicinity.

"In the world before this one, there were deities. Twelve deities, to be exact, the children of Mother Gaia and Uranus. Each of the deities were gifted in one area of life while their father ruled over the universe. They each had a part to play in keeping things intact, yet only ten were happy in their assigned roles. And so, the wrath of the deities began as the two children rebelled. One was killed in the process, while the other lived out their days avenging their sibling's death and continuing with their original plan of rebellion—world domination."

No one dares to speak. Around the fire, the soldiers bite their lips to not laugh at the Fae king who could char them all in a heartbeat. Knox's court, however, has no qualms about laughing in his face.

Axel bursts into hysteria. "Knox, you *have* to work on your delivery."

"I have not heard such an awful telling in years," Nolan snorts.

I try to hold back my laughter, I really do, but I fail miserably when Ace throws a small thumbs-up in Knox's direction, his smile looking more like a wince.

"Ace, no, spare him please."

Knox snaps accusatory eyes at me. "I'd like to see you try and keep a camp full of soldiers entertained."

My lips wobble as I try to reel in my laughter. "I haven't lived long enough to tell mythological stories. You, on the other hand, have had decades to work on it."

The soldiers study us inquisitively. Perhaps they are finally realizing that a leader does not have to equate to pain, death, and fear, but they can display love, friendship, loyalty, and trust.

A brave young soldier joins in, the first to crack a smile among his peers. "Aren't they all based on imagination anyway?"

Axel, Ace, Nolan, and Knox say, "No," in unison.

"How much truth is there to be found?" Ordelia asks.

"The Fae people cherish their stories and lineage because we believe truth can be found in all of them. Those that fabricate stories are frowned upon," Knox drawls.

I shake my head. *Faeries and their truth.*

Chapter Twenty

The bastards will burn. They will bleed for their heinous crimes.

The skin on my forearm peels, dripping with blood as I thrash against the tree they've tied me to.

The rope burns my wrists and my ankles, but I don't care. I tug and tug and tug, pulling as hard as I can. Despite the voice in the back of my head telling me it's impossible, the sight before my eyes will not let me stop.

My mother and two sisters scream at the top of their lungs as the assailants that came for us in the middle of the night pin them to the forest floor. They kill them so painstakingly slowly in a show of mockery, forcing me to watch the life leave their eyes.

They've pulled them so close to my tree that with every slash and plunge of their knife, the blood sprays my white nightgown and blonde hair.

Marking me red.

I thrash again, tears pouring down my cheeks in rivulets.

I try to note the details of their bodies, but they're concealed by the black billowing robes, the hoods that cast them into shadows. And with a piece of my sister's torn shirt shoved down my throat, I can't breathe, let alone scream for help.

Not that it'd be much use. We are so far from civilization that they didn't even bother gagging my sisters and mother.

They know no one will find them.

They will not rest until they lie dead at my feet.

Because their master isn't done playing with me. He isn't done seeing through my mind.

"Ready to watch the show, Elysia?" he purrs.

Chapter Twenty-One

A scream tears from my throat as they plunge the knife into the woman's stomach.

Knox is up in an instant, lighting the gas lamp with his flames as he rubs circles along my back. "What is it? Was it the premonition again?"

Ever since the premonition, my nightmares have been plagued with the image of Knox dying, but this…

I shake my head. "It was another premonition."

Knox frowns and watches it on the bridge between our minds.

"Up until now, I've never had a premonition of another person." I clear my dry throat. "It's always been about my future or through my eyes. I've never seen those women before."

"They're not from Azalea. They could be from the smaller towns along the border of the Essence Court, but even then…"

"You know your people," I whisper.

His eyes flit back and forth, searching for answers I can't give him.

"We don't tell a soul," he whispers.

"But we could stop it. We could help!"

His hands cup my cheeks, his thumb brushing away tears that I hadn't realized escaped. "I'll alert Lenox and my messengers to keep an ear out for hitmen, but until—"

I gasp. "You think those men were assassins?"

My stomach rolls as I think back to the three dark hoods. The way they moved flawlessly, in sync with one another… how they taunted and teased.

They had done it before, many times.

"Yes," Knox says.

My lip quivers. "So, we do nothing?"

"Did you see anything in the background that pointed to a location?"

I shake my head. It was just a regular forest and nothing to indicate which one it was. Or if it was even in the Fae lands.

"How can I go on knowing that her family is going to die and do nothing?" I ask hoarsely.

A look passes over Knox's eyes, and before he can mask it, I swear it appears to be fear.

"I think you're not the only one who received that vision."

My brows lower. "You think she's a seer too?"

"I think she shared it with you." Knox swallows. "It's not uncommon. I mean, I can share memories with whomever I please. What I'm worried about is why she sent the vision to you of all people."

"You think it's a ploy?"

"Another game…"

My eyes widen as my body begins to shake.

With the king in the picture…we have to question *everything*.

"We tell no one," I concede.

Chapter Twenty-Two

I can make you feel better, Angel. All you'd have to do is yield, Knox whispers in my mind a week later.

Moonlight glints off silver as I flick the blade in my hand. "Never," I purr.

Sparks of joy dance across Knox's eyes as he hears my words for what they are: a taunt and a challenge.

We move as one around the makeshift sparring ring we've marked beside our tents. While others choose to spend their nights unwinding from the grueling travel, Knox and I train. Not only to keep physically fit as Knox prepares me for the hardest challenge I have yet to face—entering the palace—we focus on controlling my magic as it grows day by day. Not that it's any easier of a task.

Knox assumes it's a process similar to training, that you must repeat the exercises until it becomes a process of muscle memory. I, however, can feel the difference, the way my well of magic lengthens each day. How my legs quiver and my breathing turns shallow while Knox tells me to hold the magic within.

That being said, we've made little progress this week. At

least my defense training hasn't been forgotten. And if the king has someone who can wield magic at his disposal, I need to be at my physical peak to protect myself.

Except, the one thing I want to learn is the one thing Knox refuses to teach me. *Flying*. With my growing well of power comes the insatiable itch between my shoulder blades as my golden iridescent wings *scream* to be set free. But Knox doesn't want to risk someone seeing them, on the off chance they recognize the rarity of the color, especially with the king breathing down our necks. I find I begrudgingly agree with him most of the time, other than when my wings start clawing at my skin again.

Nevertheless, the exercises aren't the only thing to occur on the mat. Despite himself, Knox can't let the opportunity pass him to touch me. Daggers may be thrown on the mat, but the touch of his heavy hands against my body, lingering for seconds longer than normal, is what truly makes my heart rate spike.

I move left, and Knox moves right, daggers in hand we wait for the other to pounce. Knox's gaze is cunning, decades of training and calculation whizzing through his mind as he waits for me to make the first move.

If I'm entirely honest with myself, I'm far too busy staring at his body to think of a move to overpower him. He knows it, and I know it.

It's precisely why he decided to train with me this evening—shirtless.

Knox's body is a honed weapon, every muscle and bone made entirely of power, and this is only a sliver of what he's capable of. He keeps the majority of himself, his magic and strength, leashed.

How beautiful it would be to watch him come undone.

Never is a long time, Angel. Are you sure about your declaration?

Knox rips my attention away from his bare chest. "As sure as I am that you're cheating," I say.

An arrogant smirk spreads across his lips. "Distracted tonight, are we?"

I feign innocence, lunging forward a step only to pounce backward, dodging his strike of steel.

Close. That was too close.

"I'm not sure what you're talking about."

Knox lunges again. I whirl, rolling onto the damp forest ground. Popping up behind him, I kick the back of his leg, making his knees buckle.

"I'm not the one who hasn't gotten any hits in tonight," I volley back.

Knox recovers quickly, jumping to his feet like a nimble cat. And so, we resume our dance of waiting for the other to strike.

"How do you want to celebrate your birthday?" he asks suddenly.

"I'm not."

I can't stop the wave of emotions that slam into him down the bond, letting him know exactly how I feel about that question.

His brow quirks. "You don't want to celebrate your birthday?"

"No," I say through gritted teeth, lunging and meeting nothing but air.

Circling me again, his eyes bore into mine. "Tell me why you don't want to celebrate."

Ignoring him, I pivot and strike again.

Knox dodges it leisurely. "Tell me," he pushes.

I roll my eyes with a huff. "Don't try and disarm me with emotional strikes."

"I didn't know it was an emotional strike," he says gently. "Although, if it's one the king knows about, you need to prepare yourself."

"I am prepared," I snap.

Knox's brows rise. "Clearly not, if you're this worked up over a simple question."

"It's not a simple question!"

I grit my teeth, his words burrowing into my mind.

How cruel to use that against me in the training ring.

Not cruel, tactical. You're about to go up against a man who knows all your darkest secrets.

Knox stands to his full height, eyes shining with sincerity and protection. "He may not have a sword in his hand, Delilah, but he knows how to inflict pain upon you without one. I want you to be prepared."

And clearly, I've struck a nerve, he adds in my mind.

"And how are you going to do that, Knox? By purposely bringing up things that hurt me?" I spit.

Knox lunges, knocking the twin daggers out of my palms far too easily for my liking. I barely have a moment to gasp in shock before he has me pinned to the ground.

"I asked one question and you got sloppy. I am doing this *for* you," he growls.

I shove him off me and retrieve the daggers. "Well, don't."

Knox quirks a brow, folding his arms across his chest. "It was a genuine question before it turned into a lesson." At my eye roll he moves forward. "Why don't you want to celebrate your birthday?"

Wrong move.

Wrong question.

I snap my leg out and sweep Knox to the ground. I pounce, the silver of my dagger driving into his neck. I bare my canines in his face. "Stop asking questions."

"I'll stop asking once you start talking. Half your problem with controlling your magic is that you bottle everything up," he says tightly.

Grunting, I shove off him, my gaze flicking to the busy camp. "Anyone can hear!"

"Have you not learned anything yet?" he groans. He picks up a small pebble and hurls it to the side.

It crashes into an invisible wall, bouncing off Knox's shields.

"Why are you doing this?" I ask softly.

If it was truly a lesson, he made his point long ago.

Knox's eyes lose the hard edge, his voice growing soft. "Does it truly bother you?"

"Yes."

"Okay, I won't ask again, and we won't celebrate." Knox stands, his shoulders stiff as he picks up the daggers discarded during the tumble.

I don't miss the hurt laced in his voice, or the way his eyes and jaws have hardened again.

I'll tell you when this is all over but please don't make me remember things about my family or childhood... I can't dissociate in front of these people. They're counting on me.

I whisper the words in my mind, pulling them from the depths of my heart because they won't move past my lips.

Before I can take my next breath, Knox is running for me, and he doesn't stop until he tackles me, his large arms around my waist. I wait for the rush of oxygen to leave me from the force of the hit, but it never comes.

Knox breaks our fall with magic, making it appear to

those around us that we're still training when in reality he buries his head into the crook of my neck and hugs me.

My eyes shudder closed at the contact. He knew exactly what I needed in this moment. And he's given it to me in the only way he can right now in front of thousands of soldiers and peering eyes.

"Whenever you're ready, Angel," he whispers.

Knox pulls back, only to capture my wrists and pin them beside my head while he sits on my hips.

I cock my head. "How did you know when my birthday was anyway?"

A memory floats through my mind, there and gone in an instant. Through Knox's eyes, I see the living room in Easton's cottage, and on his writing desk, there's a letter addressed to me, marked with the numbers of my birthday. The seventh day of the seventh month.

I gasp at the cursive numbers. That could only be Easton's handwriting.

"Why didn't you give it to me?" I ask, pulling away from the memory.

Knox eases off me, offering his hand as he stands. "You had just dissociated for days. I didn't want to send you spiraling into that state again."

I ignore his outstretched hand and pull myself up. A deep frown pulls at my lips. "What if I never make it out of this alive? How dare you take that choice away from me! I had the right to read that—"

Knox raises his hands in surrender. "Delilah, I didn't take—"

"Yes, you did! You took it from me! That was not yours!"
He's just like everybody else, always choosing for me.

Knox's menacing growl snaps my mouth shut. "First of

all, you *are* going to continue living. And secondly, I brought it with me, for whenever you're ready," he snaps.

I don't have a chance to respond. Knox storms off, heading to his tent without me.

Lying on my makeshift cot later that evening, loneliness wars with my mind and body. This is the first time I've slept without Knox in weeks, and it feels like I'm missing a limb.

The sensation thrums throughout my body as if my soul is searching for him, and the incessant tug of the bond on each end as it tries to pull us together will not concede.

No matter how my body feels, I know why he's not here. In fact, I know the exact moment I hurt him, the moment my mouth opened and struck. It's been playing on an endless loop since.

I shouldn't have snapped at him or accused him of taking choices away from me, yet sometimes my mouth takes control before my mind.

And as we near the palace, I've been getting more agitated. My body tightening, the memories attacking, as if they're trying to remind me.

No matter how many times I say to myself, *I am okay,* it doesn't make the slightest difference. Because my mind and heart know I'm going back there, into the walls of the very place that destroyed me and held me captive for twenty-two years.

My heart isn't ready to be treated how it was. Not after it's felt love and tenderness.

Love is not shown through fists and ugly words. Love is gentle touches and comforting words.

Love is not cruel. It's soft and gentle.

Ironic how I know that, yet I spoke out of irritation and anger toward Knox.

Fights, I suppose, are normal in any relationship, but it frightened me when he walked away today. So, some may call me proud, but all I immediately wanted to do was crawl on my hands and knees to him and apologize. It may take my heart a long time to reconcile how people can walk away when they're upset without coming back to hurt you.

I turn over again for another time when the hairs on the back of my neck suddenly stand on end. I snap upright, feeling like someone is approaching my tent.

Aurora wouldn't let anyone come within fifty feet of this tent. How did they get past her? Perhaps she finally tumbled into a deep sleep; she's barely gotten any since the day she saved us all from dropping out of the sky.

Creeping out of the cot, I unsheathe the dragon blade I hid under the bed in the same moment I make myself invisible. I lift my blade at the same time the silhouette of a hand reaches for the tent flaps.

A scream lodges itself in my throat as a large male figure darts into the space. I bring the sword down with all my strength. The figure catches it effortlessly as shadows fly for me, making the sword and my form reappear. Curses tumble from the assailant's mouth as crimson drips onto the floor, flowing from their palm.

"What the fuck, Delilah?"

I gasp, dropping the sword. Knox pulls his hood back, his face twisted with pain.

I panic. "I'm so sorry! I thought you were an intruder!" Before Knox can utter a word, I rush on. "I was wondering how someone got past Aurora! Of course, she would just let you walk past..."

"Delilah."

"Oh, a medical kit!" I flit around the small tent, turning over every object in my search. "Surely, they have a kit somewhere. It would be useless not to have one."

"Delilah, stop."

I rush for the bed, lifting the makeshift cot. "I mean, you'd think they'd put one in everyone's tent," I huff. Endless babble keeps pouring from me as I drop to my knees and rummage through the satchel on the ground. "Maybe it's only in higher-ranking officials' tents? You would think a princess would count as a higher-ranking official. Though, I suppose I'm not a princess anymore. Traitor? Now it makes sense why— "

Angel.

That one word snaps my mouth closed. My gaze flies to him, then flicks down to the open palm Knox holds out for me. There's no cut on his skin, only a smudge of dried and cracked blood.

Oh.

Healing magic.

I lower my head, not wanting to face the embarrassment as my cheeks flush.

Knox kneels beside me on the floor, gently taking the satchel from my hand. "There's nothing to be embarrassed about. It's nice to know that you'd tend to my wounds. In fact, it was adorable."

I blink. "That was not adorable."

"You weren't the one watching."

I bark out a laugh. "Thank the gods for that."

Knox takes my hands in his. "I'm sorry, Angel," he whispers.

My brows furrow. "What for? I'm the one who nearly decapitated you."

"Key word being *nearly*, and no you did not." Knox lifts

me before I can protest, nestling me into his lap. He rests his chin on my shoulder and looks up at me through thick black lashes. "I'm sorry for storming off. I shouldn't have walked out in the middle of a discussion."

"I know, I was in the wrong—"

"No, Angel." Knox reaches up to cup my cheeks. "I shouldn't have pushed you repeatedly, not with what you're about to walk into, and it was unfair of me not to show you the letter the moment I found it."

"But you were right. He will use any advantage he can, and he knows how to wield his words to strike the deepest."

"I used it as an excuse, though." He rubs the back of his neck, his cheeks flushing.

I've never seen Knox embarrassed. The emotion softens him, making him cute.

"I wanted to feel closer to you and I felt rejected when you wouldn't let me in. I went about it the wrong way and I apologize." His swallow is audible. "You're right, though. The moment I saw it affect you, I became overprotective and wanted to show you where an enemy could strike. I know it's not an excuse but ever since the Phoenix Rising spell...when you were in my arms..."

His voice cracks, a sheen of tears welling in his eyes. He shakes his head, unable to speak of the moment I died in his arms.

"I don't want to feel like that again, Delilah. I cannot lose you. I'll do absolutely *anything* to protect you from harm. I know it was a terrible thing to keep the letter from you, but I just couldn't bear to be the one to hurt you, to hand you something that would cause you pain."

I run gentle fingers down his cheeks. "It's okay, I understand." Leaning forward, I brush a gentle kiss against his lips. "I'm sorry I snapped at you. I just...haven't been handling the travel well, getting closer to the palace every day."

Knox's eyes soften. "I think we need to make a new bargain." At my intrigue, Knox peppers kisses up my neck until he reaches my ear. "I vow to let you into my heart fully, Angel, to everything that I am feeling and more."

My heart catches, snagging at his words. My eyes hold the truth in his words, and the promise of his unwavering vow.

"I vow to let you into my heart fully, Knox," I whisper back, chills scattering down my arms at the promise we have made to one another.

His eyes glisten. He opens his mouth but doesn't make a sound, as if the heady power of feelings choke him. Instead of words, he leans forward and captures my lips, pouring everything he is unable to speak into the caress.

His tongue licks across the seam of my lips, demanding entrance, and I give it to him willingly. The moment his tongue strokes my own, a loud moan rises from the depths of my soul. He groans his own contentment.

I've come to learn that my sounds are his weakness—the thing that can bring him to his knees.

A silencing shield snaps around the tent as his large hands grip my hips, squeezing, before settling me over his evident arousal.

A moan tumbles from my lips for an entirely new reason.

Rocking my hips back and forth, Knox's head falls backward, exposing his neck. His hands grip my thighs a little tighter.

"Good girl, Angel. Make yourself feel good."

A high-pitched sound rises in the back of my throat at his words, at the deep voice that has chased me through my dreams and fantasies.

But it isn't enough. I want him to *unravel.*

I flare my canines, scraping the sharp points across his neck, my eyes sparking with ravenous heat when the skin pebbles. His length, nestled underneath my core, pulses, growing impossibly hard.

Then with a pounding heart and a tingling core, I lick a path to his ear, letting my warm breath fall over his delicate skin. "I want *you* to make me feel good, Knox," I whisper.

White light encases our bodies, stretching time and space as Knox teleports us.

One moment I'm nestled atop his lap in the middle of the tent, and the next, I'm sitting with my legs crossed on his cot. He stands over me, peering down at me as if I'm his next meal.

Knox's grin is ravenous and purely wicked as his fingers wrap around my chin and he brushes his thumb down my swollen, pink lips.

"Say it again."

His voice is a mere rumble, a promise of the pleasure to come.

Chills scatter down my spine, making my arms pebble in anticipation. "Please make me feel good, Knox."

His thumb strokes the swell of my fluttering pulse, over my collarbones, then down to my full, heavy breasts.

He applies the gentlest pressure. "Lie back and spread your arms above your head."

His voice, that deep purr of a grumble, is a command to my limbs. Before I can consciously tell my body to move, it's deciding for me, lying back on the cot and lifting my arms.

Eagerness thrashes through me as I wait for him to move. To touch me, to do what I asked, to make me feel good. Because if there is one thing Knox is capable of, it is what I wished for. After all, he never breaks a vow.

His hands lift again, stealing my breath with the movement. Only for it to come out in a rush as he begins to unbutton his shirt, bearing his naked chest and all his glorious muscles for me. The tan honey skin shines in the firelight glow.

A pulse begins inside my stomach and then moves lower to my clit, making me squeeze my thighs together in an attempt to alleviate the growing pressure.

Knox *tsks*, the sudden break in the silence startling enough to make me pause. Discarding his shirt, he leans forward, his calloused hands grazing over my knees and pulling them apart.

"You asked *me* to make you feel good, Angel. That means no touching."

Grabbing fistfuls of my shirt, Knox pulls, ripping the fabric, the sound mingling with my heavy pants. He captures my wrists, only to tie them together with the white fabric.

His pure animalistic gaze makes my legs quiver.

He leans forward to pepper kisses along my jaw, his hands balled into clenched fists beside me.

I wiggle beneath him, daring him to grind his hard length against my throbbing core but it never comes. Instead, I tilt my head, granting him access to my neck, savoring the way his lips mark the skin as they travel lower.

The ravenous groan that tumbles from his mouth as his lips latch onto my nipple is one I want to experience for eternity.

Arching my back further, my hips lift, seeking the friction my core so greatly desires as his tongue swirls around my pebbled nipple. Then he begins to suck.

My body *burns*. A power rises from the depth of my soul at the desire to be fully joined with Knox.

And as a dark mass begins to form along his shoulders,

trickling down his back, I know my power isn't the only one rising to the occasion.

Shadows fly throughout the room. They whizz past me, slowing for a heartbeat to gently caress my skin before shooting away, leaving a tantalizing path of goosebumps in their wake.

Knox rips himself away, leaving me a writhing mess on the cot with my tied hands. In one swift motion, he finds my pants and tugs them off, along with his own, and then finally, he nestles himself against my core.

It's such a delicious feeling I throw my head back and moan, my legs wrapping around his waist as I begin to rock along his length.

"Gods, Angel, it's beautiful when you grow this wet."

I nod, though any words I had die on my tongue when the tip of his cock brushes my entrance.

His grin turns devilish. "Does this mean you concede?"

"Yes, you bastard! Yes, yes, yes!"

A rough hand slides under my ass, lifting my hips even higher as Knox enters slowly, so impossibly slow fire erupts in my eyes as they lock on his devious ones. He grins down at me despite the tremble of his body as he holds back his own pleasure.

I lean forward, capturing his lip with my teeth and bite. A droplet of blood lands upon my tongue. The taste of him makes my magic roar, blazing beyond recognition, as I stroke my tongue against his, daring him to claim me back

Knox takes the challenge.

His hips pull back, only to snap forward and penetrate me in one fell swoop. The roughness of his hips makes wetness trickle down my thighs.

I love every part of him. Every intricate side of this man has the power to undo me. The power to bring me to my knees. The power to hold my heart as its prisoner forever. And in this moment, I can see I hold that exact same power over him.

I submerge my hand into his hair and gently tug the raven strands. "Show me who you are, Knox. Come undone for me," I whisper.

His growl is so menacing it momentarily disarms me, allowing him to lift me easily and position me in front of him. But rather than facing his glorious length probing with desire and the sweat-slicked skin that glistens in the candlelight, I face the tent's opening.

My brows begin to pull together in confusion while his glorious hands slide from my breasts to my inner thighs—until he yanks me down.

My lips part on a gasp as he rips my legs open, dangling them over his own so I'm spread bare. A light wind picks up in the tent, one that smells of pinewood and ocean as it only brushes against my heated skin.

My head drops back, resting against his shoulder as his lips find my ear. "Are you dripping for me, Angel?"

"Y-yes," I stutter.

His fingers dance across my stomach, teasing me as they move closer to the bundle of nerves that scream for his touch.

"Tell me, Angel…" He pauses, and I whine at his teasing. "Are you mine?"

"Yes!" I scream.

Can't he feel it? The undulated desire pooling in my body *and* my heart? My power as it rises and dances with abandon along with his shadow magic.

I am his in every sense of the word.

"Are you mine?" I dare to ask.

"I will be yours for as long as our souls exist," he whispers.

My heart doesn't have a chance to find its rhythm after his words before his fingers are plunging into my core, his thumb pushing against that bundle of nerves. The intrusion is so welcome my core clenches around him, trying to hold his fingers inside of me as my back arches on a scream.

"You want to see me come undone, Angel, but that only happens when I touch you."

His words elicit a full body shudder, and as his fingers curve inside of me, pumping relentlessly in time with my pounding heart, a different kind of fire begins to build inside me. One demanding to be released, one burning as bright as a star.

My hips rock forward, chasing his fingers' pace as my nerves sizzle and expand, growing frenzied beneath my skin.

"I need more," I pant. "I need more!"

As always, Knox knows exactly what I need most. His hand leaves my core, replacing it with his hard length, and then he thrusts his hips upward.

I scream as I'm filled to the hilt with the most delicious sensation of him. My fingers lock around his thighs, leaving half-moon indentations in his skin.

"You want to make me unravel?" he growls. "Bounce."

The word is a command, one my body willingly obliges. In the next heartbeat, I'm rising, then snapping my hips downward, over and over and over. My core clutches him, drawing out a long groan from him.

His hands snake around to cup my bouncing breasts, squeezing and twisting the tender flesh. Sending an enchanting sense of burning pain right down to my aching clit.

"Good girl, Angel. Bounce on my cock."

Wetness leaks out of my core at his words, dripping down

his thighs. My hips pick up the pace, chasing a high only he can create.

And as one of his hands leaves my teasing nipples, snaking down to play with my clit, my stomach tightens, running for the edge of the cliff that promises a fall of ecstasy and enthralling pleasure.

"Fuck, Angel, look at you taking all of me. Just the sight of you unravels me. Now it's your turn."

His lips brush across my exposed neck, and as he sinks his canines into the skin, a scream rips from my throat.

Through it, I chant, "Come with me, Knox, come with me!"

My shaking hand travels down my body and cups his balls beneath me. His grunt and groans send me over the edge, our power colliding on the bridge and freefalling to the river below.

Knox shouts my name.

We fall, tumbling over that mighty cliff together, floating through the air of blissful euphoric pleasure. We cling to each other, mumbling praises and vows of care to one another as oblivion claims us.

Chapter Twenty-Three

Aurora's deep purr lulls me into a state of tranquility as I run the brush down the side of her stomach. Small hairs from her raven coat flutter in the light breeze as I do. Her winter coat is shedding, and she is enjoying every lick of attention.

On the next brush stroke, I lift onto the balls of my feet to reach her back. As I do, I catch a glimpse of Knox in the grassy hills beyond her. My heart lodges in my throat.

Knox's title and reign aren't revoked because he's in the human lands, but he's out there with a dozen or so soldiers doing manual labor alongside them. Knox has never viewed himself above others because of his status, though it still surprises me every time.

He has been putting in the work with the humans, not only physically but emotionally, to try and build a rapport with them, and with each passing day, he's lessening the fear in the men and women's eyes.

The veins in his forearm protrude at the weight of the axe in his hands as he lifts the weapon high above his head, then brings it down upon the tree at his feet. In one swift motion, the large trunk splits in two. He swings again, chopping the log further. He doesn't appear the least bit fatigued.

The soldiers around him stop to stare in awe. So do I.

Heat flushes down my neck and across my cheeks, but luckily for me, I can blame the red tint on the sun. It's now halfway through spring but it feels like summer has visited us early today.

My skin pebbles when Knox lifts his heavy gaze to me, his scrutiny sending a wave of lust through my body. Memories assault my mind from the other night as Knox brings the axe up again, his lips twitching as my breathing turns shallow.

He knows, he always knows.

I can also feel it, Angel.

My smile grows as I send memories of my own down the bridge. The fantasies I have about Knox, what I would do to him if we had all the time in the world.

What I want him to do to me.

Knox misses the wood on the next swing of his axe. A laugh escapes me as curses stream out under his breath.

You play dirty, Angel.

At that dangerous inflection, my eyes flick to his. I watch him lift his thin linen shirt and wipe his face, his glorious stomach muscles on full display. The lines protrude to his lower region as if it's an arrow pointing me to where I want to see most.

As if I don't know how to get there blindly already.

What a tease.

"They shed like crazy, don't they?"

I jump, ripping my gaze from Knox, my heart now pounding for another reason entirely.

"Gods, Hazel! You scared me!"

"Well, if you weren't ogling him, you would have heard me call your name," Hazel deadpans. "Three times."

I wince. "Sorry."

A small smile lights up her face as she cranes her neck. "It's okay, I understand now."

I follow her gaze to where Ace is brushing out Zephlyn's winter shedding. Ace's brows are furrowed in concentration, his focus solely on his soul pair griffin, unaware of the love pouring from Hazel's eyes and an emotion I can't decipher.

"How are you two? How's the bond?" I ask, barely above a whisper.

Happiness sparks in her blue eyes. "It's astounding. To feel this type of love again... After Luna, I thought I'd never feel it." Her eyes fill with guilt. "Nothing can compare to her and the love I had for her," she rushes on to clarify. "It's just—"

"To be loved unconditionally," I answer for her. "I understand what you mean. You don't have to feel guilty for loving someone, Hazel. Luna would have wanted you to be happy."

Hazel swallows thickly, her eyes glistening before she shakes it away. "How's the shedding going?"

Noting the redirect of the conversation, I go along with it, deciding not to push. After all, isn't that what I had asked of Knox?

"Amazing, if we're measuring by the amount of tumbleweed fur."

Hazel chuckles. "I'm not sure what's worse, the black or white hair sticking to the clothing."

After a moment of staring at each other, we murmur, "White," in unison.

Hazel picks up a brush and walks around the other side of Aurora. With the sheer size of Aurora, only Hazel's feet are visible, her voice drifting over the large creature.

"I love Zephlyn, though, so I don't mind. He's such a sweetheart."

My brows rise. "Really?"

Aurora cranes her head, puffing air out of her snout as if to say, *Of course*.

My assumption must be correct because Hazel snorts as she and Aurora share a look.

"I keep forgetting you can speak to animals," I say in awe. "It's such an astounding gift."

"It certainly is. It's also helpful with healing the—"

A deep growl from Aurora cuts off Hazel when a soldier walks by too closely. The poor man blanches, his knees wobbling as he scurries away.

"Sorry!" I call out.

Hazel frowns before an emotion passes between the two once more. In the next breath, Aurora lies down, her height now around my shoulder.

I come to stand in front of her. "Could you ask her why she is distrustful of men?" I ask Aurora more than Hazel.

I've always wanted to ask but didn't want to pry if she wasn't ready to share. But the responding slow blink I get from her has relief coursing through me.

Hazel listens for a minute. "She's not from Aloriah."

"Where is she from?"

Hazel shakes her head. "She doesn't know the name; she's saying it's made of nightmares—hell itself."

Apprehension coils around my spine. The cage around my heart tightens, bracing for impact.

"How bad was it?" I whisper.

Turning to Aurora, I plead with my eyes for her to tell me, to open her heart just a little further, so that I can maybe lessen the burden.

When Hazel starts translating again, her eyes pool with tears.

"It's horrible," she whispers. "She was born into a fighting ring that pits griffins against dragons for sport. The abuse that was inflicted upon those who disobeyed…" Hazel's features twist in pain. "You don't want to know about the brutality she just showed me, Delilah. They were all male handlers. They didn't want to waste money on lost causes, so they'd only heal the ones that made it through the night. That was part of the abuse, the mental games they'd play with the creatures."

My muscles tremble with a hatred so bright I'm surprised fire doesn't engulf me.

"How did she escape?"

Hazel's face remains motionless for a moment, and then a deadly smirk, as feline as a cat's, spreads across Hazel's cheeks.

"She feigned death during one of her fights and ate the handlers who were going to bury her."

My twinge of pride is short-lived as I swipe away the tears running down my cheeks. Mine aren't the only ones that are teary.

I reach out and run soft fingers down Aurora's lion head. "I will do everything within my power to keep you safe. You're mine now, and we protect one another."

She nudges her head against my head, and the resounding purr makes my heart melt.

"What does her voice sound like?" I ask Hazel.

The corner of her lip lifts. "Surprisingly soft, feminine. She was made to be strong, required it…learned it. In a different life, she would have been a giant teddy bear."

"I think she's still soft. Just cautious now is all."

"When are you two going to tie the knot?" Axel teases.

Ace ducks his head, not quick enough to hide the smitten smile. "Whenever she's ready."

"How about when we don't have a target on our backs?" Hazel calls, walking past with supplies ladened in her arms.

"Can we talk about this when she's not present?" Ace hisses under his breath, a flush creeping up his neck.

I chuckle as we work. It's been our job to move the heavy items that would take more than one soldier to carry. After watching Axel lift a barrel and walk past three soldiers attempting to carry one, Knox relieved the soldiers of their duties and assigned his court instead.

"There will always be targets," Nolan quips.

"Leave it alone, Nolan," Knox snaps.

Nolan, it seems, has been getting on everyone's nerves with his melancholy attitude. I can't say I blame him, though. No word has come regarding the missing Fae from the in-between. No word on the demonic army seemingly disappearing into thin air, either.

The only update from Lenox and Harlow was to inform Knox the Queen of Air had disappeared. The supposed queen has been ignoring every ruling court's letters about reinstating their crowns.

I suppose she doesn't want to hand over her power just yet.

Nolan's attitude isn't just pessimistic, it's factual at this point.

Not to mention that as every day passes, I can see the hope vanishing of finding his mother and sister. I'd be heartbroken and angry at the world in his position too.

Nolan rolls his eyes, Axel's harsh tone sliding off his back. "I'm just saying, he works for the Essence Court, so there will always be threats."

Zephlyn seems to disagree, hissing and flashing his long canines. Aurora walks by and brushes her head against his, lulling the griffin into a quiet hush. The move almost looks… affectionate.

Knox is the first who dares to ask. "Hazel…are they…?"

"Mates," Hazel breathes. "Yes."

My mind is slow to process the revelation.

"I'll be damned," Ace whispers.

"Why wouldn't they tell us sooner?" I ask.

The griffins turn to each other, emotion passing between their eyes.

Hazel chuckles. "They wanted some semblance of privacy, without our eyes on them at all times."

My heart pangs. "We would have given them privacy."

"You don't understand." Ace shakes his head, his face coated in awe. "Mates between griffins are rare, so rare I believe the last pair in our aerial legion was—"

"Four hundred and three years ago," Knox answers for him.

"What a beautiful thing," Hazel whispers in awe.

I approach the two griffins, studying the way they proudly stand together. The comfort in their closeness is eye-opening. Aurora is distrustful of males; we never saw her interacting with other creatures on the aerial legion island, and yet I looked past how at ease she was around Zephlyn.

They were made for one another.

I wonder when the mating bond snapped into place. Was it instant or delayed?

"You know what this means right?" Ace asks. At my shake of the head, he goes on. "We're practically family.

Mates can't be separated, especially animals—not when it's so rare. They go nowhere without the other."

My eyes blaze as the puzzle pieces start to make sense. "The morning we tried to leave, Zephlyn refused to let her out until you agreed to bring him."

Ace throws his head back on a deep belly laugh, the sound full of happiness. "No wonder he nearly bit my hand off for touching her!"

"And in Sector One, she was beside herself in trying to protect him! I thought it was just out of a fondness she felt toward him."

Hazel smirks as she sidles up beside Ace. "We're one step closer to being sisters now."

"We are in every sense of the word."

My heart warms at the friendship I've been able to build with Hazel. I've never had a close friendship with a woman, Annie being more of a mother figure in the absence of my biological mother. It's heartwarming, yet sad to know what I've missed out on all these years.

Knox grumbles, "I'm going to need to build a bigger stable."

Aurora huffs and Zephlyn stomps his paws.

From across the way, Annie steps out of the last tent, dismantling the material. Her soft features are such a stark contrast against the dark fighting leathers, courtesy of Ordelia. The clothing makes her appear…grim.

I miss seeing her in the nurse's quarters. Despite the horrid memories in that room, at least the display was far kinder, compared to seeing her striding amongst the rebellion army.

All I have ever wanted to do was keep her out of harm's way. Little did I know she had been secretly throwing herself into the thick of it all this time.

She clicks her tongue at our conversation. "It was about time they told the lot of you."

Ace snaps incredulous eyes at her. "You knew?"

"I could see it at the cabin. Zephlyn was protective of Aurora around the horses at first, and he shares his food with her." She shrugs, the movement rigid as she pats both the griffins, still awkward around Ace's presence. "I assumed they'd tell you when they were ready."

Ace looks away, but not fast enough to hide the guilt. "I feel horrible for not noticing."

Hazel gently strokes his arm. "They're incredibly intelligent creatures. If they didn't want you to know for a hundred years, you wouldn't have."

Annie watches on until gut-wrenching pain fills her eyes, and she rips them away from the sight of the couple.

"Walk with me," I whisper, taking Annie's hand and dragging her away.

Knox watches us with a knowing stare, sending tendrils of his shadows down my back, encouragement and support felt in the simple caress.

Annie places her hands over her pale cheeks. "How rude of me! Oh, Delilah, I'm so sorry. I don't mean to stare all the time. It's just…the uncanny resemblance is shocking. It's hard to separate the two. Every time I see him, I just flash back to Easton…and his head in the throne room."

"I'm so sorry, Annie."

Annie waves off the words, trying to smile but failing. "It's not your fault, dear." Her eyes look anywhere but at me. "Oh, it looks as if Ordelia is ready to depart!"

Happy to move away from the heavy conversation, I go along. "How far is she planning to travel today?"

"Seven hours' worth. There's a forest we can stay the night in before the rolling hills expose us."

Before we leave, I have to ask. It's been on my mind since she exited the tent. I snap a silencing shield around us. "Why did you join the rebellion? Why risk your life in the palace?"

"For you," she says as if it's the most obvious answer.

"But he would have never killed me. Was I worth risking your life?"

She lays a gentle hand on my arm. "Sometimes being kept alive is not a blessing."

Such dark words, and yet I feel them deep within my heart.

If I had stayed at the palace, I would have died. My soul would have shriveled up into nothing, but my shell would have been left for him to beat.

Nodding, I go to tell the others when Annie's gaze flicks behind my shoulder. "Will you apologize to him for me? I know he notices it."

"There's no need to apologize. He understands, but I'll let him know."

Annie leaves without a backward glance as she moves toward Ordelia and Phillip. I've noticed that on particularly hard days, Annie will travel with the pair. Though she says it's because she misses their company, I suspect it's because she needs a break from the reminders of Easton.

Ace is the first to notice me as I approach the court.

He wrings his hands. "Is she okay?"

"She'll get there eventually."

Ace rubs the back of his neck. "Perhaps I should go back and send Lenox instead. I don't want to continue causing her pain."

"Ace, that's awfully sweet of you but not necessary. Remember? We're practically family now. Where you and Zephlyn go, Aurora and I will."

Annie will soon find the differences between Ace and Easton as I did. Easton despised green vegetables whereas Ace piles them on. Ace adores the forests and woods, while Easton was always wary of them and the creatures within—especially insects. Ace's laugh is quiet and breathy. Easton's was loud and boisterous.

"You can't control it," I reiterate strongly. "There's nothing to apologize for."

He doesn't believe me, the doubt in his eyes proves that, but sending him back would be far too cruel and unfair.

Relief sweeps through me as Knox comes to my side. He can't touch me physically, but his flames and shadows fill the garden in my mind, twirling with my golden iridescent magic. Dancing along to the melody that our heartbeats create.

I never thought I would feel joyful over the mere sight of smoke. But as they say, where there's smoke there is fire, and in this current world, that dark shadow of smoke always leads me back to my home—Knox.

"They're ready to leave now," I say, relaying Ordelia's travel orders.

Ace dips his head, our conversation and his worries forgotten as he strides to his brother and mate.

"Everything all right?" Knox asks once Ace is out of hearing range.

His mask has snapped back into place, cold and passive. His lips flatten into a thin line while he stares at the thousands of soldiers mounting horses and wagons.

But beneath it all, a soft tenderness flows down the bridge.

His true feelings. What's hidden behind his charade.

I hate this, I say.

Knox moves to mount his horse. *I know, Angel. I hate it more.*

Impossible.

I pat Aurora on the way to saddling Creseda, grabbing Henry's reins to pull him along beside her. They, too, are inseparable. Perhaps the griffins aren't the only mates among us.

Knox sits atop his horse, making sure the rest of his court has readied themselves for the long journey. He fixes me with a heavy stare as well.

Trust me, it's possible.

My birthday comes and goes, and Knox respected my wishes to not celebrate it.

After the day passed, my uneasiness receded. After all, it was the first birthday I had spent without pain. Then nine days of traveling flew past without a hitch.

It lulled me, Knox, his court, and the soldiers into a state of false security.

Because what we stumble upon has most of the soldiers vomiting, crying, and fainting.

Knox's face drains of all color. Shock makes the otherwise strong Fae stumble and fall to their knees.

Aurora turns around, ramming her head into my stomach as she tries to push me back, protecting me from the sight. But it's too late.

The rolling grass hills that loom before us are no longer green but red. The brutality is so vast, that the air will be permanently stained with the metallic stench.

Never in all my life have I seen such a savage sight.

Thousands of bodies lie throughout the rolling hills, twisted in unnatural ways. Limbs are scattered, decapitated heads and vital organs thrown about carelessly.

The soldiers butchered beyond recognition.

Ordelia crumbles to her knees, weeping with abandon, screaming the same word over and over and over.

No.

No.

No.

Ordelia's men, the army that went ahead—all dead at the hands of the king.

Which means he knows there's rebels amongst his army.

As I drag my numb legs forward, my eyes widen in horror at one word written in the hills with blood. That one word makes me lean forward and puke.

DELILAH.

The king has retaliated.

The king knows I'm not dead.

The king holds the power once again.

Chapter Twenty-Four

The pain radiating throughout my body is something I've felt before. A feeling my heart knows all too well. The moment when your world is tilted on its axis, and life as you know it changes irreversibly.

The king has made his official first move, the first strike, the first public chess move, and it is in the way he knows how to punish best—taking innocent lives.

Three thousand soldiers, who had marched ahead for the rebellion cause, were wiped from this planet like they were nothing but dust.

Phillip is running, pain etched across his face. His gait is fast, surprisingly so as he skids to a stop before Ordelia, joining her in the mud-turned-crimson puddle. The shock that covers his face is nothing compared to the agony that physically crumbles his body.

I know what it feels like to lose hope, but I've never watched it so clearly in someone else before.

Phillip pulls Ordelia into his body as his shoulders heave, their uncontrollable sobs wrenching the air.

This is what the king has done.

He has brought the rebellion leaders to their knees, clinging for dear life against the grief trying to sweep them away.

Ordelia's broken voice travels on the wind, despite how frail and small it is. Her chin wobbles, bloodshot eyes lifting to mine.

"H-how?" she stutters between hiccupped sobs. "How did he know?"

I shake my head, wishing the movement could erase what he's done. "I don't know."

It's meek. An undeniably meek and awful answer, but it's the only one I have for her. He's always been like this. Ten moves ahead on the chess board while his opponent is still scrambling to fight against the first one.

The king will stop at nothing until he wins. Mercy doesn't exist in his vocabulary. His heart and soul have rotted like the Tree of Life's core.

I was foolish to think I could fight against him. The truth in that statement lies scattered along the rolling hills.

My hand reaches out to comfort Ordelia, hovering an inch above her quaking shoulders before I think better of it. The last thing she wants or needs is the daughter of the man who slaughtered her people so ruthlessly to comfort her.

"I'm so sorry," I croak.

Knox takes a step forward. Out of the corner of my eye, I can see the moment he means to reach out to me, and when he has to stop himself at the last second.

Now he sees why we must remain a secret. Now more than ever, the king can *never* know about us.

"You don't have to apologize, Delilah. This isn't your doing," Knox says strongly.

Ordelia and Phillip's heads stay bent, nothing penetrating through their grief.

"You shouldn't carry the guilt of this," Ace's soft voice adds behind me.

Sniffling, my head dips, my thoughts hollow. I don't agree. But if I don't acknowledge what they're saying, they'll continue to pour it down my throat and into my mind and I don't deserve that kindness. At this point, I'm just saving them oxygen.

Fighting breaks out behind us, a disturbance so loud we turn in sync to find a soldier, tearing through the crowd, tears streaming down his cheeks, screaming, "*Traitor*!"

The soldiers around him stare in shocked disbelief as the man comes barreling toward us, one finger raised.

"*Traitor*!" he yells again.

The tears that were pooling in my eyes fly in all directions as I rapidly shake my head. Stark realization dawns on me that the man is pointing, not at something behind my shoulders, but at *me*.

Axel takes a step toward me, his hand dropping to the sword at his side.

Knox's wings blast behind his back, shadows forming around the delicate yet strong muscle. As Knox's jaw clenches, lightning sparks, jumping between the peaks of his two wings.

Another soldier joins the first, screaming profanities. "She told the king our movements! She's a capital spy!"

My mouth opens to plead my innocence but Knox steps forward.

"Don't respond to that," he snarls.

Ordelia finally looks up. "Did you?"

Shock makes me stumble backward that she would have to ask at all. "Of course not!"

Ordelia transforms from a blubbering mess to a vindictive woman. Anger rises within her as she stands. "We have kept our movements a secret for *six* years. *How* did he find my men?"

The accusation tainting her voice rings throughout the soldiers. Their grief silences, making way for anger.

"I don't know!"

Whispers fly throughout the camp within seconds. Like a rapid forest fire, every word uttered is like throwing oil onto the flames, spiraling the soldiers into unchecked rage.

Metal groans, the undeniable sound of swords being unsheathed.

I look from Ordelia's unforgiving glare to her men, waiting for her to tell them to stand down.

The order never comes.

Even Phillip takes on the role I have always known. The one where he does nothing to stop my hurt.

Swords rise, boots march, and screams fill the red-soaked hills as the soldiers I've been traveling with for three weeks —the soldiers I've shared stories with around the campfires, the soldiers I helped feed—charge at me. Without an ounce of mercy on their faces.

After all this time, my voice holds no sway with them.

They don't even let me profess why I'm innocent, about how I couldn't possibly be in contact with the king. About how this is as much a targeted threat toward me as it is to these innocent lives.

But they want retribution, not truth. I will always be the king's daughter in their eyes.

Knox and his court have tried to convince me that the king's heinous acts don't fall on me. That the guilt of those sins isn't mine to bear, and yet I stand here, watching as three thousand of my citizens descend upon me.

No matter what I do for them, nor how I help, it will never be enough.

Perhaps it's exhaustion, or perhaps it's guilt, but when the men move closer, faster than I had anticipated they could, grief fueling their strides…I simply close my eyes.

I don't move or fight back.

This is what I deserve, isn't it?

This is my punishment for having a family member as corrupt as the king. I'll take the burden and the guilt of the lives I could not save.

They want a Covington dead.

And so, they shall have it.

With thousands of mangled body parts behind me and innocent souls departing for the clouds above me, I stand still. In the puddle of an innocent soldier's blood and squeeze my eyes closed.

I wait for death.

But anguished screams turn to terror.

Open your eyes, Angel, and so help me gods if you ever surrender again, I will chain you to Aurora for eternity.

The command in Knox's voice snaps my eyes open. I couldn't have kept them closed if I tried.

I gasp, only for the oxygen to lodge in my throat, forming a ball I can't swallow past.

A wall of orange flames and dancing shadows surround us, separating us from the soldiers. Cocooning Knox's court, the animals, and the rebellion leaders inside.

Knox turns to them, his sapphire gaze piercing Ordelia to the spot. At this moment, I almost wish I was on the other side of the flames.

Because the *look* he gives her is one of pure lethal rage.

"How *dare* you." Knox steps forward, his body vibrating with hatred. "We have done nothing but help you, and in return, you allow your men to charge at her with pitchforks like she's a *witch*."

Annie wraps her arms around me as she watches on with wide, bloodshot eyes. Her scent envelopes me, soothing the jagged edge of hurt and pain thrashing in my heart. Hazel is beside me next, her gaze wary but her stance protective in front of me.

"And *you*," Knox spits. He turns to Phillip next, and his glare is so harsh it scorches the hairs on Phillip's head. The small tips of his gray-peppered hair flutter away in the wind. "You know she isn't working for him. You saw day in and day out how he treated her. I wouldn't have forgiven you even if you had apologized profusely on your hands and knees to her, but when you have your one chance of retribution, you stand back and allow it to happen once more."

Phillip stutters, his mouth gaping open and closed like a fish. "Yes, we—"

"I don't want to hear it." Knox moves so close they're forced to tilt their heads back. "Not only will you apologize to Delilah, but you will get your humans under control." Knox spits the word *human* as if it's a disease. His lips pull back on a feral growl as his voice grows into nothing but a rumbling promise of destruction. "*Or I will.*"

They don't get the chance to speak because, in the next breath, their eyes grow distant, their features slackening as Knox drops the proof right into their minds that I'm not a spy.

I'm not sure what memories Knox had to show Ordelia and Phillip to make them believe me and I don't care. When Ordelia and Phillip come to, guilt fills their eyes. Their features drop as if the weight of their accusation pulls them down.

They open their mouths.

I raise my hand and silence them.

No matter what they say, it will never change what transpired, nor the tainted memory I have of them.

I may be a lot of things, but forgiving isn't one of them. When people show you who they are, believe them.

"Tell them to back down."

Knox lowers the wall of flames, just enough to see the soldiers on the other side.

The first soldier to call me a traitor, the one who started it all, *growls* when he sees me. Such hatred fills his features, sadness being the driving force.

He must have a loved one lying amongst the dead.

He doesn't hesitate. The moment his gaze connects with mine he lets the sword in his hand fly.

It moves too quickly.

I loosen a ragged breath, tears pooling in my eyes as it hits its mark.

An inch above my heart.

Knox's shadows capture it, swallowing the blade whole before his shadows spit it back out with a deafening roar. The blade whizzes, insurmountably faster than the soldier threw it, and it grazes the man's arm before planting into the ground. A message and a warning.

"Throw another one!" Knox bellows. "And see just how long you will continue breathing."

The soldier's face falls as he makes eye contact with the Fae king standing beside me. He clutches his bleeding arm but bites his tongue, shaking head to toe.

A Fae steps in front of me, blocking me, but what surprises me the most is that it's *Nolan*. Snarls tumble from him as he draws his sword, lightning bolts flaring down the silver.

"The next soldier to throw a weapon of any kind will be

joining the fallen behind me," Knox barks. The sharp reprimand has me greedily trying to suck air back into my lungs.

Ordelia steps forward, giving the wild Fae a wide berth as she stutters, "L-lower your weapons."

The meek whisper does no such thing, and I watch as she rises to the soldier, the rebellion leader I thought I could count on. "Lower your weapons. That was an *order*," she commands with a ferocity I've never heard until now.

One by one, the soldiers sheath their blades, grief sweeping them into its talons once more as the anger diminishes from their eyes. It's slow at first, and then they almost move as one.

The only one left is the first soldier, his gaze never leaving mine.

Ordelia steps forward, a trembling hand reaching out to touch the man's shoulder. "Elijah was a fine soldier, Oliver. A good man."

The soldier's anger begins to seep out of him. "He was proud to be selected for the scouting mission."

"He wouldn't want this for you," she whispers.

"It doesn't matter what he wished for. He's dead," he states, the words devoid of any emotion.

The fight leaves him in a deep exhale, and he turns and leaves. Walking away as a shell of the man he had been before.

Lucca comes rushing forward, pushing his way through the throes of the soldiers who remain frozen to the spot.

He pants, heaving with exhaustion as devastation lines every inch of his face. "I'm so sorry. I tried to stop them, but they held me back."

At first, I think he's apologizing to Ordelia, but that can't be right. If he tried to stop the king, he would be dead and he was with us the entire—

His eyes are on me.

Biting the inside of my cheek to stop my lip from trembling, I dip my head, too stunned for words. At least there is one human who can look at me and not see the king.

Before I can find the words to truly thank him, he takes off, embracing Marcus who crumbles in his arms and weeps.

Knox growls low and deep as Ordelia and Phillip also retreat. But what could they possibly have said? Not just one tragedy has occurred, but two.

A clear line has been drawn between the humans and the Fae, the weeks of bonding and trust wiped away with a single event. The adrenaline that was pumping through my body vanishes and I clench my teeth so tightly I'm surprised they don't snap. The pain radiating around my jaw keeps my tears at bay.

I refuse to let any of these people see me cry.

I refuse to be vulnerable before them.

"He knows you're not dead," Ace whispers.

"No need to state the obvious," Nolan growls.

Ace scowls. "How else would you like me to start the conversation, Nolan?"

Axel steps in front of them, Knox's second drowning out the argument between the two Fae with a silencing shield around Nolan. He allows himself a little smirk before turning to Knox. "Does this change our plans?"

Knox looks down at me, a glimmer of his fear flitting down the bond.

"No, it doesn't," I answer for him. "We continue on—"

"Despite the obvious threat?" Hazel asks, worry making her voice quiver.

"She's going to walk us to our deaths, mark my words," Nolan vows.

I roll my eyes, the unity he showed when my life was on the line vanishing with every glare. "Why did you drop the shield?" I ask Axel.

"He didn't. The poor bastard has nothing against me when it comes to shields," Nolan goads.

"You have one second to slam those useless lips shut before I do it for you," Axel growls.

"Don't embarrass yourself with your lack of skills we all —" Vines climb high and snap around Nolan's mouth. Thorns poke into the skin, drawing beads of blood that drip onto the thick vines.

Ace leans back, a saccharine smile on his face.

"We've given our word that we will—"

"Not trying to disrespect your opinion, Knox, but if there was any time to break one of your vows it would be now," Axel interrupts.

"Knox is right. This is for the children. This is bigger than the lack of trust with Ordelia and Phillip, not to mention we need them to save my mother, and I will *not* leave her to rot in that palace. Especially not after what he's just done." I look each of them in the eye as I say this, my gaze snagging on Nolan and daring him to try and get out of the vines to disagree with me.

"We have to proceed with caution as we near the capital," I continue. "The king will become ruthless the closer we are, and we can't trust that Ordelia and Phillip won't repeat what happened here today."

Hazel winces, her gaze flitting between me and Annie.

She splays her hand against her heart. "I'm sorry, dear. I'm just as shocked as anyone that Ordelia would do such a thing."

I wish I could agree with her, but I'm not shocked at all.

"Although we can't trust them, we cannot hold what they just did over their heads."

A chorus of obscenities fills the air.

"They just found thousands of their friends and loved ones murdered!" I argue, despite the betrayal thrashing against my heart. "Grief is a powerful emotion, and we must continue forward with their actions over the past three weeks in mind, not their moment of weakness."

"You're much better than I am, dear. I don't think I can look at my friends the same," Annie says softly, clutching her chest.

Ace's eyes soften as he stares at Annie. Likely wrestling with the deep need to comfort someone, but also not wanting to add to her pain.

"I say we kill him," Nolan drawls.

I throw my hands in the air. "Who keeps freeing him?"

Knox's eyes narrow. "Delilah doesn't want to murder him."

I note he doesn't include himself in that statement. Perhaps he disagrees.

I do. He deserves a slow, brutal, torturous death.

The violence promised in his voice makes my palms gather with sweat.

"I think you're daft for not murdering the prick."

I click my tongue at Nolan, allowing him a small sliver of truth. "Death would be a mercy to him."

Understanding dawns, my words at the beginning of this journey rushing to everyone. How I wish to make him live out his days in misery for the crimes he has committed.

He needs to feel the pain he has inflicted on others.

It's not justice if he doesn't.

Axel juts his chin behind me. "We need to scout ahead. The blood looks fresh, so they can't be too far."

Hazel's eyes widen. "You think they could have laid a trap for Delilah?"

I shake my head. "He may have set a trap, but he didn't get his hands dirty. He isn't anywhere near this. Especially not if he knows that I'm with Fae who possess magic."

"So we're just going to move forward as if nothing happened?"

I shrug. "We may not have the upper hand now, but he still doesn't know about this rebellion unit. If he did, we would all be dead."

"Go inform Ordelia of our plans and that we will return in an hour," Knox says to Axel.

A shutter closes over Axel's eyes, a mask slipping into place—an impenetrable wall—as he strides to Ordelia.

Every soldier within the vicinity moves away as if Axel possesses a contagious disease.

Water moving around a rock.

No matter what happens, there will always be a divide, drifting whenever the King makes his move.

We're in the air twenty minutes later, me astride Aurora's back and Knox flying beside me. The rest of his court is spanned in front of us, deciding to not leave one another after earlier events. Even Annie considered getting on Aurora's back, but in the end, her fear of heights won out and she decided to tend to Creseda and Henry, readying them for the journey.

Despite needing to scour the land below for any sign of the king's soldiers, my gaze continues to slide to the Fae beside me. I tilt my head, my hair fluttering behind me, the black hood that has been concealing my face long forgotten.

Knox's rigid jaw and pinched eyes draw me in closer with an anxious need to soothe whatever has him bothered. The taut muscles of his back may make my legs tighten with anticipation, but I know it isn't out of pleasure. Knox's body is coiled tight, brimming with a viciousness I'm unsure of how to handle.

With my hands around Aurora's harness and her golden eyes on the ground below, I go deep within my mind. Walking through the garden, my feet soak up the cloud-like feel as I swing open the door to the bridge. I pause as I find his side not colorful and joyous but shrouded in shadows so deep that dark thunder and lightning strike within the gray clouds.

A sharp gust knocks into me and I'm forced to grip the railing of the bridge as it swings from side to side. My hair billows in my face, partially blocking my view.

Knox!

There's a moment of reprieve and then it intensifies to the point that the bridge shakes beneath my feet. Gasping, I fall to the wood, clinging to it with a death grip. Between the planks, I see the usually calm river below raging with rapids that make tears pool in my eyes.

What happened?

What happened? WHAT HAPPENED?

Knox's voice thunders over the storm he's creating, leaking from the depths of his mind as he tries and fails to control his emotions. The tight restraints he usually confines them in have been shattered.

I know all too well what happens when you bottle emotions up. At some point, they explode.

The wood beneath me creaks, shaking with ferocity as bootsteps storm down the bridge.

Leather combat boots stop an inch from my face.

Peering up, I expect to find Knox's soul, the bright star shining. Instead, it's dimmed to the point that his soul is made entirely of shadows and flames.

What happened was you gave up. On me, on Aurora, on us! His chest heaves, anger cracking to give way to heartache. *You gave up on life. You closed your eyes.*

And I do so again as I can't dare face him.

In the moment I felt helpless—exhausted of being weighed down by the king's actions and cruel shadow. I was tired of the life I was handed.

It was the coward's choice, Knox snarls.

My eyes snap open with a kernel of hatred, for the first time directed at Knox. As I stand, using golden tendrils around the bridge to stabilize it, I take a step forward, shoving my finger into his chest.

Don't you dare say that to me again. Ever.

Shadows push against my golden light, striking it like a serpent until I'm forced to retreat.

You gave up.

My jaw hardens. *Can you stand here and tell me that in all your one hundred and fifty years of being trapped, you never once wanted to give up?*

Something flickers in his eyes, shadows parting to let me see his soul.

With just one look, I know within the marrow of my bones that Knox has once felt as exhausted as I did earlier today. His anger isn't entirely because I decided to close my eyes; it's because he believes he failed me when I did so.

There is a part of me, Knox, that will never go away. I could be the happiest woman in the world, and I would still have a small kernel within myself that would want to close my eyes.

I walk forward, laying my hand gently atop his heart.

I wish I could say it will go away, but it's not something that ever leaves. Perhaps it is my father's fault for planting this within me, but I cannot change it.

The shadows around Knox's arms dissipate, giving way to starlight.

You are not a failure. There is nothing to fail at, Knox. This is a part of who I am. One that I used to be deeply ashamed of, but it has also helped me grow. Sometimes its voice is loud and sometimes it's quiet, and you can't control the volume. Sometimes, all you can do is roll with it. Today was simply a moment of weakness, a day that the volume was broken.

A tear rolls down his cheek, dropping onto the bridge, and as it does the shadows recede completely. The rapids stop, replaced by the calm river once more, and the bridge shines with rays from Knox's starlight.

I don't want you to feel that way, he admits. *I cannot stand the thought of you wanting to harm yourself in such a manner. It breaks my heart.*

His voice cracks like the broken organ.

Taking his hands in mine, I place gentle, featherlight kisses across his palms.

I will make a bargain with you.

He snorts despite himself, his eyes sparking with mischief. *You truly are a Fae.*

Ignoring his teasing tone I say, *What if I tell you when the voice is loud? You won't be able to change it, but I will spend that time with you.*

Hope blooms in his sapphire eyes.

Your very first Fae bargain. His lips lower to my forehead and my eyes close on their own accord at the comfort that races straight to my heart. *I vow to be beside you, not just on the days when the voice is loud, but for every day it wishes to sing.*

The bond between us pulls taut as the feeling I haven't dared say aloud—love—grows deeper between us.

Promise me another, he breathes.

The word strikes me. I suppose I truly am a Fae, because, through it all, Knox never acknowledged I didn't say *promise* or *vow*.

I never want to fail another loved one again with an unfulfilled promise.

Licking my suddenly dry lips, I blink impossibly slow, waiting for him to speak.

Don't lock me out. You can withdraw, you can retreat, and you can ignore me...just please don't lock me out.

My heart catches at the intensity of his plea, one that despite my burning throat I know I cannot ignore.

Anything for you.

A radiant smile brightens Knox's face. His joy is contagious, making the corner of my lips tug until the moment is torn from us with a small whine of fear from Aurora.

Axel's flying form is a silhouette along the horizon, his wings flapping rapidly. Knox's body tenses, the muscles straining as he soars for Axel. The court stops, hovering midair as the Griffins circle, predatory eyes watching everyone's back.

In one fluid motion, Axel dives into the circle, his chest heaving.

"What is it?" Knox asks.

Axel's eyes flick to mine, there and gone in an instant, the move making my spine straighten.

"The lake," he spits out, his breathing ragged. "They're at the lake."

"Who is?" I dare ask.

Anxiety sinks its teeth into me quickly and without reprieve as Axel's eyes fill with fear.

"The king."

Chapter Twenty-Five

Phillip hurriedly unrolls the map of Aloriah on the back of one of the wagons.

Despite earlier events, Ordelia and Phillip followed Knox's bellow as he landed from the sky screaming, commanding the rebels to halt, as he explained the army waiting to attack at the lake.

Not a group of soldiers—thousands. Stationed around every inch of the water. The king's tent sitting on the edge, heavily guarded by hundreds of his most trusted men.

"Are you positive you saw him?" I ask Axel. "You could be confusing him with one of his commanders or maybe—"

Axel cuts me off. "It's him, Delilah."

My ears begin to ring, numbness crawling over every inch of my body. Worry flashes in Axel's eyes with a dip of his chin. He knows the tirade of emotions and the manipulation and abuse stomping through my heart and banging at the door I try to keep sealed at all hours. The place where I lock every emotion and memory of the king away.

It's now bursting at the seams.

"He won't come near you, Delilah. We'll make sure of that," Axel vows.

Ace nods in agreeance and Hazel…the vengeance in her eyes makes me want to watch *her*. In case she tries to go after him.

I won't let him so much as breathe in your direction, Knox adds in my mind.

I swallow thickly, the support coming at me from all angles an unfamiliar feeling. I may have had Annie and Easton during my time in the palace, but never a group of people. People willing to rise to defend and protect me. This is a different type of heady power than the one the king chases.

Phillip's frazzled voice pulls our attention to the map. "There's nowhere we can go. If he has the river surrounded, they'll see us moving."

"No matter the direction?" Annie asks, wringing her hands.

"Not with the number of soldiers we have."

Ordelia shakes her head. "I'm not risking another army of rebels."

How did he know? How does he always know? How is he always one step ahead?

"Can we teleport them?" I ask Knox.

"We'd run ourselves ragged trying to get everyone across. If anything happens, none of us will have magic."

Voices rise, shouting over each other. They all speak to be heard but none listen when spoken to.

I rub my hands over my face, a dull pounding in the side of my head growing with the volume and the risk that we must take if we want to move forward.

There's nothing I wish for more than the king to simply vanish.

My breath jolts from my lungs. Ceasing to exist.

Knox's eyes are already on mine, always aware of what's happening in my mind before I am myself.

"What's your idea, Delilah?" Knox asks loudly, his voice cutting through the shouts like a sword.

The move almost makes me smile, reminding me of those very first days at his home with his court. He heard the thoughts in my mind and forced my hand in spilling them exactly as he is now.

"Invisibility," I say, finding my breath.

Nolan scoffs. "You don't have enough power to make all the soldiers invisible, let alone touch them all at the same time."

Only Knox and I know the true depth of my magic, or how it's grown by the day—so much so that Knox has had to help me burn through the excess of it during our nightly training sessions. To ensure it doesn't consume me from the inside out.

All anyone has seen is our training in the ring, courtesy of Knox's glamours and shields, but no one has glimpsed my golden power since my outburst in Sector One.

I lower my eyes. Nolan's right on the last half, though—I haven't been able to master making others invisible without touching them yet.

The tender shadow hand that runs down my back sends comfort through my blood but also an idea into my mind. I don't dare look at him as I speak down the bridge between our minds.

You used my invisibility once before, in Sector Four's town center.

Not to mention the daily trips he takes down to my well.

Knox points to a path on the map, looking immersed in

the conversation happening out loud while he responds to me mentally.

I can't take your magic to make the soldiers invisible, not at this magnitude.

But what if you didn't take it? What if you simply enhanced it?

Knox leans back, crossing his arms over his chest. He nods to Axel, having his second distract Ordelia and Phillip.

Then he flicks his eyes, shining with pride, to mine.

What do you have in mind, Angel?

Chapter Twenty-Six

Sliding my hand into Aurora's raven fur sends a jolt of pure euphoria through me. To feel the muscles working beneath my legs, the wind assaulting my hair, and the crisp air making water pool in my eyes.

Being connected with her like this has my body singing one word: *home, home, home.*

That is what Knox and Aurora are to me—home.

I have never been as grateful as I am now to have these people in my life. That in a moment of fear, I have Aurora's strength beneath me and Knox's warmth at my back, protecting me.

With his arms wrapped around my waist, I lean back into the hard ridges of his stomach and chest muscles. Being as high up as we are, no one below can see us, allowing us to *finally* be ourselves.

Knox's hand slides along my jawline, pulling me to him, and I fall into him as he captures my lips in a tantalizing kiss. The softness of it and the tenderness makes my heart melt. The anxiety that paces in the corner of my mind, ready to pounce at a moment's notice, is locked away for a moment—held at bay as Knox holds me.

Home.

"It's time, Angel," he whispers softly.

When my eyes flutter open, the sight that looms along the horizon has my anxiety pouncing again, the beast latching onto me and refusing to let go.

The glistening blue water of the lake is tainted by the black and gold glinting in the midday sunlight. Horses and tents line the perimeter, and soldiers stand to attention as they guard the river and land surrounding it.

Waiting for an enemy that will never arrive.

My skin buzzes, my chest burning with the need to get out and get away. The force of it steals my breath away.

"Are you ready, Angel?"

Catching my voice before it cracks, I say, "No, but I have to be." I lean forward then and whisper in Aurora's ear. "Lead them to safety."

Taking a shuddering breath, Knox's arms wrap around me once more before we join hands, clutching one another as I open the door between our bridge.

As I step onto the wooden platform, the sight of Knox leaving his mind open and vulnerable for me to guard knocks the breath from me.

Knox's essence—his soul—is beautiful.

It's Knox, in all his six-foot-five, muscular glory of grace and power. The strong jawline, twinkling sapphire eyes, and high cheekbones. It's everything he is and yet more. He glows, a beacon shining bright even amongst the beauty of my garden's mind, sparkling as if he was created by the stars themselves.

I've seen him glow before, a sliver of this form, but nothing compares to his true self.

He walks toward me, his hand lifting to stroke my cheek. My head turns into his warmth, his touch. His beautiful soul.

You are just as bright, my golden light.

I blink. *I shine too?*

As if my very own angel.

He leans forward, his lips capturing mine. Electricity hums, passing between our lips.

Knox pulls away at Aurora's warning growl. We're getting closer.

Be safe, I whisper.

Always am.

I watch Knox walk away, allowing my heart to open to him further as he descends into my magic well.

While Knox is in my mind, using my well of power to create an invisible shield from the king and his army, I'll be in his, guarding its beauty.

Knox had to weave a web of lies about why we had to be in the air together, but it worked to our advantage that Ordelia and Phillip are naïve and uneducated about magic. Especially after recent events, I don't trust those two knowing we're mates.

Pebbled stones greet me as I open the metal door, the black stones paving a path through a lively green forest. Plants and trees arch over me, as if trying to conceal what lies behind the branches.

The metal door slowly seals shut behind me, and in the wake of silence, I hear the gurgle of rushing water. A light shines at the end of the pebbled path, the orange hue twinkling as if beckoning me to follow.

Fireflies greet me as I turn the corner and discover a beautiful garden maze. Flowers blossom from all directions, and the flower trail leads me this way and that until I stumble upon a stone archway. I lift onto my toes to read the faded inscription covered by grime and dirt. *Holloway*.

Walking through the arch, tingles race down my back as if he just shuddered at my entrance. The temperature grows warm, making perspiration drip down the back of my neck.

A trickling river flows before me, running down a stream to my right and gliding into the garden beds. I follow the path of the water over rocks and riverbeds until I find the source of its flow—a beautiful waterfall.

The waterfall starts on a large rolling hill, cascading over obsidian rocks. Occasionally, a break in the stream offers me a peek to what it's hiding—a cave.

It takes me a moment to fully grasp what I'm staring at, and when I do, the realization brings me to my knees.

Knox has recreated the waterfall where we hid for hours from the demonic hounds. The hours in which we spent glancing at one another, unable to use words in fear the hounds would hear us. But we didn't need words, we never have. Our eyes have always been the way we truly communicate.

More so for myself.

I have a thing for eyes. When I was younger, I believed it was my superpower. They've always been able to talk to me, the way a quick glance can give you a look into one's soul. It began when my father started beating me. I learned from a young age that when he was about to pounce and strike, his eyes would change, so I began looking into them at every chance I could—despite the fear that made my bones quake.

Perhaps that time in the waterfall was when I started to process I could trust Knox.

I circle the waterfall he created, and I cannot stop my heart from filling with awe. Every intricate detail sends a rush of warmth through my blood, and when I reach the top of the waterfall, my heart stumbles, tripping over itself.

I find a forest—the one where we first met. It's easy to spot the circular clearing that I lured the soul eater into, only for Knox to laugh at my swordsmanship after I killed it, his dark chuckle rumbling through my bones as he toyed with me.

I will never forget hearing his voice for the first time—at least, in person. Before that, I had dreamed of him and his voice for years.

Love catches my breath, the oxygen in my lungs stuttering at the evidence of his care for me.

Shaking myself out of shock, I will myself to focus.

I can obsess over this at a later time, perhaps show him what it means to me to find his mind like this. To know that he has filled his inner sanctuary with memories of us and the story of how we found each other.

Standing in the middle of Knox's mind, the middle of the forest, I make myself invisible. Before me, my creamy skin and long slender fingers disappear.

From within Knox's mind, I tap Aurora with my physical body, signaling for her to fly, leading Knox's court as they guard our vulnerable bodies in the sky.

I feel the moment Knox connects with my magic. It practically hums through my bloodstream, ecstatic to play. The bond between us tugs, reveling at the feel of our souls joining and becoming one.

Our magic works in unison—yin and yang.

Knox submerges himself into my well, using the invisibility magic running through my blood to enhance the protection and silencing shield wrapped around the army marching below. As long as I continue to remain invisible, Knox will be able to access it, spreading it to where I cannot.

His court, flying around us, uses their own power to make the large silencing and protection shield hold steady, impenetrable, while Knox concentrates on concealing the soldiers.

The days and weeks of saving our energy reserves have paid off for this exact moment.

Inside Knox's mind, I widen my feet, grounding myself, while he spreads my magic out, stretching it for miles around the troops now marching toward the king.

The release of magic is an instant relief. The burning, indescribable itch that has been humming under my skin slowly dissipates. The tension around my shoulders loosens for the first time in weeks. I tip my head back, reveling in the feel of not having the weight of the power trying to burst from deep within me.

Time warps, passing through my fingers.

I don't dare open my eyes to see how close we are to the king and his men. How far away death lies if we are caught, how swift it would be if my magic falters.

Curiosity brims in my mind, but the feel of Aurora below me and Knox behind me gives me the strength to focus. If something is amiss, I know they'll inform me. Other than that, I refuse to look, especially for the one face that still haunts my every waking moment.

Instead, I marvel at the feel of me and Knox joining. How our magic caresses one another, golden flames and shadows entwining.

A smile is playing on my lips when a sudden force slams against the walls of Knox's mind so forcefully it jolts me, knocking me to the forest floor.

Then it's silent.

I pick myself up and roam the forest, trying to figure out what could have physically thrown me off my feet when a second wave smashes into the walls of his mind. This one makes me stumble and hit my head, the force so hard I see stars.

The canopy of leaves above me swims, blurring as they sway. Everything in my sight doubles as I rub the back of my head, trying to soothe the ache with a gentle touch.

Shock evaporates, adrenaline pumping through my system when worry begins to gnaw at me. With Knox not being in his mind, he can't break concentration and speak to me. Sending a flurry of soothing air down the bridge and into my well, I try to calm whatever worry he might be feeling.

I've gotten to my knees when another force slams into his walls, this time from behind me.

Another mind reader.

It must be, there's no other explanation. No other magic has the power to attack like this. Which means they know Knox isn't in his mind, but not that I'm here to guard him at his most vulnerable.

Sprinting to the entrance between our bridge, I throw my hand out, slamming my own mind door shut. Trapping Knox within my mind, and myself in his. I wind back up the black pebble path, through the flower maze, and past the waterfall, and then at the top, I lift my hands to secure his fortress walls with walls of flame. The flames don't singe what's already inside, but if something manages to get through his defenses, it will burn them instantly.

The flames lick along the circular walls, searching for whoever dares to try and enter.

I widen my stance once more, tethering myself to Knox's mind as I allow a part of my essence to search, gliding through the golden iridescent flames guarding his sanctuary.

Knox's fortress allows me to pass, not creating a gap but letting me walk *through* as if aware of my presence and intention. Permitting me to become one with the fortress wall. The forest surrounding me disappears, replaced with what's beyond the walls.

My jaw snaps closed to stop my sharp gasp.

Slick darkness, like night itself, slithers around the walls of Knox's mind. It pulls back only to strike against the steel again. It barely leaves a dent but the relief I feel is short-lived as it continues to grow, its thickness deepening by the passing seconds.

It acts like oil. Slippery, slimy, and rotten.

The stench it emanates tickles a part of my brain, as if I should know its decaying source. It's akin to the demon hounds and yet entirely different.

The next hit makes me wobble, forcing me to grit my teeth and dig my feet deeper into the forest soil. When I steady and peek my essence out once more, I find a scratch along the iron walls.

The darkness sings its praises, sizzling with elation at its damage. At that moment, I know it will come back for him, pouncing when he least expects it—when he is at his most vulnerable.

I cannot let that happen.

My magic conforms, morphing into whatever power I deem necessary. With my mind running wild with imagination, I form fire shadows of my own to mimic Knox's power and his steel iron walls, except mine have a face.

The abyss pulls back, readying itself to launch once more, and when it's poised to strike, coming close enough for my fingertips to reach out and touch it, I strike.

The head of a cobra lunges from the iron walls. Its mouth opens, a deep hiss tumbling from between glinting fangs. The sound reverberates through Knox's mind, making my legs vibrate with the force.

I slam into the darkness, then retreat. I don't give it time to inspect its enemy. They cannot know it is my power and not Knox's defenses.

The entire wall becomes a nest of cobra heads, the hissing turning so loud I shake from side to side. The dark oily abyss vibrates as well, unable to escape the wrath of my power. Then the cobra heads pull back, pouncing all at once, fangs glinting and tongues slithering. The abyss shrinks and disappears, its lingering stench of death and corrosion coated in fear.

Aurora suddenly drops, making my eyes fling open while I fight to stay rooted in Knox's mind and cling to my invisibility magic. I will not have the deaths of three thousand more innocents hang on my consciousness.

This time, I will prevent their tumbling heads.

My gaze is wild and crazed as I search for what Aurora reacted to.

We've passed the lake. Orders are being issued behind us —from the king's men. Readying themselves for an attack that will never come.

Warmth pulses at my sternum. I startle, digging out the crystal necklace brimming with white light. *The Veil of Truth.*

It's been so long since it's reacted, but if it's burning now, that means—

Something's being concealed.

It must be from Knox and his court's shields and glamours…right?

Nothing else reveals itself, and I breathe a sigh of relief as the rebels climb the large rolling hill, while the lake and king's soldiers grow smaller behind us. My lips twitch into a smile, spreading quickly, before vanishing in a heartbeat.

It can't be.

My hand in Aurora's fur shakes, the color draining from my face.

I stop breathing, stop feeling the wind brush across my skin, stop hearing the beat of my heart…I simply stop as I stare at my father.

The king, I remind myself. He was never a father nor one that deserves the title.

Everything continues, which means time hasn't stopped even though it feels like it has. The soldiers continue to move under the guise of my invisibility and Knox's shield. Aurora continues to fly. Knox continues to hold me, and despite what I felt earlier, my heart continues to beat.

Looking at the face of the man who haunts my dreams and waking life, I feel like those around me should also notice. Should be screaming for their lives, running with terror in their eyes, and yet nothing changes.

But everything within me does.

It's impossible, and yet we continue to stare at one another. Despite the distance, the height, the invisibility, and his human eyes, I can feel it. His cold stare and disgust.

I can feel it.

And when the corner of his lips tug into a malicious smirk, showing the rotten soul residing within, I know I'm not insane.

The king can see me.

Chapter Twenty-Seven

My gait is dazed as I walk through the camp hours later, passing by the thousands of tents raised for the night, hidden within the deepest part of Sector Six's woods. The numbness that overcame my body when my eyes connected with the king has stayed with me, haunting me like a ghost I can't shake.

Numbness has graced me with one thing, though—oblivion.

Faces and features all blend into one. I scarcely make out the soldiers' grim expressions as I pass, the wide berth they all seem to gift me. Whether out of gratefulness for saving them all or out of their wary trust in me, I do not know and can't force myself to care.

Everyone's perception has shifted, drifting into endless streams of emotions.

Whereas my mind has narrowed into one stream, one thought, one current. The image of the king, the moment his lips lifted into that horribly sickening smirk. The one that sent chills down my spine, had my stomach lurching and heart bottoming out.

He appeared to know something I did not.

And *that* is what terrifies me the most.

The sordid ordeal is impossible to fathom because he couldn't have possibly *seen* me, not behind the force field of invisibility. If he had, he would have sent his troops after us. It would have only taken them a short time to catch up to the rebellion army.

He wouldn't have let us simply walk past them.

Despite the logical side of my brain arguing these points, I can't shake his look, the cold detached victory that shone in his beady eyes.

I place a hand over my stomach and grimace at the nausea churning there, willing my anxiety to settle for a moment.

Forcing myself to breathe in deeply through my nose and out through my mouth. Trying and failing to dispel the dizziness that wracks my body.

A familiar calming sound whispers through my mind.

Angel?

Spinning around, I come face-to-face with Knox, and my heart sags with relief. I open my mouth to speak, only for him to gently place a single finger over my lips, silencing me.

His eyes flick to the side as leaves rustle in the distance.

My eyes narrow as I make us invisible, my hand clutching Knox's wrist. His pulse jumps beneath my fingers.

Three soldiers walk past, harmlessly bantering as they search for firewood. I breathe deeply as Knox removes his hand from my lips once the soldiers disappear around the corner.

Once they're gone, Knox slides his hands into his pockets and leans against the thick tree trunk. "What happened?"

I snap my gaze to his, the soldiers long forgotten.

Despite knowing I can trust him, with my heart screaming to let him in…I hesitate. Fear sewing my mouth shut.

I despise that the king has this power over me, even when he's not here. His voice is lodged in my mind, his terror and control residing in every recess of my consciousness.

"Angel, what is it?" Knox asks again.

Tears pool in my eyes without my consent. My jaw clenches and I bite my lip to contain the emotions threatening to explode, but all I manage to do is bite my lip and draw blood.

It takes all the willpower within me to retain some semblance of control, but it shatters the moment Knox's gentle hands touch my cheeks, his voice growing impossibly soft with worry.

"Angel, please tell me so I can help." At my continued silence, Knox whispers, "As one."

The words release me, unlocking the cage around my mouth and mind, making the king's voice small. Taking a shuddering breath, I place my hands on his hips, needing his strength and touch to ground me.

"He saw me," I whisper.

Knox frowns. "Who did?"

"The king."

One moment Knox is staring at me with disbelief and in the next I'm watching what happened earlier unfold. The smirk that came across his face, the knowledge he seemed to hold, teasing that he had already won.

When the memory vanishes, I instinctively step back, squeezing my eyes shut tightly.

"Angel, I'm sorry," Knox whispers, wrapping his strong arms around me. His warmth and scent encompass me.

My breathing quickens as the memory lingers.

"That's impossible; the force was impenetrable. If he had seen us—seen *you*—he would have come after us." Knox shakes his head. "He would have tried to kill us."

"I know, and that's what I've been trying to tell myself, but…you saw it. He knows something, Knox, and whether he saw us or didn't, he could feel that we were near."

And while we're on the subject… I swallow the lump of emotions rising in my throat and whisper, "Someone attacked your mind while I was in there."

Knox's eyes widen, then give way to a fierce scowl. "Show me."

I let him in again. My eyes glaze over as I show him every single moment that horrid oily darkness attacked him, the fear I felt over someone conquering his beautiful mind.

Knox pulls back with a slight shake of his head. "Someone is beside him wielding magic. They had to be close by to attempt an attack like that." Knox's eyes turn calculating, the warrior within churning. "We need to get to the palace."

"What aren't you telling me, Knox?"

"I think the sooner we get your mother out of that palace, the better."

My chest constricts. "Y-you think he's *done* something to her?" I stutter out.

Was that why he looked triumphant?

Knox rests his chin atop my head, running his palm up and down my back in soothing circles, making the tightness lessen. "Whatever he has or hasn't done, we will get through it together. As one."

"I wish I had your confidence," I say begrudgingly.

I can hear the smirk in his voice as he drawls, "It takes years of practice being the most sought-after warrior."

Rolling my eyes, I chuckle, the sound dying off shortly after. Silence falls over us like a blanket, but we don't need words to communicate what we feel, what our hearts desire.

Knox's cockiness is his ultimate armor, and despite what he said, a small kernel of fear resides within him.

We all have a reason to feel dread. The dream I had weeks ago, the premonition of our deaths and Aloriah's end, being one of them. But if the king continues to rule, there's no telling what he'll do. Who he will enslave, who he will kill, how many children he'll turn into mindless killing machines.

He's taken two sectors down, and there's no telling how large his army's size will grow as he burns the others to the ground.

It's what he did to me—making me weak, vulnerable, and susceptible to information. Breaking me into a shell of the person I could have been so he could fill it with his ugly words. He's made it so the orphaned children rely solely on him for food, clothes and shelter.

It's how he manipulates.

He made the children vulnerable to make himself *needed*.

He will be able to create monsters from the very travesty he created, but the question remains, why do any of this now?

"How far would he go to win?" Knox asks hoarsely.

My blood turns cold. "He would sell whatever is left of his soul for victory."

With just a simple look Knox scoops me into his arms.

The tension leaves my body as he shoots off. To where, I don't care. So long as it's far enough away from the camp that I can forget about what happened earlier, forget about the king, forget about what we're about to do… I just want to forget.

"Am I selfish for wanting that?" I ask, knowing Knox can already tell what I'm feeling. "Thousands of people died and here I am begging my mate to whisk me away. I'm running from a trauma that isn't even my own. What those people went through—"

"Is a tragedy," Knox cuts me off. "But one tragedy doesn't take away from another."

His gaze narrows as he suddenly drops, and I don't have to wait long for answers as to why. He lands a minute later, setting me down gently only to maneuver me against his back.

One of his favorite positions. His arms wrapped around me, his powerful legs beside my own.

This is quickly becoming what we do—perhaps what will be intimate between the two of us for as much time as we have together. Knox sweeping me away into the air, secreting us off to a secluded spot.

Pink hues dance across the sky from the setting sun, lighting the forest and rolling hills. The small rivers mirror the sky in their reflections, blue and pink swirling together.

Birds soar past, chirping as they soak up their freedom.

"How can something so beautiful hold such a great deal of ugliness?" I ask.

"One cannot exist without the other."

Duality is the promise of life, and change. Everything that exists within the universe must be balanced, equal to its counterpart.

I should feel comfort in that prediction, but it isn't stable. Duality will find its balance when it wants, and when I feel high, soaring on the happiness of life, I can't help but wonder when it will end. When duality will come crashing in to claim the balance life demands. When exactly the rug will be pulled out from under me.

That's what's happening now.

I enjoyed peace, happiness, and freedom for months in the Fae lands. Now, duality has come to claim its dues. I'm free-falling, life throwing just as much sorrow and sadness as it offered me elation.

If it's any consolation, it's comforting to know I'll rise again, and that happiness will have me soaring in the future. I just hope I experience it before the premonition claims me.

"You're not selfish," Knox reiterates, drawing me from my thoughts. "In fact, I believe you're the opposite. You're not only going up against the king, Angel, you're fighting against someone who abused you your entire life. That's no small feat. It takes courage." His lips press against my temple. "It's also normal to want to take a minute to breathe, to process your emotions and clear your mind."

"How often do you feel the need to take a moment to decompress?"

Knox may play the role of a cocky king—at times he truly is—but I see past it when he's not. The night he opened his heart and soul to me, the times in which he's shown me all of what he went through. What he felt for himself and others.

That is not the acts, thoughts, and feelings of a king who only pursues power and victory.

It's the actions of a deeply empathetic person, one with a heart made of gold.

One that I've fallen in love with and continue to every day.

"More often than you'd think." His voice grows quiet, mingling with the sounds of nature surrounding us. "Views like this are what kept me together after the loss of my parents. Of course, my court helped, but when they were asleep, and the house grew quiet...it was this that gave me the reason to breathe again."

Turning around in his arms, I slide my palms up his cheeks, my thumbs brushing back and forth. My heart skips a beat when he leans further into my touch. His lashes flutter closed for a moment. "You are so strong," I whisper. "Thank you for all that you do. I don't know what I'd do if I didn't have you by my side through this."

Knox's lips part as a rush of air leaves him. Energy crackles between us, growing heavy with the emotions that bounce between our hearts.

"We will get through this," he says. "And when we're on the other side, we are going to drink *a lot* of faerie wine." He chuckles darkly, lessening the tense energy.

A deep belly laugh escapes me. Knox stops and stares at me, as if greedily soaking up the sound, and then steals my breath when he flashes me a devious grin.

I knock my shoulder into his chest and return to resting against his back. "Soak up the view while you can. We don't know when we'll be able to sneak away again."

"As long as you're by my side, I don't care what the view is."

And just like that, Knox steals another sliver of my heart.

Chapter Twenty-Eight

Beautiful sunflowers bloom between Hazel's hands four days later. Then the radiant yellow petals wither into nothing as death claims the stalk. Her face is twisted with concentration, perspiration dancing along her brow as it unfurls once more, growing from a husk to the once beautiful sunflower again, brimming with life.

My smile twitches. She's grown over the past few weeks, the time to resuscitate plants and flowers shortening as she masters the gift.

"How come I haven't seen you use your magic?" Hazels asks once she wipes her brow and sets the flower aside.

"I feel as if my outbursts have been enough of a demonstration of my abilities," I joke.

Knox and I agreed to keep my…*issues*…between us. I trust Hazel with my life, but the last thing I need to do is add to everyone's stress and worries. The second I mention *uncontrollable* and *magic* in the same sentence, all hell would break loose, and we need everyone focused as we quickly approach the palace.

Hazel chuckles along with me. "This is true, but your power is so beautiful. I miss watching you in action."

My cheeks tint pink. "Thank you."

Ace jumps in front of me, drawing my attention away from his mate. He holds out his hands, both closed into a fist.

"Choose."

I pretend to ponder before tapping his left.

He opens both his palms to reveal small cuts of milk chocolate. "Surprise. I keep seeing you eye all the soldiers when they have some." He lowers his voice to a mere whisper. "I snatched a few when they weren't looking."

My heart pinches at the kind gesture, and that from all the people in Knox's court, it had to be Easton's doppelgänger handing me what Easton adored most in life.

My voice cracks as I whisper, "Thank you."

His eyes drop, and it makes guilt slam into my mind from ruining this moment. Shaking the sadness away, I pluck one of the squares of chocolate, leaving the other. "Share with me?"

He shakes his head adamantly. "No, they're for you."

"Think of it as payment."

"For…?"

I flash him a sheepish smile as my eyes flick to the area behind our tents. "Help me prepare the lamb for the griffins?"

He chuckles, plopping the chocolate in his mouth and speaking around his chewing. "You don't need to bribe me for that, but I will accept."

Without wasting any time Ace passes me a butcher's knife and we get started on our task. I wrinkle my nose despite myself. Ace laughs at my expression until his mood turns somber.

"Do you think Hazel seems happy?"

My head snaps up at his question. "Of course! Despite the

predicaments we're in, did you not notice the grin plastered to her face?"

"Yes, but…"

I cock my head at his hesitancy. "You can ask me anything, Ace."

"If I ask you something, swear on your life you will not tell."

Even Aurora and Zephlyn huff at his sudden seriousness. The utter conviction in his tone. Stepping between the two griffins, I hide behind their enormity to give us some privacy.

"Ace, you're beginning to frighten me."

He rolls his eyes. "Just swear it."

"I promise," I say without a second thought. The words remind me of what I told Easton when he asked if I trusted him. I told myself I wouldn't promise or vow something again, but it came so naturally with Ace.

Ace glances around, peering below the griffins' bellies to check for those who pass. Once he's satisfied that we are alone, he reaches into his pocket and pulls out something so blindingly beautiful my breath leaves me in one gasp. The knife in my hand clatters to the ground, splashing into a puddle of mud, as my hands snap to my open mouth.

"Oh, Ace! It's beautiful!"

An oval-cut ruby sits atop a silver-banded ring, with sparkling flecks of white diamonds surrounding the gem. As if a rose clustered by leaves. It's the ring of Hazel's dreams.

"Do you think she will like it?"

"Like it?" I say, still struggling to breathe past the magnificence of the ring. "Ace, she will adore it—love it beyond reason! How long have you been carrying this around?"

Zephlyn puffs up his chest, a breath blowing out of his snout. Aurora brushes her head up against his, as if they're chuckling at an inside joke.

Ace's cheeks tint a ferocious red, mirroring the ruby in his hand. "Ignore those two. I was just beyond excited when I got it, I had to tell someone…" His voice drops so low I can't even hear him with the enhanced Fae hearing.

"I'm sorry, what?"

Ace lowers his head. "After the eclipse ball," he mumbles under his breath.

My lips spread into a smile so wide I'm sure my cheeks are about to split wide open. "That's beautiful, Ace. I wish words could describe how happy I am for you, for the both of you."

"She hasn't said yes yet," he reminds me as he places the ring into the black satchel attached to his pants. The utter care in his movement makes my heart pinch.

"She will, I'm certain of it. Do you know how you want to ask her?"

His eyes alight, sparking with an enthusiasm I haven't seen for a long time. "Yes. I plan to surprise her with a mating ceremony by Luna's waterfall. That way, she will feel like she attended in some capacity."

My hand clutches my chest as silver pools in my eyes. "She will love that," I whisper.

A soldier walks past, and Ace immediately heaves another cut of lamb onto the table, trying to remain as inconspicuous about our conversation as possible.

After a moment, I have to ask, "What are the Fae weddings like?"

"The Fae call them joining ceremonies." Ace doesn't even grimace as he starts cutting in. "It's a ceremony in which we celebrate the joining of two souls. The high priestesses are quite poetic about them."

I sigh, wistfully imagining such a beautiful event.

"What are the ceremonies like in the human lands nowadays? Is it still a marriage of opportunity and wealth?"

I frown. "I wouldn't know... I've never attended one." Although I've read about plenty, all varying from true love to merging family wealth. The longer I think about Ace's question, the more I realize, "I don't think I've ever met someone in love with their spouse."

Ace's jaw drops before he quickly catches himself. He tries to hide it, but he can't fully conceal the pity in his expression. I suppose it is pitiful to not have experienced such a mundane life event.

I shrug. "Perhaps I was just sheltered?" I state it as more of a question than the fact it is.

"Well, when we go back to Azalea, we'll dine and people watch in the city. You'll notice the rings, matching necklaces, and the love in their eyes."

If I make it back to Azalea, but I don't say that thought out loud. Unlike Nolan, I have control over my pessimism that others don't want to hear.

"Did Annie never marry?"

"No. Actually, I don't know if she's ever been in love. She's never talked of such things."

"Who has never talked of such things?" Annie asks, startling me to the point a yelp rises from my throat. Sometimes, I wonder if Annie has a preternatural ability to sense when other people are talking about her.

Quickly resuming my duties of slicing and dicing, I clear my throat. "Aurora. She's never said if she likes anything other than the fattiest pieces of lamb."

The lie rolls off my tongue, which isn't a lie at all. She truly does huff about which animals Ace and I choose. The deadpan look she gives me tells me she can sense the sincerity in what I said.

My brow quirks, daring her to challenge me. "You do like them fat," I whisper.

A gentle nudge is all I get in response, yet it speaks a thousand words. Especially as her eyes appear to glow with humor.

"Uh-huh." It doesn't seem like she believes that's what we were talking about, but she drops the subject. "Care to help me line the wet clothes?" she asks.

I squeeze Ace's shoulder as I move past him, slyly winking before I take one of the baskets out of Annie's arms and follow her. "Of course. Should we get Knox to heat them?"

She waves her hand in the air. "He's busy helping some of the soldiers and I don't want to bother him."

"I'd do it myself but…" My cheeks flush. "I'm certain I would burn the material to a crisp."

Annie drops the basket at her feet and grabs a piece of linen off the top, throwing the material over the makeshift line one of the soldiers hung up between two trees. "Don't worry, dear, I've been drying clothes like this for over forty years. I can do it one more time without magic."

The guilt and shame that were beginning to coil around my heart lessen, drifting away with each of Annie's words. She's always been able to do that—calm me with the mere sound of her voice.

As if a medical balm.

"Do you miss making your tonics?" I ask. She had mentioned when we left the cottage that she had been practicing but hadn't been able to bring her supplies on the road.

Her shoulders sag as if the tension in her shoulders is lifted with just the mention of medicine. "Yes, very much so. I thought perhaps I would be distracted and busy… I didn't realize how much time was spent traveling with only your thoughts."

"You could offer your services to the healers?" I suggest.

She shakes her head. "I've already done that; they've got it covered. I'm grateful no one has been hurt beyond the usual injuries of travel, but with nothing else there isn't anything to do."

It's a good thing we haven't had any injuries or battles to fight, but I know how Annie feels. Travel does feel tedious day in and day out. There may be thousands of people around you, but it gets awfully lonely when you're left to your thoughts, whirling and twirling as messy as a hurricane.

"I was wondering though…" Annie trails off, the words lodged in her throat.

"Yes?"

"Perhaps when this is all over, I could study the medicine of the Fae? If Knox has any books to spare, of course."

My eyes alight for another reason entirely. Is she planning on coming back with us? "Of course, Annie! He wouldn't—"

"Wouldn't mind in the slightest," Knox drawls behind me.

Annie and I jump in sync. Behind us, his eyes are aglow, shadow fire rippling amidst the deep ocean blue. That fire moves to his fingertips, and in an instant, the clothes are dry. Not a single item is burnt or shrunk.

Annie places a hand over her heart, her cheeks flushed. "Oh, Knox! I'm sorry, I didn't mean any disrespect. I was going to ask you, I just thought—"

He cuts off her nervous babble. "My books are yours," he says. "You can take whatever you need. It's an honor to have you interested in the Fae medicinal practices."

Hope burns as bright as the setting sun in her golden eyes. "Thank you. I look forward to learning them all."

Annie turns to me, a question lingering in her eyes and

burning on her tongue. I can read between the lines, and elation erupts in my chest.

Squealing, I throw my arms around her, mindful not to crush her.

"Yes! A million times yes!" I turn to my mate, still holding Annie in my arms. "Isn't that right, Knox? She can stay with us for as long as she wants!"

Happiness dances across his features, love pouring down our bond. "My home is yours, Annie."

"Oh, Annie, you will love it! It's magical! The cities are so full of joy it's contagious. People sing and dance in the streets! And the libraries…oh, there are so many books it will take you a lifetime to read about all the tonics and medicinal spells."

Annie lays her hand on my cheek, halting my words entirely. "I look forward to you sharing your home and new way of life with me, Delilah."

Tears spring to my eyes, burning silver against the ice blue. I swallow thickly. Easton never got to experience what he hoped for most in this world, but perhaps he's looking down on us and smiling that Annie finally gets to experience the life of freedom she so greatly deserves.

The freedom we all deserve.

Chapter Twenty-Nine

That moment—one of happiness and joy and new beginnings—feels like a lifetime ago, even though it all comes crashing down just the next day.

Knox's knees give way. On the ground, he shoots out his arm, trying to stop me from seeing the inevitable. "Delilah, don't look."

I'm not listening. My feet are propelling me forward. After Knox fails, Axel is the next to try, encircling his arms around me and pulling me back.

"Delilah, don't. You don't need to see this."

His words are just like the rest, simply floating through the entrance and exit of my brain before they can register.

I feel nothing as I splay my palms against his skin and singe him, the sound of his hiss in my ear as he yanks his burnt arms away, but it doesn't compare to the pounding in my ears.

I've spent seven hours preparing for this. Prepping my mind for what it was going to see. Allowing my imagination to run for miles. To make it worse than what it truly was so that it wouldn't hurt as much.

And it was all for nothing.

The sight before me is even worse than my wildest imagination.

Thousands of bones lie before us.

Skulls litter the floor, the jaws hanging open as if they all died screaming. The energy is palpable. The sadness and fear that terrorized these innocent people will forever be imprinted on this land. Or what's left of it. A proud fishing sector, now death's backyard.

Buildings are now ash fluttering in the wind. Houses lie decimated. The lively forest that once grew here now is nothing but bleak blackness and charred ground.

It's not even burnt. It simply has ceased to exist.

I thought I'd feel anger, hatred, grief…but I feel nothing. My body is utterly numb as my heart abandons me. Unable to stand the sight of what the king inflicted. The amount of people that died.

The suffering…it's too much.

It brings me to my knees, though all it does is crush the bones beneath me.

This is what he wanted. The heir to the throne on her knees before the man who destroyed her kingdom.

I crawl forward, only for something to crunch beneath my hand. I yank it back. There's now a fine fracture between the eye sockets in the remains of someone's skull.

I cracked someone's skull.

Sucking in a breath isn't enough. The rise and fall of my chest is useless. *Why can't I get oxygen?*

"Delilah."

I hear my name, and I feel the bond within me tug, but I can't deal with it.

There's a small version of myself, a child-like version of me, that's trapped within the confines of the cage I built for her in my mind. She's screaming and kicking, and with every pound of her fist against those walls, the dam I've been building for years leaks just a little more. And with one more agonized wail, it shatters.

This is the break. This is the end of the dam. For I am not swimming I am *drowning* in its wreckage. Suffocating under the weight of my memories of what was done to me.

One after the other, they pummel me, uncontrollably like a wave.

The first time he wrapped his hand around my neck and squeezed. Spit flew from between his gritted teeth. My eyes had bulged, because it wasn't enough to see me turn purple. It wasn't enough that I wheezed. It was never enough.

He wanted me dead.

The only reason he stopped was a guard had broken a vase, the sound reminding him of our public audience. It wouldn't have looked good if the king killed his sweet six-year-old daughter.

I wish I could say he grew smarter about where he hurt me, but he didn't. He just grew to not care. He built his empire large enough that he couldn't be touched.

The little girl's fist pounds against the cage again. Another memory.

The day he realized he was powerful enough to get away with anything. He had hit a servant, a young twelve-year-old girl who had to work to support her family because she dropped a fleck of potatoes and gravy on his lap while serving him.

It broke my heart to see the cut that marred her clean, fresh skin.

So, I took a stance, one that I knew would get back to my father.

I took my most expensive jewels, rubies, and coins and

placed them in a sack. I handed it to her and pleaded with her to leave Aloriah. I told her to take her family and use the money to run. To never look back.

I was fourteen myself, but I was old enough to understand. I always had.

I was only proved right when he marched up to me and punched me.

Slaps were for women, he would say, and I was not one yet.

His people simply stood aside and did nothing, as if they had turned to stone statues in the middle of the room.

Easton was the only one who opened his mouth and attempted to stop the beating. Then the king had unsheathed his sword, threatening to slit him from ear to ear if he interfered.

Even months later, I wonder if that's why he had killed Easton in such a manner. To fulfill his vow.

Easton's father, the captain of the guard, had dragged him away without a word. My own father then turned me over in my pool of blood, used his blade to slice open my corset, and created my first scar—the one of many that now decorate my back.

He sliced me so deeply it awoke me from unconsciousness, only for the severity of the pain to send me tumbling into darkness once more. Fourteen years old, his own flesh and blood, and he carved me like a turkey.

I couldn't lie on my back for a month without wincing and flashing back to his face full of rage. The monster he became in that moment haunted me for years. It still does.

But this day was the turning point. The monster within him had been unleashed entirely, and I had lost all hope he would ever change. That he would ever love me. And once he saw that not a single person within his court stopped him, it was the beginning of the end.

The little girl kicks her feet against the cage. I spin into another memory, the one haunting me as of late.

The true reason I hate my birthday.

I was sixteen, finally turning into a woman, and I had hope for the first time in years. My body was changing and growing, and my muscles were finally blooming after all my hours in the training room.

I had hoped he would stop. After all, he said slaps were for women and I had finally turned into one. Slaps were much easier to deal with than his fist. But I was clearly not a woman yet, still daring to dream and hope like a naïve, foolish child.

That evening at my birthday dinner, seated beside my unseeing mother, I dared to ask about the prisoners I had found in that gods-awful prison on the outskirts of the capital. What he was to do with so many people, and why he had herded them like cattle. When the king shared his plans to execute them, children alike, I couldn't hide my disgust.

Later that evening, I would soon look back on that moment and chastise myself. I knew better. I had been schooling my features for years, but when it counted most, eye to eye with the king, I had gasped at such a horrid idea.

In retaliation, the king tied my wrists to the post in his room, cut my corset, and whipped me seven times. I got through the first round without a sound. After enduring the whip for years, I was beginning to withstand the pain and bite my tongue. He didn't like that.

His cruel wicked laugh had snaked down my spine as he declared that being it was my birthday, he would bestow upon me the honor of fulfilling the date with his punishment.

Seven whips…seven times.

Forty-nine in total.

Two hours and thirty-nine minutes later, I was forever marked by that post, and my birthday was no longer my own.

Standing on the rubble of Sector Six—standing on the remains of the innocent people of Aloriah—my blood boils. Magic builds.

Wrath.

Vengeful wrath.

It twists and writhes through my body, and instead of trying to control it, to leash the fury demanding to escape, I allow it to run as wild as a wolf.

When I look down and see a small skull barely the size of my palm—belonging to that of a newborn infant who was left behind—I roar. My magic howls alongside me.

Golden power explodes in all directions as it aims to fight a battle that has already struck.

Knox rushes down the bridge. "Give it to me, Delilah!" he screams. "Blast it down the bridge!"

As if my magic has a mind of its own, it turns, blaring down the bridge into Knox's awaiting arms.

He stumbles back, screaming with the power needed to devour it. But it's not enough. My body ignites, golden fire erupting along every inch of my skin as the rage within me climbs to a higher feat.

My magic doesn't swallow me whole thanks to him, but it does continue to shine bright, fueled by the unforgiving indignation within my heart.

It demands justice.

And for once, I feel it.

The strength to fight back.

Chapter Thirty

Aurora flew me far, far away.

Allowing me to take the coward's way out.

While Ordelia, Phillip, and her rebels walked among the remains of the fallen, I flew high above, so high that the bones of the innocent looked like nothing but a speck of dust.

It's been days since I've seen the remains of the sector, and since then, we've made our way into Sector Seven.

When Aurora, Knox, and I landed every night to set up camp along the forests and soldiers made eye contact with me, it was not distrust or disgust that I found lining their eyes, but respect.

The shift within the soldiers was palpable, and I couldn't fathom it. I was a coward. I couldn't stand to see another bone, and yet they looked at me with admiration. It never made sense until Axel explained one night how seeing the anger and power that overtook my body restored hope in their hearts of my allegiance.

Change, it seemed, was coming, whether the king wanted it or not.

Despite my newfound hope over the soldiers, Knox still grumbled about how I had always been helpful and on the side of the people of Aloriah. How it shouldn't have taken me exploding with anger for them to believe where my true loyalty lies.

He switched perspectives when he saw how happy I was about it, at least out loud.

When Knox and I land again for the night, soldiers dip their chins in greeting. We return the gestures and seek out Ordelia and Phillip's tent. Tomorrow, we infiltrate the palace.

Knox's court, Annie, and Lucca are also waiting for us.

"Oh gods, I thought you went missing! You've been gone for so long. How was the flight?" Annie gushes.

My cheeks turn pink as Knox's shadows draw a tantalizing caress down my back, the memory of our steamy detour playing through my mind.

"Can you fuss later?" Nolan grumbles, boredom etched across his features. "We have a palace to break into."

Annie clicks her tongue. "You may be older than me, boy, but you don't rush a mother."

Mother.

Annie is, in every sense of the word. But it doesn't detract from my own biological mother. One love doesn't diminish the other.

One of Knox's dimples appears as he splays his hands to the maps littering the makeshift table. "Shall we?"

Annie, to my delightful surprise, takes up a spot beside Ordelia. Relief is a powerful emotion, and it knocks the breath from me at finally seeing the two begin to make up.

What Ordelia did is not excusable, but with the premonition lying heavy on my heart, the last thing I'd ever want is for Annie to lose a dear friend. Things are already peculiar; we need to be cherishing these quiet moments before we find ourselves staring down death in the name of the king.

Phillip begins talking strategy, drawing my attention to the detailed map of the capital and palace grounds. In the northern half sits the rich citizens of the capital, along with the king's soldiers and their families. The southern half holds the palace grounds. The mere drawing of the building has ice scuttling down my spine.

Axel's finger lands on the northern forests of the capital border. "We'll send troops out to the forest to light fires as a diversion. Have a hundred create altercations with the soldiers patrolling the area."

My eyes spark with glee. "Tell them to burn the prison to the ground."

If you can even call it a prison. It was a metal container with four walls and one entry and exit point, where people had to sit and breathe in their own filth.

Seeing that gods-awful place burn into nothing but ash will be a blessing.

Perhaps we should leave it to lock him in there.

"The king will send his men to squash it as quickly as possible. He won't condone having the rebels attack the capital. It makes him look weak," Phillip continues, his brows knotted in concentration.

Knox juts his chin across the table. "Nolan will go with them, hiding in the treetops." As Knox slides his eyes to Nolan's hazel ones, they take on the glint of a king ordering a member of his court. "You'll use your air magic to keep the fire spreading northward, away from the capital citizens. We will not be the ones responsible for causalities."

"We are *not* the king," I say.

"Understood, Your Majesty," Nolan drawls.

I roll my eyes, ignoring the teasing tone. Some have

anxiety attacks when stressed, others overindulge or become irritated, and then there's Nolan, annoying everyone within the vicinity.

"He won't send all of his soldiers, though," Axel interjects.

"Only the soldiers around the palace have orders to follow against threats such as this. The soldiers stationed inside the palace will remain," Phillip answers.

"That part I will handle," I cut in. "Aurora and I will land in the western wing of the palace roof. I'll enter through my old quarters."

"I'll accompany you," Knox says.

Clearing my throat, I send calm energy down the bond, praying he won't make a scene with this. "No, I am going into the palace alone."

Knox's spine stiffens as his head slowly turns to me, the move predatory.

"It's enough risk with one of us entering," I add.

His eyes harden before he blinks it away, the only shock he will show. "I'm going with you. You'll need my assistance."

Annie interjects on his behalf. "Delilah, you cannot go back there alone."

"Why do you have a morbid obsession with going in alone?" Knox asks tensely, his teeth gritted.

My tongue clicks. "It is not a morbid obsession, it is an order. You are in the human lands. This is my territory and, traitor or not, I still possess the last name, Covington."

Annie doesn't hide her gasp at my harsh words. Knox's court awkwardly shuffles side to side, finding sudden interest with the floor.

But Knox needs to understand I'm not backing down on this.

What the fuck are you trying to do? he chides in my mind.

You are not going anywhere near the palace walls, I say, then continue my argument out loud. "The last thing we need is him capturing a Fae king. He will kill you on sight or, worse, use you as a bargaining chip against the Fae courts."

Why did you not speak with me about this before the meeting? he hisses.

Because I knew you would change my mind and I am not risking your life.

"I think you're underestimating my abilities to not get caught, *Princess*," he says through gritted teeth, answering me out loud.

I quirk a brow. "What if he has wards blocking magic around the palace?"

"I'll go with her," Axel cuts in, halting the argument which is quickly devolving into a lover's quarrel. He straightens, holding his arms behind his back. "As your second-in-command, I'll go. I can't be used as a bargaining chip and I will protect Delilah with my life."

Tension fills the tent so thick no one breathes as a look passes between Knox and Axel. I know he's speaking to him in his mind.

"I can't make all of you invisible, and I've snuck in and out of my room through that roof for years without detection," I say, hoping to ease Knox off from reprimanding Axel too harshly. "I can do it again—alone."

"This is ludicrous," Knox growls.

Ignoring him, I plow forward, hoping that with further information and details, the warrior inside of him will recognize this is the smart decision. "While the forests are swarmed with Ordelia's rebels, Knox and Ace can infiltrate the palace through the food delivery wagons." *In case some-*

thing goes amiss, you will be close enough to read my mind and teleport to me, I say to appease him.

But that will be my absolute last resort. He *cannot* step foot inside that palace.

I open my mouth to administer Axel's duties, but the look he sends me freezes my jaw.

"Whatever orders you are about to tell me, don't. I am not letting you go in alone."

Knox snaps a silencing shield around us, leaving Ordelia and Phillip on the outskirts, their widened gazes and pale faces letting me know they can't hear a word. Knox turns to me and hisses, "What are you doing?"

Axel's accusatory eyes snap to Knox. "How could you let her do this alone after last time?"

Understanding dawns on me, why Axel is so incessant on accompanying me. The last time we all split up like this, I died in Knox's arms, only brought back to life by the sheer strength of his magic and his stubbornness to not let go of our bond.

My voice softens, remembering Axel's silent confessions in the forest. "Axel, I will be fine—"

"If you believe that, then you shouldn't be going alone." He directs his focus to his king. "I am going with her, and that is final."

Gasps spread around the room. If I had to guess, this is the only time he has ever spoken to Knox in such a way or questioned his authority.

Let him come, I whisper.

Absolutely not. If anyone goes with you, it's me.

No. You are not going anywhere near the palace in case he already knows we're mates. I am not handing you over to him.

Delilah, I can handle—

NO!

The exchange takes place quickly, no more than twelve seconds, and yet a certain terror has overcome Axel while he waits.

"You can accompany me," I rush out before Knox has a chance to say anything.

Disbelief courses through him, along with a tremendous amount of pain, rushing for our bridge.

Please forgive me, but it will kill him. He will be more useful by my side than distracted and failing at another isolated task.

It will kill me *to be separated from you and not able to help if you need me.*

No, Knox. If you walk into that palace, you will be sentencing your own death. I send a wave of tenderness down the bridge, hoping to convey just how much I believe his safety could be at risk within the palace.

His glare could light a building on fire, but Knox drops the shield, his body thrumming with hurt and rage. He turns to Ordelia and says coldly, "My second will accompany Delilah."

Ordelia merely dips her head, in acknowledgment and probably also fear, not wanting to look Knox in the eyes. Phillip watches on with, dare I say, guilt. Over what, I have no idea—there are too many things to choose from.

"How will you find your mother once you're inside?" Annie asks, breaking the tension growing in the room. "Nobody has seen her in months. What if she's no longer in the palace?"

"She's still there. He wouldn't risk moving her to another location," I say with conviction. I close my eyes. "I'll demonstrate: Everybody move around the room and take up a different position." When I hear no feet shuffle, I open an eye. "If you wish to know how I'll find her, move."

They finally scramble, and once they settle, I ground myself, concentrating on the magic within me. This is what Knox and I have been training for all these weeks, to gain control over the growth. I let a little bit slither out of the well, just a small trickle of power, and sear it out into the tent, weaving it between the warm bodies until I find the one I want.

And when I do, I pause, my lips parting on a small exhale.

"Annie," I say, tapping her shoulder with a golden hand of magic.

She gasps, and I know I've gotten it right.

"That's incredible!" Annie says when I blink my eyes open.

I smile, but it falls flat. "That's how I'll find her. I can discern her essence with my magic. We should hopefully find her in the palace within minutes and get out."

"Yes, fascinating, but *how* will you get your mother out?" Nolan drawls. "What if there are wards against magic?"

That's Nolan, always being sarcastic, but also always asking the tough questions we need to consider.

"I'll be able to detect them," Axel growls low, glaring daggers at Nolan.

Looking around the room, I take in the moment before I truly become a traitor of the crown. I'm surprised I find it so easy to speak, so easy to betray the very thing I have been born to protect. "There are underground tunnels. It's the king's escape route if there were ever an attack on the palace. Even his most trusted guards don't know about its existence. Only those in the royal family."

Phillip blinks, the only surprise he shows. "Where?"

"The family vault passageway. There's a hidden door

along the wall." I lean forward, tracing my finger along the western palace grounds. "The tunnels lead to the edge of the forest. Where the mountains meet the capital." I flick my eyes to Knox. He still won't look at me. "That's where Axel and I will meet with Knox and Ace, hopefully along with my mother."

At least Ace nods and agrees with me, a friendly face that acknowledges my presence, so I address him instead. "You two will sneak into one of the morning supply wagons. They leave from the food distribution in the outskirts of the capital, then travel underneath the palace through the servants' entrance. From there, it's a short walk to the tunnels."

And this way, if Nolan's right and there are wards around the palace and teleportation isn't an option, they will still have a way to be there. Plus, this needs to look like a rebel attack, not a Fae one. The last thing we need is a war between the races too—if that's not already within his plans.

Phillip nods his head to the Fae king brooding beside me. "Why do the men need to venture through the supply wagons?"

"We need someone else on the grounds who possesses magic and I'm unsure of whether the tunnel exit will be laden with wards of magic."

"Surely there are checkpoints for stowaways," Ace cuts in.

"They check the back of the trucks, not the drivers." I point to their ears. "You'll either have to find a hat or "

"I'll glamour our Fae features," Knox says, finally breaking his silence.

Nodding tentatively, I move my gaze to Hazel. The order I've been dreading to utter. "I need you to guard the tunnel's exit. Just to ensure we have no surprises waiting for us as we escape."

A spark lights in Hazel's eyes. Pride, possibly, at being able to help, or perhaps contentment that I've stopped coddling her. "Absolutely!" she chirps.

"Can you spare two soldiers to accompany her?" I ask Ordelia.

Hazel grunts. Okay, perhaps baby steps with coddling.

"Of course, I'll give the orders tonight."

Taking a shuddering breath, I stare at the map, my mind already running through a thousand variables of what could possibly go wrong and what to do if they occur.

"It's a great plan," Axel says, noting my anxiety.

"Thank you," I murmur.

"We'll move out at first light tomorrow," Phillip orders, rolling up the map of the capital grounds and palace.

Knox leaves the tent before Phillip even finishes issuing the order.

I give him a couple of minutes, allowing the others to distract Ordelia and Phillip before I sneak away. The moment I enter his tent, he whirls on me, not bothering to wait for the tent flap to close fully.

A silencing shield snaps around the perimeter.

Chapter Thirty-One

Knox bares his canines as he hisses, shoving me against the tent pole, "Do you want to die?"

"Do you?" I spit back. "Because that's what will happen if you step foot in that palace. It will not be Easton's head on a spike in the throne room, it will be yours!"

"You cannot keep me from going."

"I just did. This is my territory, Knox, and I gave you an order."

"Don't you dare get political on me," he snarls.

"I will continue to do so if you keep up this foolish nonsense!"

His Adam's apple bobs. "Every time I think about you entering that palace, I see you lying dead in my arms. *Every. Single. Time.* Can you imagine how that feels? To be *demanded* to leave you alone in a place that is not only dangerous but houses the monster who abused you all your life? It is gut-wrenching that you will not allow me to help you through this."

A crack breaks through the anger caged around my mind and heart.

I lay both my palms flat against his chest, allowing the electricity that always lies in wait to connect.

"I'm sorry. I'm sorry you have that image and that your mind uses it against you—I truly couldn't fathom seeing you in such a way." Although I do know, my premonition made it so I know how it feels to lose him. "And that is why I cannot let you come with me, Knox. Please do not force me to concede this."

His eyes flick back and forth before I watch them slowly lose their hard edge. He lowers his forehead to mine with a deep exhale. "You're never going to let me go, are you?"

"Never."

He pulls back, flopping down onto the cot. His head falls between his knees. I kneel before him, sliding my hands up his cheeks. My heart pangs, guilt filling me at the devastation and worry in his sapphire eyes, but this short pain would be nothing in comparison to his death.

"Axel will protect me," I say. My thumbs brush back and forth. "You heard him."

"I cannot lose you again, Angel." His voice cracks, forcing him to clear his throat. "I don't ever want to go through that pain again. It was *excruciating*. And I only experienced it for a few seconds. I couldn't imagine living like that, without you, for thousands of years."

"Maybe we should stop putting ourselves in these situations then," I tease.

"This is no time for humor."

I duck my head, catching his gaze. "I think it's a little funny." When he doesn't respond I push him back, straddling his hips. His eyes snap to mine.

That got his attention.

I place my hand on his chest, marveling at the way his breathing stutters from my touch. "There are going to be moments in our lives where we are separated. We need to trust that the other will return." The anxiety in my chest despises my words but I force them out regardless. "We both can't live in fear. I'm tired of anxiety ruling my actions and thoughts."

My words may be hypocritical, but I will not budge on this.

I cut him off as his mouth opens to surely protest. "I'm not asking you to not worry or to stop caring about my whereabouts and whether I'm safe. I do the same for you. What I'm saying is I don't want to make decisions based on fear. That's how we will end up getting hurt or manifesting the very thing we fear the most—losing each other."

A sly smirk comes over his lips. "Your biggest fear is losing me?"

"Of course that's the part you acknowledge," I say, whacking his shoulder playfully.

His hands capture my own during the movement, faster than I can blink. He spins us, pinning me beneath his weight. "I care for you more than you could ever imagine, Angel," he says on a whisper, the vulnerability shining in his eyes enough to make my heart trip over itself.

My breathing stutters as I become aware of every inch of him. And the little space between us. The way my nipples brush against his chest on each inhale. How our breathing falls in sync with one another.

Electricity zips down the bridge between our minds, jumping between our fingertips where we touch.

"Do you feel it?"

"Yes," I breathe.

"Good," he growls and smashes his lips to mine.

The kiss is anything but gentle. It's hungry, urgent, and full of fire.

His hands wrap around my wrists, sliding up and through my palms to link his fingers with mine.

His tongue strokes across the seam of my lips, begging for entrance. I open willingly, happily, and the moment his tongue touches mine in a toe-curling caress I moan. The sound makes him groan in response.

Every time we kiss it's as if I finally return home. The butterflies that nervously flutter in my stomach can finally settle onto a quiet branch and breathe. The excitement of having him touch me never fades, and I know, as sure and steady as our bond, that it never will.

I know he feels the same because the emotions flooding my heart are his too. The weight of what we feel for one another is pure and as light as a feather, and yet so filling that it grounds us in the strong emotions that would otherwise sweep us off our feet.

Knox pulls back only to pepper kisses along my jaw. My head falls back to allow him more access, and as he travels down, his canines scrape the apex of my neck, making goose-bumps pebble my skin.

His hands slide down my forearms, the rough callouses sending a chill down my spine. My breath sharpens as his hands continue to move south. My back arches like a feline, almost on its own accord, seeking his touch.

A delicious sigh of relief escapes me as his large palms cup me, the gentle squeeze eliciting a whimper from my lips. The gentle teasing and strokes against my breasts make my hips roll, and his large length hits the spot between my thighs that makes my toes curl.

"Do you like ordering me around, Angel?" Knox purrs.

Knox lifts his head as he waits for his answer. His hands pause on my breasts, his hips no longer grinding, as his eyes seem to taunt me.

"Y-yes," I stutter.

Knox peers at me through thick black lashes, a devilish smirk pulling at his lips and making me catch my breath for another reason entirely.

"Order me then."

I blink. "Order you?"

I lift my hips, seeking out the friction he so greedily is keeping from me.

Why isn't he moving?

"Yes, Angel, order me."

I pout. It's such a childish thing to do but the sight makes Knox throw his head back on a deep laugh, the veins in his neck straining. The sound is like heaven to my ears.

"I won't move until you order me, Angel."

Shaking my head, I ignore his words and lift my hips. "Please don't tease me, Knox."

He lowers his head, his canines scraping my ear gently before his breath whisps across it. "Order me," he growls again.

"Touch me and I will," I pant.

Before I can blink, his hands are moving again, gripping the leather corset covering my stomach and breasts. Knox pulls and the material shreds instantly, the remains getting thrown behind my shoulder. I gasp in shock, the cold air brushing against the sensitive flesh and making my already hard nipples pebble further.

His large palms cup my breasts once more, and instead of just squeezing as he did last time, his thumbs reach up to swirl around the puckered nipples.

My neck strains as my back arches impossibly high.

"Do you like that, Angel?" he asks, pinching the sensitive buds.

"Yes," I say breathlessly.

My hips lift, wishing more than anything for his touch.

Knox *tsks* above me. "You know the rules, Angel." He lowers his head. "I've held up my end of the bargain."

I shake my head as images float through it, one after the other and each one filthier than the last.

Knox chuckles and captures my lower lip between his teeth.

"I'll make it easy for you." His eyes spark as he pulls back. "Do you want my tongue or my fingers on your clit?"

The husky allure of his voice breaks through my pride and stubbornness.

"Tongue," I rasp. "Tongue!"

My clit throbs, electricity swirling between my thighs, wetness coating my pants. My chest rises and falls rapidly as he slides down my body.

His eyes fill with liquid heat as he pulls down my leather pants, the lids drooping. He stops to take it all in. "Perfect, Angel."

The cold air that brushes across my core makes my body feel alive. Every nerve ending alights in wait, pulsing for his touch.

Shadows twirl behind his back, and as Knox slowly lowers, they lunge for me, grabbing my wrists and ankles and spreading me bare in a tantalizing position. His eyes never leave mine as a quick lick strokes against my entrance. I throw my head back at the sudden sensation it provokes.

His arms snake up my skin, over my hips, up my stomach, and finally stopping at the swell of my breasts. Knox's deft fingers latch onto my nipples, pinching while sucking my clit with abandon. My head twists to the side on a scream, the sensation so intense my legs begin to quake.

Thank the gods for silencing shields.

Knox groans, the vibrations in my core only enhancing

the sensations. He pauses, giving me a moment of reprieve, before sucking deeply once more. It isn't long before my pleasure begins to climb.

"Knox, I'm close, baby. I'm so close," I moan.

My legs begin to shake, and on my next breath, he thrusts a finger inside me. Then two. I whimper at the intrusion, and he starts pumping harder. His vigorous pace is heightened when I start rolling myself against his face.

His groans send my pleasure higher. "You taste like fucking perfection."

His fingers crook inside me, stroking that place only he can find, and I tumble. My entire body shudders against his face, my legs clenching around his head, and I chant his name as I come violently.

The shadows around my ankles seem to stroke the limbs to hold them still. Knox's tongue doesn't stop his pace and his fingers continue coaxing the orgasm until it builds so high my body floats until it's nothing but stardust in the sky.

When Knox finally pulls back, those sapphire eyes glint with pride in the low lights of the gas lamps. The flame dances in those gorgeous irises and across his cocky smirk as he brings his dripping fingers to his drenched mouth and sucks.

It's a primal move, possessive, and yet it only results in another low hum gathering deep within my belly.

It's in this moment—with him standing over me, his stomach muscles flexing as he rips off his linen shirt to reveal the sheen of sweat beneath, his glorious large ridge tenting his underwear now that's pulled his pants off—I know I will never get enough of him.

Knox cocks his head. "Care to share what's on your mind, Angel?"

Sitting up on all fours, I reach out and capture his hand,

elation sparking in my eyes when electricity jumps between our fingers like I know it always will—our own lightning storm.

"Lie down," I command, surprising myself at the sultry tone.

The heat that fills Knox's sapphire eyes would have brought me to my knees had I not already been sitting. The pure desire in them makes heat coil between my legs again.

He smirks. "I see you've come to understand the rules of the game now, Angel."

"Oh, you have no idea, Knox."

Once he's lying down, his glorious body on display, I pause, taking in every intricate detail. The soft pads of my fingers skim over the tight muscles of his legs as I commit them to memory. The way they dance and bunch beneath my touch, the way his large thick length pulses, jumping as I draw near. A smirk plays on my lips as his chest begins to heave, his breath hot and his gaze hungry on me.

I move to sit between his legs. I start by latching onto his underwear and slowly pull the material down, my breath leaving me in an audible whoosh as his large velvet cock springs free. The thick girth pulses, the tip almost purple with how hard it's straining from the pure need of wanting me.

My mind spins, overwhelmed by the desire to taste every inch of him.

I feel the moment his cockiness fades when both my hands land on top of his thighs and slowly slide up toward his hips. His lips part, eyes growing heavy and wide as I lower my head.

My breath fans across his sensitive tip, making the hairs on his legs beneath my palm rise. I mirror his earlier grin, allowing myself to let go, to unleash myself with him.

Only him.

Satisfaction courses through my veins as I dart my tongue out, stroking him from base to tip, his resounding twitch and groan music to my ears. His stomach muscles strain, all pretenses of bravado fading, then entirely disappearing as I dip my head, my tongue darting out to lick the tip, before devouring him whole.

The deep purr of his husky groan fills the tent, my body, my soul.

I take him deeper in my mouth, my saliva dripping down the thick base, lubricating my fists stacked on top of each other to stroke him fully. Both working in tandem and yet moving in opposite directions.

I can't help my lips from curling as I watch his eyes grow comically wide.

His hands dive into my hair, gripping the strands roughly, though gentle enough not to harm me. Even in this wild moment, he knows the limits of his strength.

I swish my tongue side to side and take him deeper until he hits the back of my throat. At the sound of my gag, he throws his head back on a deep moan. The sight of him withering beneath my touch has liquid pooling between my legs.

It isn't until one of my hands leaves his base, snaking down lower to cup his balls, does he snap completely.

On a deep growl that reverberates down to the depth of my rib cage, Knox yanks me off him, his hands under my arms, and pins me beneath him.

"You like making me come undone, Angel?" he pants. His eyes are molten with heat as his body hovers over mine, taut and stiff with restraint.

His hands reach down, gliding up my inner thighs, the soft tantalizing touch sending chills throughout my entire body and contrasting it with the burn of my nerve endings.

"Yes," I breathe.

I widen my legs, spreading myself bare for him as his fingers trail higher, my body growing impatient with how slow his fingers are moving.

Knox's nostrils flare. "Are you wet for me, Angel?"

"Yes," I repeat, my voice hoarse.

Knox's fingers finally reach where I need him but he doesn't touch my clit, never so much as grazes it. I whimper impatiently, my cheeks heating at how demanding my body is growing. My hips lift to try and make him touch me.

Knox's knees pin my thighs apart, my body unable to move beneath him.

"Uh-uh," he *tsks*. "Not until I say so."

"What happened to me being in control?"

Fire sparks in his gaze. "You never were, Angel." His tone is dangerously dark, his fingers matching. They graze the side of my core, drawing circles through the wetness there.

He's mastered the art of torture—not just in a war tent but in the bedroom.

I jut my chest up, my heavy breasts and hard nipples begging for him, for what they just experienced.

Finally, his hand palms me. His heavy hand squeezes my breast roughly, while his fingers pinch the pebbled nipple until it stings with pleasurable pain, making me cry out.

Gone is the gentle and soft Knox. In return is the man staring at me as if I'm a meal he's about to devour.

"Knox," I plead.

"Do you want something, Angel?" His voice is hoarse, rough and grating.

I may be the object of his teasing and torturing, but he's turned on just as much as I am. His large cock strains between his legs, his purple tip evidence enough.

I lock my heavy-lidded gaze on him, watching as the

breath leaves him. I know my cheeks are flushed, hot to the touch, and I know my hair is a wild tangled mess, thanks to his hands roving through it as I sucked him. But it's my eyes, begging him to pleasure me as much as my words, that makes his lip curl back on a feral, deep growl as I whisper, "I want your cock inside of me."

Knox is entering me in one deep, hard thrust before the words have fully left my mouth.

His large size stretches me more than it has before. I throw my head back on a scream at the sudden intrusion, and yet the slick wetness of me has him gliding in all the way to the hilt. His tip probes me, brushing the walls as he fully seats himself inside.

Knox buries his head in the crook of my neck, his deep satisfied groan rumbling all the way down to my toes.

He chants my name like a prayer in my ear as his hips begin to pick up, setting a relentless pace, and when his hands slide under my ass, he drives impossibly deeper.

But it isn't enough.

My nails scrape down his back, crimson following in their wake.

A deep growl leaves Knox's lips as he spins me onto my stomach, and pushes my chest down onto the cot, my ass in the air.

When he slides in behind me, I thank the silencing shield for its presence, for if it weren't here, Knox's groan could be heard for miles. His thighs quiver behind mine at the ecstasy that fills our bodies with his entrance. The new position and angle allowing him to drive in further.

"The most perfect pussy," Knox grunts. "So wet for me."

Even his words make more wetness trickle down my thighs as his body worships mine in the best way possible.

"My perfect angel."

My hands glide in the rough sheets, scrunching the fabric between my fingertips, and I cling to the bed for dear life, the fullness of him like nothing before. I push back, meeting him thrust for thrust as I chase the ecstasy dancing along the horizon in my body.

Knox's groan is deep and long. "Bounce, Angel. Show me what you want most."

The tip of his cock brushes the spot within me again, a spot so deliriously glorious it makes my knees buckle and has a moan falling from my lips. Turning my quivers into shakes as he hits it, over and over and over.

His hand wraps around my throat, gently squeezing, the feel making my eyes close as an orgasm looms. I try to put it off, wanting his touch to last forever, wanting to dance with him along the edge of this cliff that we climbed together.

Wanting to feel his gloriously strong body moving behind me for the rest of our days.

"Gods, you're perfect, Angel. Made perfectly for me and my cock." He grunts, moving a hand to pinch my nipple before massaging the heavy breast. "Look at you, bouncing on my cock like you were made for it."

My core clamps around him, eliciting a full body shudder from him. His head falls forward into the crook of my neck, his canines scraping against the sensitive skin there.

The overwhelming sensations continue to build, tightness coiling in my limbs. And as Knox's hand leaves my breast, trailing down my stomach to my core, his magical fingers brush my clit, playing my body as if I was an instrument, custom made for him.

Then his canines sink into my neck.

Marking me as his.

The possessiveness throws me over the edge and makes

my body's nerve endings explode. Coming around him in endless waves of pure ecstasy.

The feeling is addictive, my body soaring like no other. My core clenches and convulses on his large cock while I rock my hips, drawing out my orgasm, until I twist my head to the side on a whimper and moan the words that are his undoing.

"Come inside me."

Knox growls under his breath and captures my lips. His hips thrust deeply once more and stop, holding himself seated to the hilt as he shakes, moaning my name into my mouth as our orgasms dance together and dive over the edge of the cliff, submerging into the water of ecstasy that are our joined bodies.

It is a moment I will cherish forever, because I can distinctly look back at our time spent together and know that this was the moment, I became addicted to the feel of Knox Holloway, and I will never search for the cure.

Chapter Thirty-Two

Leather sticks to me like a second skin. The corset wrapped around my chest beneath my fighting leathers pulls every inch of my stomach together, cinching my waist as if the material can keep the vital organs in their respective place against an attack from steel, while also accommodating my ribs to flare when I need to breathe.

Pulling the leather strap against my thighs, I tighten the sheath holding my blades. One by one, tug by tug, I layer my body with silver.

Blades, swords, daggers—every single inch of skin that can carry a weapon is filled.

Before I head out, I quickly lather oil on the small cut of cloth and wipe down the length of my dragon sword with ease. I can't help but feel close to Easton with it, which is peculiar because he never once saw it, but I can remember his love and excitement for dragons. The hope he held in his heart.

Once I strap the blade across my back, the heaviness that is always weighing on my heart when it comes to Easton lifts slightly, as if peeking an eye out and smiling at me.

Boots stomp across the camp, the power in the footsteps raising the hairs on the back of my neck, and for good reason. Knox's gait is full of strength as he walks around the wagon, joining myself and his court as we ready ourselves.

It's hard not being able to touch him as we're about to part. I know he's still upset with me over that, especially now that he must leave me behind with Axel and Aurora.

I can tell he's dipped into that place, into the mind of the warrior, which is just as lethal and sharp as his honed body.

His steely gaze snaps to Axel, and without so much as a word, Axel strides up to him. They grasp each other's forearms as Axel leans forward and whispers in his ear. Those steely sapphire eyes find mine, sending a chill down my spine.

Even after Axel walks away from him, our gazes don't pull away from one another.

I can feel the anxiety pulsing off him in waves, the hesitancy in his gaze, the utter terror filling his heart—all through the bond, allowing me to see what's beneath his current mask.

To all that walk past, we appear to be readying ourselves for the task at hand, but I couldn't be further from my physical body.

Opening the door to the bridge between our minds, Knox's essence appears on the other end. He radiates warmth and light as if the very stars are held within his soul.

We walk in sync toward each other.

My breath quickens as he nears, and when our hands reach out and our fingers slide together, electricity strikes between us. We collide.

Knox engulfs me in his arms. My cheek rests against his chest, the energy of his soul making it tingle.

Please be careful, he whispers gutturally.

I always am.

We don't disentangle as I tip my head back to stare at him. *You are my reason for breathing. Don't let them take you from me.*

Knox blinks, shock overtaking his features before tenderness returns.

I'll come back to you, Angel. I always will.

Axel jostles my shoulders and brings me back to reality.

I blink rapidly, my eyes finding Knox as he seems to do the same. He departs, but he doesn't stop staring at me until the very last second, having to almost rip his gaze away.

Ace runs to join him but pauses at my side. "I'll have his back, Delilah, I promise," he whispers in my ear.

Thank you, I mouth, as he's already gone and after Knox.

Aurora and Zephlyn are also saying goodbye, caressing each other's heads, and when she walks away the panic that infiltrates Zephlyn's eyes gut-punches me.

Knox and I aren't the only mates separating today. Including Hazel, who flew away with a watery gaze just moments before. They're all putting their lives on the line, their mates' lives, and their loved ones' lives for my own family.

I shove the guilt away. I cannot go into this with a losing mindset.

Aurora sidles up next to me, her spine straight and head held high. I don't think I'm the only one putting on a brave face today.

I sink my hands into her fur and mount. Axel gets on behind me. I lean forward and whisper in her ear, "I'll do everything I possibly can to reunite you two." At her small purr, I say, "Now take me to the king."

The palace that looms before me was never my home.

A home is a place, a person, a creature or a book, that makes you feel safe. Cared for and comfortable in your own skin. A home is something that simply makes your soul feel alive. A home is what your heart sings for.

My home was Easton. My home is the stars that wink down upon me as we fly under the cover of darkness. Now, I've found a new home with Knox and his court.

It is because of them I know what a loving home feels like, and I know without a shadow of a doubt that this stone palace is anything but my home.

I spent the past two hours on Aurora's back invisible, Axel's hand on the middle of my back, trying to prepare myself. The trip was silent, the usually quiet Fae behind me soundless for another reason entirely today.

I know he can feel it. The anxiety rolling off me in waves, the tension in my body. At one point, I figured he could even hear my ragged heartbeat thumping wildly.

But when we climb over the mountain peak, everything falls, my breath escaping me entirely, bile lodging itself in my throat. Tears spring to my eyes as the palace comes into view. The stunning architecture masks the horrendous events that occur within the walls and the monsters that it holds.

"I wish I could tell you something comforting right now but I know it wouldn't help," Axel says behind me.

I nod, recognizing the way his kindred spirit wants to help. Instead, I breathe in deeply through my nose, holding it for several beats before eradicating the toxic air from my body. Imagining I'm expelling all the memories with it.

I can do this.

"He can't touch you, Delilah, not now. I won't let him," Axel vows.

I say nothing, knowing that if he wanted to hurt me again,

he would find a way. After all, he already has with the sectors, with the citizens.

When Aurora lands, Axel and I waste no time jumping off and waving her away, but she pauses. Her golden eyes snap to mine, almost pleading with me not to go inside.

I pat her head, laying my forehead against her own. "I can do this," I repeat out loud, willing strength into my veins. "I'll see you soon."

Perhaps it's the training Knox has been putting me through each night in the confines of his tent, or the endless hours spent in our makeshift rings in the forest, or the fear of not wanting her to be discovered, but when I watch Aurora beat her wings and ascend into the sky, I will my invisibility to spread to her, and it does.

Before my very eyes, Aurora's large raven-black frame disappears above our heads.

It's as if my magic transformed the very air around her, willing the power of air from the court of Entrile to whisper to the particles surrounding her, begging for them to allow me to hide the glorious creature.

It seems as if Mother Gaia granted me my wish.

Axel gasps, and for the first time since I woke up this morning, I feel a slither of relief.

He will never get to her.

It takes every ounce of strength within me to turn around and face what's ahead. I'm grateful that I don't have to explain to Axel the turmoil raging on within my heart, the emotions rising from the depths of my subconscious.

Axel looks out over the palace grounds pensively as he asks, "Are you ready?"

My chest rises on a deep, shuddering inhale. "As I will ever be." *Which is never.*

As my eyelids flutter closed, I will my magic to spread,

not just to Aurora whose energy flies steadily back to safety in the campgrounds, but to Axel beside me too. When I open my eyes again, the Fae disappears to everyone except myself, as my magic allows me to see the warrior ready to strike.

My magic has never been this carefully controlled before. *Why is my magic stronger here?*

Screaming breaks out behind me, pulling my attention away. Axel and I rush for the side of the roof, watching as hundreds of men pour from the palace and the forest surrounding it. *I didn't even see anyone in the trees. How were they so well hidden?*

Orange flames dance brightly along the northern forest, climbing so high it appears as if it's reaching for the rising sun, feeling drawn to a kindred spirit.

The fact that we can see the flames from this far away…

Axel grins. "Nolan is wreaking havoc."

Frazzled soldiers scream orders, running to and from the palace, before rushing toward the burning forest.

Pure chaos has erupted and for once the screams of the soldiers make me smile as I hear the words, *rebels* and *capital attack.*

They've walked directly into our trap.

"Let's go," I say, leaving the sight of the capital's forests burning into nothing but char behind me.

I reach into my pocket and lather my hands with chalk, Axel doing the same. I marvel at how my muscle memory kicks into gear easily, how I did this for most of my adolescent and adult years.

Even so, it would be easier to teleport into the room but after hours of discussing the risks in detail, we decided to try and keep all magic to a minimum. We don't know what we're walking into, whether or not whoever put the magic ward around the lands and attacked Knox's mind is within the vicinity and working with the king.

It's daring enough to use my invisibility. I just pray Axel will be able to detect any of the wards before they detect us.

I descend first, the tip of my leather boots stretching to touch the stone wall. My fingers tingle as I dangle, pain racing along my bones. It's easier than it used to be now that I have Fae strength, but dangling from five stories high is still a feat.

At least now I have the knowledge and comfort that if I fall, Axel can fly and catch me or I can teleport.

I clear two floors, then pause at the familiar veranda. The intricate stonework spikes my heart rate.

The doors are open, the curtains fluttering in the wind.

It shouldn't be open.

Axel comes beside me, freezing as he sees what's snagged my attention.

My energy spears into the room, searching for anything with a heartbeat, while Axel's power searches for glamours and wards.

We both dip our heads, indicating that the room is clear. Then I swing my body over the stone wall and land on the veranda, my bones vibrating with the impact.

Even after Axel lands beside me, I don't dare turn around. Out of fear of seeing my old life and the memories every inch of this palace holds. As if standing still can fast forward time, transporting me to a future in which I have my mother beside me, and everyone I love unharmed and *away* from this gods-awful palace.

I just want to move time.

"Holy shit," Axel says under his breath.

The statement has me whirling.

I wish I hadn't.

What was once my sanctuary in this wicked and cruel world is now destroyed.

Stumbling through the door, I can't help the tears that spring to my eyes. I slap a hand over my mouth to stop the scream of shock from escaping my throat.

The books that I cherished throughout my entire life lay ruined. The pages torn from the binding, the bookshelves that held the many loves of my life, the lives I devoured and thought about for years lay shattered.

The wood crumbled into nothing but dust, barely able to tell what it once used to be, the stories it held. Some were even thrown in the fireplace, the covers of those that escaped their end sit haphazardly to the side, away from the charred remains of the stories that didn't escape the flames.

Feathers litter the area from the pillows that were shredded. The intricately carved wooden frame that once used to be my bed lies in shambles, the mattress torn beyond repair.

Clothes even trail from the closet, fabric and corsets and wires all ripped and tattered, tossed haphazardly around the room.

Everything in the space is coated in a thick layer of dust like no one has deigned to enter here since.

Axel's heavy hand lands on my shoulder, his voice holding every ounce of sadness that's in my heart. "Delilah, I'm so sorry."

My mouth opens and closes. I truly don't have any words for the heartbreak wracking my body. Which is ridiculous, I shouldn't be so torn over a room in a palace that I despised for years. But this was the only place he hadn't entered, hadn't tainted with awful memories. It was my sanctuary, and he defiled it—violated it beyond repair.

I know exactly who ruined this space. Who continues to

break the things I love most. Who takes away everything precious in my life.

And it terrifies me that I share blood with him.

I shove the turmoil racing through my veins down deep, below the surface of my consciousness to the dark abyss even my thoughts can't find. I need to have a clear mind when I walk through those doors and into the hallways of the depths of hell. I need to find my mother. That is all that matters right now.

I shake it off and whisper, "I'm all right. Check the hall for wards."

Axel pauses, contemplating my words until he decides better than to say anything and walks to the other side of the room.

"Clear," Axel says, slowly opening the bedroom door.

Revealing the bedroom across the hall. Easton's old room.

Axel doesn't stop me as I approach and open the door, but my foot stops mid-air on the threshold. The room is empty, holding nothing but darkness that mirrors the feelings berating my heart.

There's not a speck left of him, not a single trace that he even once lived here. It's as if he never existed, created just by my imagination.

The only belongings I have of him are what I took the night we ran away. The small satchel bag contained a few pieces of his clothing. I left a handful of them untouched in the bag, hoping his distinct smell would linger for years if I kept them in there.

Seeing his belongings gone is like a slap to the face.

Heavy boots march toward us on the marbled tiled floors. My head swings to the side as they grow closer. I pray to the forgotten gods, to whoever will listen, that this works. That there aren't any hidden wards placed around these walls.

Two guards round the corner and pause. My heart hammers wildly in my ears as their eyes bore into us. My breathing stutters out of me when the nearest soldier walks forward, his gaze piercing.

My entire body begins to shake as viciously as a leaf tumbling around on the forest floor.

The king must be right behind these soldiers. He's going to walk around the corner any minute. He knows we're here, and he's ready to intercept us.

But the soldier walks right past us, simply closing my old bedroom door.

They turn to each other with puzzled expressions.

"Did you enter the room?"

The soldier's frown deepens. "No, did you?"

"Obviously not if I'm asking you."

He rolls his eyes. "It was probably Lenard. He was on rotation last night. Nosey bastard."

They continue down the hall and take up positions at either end. My gaze whips toward Axel's, relief a tangible taste upon my tongue as he signals to move forward. A silencing shield snaps around us courtesy of Axel as we begin to walk, masking our sounds.

Despite it, we keep our steps light and although the soldiers stationed can't hear or see us, I still hold my breath as we pass them.

Without a backward glance, not daring to hurt my heart any further, I don't say goodbye to Easton's old room, to the life we shared. I can't bear to right now.

I spear my power out, allowing the iridescent golden magic within me to search for my mother. It moves through floors, walls, and people, past every living being until it finds its mark.

The halls feel colder somehow. As if evil has spread

further and consumed the entirety of the palace. And the further we descend through the south wing, the more differences dawn upon me.

It's silent.

Where it was once filled with scuttling feet, workers running around the halls with heads bent low and eyes on the floor, it's now just empty.

In fact, we haven't passed a single server or maid. The palace isn't dirty—the marble floors sparkle and the rugs have been dusted—so I know the king hasn't fired the help while on a rampage. Yet I can't help the niggling feeling racing down my spine.

Something has changed. I just don't know what.

What happened here since I left?

A deep cough fills the long narrow hall, pulling my attention to the left. The hallway I know all too well. The one I'd visited frequently, never being able to escape the king's fists.

The hall that leads to the nurse's quarters.

Swallowing past the thick lump in my throat and ignoring my suddenly burning eyes, I walk past.

I'm not going down it today.

That's a victory in itself.

But a new kind of terror stops my heart. Axel leaps in front of me as three soldiers come racing around the corner, marching quickly to the west wing, their swords clinking against their armor.

"Hurry, they've infiltrated the capital border!" one of the soldiers shouts.

My eyes widen in shock. They weren't supposed to infiltrate the border; they weren't supposed to even come close to it. There are innocent families in the capital.

I signal to Axel and run, my steps light and hurried. We need to get out of the palace as quickly as possible. We need to stop whatever movement the rebels have created. We planned for a distraction, not an outright war in the capital.

I stumble over my own feet when I feel a tug, not within my bond with Knox but a tug from my *magic*. As if it's a creature of its own, summoning me, telling me to hurry. I pick up the pace, my heart hammering wildly as it leads me to the council meeting room. There's shouting leaking from behind the black mahogany doors.

I gulp but breathe with relief when I don't find the king's personal guards outside the door. It's a relief and yet a fear to not know where he is.

I suppose he could still be back between the sectors, at the river, but I highly doubt it. And if he is, he won't be for long when he finds out the rebels infiltrated his precious palace.

I don't dare think about who he will blame, who he will take his rage out on now that my mother and I will no longer be present.

But one thing I didn't prepare myself for, the one thing I had managed to successfully block from my mind, now halts my steps as I come face-to-face with the looming hallway that leads to the throne room.

And a choice.

One that will not be taken away from me.

Rescue Easton's head or go on without him.

Chapter Thirty-Three

Axel doesn't have to ask. He simply places his hand on my arm and says, "Whatever you decide to do, Delilah, I'm all in."

Words tumble from my parted lips in a garbled mess of sputtering coughs.

It is the one choice I wish could be made for me, because looking down that pristine hallway, all I can hear is my head telling me to run.

I hear the ticking of a clock as I stand there, suspended in time.

Until the ticking finally stops. To pay its respect as I whisper, "I'm sorry, Easton."

I turn, spinning away on my heel as a tear escapes, rolling down my cheek. My magic tugs again, hard enough to make me stumble away from the hallway, leaving behind the memories that threaten to swallow me whole, and the friend that I don't have the courage to see in that state—as a trophy the king conquered.

I follow it blindly, letting my power lead me down endless corridors, past rooms holding gods knows what. Axel is silent beside me the entire way. But the magic takes us somewhere I didn't expect—outside.

Coming to a stop at the end of the hallway I pause, frowning at the endless forest that greets us.

"What is it?" Axel asks.

I shake my head. All the while, my magic beckons me to enter the western woods before me. "It wants us to leave the palace."

Axel gazes toward the woods as if it holds the answers. "Would he take her off the property?"

"I wouldn't in a million years think…" My words die off as curiosity has me following my magic's path. Past endless trees and branches that scratch against my leathers.

My breathing picks up, following the pattern of my hurried footsteps, and the moment it dawns on me where my magic is leading us, my heart drops.

The dungeon.

Where no one who enters is seen again.

It's where the king places who he believes are traitors. Where those who speak ill of the king lose a tongue, or worse, lose their head. The torture inflicted inside is unimaginable.

I've never stepped foot inside, for fear of the king locking me down there as a form of punishment and humor.

Axel and I come to a stand before the impending stairs cloaked in darkness. The groans and screams emanating from the space below send a chill down my spine.

Axel cringes. "What's down there?"

"The dungeons. It's where he sends traitors of the capital."

The smell emanating from the space makes us gag, the stench of human filth stuffing itself down our sensitive noses.

How can any of the soldiers tolerate being down there?

The smell alone would send those with a weak stomach running. How can any of the people *survive* this?

Because they're not meant to.

"Do you know how many soldiers are stationed in there?" Axel asks around a gag.

"No. I can't even see with my magic. There's…so many prisoners down there."

Axel unsheathes a blade from his back. "Then only one way to find out."

Mirroring him, I unsheathe the dragon sword.

Axel leads, his back tense and shoulders rigid as he moves down the cobbled steps. His eyes rove every inch that the dark corridor allows us to see.

The intensity in his gate makes my heart pinch. He took his vow and word to Knox to heart.

Dark rumbling murmurs float to us as we walk down and around the spiral steps, the stones growing wet the farther we descend, water dripping down the thick walls.

Down this far, the steps appear to shrink, the walls on either side of our shoulders caving in. The stairwell grows narrower until Axel's shoulders graze the walls, and he has to shuffle sideways to continue.

The next words to fill the narrowed staircase have Axel and me freezing.

A scuffle breaks out, the sound ceasing when a resounding slam rings through the hall. A long harrowing howl of a moan breaks out, along with snickers.

"Another one kicks the bucket, Jarod?" a man calls.

"Yes," another grumbles.

Laughter rings out. "Just don't know when to stop, do you?"

"Want to go take care of the tint in your pants?"

"Shut it, Lancaster. Your legs trembled the first time you took a life," the soldier snaps.

Howls bounce off the stone walls. "Yeah, and it wasn't in fear was it, Lancy?"

They say this as if it's a humorous thing, a running joke of how the soldiers take pleasure in the screams and terror. As if a sadistic man who cannot stop himself is the funniest thing in this world.

How could anyone find *pleasure* in torturing another life?

Axel's eyes are soft as he asks, "Are you all right?"

"I don't suppose we can lock them down here, can we?"

"Unless we want to quickly tip people off that your mother is gone…no," Axel says solemnly as if he's already thought about it.

I block out their words, the laughter and the cheers. My magic beckons me again—my mother beckons me.

I also block out the fact that these have been the men watching over her.

Axel and I walk side by side down the corridor, our gazes snagging on every cage and cell. They're all filled with men, women, and *children*. The king doesn't care. He doesn't discriminate, nor does he show mercy.

My feet stumble over nothing but air as a dreadful thought occurs.

Are some of Ordelia's men here in these cells? Being interrogated?

Not that you can even call these cells, or cages—they're holes of dirt. No beds or buckets, just dirt holes in the ground and the iron bars to keep them in their pits.

"Are you sure you felt her down here?"

It's the last place I would have ever looked, and with that thought in mind, it fuels my response. "Absolutely."

Axel doesn't doubt me, but the worry that enters his eyes

makes me fear for what we will find. Especially as we descend farther into the dungeons, past the cells of prisoners and to the rooms with wooden doors hanging open. The metallic smell that emanates from them tells me all I need to know. The sight that I find only confirms it.

Each room is designed for torture.

We pass a room with a prisoner, his hands and legs tied to a chair that's tipped back. A rag covers his entire face, and a guard stands above him, smiling, just as he dumps a bucket of water over the prisoner. He gargles and chokes around the rag, and the sound buries deep into my brain.

More rooms, more torture devices. Posts, chains, and ropes dangle from the ceilings. Whips lie scattered on the ground, splatters of blood decorating the walls. I swallow as we pass standing iron coffins, blades sticking out on the inside of the doors, making whoever stood in the contraction unable to move. The blades would pierce their skin if they even breathed.

How long do they force the prisoners to stand in it?

Every step is harder than the last, more bile churning deep in my stomach.

Screams of pure agony come from one of the deeper rooms. I can't not look…yet I wish I hadn't.

A guard chuckles darkly as he stands over a young man tied to a metal slab table. At first, I wonder what's happening, making my steps slow. Axel wraps his hand around my arm, urging me forward a moment too late.

My eyes widen as the guard starts to peel off the man's skin.

Axel moves just in time for me to twist and vomit. Missing his leather pants by mere inches.

The puke vanishes within a blink of an eye, a snap ringing through my ears. I suppose I now know who cleaned up

Hazel's mess the night the guards injected the Fae with poison.

He wraps an arm around me, dragging me forward as I continue to dry heave. He tries to rub my arm in a soothing motion, whispering in my ear to keep my head down, but nothing can stop the sounds and smells from bombarding me.

"We have to save them," I whisper. Lifting my tear-filled face to Axel, I see the answer to my question burning in his eyes. "We can't leave them here to die."

"It's too many people, Delilah."

I shake my head. "No, please let me save them."

Axel is torn, his gaze searching, a warrior plotting and planning. When his green eyes come back to mine with a slight sheen, I know it's hopeless. It's a suicide mission to rescue one person. To try and free hundreds…it would be impossible.

"When all of this is over," I say between hiccups, "I'm coming back for them."

The people in here may not hear me or know it, but I vow it to them. Let this be the one promise I make, the one I take to my grave.

I won't abandon them.

Most, if not all, of the people in here are innocent. Just like the people he's burnt to a crisp in Sectors Six and Seven.

Axel dips his head. "I'll help you. When the time's right."

Axel and I don't exchange any more words as we continue, but I do heed his earlier sentiment and keep my head down. I don't care if that makes me a coward. I need to be strong right now, and the sight around me is threatening to bring me to my knees.

It isn't until we reach the bottom of another rounding staircase do I *feel* her.

My necklace burns, sizzling my skin until it makes me

yelp. I pull the crystal away from my chest, finding it radiating as bright as a star. Brighter than I've ever seen it before.

There's magic down here—one that's extraordinarily powerful.

Axel frowns deeply at the burn mark on my chest. Both of us watch as my magic heals it, new skin overtaking the dark angry welts the pendant left behind.

Our eyes collide, but both of us know what it means. We need to be careful. The invisibility may not continue past a certain point, and by the cold darkness emanating from within, I know we're not alone.

"I'll go first," Axel announces.

Without giving me a chance to debate him, he steps out of the stairwell. After a moment, Axel pops his head back into the stairwell, beckoning me to continue. A smile threatens to escape—even in a place so vile—because the invisibility is still intact.

Descending the final steps, my leather boots cling to the damp stone. Dark murmurs from down the hall spur us forward and, rounding the corner, we find six soldiers stationed in front of a large wooden cage door. The hallway is short and narrow, making the burly men stand sideways to face each other.

"Did you hear about the rebels?" one asks.

The soldier standing across from him rolls his eyes. "They'll never get through the capital."

The soldier blinks. "They're already through the walls. They were heading to the capital's center last I heard."

"No, Simon said they were *at* the border, not *through* the border," he *tsks*. "Gods, you are a drama queen."

"Quit it, Arthur," another soldier snaps, his gaze deadly.

Arthur kicks off the wall. "Whatever, we need to rotate shifts. Go up to Lancaster."

My stomach sinks as the two soldiers walk past us. *Those sadistic bastards have been standing watch over my mother too?*

Axel grabs my wrist. One moment, my feet are on the damp stone floor, candlelight illuminating the way to the cellar door, and the next, we're shrouded in darkness. Axel teleported us into the room past the guards.

It's peaceful for a moment. Silent.

That only lasts so long.

Sirens blare throughout the dungeons, so loud it makes Axel and I drop, covering our ears with our hands. I'm not sure if I'm the only one who screams.

Flames erupt throughout the room, one by one, candles ignite, illuminating the circular cage.

The sirens stop abruptly.

The moment my eyes connect with heavy-lidded brown ones, I detest that I was right. I *loathe* that I was right.

I suck in a choked breath, screaming for two reasons.

Axel's shock roots him to the floor before he shakes himself out of it, jumping into action and walking toward my mother. Who is chained like cattle, beaten, and bruised to the point of being unrecognizable.

But I know her brown eyes. I know the color distinctly, the soft ring around her iris.

Except, it's not just the color. Her eyes are *clear*. I memorized that look for years, read the telltale signs of her body and prayed for moments like this.

My mother is lucid.

And what dangles in front of her is a body I will always recognize, even without his head.

Chapter Thirty-Four

I don't know where to look first—at the decapitated body, or my mother.

Easton wore a brown leather bracelet every day, a gift from his lover. He never took it off, and as my eyes glide down the body's left arm to see it still attached to his wrist, I know it's Easton…what's left of him.

They've preserved his body, with magic I assume, to torture me.

He knew I would come for her.

I turn to her, welts around her wrists, and the fluid between her feet both indicate she hasn't been moved from this position in a *long* while. My poor mother is spread bare, completely naked and dangling from the chains. Her once-soft skin is peppered with bruises and cuts and covered in dry blood and filth.

Only one brown eye is visible, the other swollen shut, her lip cut and cheekbones both bruised and bleeding. Her chest barely rises, the wheeze coming from her throat making tears pool in my eyes.

I swallow bile over and over and over again as my gaze slides to Easton's body once more.

I don't have time before the doors blow in behind me, not just from the six soldiers who were posted outside. It's all the soldiers within the dungeons.

And they're not looking at my mother or the body—they're looking at Axel and I standing in front of her.

Magic wards.

I stand, Axel drawing the sword from behind his back. My mother whimpers and the chains rattle behind me. Even in this state—chained, gagged, and wounded—I know she's trying to get to me.

With a flick of my wrist fire erupts along my forearm, spreading to my fingertips. I unsheathe my dragon sword, pouring flames down the steel as if the pommel is a living dragon breathing fire.

I've never been more grateful than in this moment for Knox and his grueling training sessions as thirty-six men pounce.

Knox is on the bridge between our minds in an instant, his agonized emotions pummeling me.

Fight, Delilah! Fight!

Three men fall in first, the ones who were gloating over being aroused by their kills, and I'm more than thankful it's them. I need someone to take out my rage on after finding my mother—*Easton*—down here, and I beat them to a bloody pulp.

The room works to our advantage, with only enough space for three or four soldiers to fight at a time. Axel takes on the two closest to the door, his long blades of steel slicing into their abdomens and throats before the men so much as raise their swords.

A soldier lunges for me, his steel coming down and

meeting my own. Sparks of flame dance off the swords as they clash.

Disgust coils through my entire body when I notice a tint in his trousers. Jarod. The man who gets off on torture and pain.

I sneer and pivot, shrugging off the weight of his sword and bringing my knee into his groin. Satisfaction rushes through my veins as his breath leaves him in a whoosh. I don't allow him a moment to recover. I bring my knee up once more and drive it into Jarod's nose, reveling in the sickening crunch that follows.

Golden hands wrap around his throat, and with all my might, I fling the man across the room, ignoring the way my shoulders flinch when he hits the stone wall with a resounding thud.

I don't have a moment to catch my breath. In the next second, another soldier is hurtling for me. With two daggers in hand and a sickening scowl, he descends upon me, flinging the daggers through the air. I whirl to dodge, but the steel grazes my cheek. Warm sticky blood drips down my face as I now stand before the dagger thrower and another menacing soldier, beady eyes boring into me.

Rage erupts down the bond. *Kill him!*

I use the moment they unsheathe more blades to my advantage and slide across the floor, directly for them. Sweeping my leg out in a wide arc, my boot connects with both their shins and knocks the men to the floor. I jump to my feet, snatching the dropped blades and embedding them in their thighs—then through the floor—impaling them to this rotten room they call a cell.

The men squeal like pigs, trying to wiggle their way out, but finding it impossible.

Without stopping, I reach for the swords strapped to their

hips and hurl them toward the door. The blades find their marks in the shoulders of the two men running for me.

Axel bares his canines, the two blades in his hands dripping with dark crimson blood. He whips out his arms to the side, slicing their throats in one movement. They crumble to the ground, gagging around their blood.

With four men left, their faces turn a molten shade of red as they take in their dead comrades lying in a heap in the room. Even the men I pinned to the floor lie dead as well, all with slit throats. I suppose I have Axel to thank for taking the lives I couldn't.

The ones remaining herd Axel and I together, our backs collide as we try to keep them away from my mother and Easton's body.

I dive deep into my well to finish them off, but—

It's empty.

What is wrong with my magic? Where has it gone? I look around the room. *Is there a siphon?*

The shock incapacitates me just enough to catch me off guard. The men lunge, but not with fists or steel. They latch onto my wrists and yank me so forcefully that my head snaps back with a resounding crack.

Their nails dig into my forearm as another emerges from the shadows, one neither Axel nor I spotted, and I am left utterly helpless as he drives a blade deep into my stomach. My breath expels from my lungs in an instant, replaced with a burning fire of pain spreading from my abdomen to my entire body.

The soldier's beady eyes never leave mine, pleasure filling the cold depths of his soul, as he begins to twist the knife in my gut.

I scream, spasming in their hold, wondering why time decided to slow for me in this instance.

Knox's scream of agony barrels down the bridge, so potent it makes my head rear back in shock.

Liquid rises in my throat, crimson dripping down my chin.

No, no, NO! he roars.

The room spins and turns, and suddenly, I'm no longer looking at the soldier but the ceiling. For a moment, I think I hear my mother calling my name, crying and screaming it.

Air whooshes through my ears as if I were dumped in a tunnel.

Then Axel is hovering above me, blue light pouring from his hands, fear lining his features.

The last thing I see before shadows claim me is my mother rattling her chains as she cries for me.

Chapter Thirty-Five

My head pounds a ferocious beat in my skull when I wake up again. I sit up to find Axel unclipping the chains that hold my mother. The movement makes her crumble into his awaiting arms and the relief that washes across her features is enough to make me cry.

Phillip and Ordelia said no one had seen her since I left… Has she been here ever since? Has Easton been here since he died?

Rising to my feet, I'm shocked to only feel slightly dizzy with a twinge of nausea. There's still the slice in my fighting leathers, along with the wet blood slicking the material, but where there should be a blade embedded in my stomach, I find nothing but smooth skin. Instead, crimson blood leaks from the now-dead soldier's throat.

I rush for the bridge. At my entrance, Knox falls to his knees and weeps.

I thought I lost you, I thought—

Shh, I'm okay, Knox. I'm okay, I soothe, running my fingers through his hair before cupping his cheek.

I'm coming as fast as I can. The tunnels have wards against teleporting.

Why are there so many wards? Why is he prepared for magic?

Before he can respond, Axel rushes toward me, his face strained as he carries my mother in his arms. "We need to move now, and you need to use your magic to get us out of here before more soldiers come."

The second the words leave his lips, shouts come from above.

"What about Easton? I'm not strong enough yet to carry him!"

Axel's eyes connect with mine, and I see the exhaustion there in them.

I have to leave him. I have to abandon him all over again.

A sob flies from my lips. I turn to his body and cry. "I'm so sorry, Easton."

It seems like I have uttered those words every day since he died.

Picking up my blade, I wipe the blood off. Heavy boots fill the stone hallways, shouting voices a deafening promise of death.

Lunging, my hand clutches Axel's arm and I dive deep into the golden well within me. Submerging my entire being, I swim in the small ounce left at the bottom and push with all my vigor.

Chancing one last glance, I whisper, "I'll come back for you, Easton. Together forever."

I close my eyes as the door behind me flies open, and my mother's scream pierces my ear before we teleport. It's harder than usual, as if I'm trying to walk through quicksand.

A hand scratches my back as we disappear, the sharp nails tearing the skin. The pain propels me forward through whatever wards were placed around my mother's room of torture.

Suddenly, I'm shaken violently. My eyes fling open, only to squint against the burning sunlight.

Axel's panicked face blocks my sight. "Hurry! I can't carry you both."

Adrenaline comes crashing down upon me once again, but it's not enough. Everything feels so heavy. My head flops to the side, and I see my mother now in the light—the brutality and the wounds she received…gods I'm thankful the monsters who did this to her are now dead.

How will she ever recover?

"*Delilah!*"

Axel's panicked shout snaps my gaze to his. The hollow ringing in my ears subsides, giving way to the sound of hooves, feet, and the rumbling forest floor.

My eyes widen, horrified. I was only strong enough to teleport us up and above the dungeons, not away from them.

They're coming.

"I barely have any magic left," I admit in a panic. "I can't teleport us. How are we going to get back into the palace?"

I run through my mind, flinging open the room that holds my magic well. It's almost depleted. How do neither of us have magic? What was inside the dungeons to siphon such power in such a short period of time?

Axel's eyes strain toward the forest. "Is there no other way into the tunnels?"

"Only one way in and out—the palace and the forest where Hazel is—but it's too far."

Axel lifts my mother higher as her lips part, a small wheeze leaving her chest. If I didn't have Fae hearing, I never would have heard the small sound. I lean forward, my brows furrowing as my mother's lips begin to move.

She's not wheezing…she's whispering.

At whatever she said, Axel's eyes widen. Then he grabs my arm and pulls me forward into a run. He doesn't say a word as we do, trying to keep our steps light as the king's soldiers hunt us.

Axel and I run along the outer edge of the forest, circling to the northern side of the palace grounds, and then he stops. His chest heaves as he stares at the open field looming before us, the stables on the other side. I begin to wonder what exactly my mother whispered to him.

"You can't be serious," I say flatly. "We can't run across an open field."

"Do you not have any magic left either?"

I shake my head, my gaze moving to my mother, passed out but still breathing in his arms. We need to get her help. It makes the words tumble from my mouth before I can think through them. "I have a little, we just need to be quick."

I don't dare tell him that my bones are tired, that I feel as if I'm on the verge of burnout.

It makes no sense that my wildly growing power is now empty. Even my invisibility magic barely takes anything out of me. So *where* did it go?

Pleading with the small drops of golden light, praying for it to hold on just a few more minutes, I cup my hands in it and make us all invisible. I don't dare waste a second. I'm on my feet and running as soon as Axel disappears beside me.

I can't see him anymore, not daring to waste another drop of magic on revealing him, I place my full trust in his hands that he's still running with my mother alongside me in this field.

I just pray he's moving as fast as I am.

The three minutes it takes me to run across the field are

the longest ones of my life as I push my Fae senses, ability, and power to their limit.

I've never been more grateful for the stables than I am now as I fling myself through its doors. The invisibility drops the moment my feet touch its flooring. Relief and tiredness make my knees buckle as Axel stands before me, breathless with my mother in his arms.

Scrambling to my feet, I grab one of the nearest hunting horses and mount it bareback. I use my legs to steady myself as Axel carefully hands my mother to me, her body limp, weak and fragile. Her bones stick out, and beneath the dirt and blood, her skin is a sickly gray color.

Axel snatches a horse blanket from the tack and hands it to me. My hand trembles as I accept it, wrapping it around my mother's naked body, maneuvering her just right so she doesn't fall off the horse.

Axel mounts another horse just as his head snaps up.

"They're coming," he whispers, kicking his heel into the horse.

I follow his lead, shooting off and out of the stables. I can't make us invisible, not without draining myself to the point of burnout. Wherever my mother told Axel to go, I pray that it works, that we can get there in one piece.

Easton's lifeless face flashes across my mind, his limp dead body lying in the grass feeling all too similar to how my mother feels in my arms. It feels like the night I lost Easton, how we ran away believing we had escaped, only to be attacked.

It feels like I'm losing him all over again, and when I see where my mother sent us a few minutes later, another sob flies from my mouth.

Three empty buildings loom on the horizon.

I snatch the necklace around my neck, nostalgia washing

over me as we ride to the compound, the treehouse hiding beneath the glamour.

I shake my head, trying to dislodge the memories of me and Easton with the movement.

It's too much.

Axel jumps off his horse after easing it to a stop near the old run-down well.

"Why did she send us here?" I ask, wiping tears from my cheeks. "The king knows about it. He'll come searching soon."

Axel starts ripping the old, rotted wood placed over the well. "There's another entrance."

Shock freezes me, my mother's chest rising shallowly against my own, and when Axel tears the wood away to reveal a set of stone steps, my mouth gapes open.

Was this what she told him?

He gently takes my mother off the horse, holding her with such care against his chest I know I will forever be grateful to him. I dismount the hunting horse, then tap their butts to send them back to the palace. If anyone is treated well in that horrid palace, it's the horses. They serve a purpose that the king cannot deny.

Axel begins descending the stairs carefully and I can't help turning to say goodbye.

Removing the pendant from my neck, I watch as the compound disappears, and in its place, the treehouse appears. The only place I had a sense of peace throughout my childhood.

Perhaps one day I'll be back under different circumstances, but for now, I have to say goodbye.

Shoving the pendant back over my head, I place the old rotting wood over the top of the well, covering our tracks.

The sunlight disappears, shrouding us in darkness. Sealing us in.

I can't believe all this time, so many answers lay beneath my feet, within reach of my hands.

The Fae in-between, and an escape.

I wonder where those Fae are now, if they're still being held captive, tortured even…or if they're somehow okay.

My mother doesn't stir in Axel's arms. She continues breathing, and as shallow and slow as it is, it at least never stops rising, and I thank the forgotten gods for that small miracle.

It feels as if Axel and I have been walking for hours down this dense path. The musty wet mold clinging to the air makes breathing difficult. And it's dark. So unbelievably dark.

Axel hasn't asked why I haven't lit a fire, and I haven't asked why he hasn't used any magic.

My feet stumble as the hairs on the back of my neck rise. Goosebumps burst down my spine, and I lunge forward. There's only one person that can elicit that reaction from my body, without me so much as laying eyes on them.

I hear his gasp of relief and the shadows around me that breathe a little easier as they run with me. The tendrils wisp across my face, stroking my cheek tentatively and searching my body for injuries.

Axel's footsteps pick up behind me as he feels it too, understands what has joined the darkness, that the shadows surrounding us aren't mere shadows but magic.

I fling myself into Knox's awaiting arms.

I can't stop the sobs that escape me as he crushes me to his body. Pinewood surrounds me. His fast and heavy heart thumps against my chest. Our skin sparks where it touches as he nuzzles his face into the crook of my neck.

"Angel," he breathes.

I run my hand over his head, tangling my fingers into the thick raven-black strands before running my hands all along his body.

He's here, he's here, he's here.

I know the separation was my own doing, but in this moment, in the comfort and safety of his arms, I cannot for the life of me remind myself why I made the choice. Why I forced us to part. Why I made myself go through all of that without him.

The tears streaming down my cheeks drop onto his shoulder.

Knox pulls his head back, those sapphire eyes searching my tear-filled ones. A small fire lantern sits behind him, Ace lighting it now that we've reunited.

The moment the tunnel is filled with the soft orange glow of the flame, the moment I can truly see Knox's face, his sharp jawline and his cheekbones and the worried gaze that pierces mine, I breathe.

"Have you healed all right?" Knox asks gruffly, his eyes dropping to my stomach and the hole in my fighting leathers from the blade.

I open my mouth to ease his worry, but Axel cuts me off. "She was sliced and stabbed. I healed her with what I had left."

The darkness in his eyes gutters to a new ferocity. "Is whoever did it dead?"

The shadows that were kept at bay by the lantern flame begin to crawl closer, vibrating with tense energy.

"I sliced their necks myself," Axel says coolly.

I place my hand on his cheek, happy when my touch

makes him refocus. "I'm not the one we need to worry over." Knox follows my eyes, his face slackening when they land on my mother.

"Oh my—" Knox clears his throat, his hold on me tightening. "We need to get her to the base. Annie can help us heal her."

Ace steps forward. "Hazel can heal her. She will know where to start first, and she's closer."

Hazel.

Her magic can see deeper into the body, guiding her to what needs attention and how to repair it. Knox and Ace don't suggest trying to heal her, because without Hazel's gift, we could end up damaging her further.

Knox lets me down but doesn't let go. Instead, he walks with me in the crook of his arm while Axel starts forward with my mother still in his arms.

"Axel," I call.

He turns.

"Thank you," I whisper hoarsely.

For everything. For myself, for helping me through the palace. For my mother.

Something flashes across his green eyes, perhaps understanding, because he doesn't say anything. He simply dips his head and continues moving.

As we walk, Knox wraps an arm around my shoulder, turning his head to the side to kiss my forehead.

"I'm so sorry, Angel," he whispers hoarsely.

I don't even have to say anything. He would have felt my emotions throughout it all, especially seeing Easton's body.

I return his gentle kiss before sliding my gaze to the silent Fae beside Knox.

Ace walks slowly, his brows furrowed and his eyes concentrated on the ground. Even Knox does the same.

"You haven't spoken about what it was like in the capital," I broach carefully. "Anything you care to share?"

Ace's forest-green eyes flash to Knox, an emotion in them, disappearing so quickly that I don't have time to discern what it means.

I whip my head to Knox. "Tell me."

The command in my voice makes Axel stumble before he picks up the pace once more.

Considering what I saw today...nothing would surprise me.

Knox opens his mouth but falls silent as footsteps echo off the tunnel walls in front of us. Everyone freezes, ears straining toward the dark hallway.

Ace shoves the fire in the mud, stomping his foot over it, and plunging us into darkness once more.

I cling to Knox as if my life depends on it.

All things considered, I feel it's childish to be afraid of the dark, or perhaps it's because of what I've seen that I'm afraid of it. The monsters that lurk within the shadows, waiting to pounce.

Darkness holds secrets.

The only darkness I have ever been safe in is Knox's, and he takes a step in front of me, maneuvering me behind his back. Axel falls behind us, protecting my mother.

We wait in the middle of the tunnel for what feels like hours with our swords unsheathed and our breaths mingling. We can't hide in this tunnel, nor can we turn around at this point. And with no power, I can't spear out my magic to identify them.

The footfalls pick up, heavy boots marching against the damp, muddy cobblestone.

One set of footsteps.

My brows furrow as they draw closer, their breathing so sharp and heavy it feels as if they're panting in my ear.

Knox's shadows spread through the tunnel, his shoulders tensing, only to lower in one quick exhale. He quickly sheathes his sword and swears profusely.

A kernel of Knox's shadow fire lights the wood in Ace's hand again, making my heart drop into my stomach as the tunnel is illuminated once more, just as Nolan rounds the bend. His face is drained of color, hazel eyes wild and frenzied with fear.

He doesn't stop until his gaze lands on Ace, and the look that passes across his features has Axel gently lowering my mother to the floor and stepping beside his twin, his shoulders squared and ready to fight.

My voice is hoarse as I ask, "Why are you here? You should be with the rebels controlling the flames."

"Nolan, what is it?" Knox demands when he doesn't respond.

Nolan's gulp is audible, and despite the command in Knox's tone, Nolan's gaze never wavers from Ace.

"I'm so sorry."

Ace's face slackens. "What for?"

Despite the question, everybody in this tunnel can *feel* why. The energy shifts, dread curling in our guts and swirling in the air.

We all know.

And for that reason, I don't feel shocked when Nolan speaks.

"They've captured Hazel."

Chapter Thirty-Six

I haven't felt this human in months.

The pain that radiates through my joints from my pounding feet on the cobblestone ground feels foreign. Singing a painful melody that makes my chest heave.

I must remind myself how to breathe as I round the corner and light flows into the darkness.

I must remind my body that this is normal exertion while you run. At least, it used to be, but it's a feeling I'm quickly relearning as I follow behind Ace, struggling to keep up with him.

Knox and Axel's steps fall beside me, the air flowing effortlessly into their lungs teasing me as we follow Hazel's scent trail. The rhythmic fall and rise of their chests point out the stark difference in mine, how my breath is choppy and wheezy.

This is not just exhaustion—this is what it feels like to be on the brink of burnout. How I felt inside the Tree of Life.

Considering a fear of mine for the past two months has been about my magic growing to the point it consumes me, I can't help but wonder where it all went.

Why am I struggling to breathe? To run? To function?

And beyond that, my head is light and dizzy, and my palms are clammy for an entirely different reason. It's panic, my fear for Hazel, the avalanche of emotions swallowing me whole.

I just had a front-row seat to their torture chambers in the dungeons, the torture they will no doubt inflict upon Hazel.

By the way the color leaches from Axel's face, the way he can't hide the fear engulfing his green eyes, I know he's thinking the same thing. Hazel may be strong, but she won't survive that kind of torture.

Coming out of the tunnel, Ace sprints past the two rebel soldiers who lie beaten and unconscious, the ones who were meant to protect his mate. He all but flies into the forest beyond, moving so quickly I can't keep up.

Knox's brows dip as his head whips to my mother and then down to his chest.

Why is no one teleporting? Why is no one using magic?

Ace skids to a halt, chest heaving, dirt and forest debris scattering, then drops to the floor, signaling for us to do the same. Axel gently lowers my mother once more, her breathing shallow but even.

Crawling across the dirt, I stop next to Ace, my breath stuttering as I watch dozens of wagons travel up the mountainside, toward a looming building twice the size of the palace. Its dark features lie hidden within the large canopy of trees.

The complex is a monstrous building.

It runs on for several miles, and without the aid of my Fae sight, I wouldn't be able to tell where it ends or begins. It's a building of camouflage. A building of secrets. A building of children…and now Fae.

The dozen wooden wagons are adorned with iron bars.

Those aren't humans in the wagons; I spot their elongated ears immediately. The ones that aren't adorned with Fae ears are hauled in wagons that shine. The iridescent color shimmers when the sunlight hits it.

My chest burns, the skin sizzling before I yelp and pull away my glowing pendant.

"Is that…?"

"A glamour," Knox muses, his brows furrowing.

The glamour not only conceals the outside to those within, but hides who lies behind the iron bars.

"The king is using someone very powerful to wield this type of magic," Nolan whispers, awe and fear dancing in his voice.

"If we didn't believe before that he had someone wielding magic, today confirms it," Knox says darkly.

"It's why we're all out of power. Something is siphoning our magic," I murmur.

"My magic wasn't drained until after we left the tunnels, though," he says.

Ace's gasp drags our attention away, his eyes flitting between the wagons and the complex. In the next breath, he launches himself off the mountain face, his legs pumping so fast it's as if the very wind carries him.

Axel and Nolan are the next to move. Their figures disappear then reappear a few feet in front of Ace, using whatever last reserves of magic they have to catch up. The pair collide with him, their arms latching around Ace's as they restrain him. He scrambles against their hold, his fingers clawing to get free.

Axel pleads with his eyes, his voice as soft as a feather, but nothing can get through to him, not even the bond of his twin.

"She's gone!" Nolan barks in his face to subdue him.

The words hit their mark, freezing Ace's wild limbs. His eyes pool with tears as they lift to Nolan.

Nolan droops, weighed down by guilt. "I saw them take her away. Iron shackles and muzzles."

Iron shackles and muzzles.

The words make him absolutely feral. "Why didn't you stop them?" Ace screams incredulously.

Knox snaps a silencing shield around us, using whatever last drops of magic he can spare.

"It was one against fifty…I couldn't do anything."

Ace's eyes narrow at him, distrustful. "Why were you there?"

"What?"

Ace grits his teeth. "Why were you close enough to watch her be taken?"

Nolan stumbles backward. "Some of the king's soldiers were taunting us about captured rebels. I was worried." Nolan places his hand over his heart. "Ace, I didn't do anything, I would never."

"I know you didn't do *anything*," he spits.

Nolan's face crumbles. Getting slashed with iron wouldn't have hurt as bad.

Knox steps between the two, his presence demanding Ace's attention. "We will do more harm than good going into that complex blindly. None of us have magic and we're exhausted beyond reason." Knox's eyes bore into Ace's. "We will kill her if we go in now."

"We'll get her back, Ace," Axel reassures him.

He shakes his head. "I saw the look on yours and Delilah's face when you came back from the dungeons… I *smelled* the rotted flesh and blood." Ace's voice cracks as his shoulders start to shake. "They're going to hurt her beyond repair."

I don't dare contemplate why the king is capturing Fae, or *how*. All I know for certain is that we need to get into the compound now more than ever.

A small whimper rises behind me.

We all turn to see my mother come to, her eyes bloodshot but still clear.

I rush over, kneeling before her. Her brown eyes flash with recognition before tears begin to pool in them.

"We need to get her medical attention," I whisper. My chest pangs with guilt, my heart physically hurting at the next words I force myself to speak. "We need to leave, Ace."

His eyes flare with indignation and disbelief. "What did you just say?"

"We can't do anything for her right now. I barely have a drop of magic, and we can't go in there without it." I fling my arms toward the wagons that disappear into an open door in the complex. "Especially when they're using magic."

I hate the betrayal that darkens his features. The twist of his lips. The gasp of shock.

"She's right, Ace," Axel whispers.

He shrugs out of their grasp as if he was burned. The movement fills Axel's face with pain.

"I can't leave her," Ace croaks.

My heart breaks at his anguish. I don't blame him. If that was Knox, they'd have to physically drag me all the way back kicking and screaming. I *know* what I'm asking. I understand the ramifications. It will hurt him, hurt everyone, to leave Hazel in that gods-awful complex. But we don't have a choice.

"I would do anything for her. *Anything*," I repeat. "But even I know that if we go inside right now, we will not only kill her but ourselves." I pray the conviction in my voice carries what I feel in my heart. "We will get her back."

My mother cries out in pain, and I do everything in my power to not move. To keep my gaze locked on Ace, to not break the connection. I don't want him to think I'm choosing, to think I'm prioritizing anyone. Hazel is my family, just as much as my mother is.

I gulp as her whimpers grow louder.

"Please, Ace," I beg. The sounds of my mother's pain mingle with my voice. "We are no good to Hazel dead."

Knox places a hand over his heart. "Ace, I swear to you we will return the moment our magic is replenished and we have a plan."

Ace doesn't utter a word as he stalks past Knox and me, silent tears rolling down his cheeks. His wings unfurl, beating wildly as his chest heaves on a mournful wail.

"I-I'm so sorry," I whisper.

I don't know who I say it to, but I feel the need to voice the words.

We're all here because of me, because I wanted to save my mother. *Hazel* was here to help me. And now it feels like we traded my mother for her.

Axel lays his hand on my shoulder. "He'll come around."

But even as Axel says it, I know he doesn't believe it. Again, if that was Knox...*I'd hate me too.*

"Nolan, take over for Axel," Knox says, indicating to my mother.

Without hesitation Nolan moves, picking her up with such careful tenderness it shocks me. Perhaps it's because she's a mother and reminds him of his own...or perhaps it's because he doesn't hate me after all. For whatever intention, he holds her tight, yet softly enough not to harm her, as he flies her back to the base.

They all take off through the canopy of trees to avoid detection, but I can't seem to make my feet move. It isn't until I feel Knox's large hands, the warmth from his palm singeing my back, do I break.

My knees buckle, but he never lets me hit the ground. He scoops me into his arms and I lay my head on Knox's chest as I finally—*finally*—allow myself to feel.

The sounds coming from me aren't pretty, the sobs wracking my body sucking the life from me.

This is what I have always feared most with Hazel. I feared that I would drag her to her destruction because I brought her into this mess. I told myself that I hadn't pulled her into harm's way when she met Ace because something so beautiful and precious came out of it. She had found her mate, her life partner, her love.

As Knox flies us back, the heavy silence between us grows, the bond tugging relentlessly.

I'm too tired for words, but we don't need to speak.

Knox plants a featherlight kiss against my temple when we reach the rebel base. The makeshift tents hide within plain view. It's the only leverage we have against the king. He's completely unaware that his enemies sleep under his nose.

Annie runs toward us when we land, beckoning us, her gaze wild. "Hurry! You need to come quickly."

Without hesitating, I shove my exhaustion aside as we sprint for the medical tent, all while my mother's pleas echo throughout the camp.

We burst into the tent, taking in the chaos of nurses and soldiers bustling around.

My eyes roam the room, searching. "Where is my mom?" I ask the nearest nurse.

Her wide eyes meet mine as she points to the woman sitting on the cot.

"Mom?" I ask.

The nurses tending to her whip their heads to me,

panicked before they begin to back away from the woman. As they realize she isn't just a hurt citizen, but the Queen of Aloriah.

Except, the woman on the cot is not my mother.

"Delilah."

That voice…

"Mom?" I ask, confusion slamming into me as I stare.

"Delilah," she calls again.

Gasping, I stumble forward and sit on the cot, my knees giving way to the shock of her changed appearance.

"Everybody out!" Knox snaps. "Everyone but my court and Annie."

I'm grateful that he knows I'd want her here with me. She's the only familiarity I feel in this moment with my old life because the woman sitting before me is supposed to be my mother, but she looks completely different.

Where her hair was once brown and short, it's now long, so beautifully long, and matching the color of her changed eyes. Her *violet* eyes.

Mere moments before, she was covered in filth. Bruises and cuts marred her skin and her bones were protruding. Yet now all I can see is the faint outline of her collarbone against her clean, pristine skin.

I stutter, no coherent thought or words escaping my lips as my mother allows me to stare. As if she knows the shock and was expecting it.

"I don't understand," I say.

She reaches forward and I can't help but note that her fingers are *webbed* together. I'm so utterly stunned I don't flinch or pull away as her silky fingers graze my tipped ears.

"You grew up beautifully," she says in awe.

Knox slowly approaches me, his arms reaching for me, but his gaze focused on the woman before me. He doesn't make it within several feet before my mother shoots out a hand, purple light flowing from her palms. She cocks her head, her own gaze never leaving mine.

"Let her be. She is safe."

My body begins to tremble, my mind refusing to believe this is happening. I swallow thickly as she stands, her movements graceful and elegant as she steps over to the makeshift tub in the corner.

When was that prepared?

Her eyes never stray, her palm never wavers, the violet light never dropping as it holds everyone back while she lowers herself into the water.

"It's nice to officially meet you, Delilah," she says as she submerges.

A violet tail propels out of the water.

Chapter Thirty-Seven

Annie stands behind me with her mouth gaped, jaw hanging low, the medical kit in her hands shaking. The woman in the tub turns to her, a humorous smirk dancing across her lips. "There's no need for that, love. You can place it down now."

Her voice, her words, her *mannerisms*—everything has changed before my eyes.

The moment the purple light drops, Knox is next to me within a second, his back as tense as a rock. He pivots just slightly to get me behind him as I stare at...a mermaid.

My ears start to buzz, a thousand hummingbirds taking flight and drowning out all the chatter in the room. Knox tenses further, his head snapping to the right as he hisses something and flares his canines.

The sight makes the hummingbirds die in my ears.

Blinking rapidly, I feel nothing but utter disbelief. I can only focus on violet—the color of her hair and her eyes and her *tail*.

"My mother's a mermaid," I murmur to no one in particular.

Silence falls over the tent.

Off to the side, Nolan helps Annie to a seated position on the floor as she fans herself. Her once rosy cheeks are leached of all color.

"Hello, Delilah," my mother whispers.

I don't dare open my mouth, not even to the women who taught me it was impolite to ignore others when they spoke to you. Not as I let my eyes roam her body…or what's left of her once-human form. Even her ears have elongated to look like mine, though hers are made of scales.

"How?" I croak.

She cocks her head, seemingly assessing me right back, cataloging what's changed within myself.

"It's a long story," she muses.

"We have all the time in the world," Knox cuts in sharply.

Her violet eyes steel as they slide to him. "No, you don't." A smirk plays on her lips. "Those mind tricks won't work on me, King. Although you already knew that."

"Was worth a shot." He leans forward, resting his arm over my legs. My mother also doesn't miss the protective movement. "However, you also know that I won't take your word for whatever story you're about to spew."

"How do you—"

"She can see it," he says simply.

I snap my gaze to my mother, the details clicking into place.

"You're a psychic."

Does she know the mermaids who led me to Knox? Is that why they helped me that day? Is that why they're helping me now?

I can see the same questions swirling in the minds of Knox's court. Even Ace looks at me with sympathy. Another kernel of my life that was never true.

"Was any of it real?"

The softness in her violet eyes is comforting, despite the tidal wave of truth that comes crashing down upon my heart.

"No."

My body jolts backward as if I was physically struck. The deep breath I try to inhale feels like blades being shoved down my throat. Knox abruptly stands, a menacing growl ripping from his mouth. Even the twins take a step forward. Annie's golden eyes fill with unshed tears as she turns to me.

My arm reaches out and latches onto Knox.

I need to hear, I say to him in my mind. The key word in that statement being *need*, not want.

"No?" I repeat out loud.

"No, none of it was real," she says calmly.

All the oxygen in the tent seems to evaporate.

"Are you even my mother?" I ask around the painful lump in my throat.

Logically, it would make sense for her to be my mother. After all, I had to receive these powers from somewhere. Her being a mermaid with magic wasn't exactly what I had in mind, but it's possible. At least, that's what I repeat to myself in the tense moment of silence as she stares at me, unblinking.

"No."

The word physically hurts, more so than before. My lungs stop moving, my heart stops beating, and for a moment, everything around me seems to pause. Time freezes as my world is pulled out from under me. Everything I ever thought I knew about my life—gone in the blink of an eye, destroyed by one syllable.

How did I never see it before? The more I stare, the more I notice her features and how different they are in comparison to mine. Where my lips are full, pouty, and heart-shaped, hers are small, a larger bottom lip to her top. Where my face is round, cheeks full and peppered with freckles across my small button nose, her face is sharp, angular. High cheekbones and a straight nose.

It was all an illusion. Her face, and my life.

The fairy tales my mother—no, *Eleanor*—told me as a young girl come flooding back through my mind. Every time she spoke of the Fae, mermaids, and their lands. The way she worshipped the forgotten gods, the universe, and the lunar cycle. Her wistful tone in the stories I now know was about her home, her *people*.

This is how she knew so much when it was forbidden to speak of them. How she knew such information when their stories and books were removed from the libraries of Aloriah.

The Queen of Aloriah, married to the king who detests magic, is a mermaid.

The reality around me only begins to move again when all the air in my lungs rushes from my mouth in one large whoosh. And then time is speeding up, uncontrollable and unpredictable.

Bodies move around the too small tent in a flurry of activity. Their mouths run a million miles a minute, their words blurring and mixing as one. And as the rope wrapped around my heart begins to tug, slipping from my grasp, I know who sped up time.

Me.

My body starts to float and drift, flying high as my heart abandons me once again, despite how tightly I gripped that rope.

My mind spins, dizzy and yet empty all at once. The pressure of the world around me caves in, squeezing out the small inner child until she steals my heart, the little thief running deep into my mind, the small pitter-patter of her feet akin to the erratic beat of my heart. Until she slams a door shut, submerging me in darkness and silence.

Her small sobs leak through the bottom crack of the door.

I try to open my mouth to speak, to beg the little girl to come out and convince her that she's safe, but it's useless. I can't continue to lie to her, not when I don't feel safe myself.

My body sways, floating higher.

I crane my neck behind me to check if my wings propelled me into the air, but I find nothing but the top of the tent. Furrowing my brows, I peer below, shocked to see myself sitting on the cot. As if I haven't moved, Knox sits beside me, unaware of the shell of a person his arm is wrapped around.

It's odd to watch myself.

The utter devastation on my face is surprising, considering I can't feel anything emotionally. Perhaps my body knows what's happening and my mind simply can't process or *doesn't* want to process the truth.

Eleanor's voice floats to me as if she's the only one who can penetrate the shield I've created. I used to find her voice comforting, her clear eyes a blessing. Now all I feel is dread when she opens her mouth.

"I've watched you grow since the moment you were an infant." Her voice softens. "I'm not sure who your mother is, but I wish I did."

If Eleanor is not my mother…then who is?

I watch my eyes glaze over, tears rolling down my cheeks, but there isn't an ounce of emotion on my face anymore. Just my body trying to process what my mind won't let me feel.

"I was taken for one thing and one thing only." Her violet eyes slide to Knox. "To be controlled and used as a weapon.

That's how no one could kill him, how he got away with everything."

"He was always one step ahead because he had you," Axel murmurs.

Eleanor's lips flatten into a line. "His personal seer."

My stomach drops, rising into my throat as I suddenly fall. My body is propelled back into the world, along with my heart.

It slams back into its cage once more, but an electrical storm explodes within me. Lightning flashes in my mind, words replaying in my ear, throwing sentences at me as if someone cut up lines from a book and chucked them at my head.

Gold is the song she sings.
The ones with scales see all.
Black as night yet not alive.
Busy, busy mutts.
The truth will be set free.

Everything she's ever said to me over the years, the ramblings before I left—they were all messages, *visions*.

Gold is the song she sings. My golden magic as it spoke to me.

The ones with scales see all. The psychic mermaids who reside in the Mason River.

Black as night yet not alive. The demonic creatures and their rotting black blood, their darkness.

Busy, busy mutts. The demon hounds that hunted me.

The truth will be set free. Which is now. My world being pulled out from under me.

My mother never spoke in ramblings. They were riddles. As the mermaids do.

"How did you break the spell placed over you?" I motion to her tail, utter disbelief coursing through me despite seeing it for myself with my own eyes. "The spell that made you human?"

"I wasn't made human. It was a form of torture, being trapped in that horrible body. It was a gods-awful spell and I'm thankful to be rid of it." She grimaces. "Made using my power feel as icky as oil."

I quirk a brow. "Again…how did you break it?"

Mermaids and their words, always swimming around the truth.

She rolls her eyes, flicking her wrist to point at all of us. "Where do you think your magic went?"

Knox's eyes darken. "You siphoned our magic?"

"How else was I supposed to break that horrid spell?"

"Did you really have to take all of it?" Axel growls.

"Why didn't you tell me?" I blurt. Knox's hand tightens on my leg. I lean forward, my hand clutching the pendant I keep hidden beneath my clothing. "When you gave me this, you were lucid. Why didn't you—" I pause. "Was there ever anything wrong with your mind?"

I clutch my pendant tighter for another reason entirely. This is not an heirloom that ran in the family, nor was it found by us… It was Eleanor's.

"That would be a lovely spell your father had placed on me after he found out about the little stories I read to you." She huffs. "He didn't appreciate someone trying to undermine him. However, as you might have noticed, it didn't take him long to figure out the kinks in the control he had over me." Eleanor's eyes shift, tracking my white-knuckled fingers holding the pendant. "I'm glad you've managed to keep that, though. When my mother gave it to me, I lost it seven times." She chuckles as if it's the funniest thing in the world.

My throat grows impossibly dry. The pendant that has been wrapped around my neck, guiding me through all this monstrosity, the one that helped save the Fae race…is a mermaid heirloom. It could be thousands, if not *hundreds* of thousands, of years old.

Knox cocks his head. "If you were his source of magic, who placed the spells on you?"

"I wish I knew, boy. Another little trick that minx has figured out—how to stay hidden and out of my sight."

Boy. I nearly choke at the word.

"How old are you?" I find myself asking out loud.

Eleanor *tsks*. "Didn't anyone ever teach you that it is rude to ask such a thing?"

"Forgive me," I drawl sarcastically. "My mother was never around to."

Eleanor swims forward, water splashing over the side of the tub. "I truly am sorry, Delilah. I tried all I could to shield you," she says, her gaze dropping to the pendant. "The king is a master of control…always one step ahead of everybody."

"No thanks to you," Nolan mutters under his breath.

"I'm ten times stronger than you. Don't forget that when speaking to me," she snaps.

Nolan's lip curls back in distaste. I suppose the cocky attitudes of mermaids are hereditary. The woman I watched growing up wouldn't hurt a fly. She was docile, tame…everything the king made her to be.

The woman I thought was my mother never even truly existed.

Nausea swirls in my gut. I place my hand on my stomach as if I can contain it, keep it within me just for a while longer. I just have to get through this. Then when the time is up…I have to try and live with the truth that has been dumped into my lap.

"Were you the one that placed the spell on me? To contain

me?" I try to steel myself for the answer as I push past the lump in my throat. "Was I truly never a human?"

Eleanor at least has the decency to whisper her response. "Yes."

"Why? Why would he do this?" I explode and jump to my feet. "Who is my mother? Another Fae masked as a human under his thumb because of the spells *you* placed on others?"

I can't contain the tremble in my hands as my voice rises, anger flooding my veins, threatening to take control of my actions and words entirely.

"You think I *wanted* to be contained and imprisoned on land? To be controlled like a puppet, moved as he wished, used as he desired? I was a *toy* to him. A weapon to be used at his disposal."

"You weren't the only one. You made sure of that," I spit. "You are part of the reason he has so much control and power!"

I watch my words hit their mark on whatever guilt resides within her for the harm she's caused. She may not have had a say in it, but it was her hands, eyes, and power that helped shape the king and his influence today. The supposed mighty kingdom that he built.

It's all a lie.

An entire kingdom and crown, his *throne*, built atop deception.

I close my eyes with a deep sigh as I try to tame my emotions. "I'm sorry for what he did to you. But I cannot look at you right now. You represent everything that never existed in my life. You represent the illusion he created, the lie that was my life for over twenty years." I walk out, keeping to my word and avoiding looking in Eleanor's direction. The court follows me, and I turn to Ace. "We need to come up with a plan on how to get into that complex."

Without saying another word, I walk off. This time, they let me be to mourn the shambles of what used to be my life.

Annie's voice carries to me on the wind, courtesy of Knox. "Perhaps today is a good day to bring out that fancy Fae wine Nolan smuggled in his satchel."

Chapter Thirty-Eight

Hidden within the depths of the rebellion tents I pace…and pace…and pace. Unsheathing the swords strapped to my body, the blood dripping off the silver onto the muddy floor reminds me of the dungeons and the atrocities we saw.

Hazel…the torture they would be inflicting.

I jerk my head forcefully as if it can shake the thoughts and memories away.

Not now.

Grabbing the nearest canteen, I start pouring water over the silver. The dragon sword lies heavy in my palm. Another thing I failed at, *Easton*. I scrub the blood off the sword as if it has personally wronged me.

I'm on my hands and knees grunting, my hand wiping vigorously when Knox walks through the open tent flaps. Pinewood and ocean float to me, carried by the wind.

His footsteps are light, almost dragging as he kneels before me. His large, tanned hand wraps around my own, halting my movements. The small reprieve that rushes through my body at his touch is short-lived because my mind

—no matter how badly I want to forget it, how badly I want to move past it—won't stop replaying my mother's—*Eleanor's*—words on repeat.

It won't stop churning, spitting out thoughts and questions faster than I can handle.

It simply won't stop.

"Angel."

Knox walks through my mind, his soul pure and light, whereas mine feels heavy and ruined.

Tainted.

I'm crouched in a corner of my mind, Eleanor's words and the memories of my fake childhood swirling around in the once bright and happy blue sky of my mind.

It's endless.

I don't know where one lie begins and where others end. I suppose they never do, as if created by time itself to be limitless.

Knox's fingers are gentle as they brush under my chin, slowly lifting my head to his. My eyes collide with his heavy sapphire depths.

"What do you need?"

I repeat the words he said to me all those months ago.

"You. I just need you."

Knox wastes no time and hauls me into his lap, letting me nestle my face into the crook of his neck. I don't mean to; I truly try with all my might to cling to the semblance of control I thought I had over my emotions. Yet when Knox begins whispering in my ear about how everything will be okay, how he will be with me every step of the way through this while his gentle hands stroke my hair and back…I simply fall apart.

I feel as if I'll forever be the girl who breaks down. I should be used to this by now, the chaos that comes with having the last name Covington, but every time it still shocks and stings.

In a muddy tent, the blood of others dripping off my skin and leathers, swords, and knives scattered around us, I crumble.

I break for the little girl within me who never understood why her mother stopped speaking to her. For the little girl who felt abandoned. For the little girl who would look at passing families, picking out the differences between her own and wonder, *why can't I have that?*

For the little girl who believed she didn't get it because she wasn't good enough to be loved.

For the little girl who believed she deserved to be beaten.

For the little girl who wanted her father to hug her.

For the little girl who wanted to hear one more bedtime story from her mother.

For the little girl who simply wanted to be loved.

The tears that pour from me, the sobs and the piercing wail that wrack my body, are all for her. The injustice of it crushing. The weight of what was truly reality suffocating.

My life was never mine—not truly.

It was crafted and molded by the hands of others who never had the intention of filling my world with love.

But with the endless plans we have for the complex rolling in my mind, I take pleasure in the fact he's not the only one who can twist fate.

Pulling back, I look into Knox's eyes, just as heartbroken as mine.

"Can we trust her?" I croak.

Knox brushes a lock of hair behind my ear. "I'm going to try and look into her mind."

"But she will know. You already tried."

Knox shrugs, averting my eyes. "I'll sort something out."

"No lies."

I can't handle any more lies, even if it's Knox withholding information to protect me. I'm sick and tired of people hiding the truth from me.

He sighs. "I'll make a bargain."

I shoot up, scrambling out of his hold. "You can't! Bargains with a mermaid are suicidal, even if the woman was my pretend mother at one time or another," I bite out. "Mermaids words are twisted and wicked and cruel. You taught me that. Do not make a bargain with her, I beg you."

"She was being controlled, Delilah, very similarly to how you were."

"I don't care. She is the reason why he is as powerful as he is, the reason I never knew I am a Fae." I swallow thickly. "Don't push me on this, Knox."

He leans forward, his soft lips landing on my forehead. "Okay, Angel. Whatever you need."

I run to him down the bridge as shadows swirl and dance around me. Flinging myself into his arms, I let him hold me, the warmth of his soul comforting mine. Shadows consume me, stroking what little golden magic remains.

Every time we leave these tents, I fear that you will be harmed.

Knox pulls me back, his hands never leaving mine but he dips his head, forcing me to stare into his sapphire eyes.

Don't you know I feel the same? That I want to protect and shield you from the dangers of this world? It took every ounce of strength within me today to walk away from you. To let you go into that palace without me. My body was shaking with the restraint needed to stay away. My thoughts tried to convince me every second that you were dead. It took everything within me to keep your promise and to give you what you wished most.

Knox's hand burns brighter with every word, his chest emanating stardust light.

I do not care if I get hurt to protect you. I will bleed for you, die for you if it means your safety. There is not a thing in this universe I would not endure to keep a smile on your face, Delilah.

A thick sheen of tears coats my eyes, blurring my sight. I blink rapidly to memorize this and the words. The way his eyes grow wider, the sapphires burning brighter, and how his soft hands never stop caressing my skin.

How Knox's words make my heart beat for life. He replaces the hollowness in my chest with thoughtfulness.

Everything is brighter with Knox. Life is easier—lighter. As if his stars shine within my mind, lighting up my world from the inside out.

One word, one syllable, and four letters come to the forefront of my mind. It's a feeling that pounds through my chest when I think of him. It has my heart skipping wildly with anticipation. It has pure happiness radiating from me.

Love.

A small word that holds a significant meaning. How could something so simple represent something so extraordinary?

My lips part, ready more than ever to tell him exactly what burns through my heart for him, but nothing escapes. I'm left feeling jarred by overwhelming panic that I cannot find the right words to express how deeply I care for this man.

That hurt spreads throughout my chest, blood spilling from a wound, as Knox's light dims.

I lay my palm against his cheek and apologize with my eyes, begging him to read my mind, my thoughts, my heart. But for once, Knox shakes his head, not wanting to spoil the words he so desperately wants to hear.

Those words scare me more than anything, and at this moment, I cannot seem to shake it.

Clearing my throat, I pull away into my physical body. "We *have* to get Hazel back, Knox." My chin trembles as I try to hold back more tears. "I cannot let him harm her because of me."

"I'll do everything I can to get her back."

I move off his lap and he rises to his full height, his body imposing. I tilt my head back, savoring every inch of him. I reach up and lay my palm on his cheek, my heart galloping as he closes his eyes and leans into my touch.

"I am so grateful to have found you," I whisper, continuing in my mind. *I couldn't face this without you.*

My whispered words have his eyes snapping open.

"The real gift is you, Angel."

Lifting onto the balls of my feet, I reach for him, my toes curling as he lowers to meet me halfway. His lips brush mine, his warm breath fluttering across my skin.

"As one," he says gutturally.

"As one," I echo.

I savor his kiss and touch, letting the contact ground me, and soothe me. When I pull back, I wish I could return.

I hate that we must hide who we are to each other.

Knox's smirk is purely feline. *Don't you like all the sneaking around, Angel?*

My mirroring smirk is answer enough.

I shove his shoulder playfully before leaving the tent, feeling his heated gaze on my back. Once he falls into step beside me, the amusement fades from his eyes, replaced by cool indifference. His cold mask of a Fae king is restored.

"Do you think Ace will ever forgive me?" I ask quietly.

"In time. Once Hazel is back in his arms, he will be able

to think clearly once more and see that it was a suicide mission to go in when he wanted to."

"Until then, I wouldn't blame him if he hated me," I murmur.

You are not to blame for her disappearance, Angel.

I click my tongue. "No, I know exactly who is to blame for this."

When we reach the medical tent, I fling open the tent flaps, marching for the woman who lied and betrayed me every day of my life.

My entrance silences everyone, including Eleanor.

I need to talk to her. If anyone knows how to get into the complex, it's her. Gods know she owes me.

Ignoring everyone else, I stride up to her tub. "What magic resides in the complex?"

Eleanor leans over the edge of the tub, resting her chin in her scaly hands. "That, my love, is a mystery to even myself."

"You're a psychic. I know you can see it."

She rolls her eyes. "Just because I possess the gift to see does not mean I see *all*."

"This is not the time for riddles and games. You'd think after hiding my true identity, you'd show me the decency of answering my questions."

Her violet eyes flare to the whites of her eyes until she blinks, and it recedes. "I cannot see anything to do with the king. I never have."

Knox steps forward. "He has someone else?"

Eleanor grimaces. "He always has someone else. He has to, to hide his movements."

The attack on your mind at the lake, I remind Knox. *Eleanor was in the dungeons; it couldn't have been her.*

This means it also couldn't have been her who sent the premonition of the women being assassinated in the forest.

Was it real all along? Am I now receiving visions of others lives?

Eleanor's eyes snap to Knox as his own narrow, a silent conversation passing between the two minds.

"Do you know anything about the complex or not?" Ace asks, his impatience growing.

"No."

It wasn't her at the lake, Knox says after seemingly conversing with her.

"What *do* you know?" I ask.

Eleanor leans back, making herself comfortable. "Honestly? Not a lot. He's one of the very few people in this world I cannot see." Her head slides against the tub as she turns to me. "There was a reason he chose me, plucked me from the river."

My head cocks. "How were you taken? The entrapment spell was in full force."

Anger shutters over her violet eyes, as if memories are assaulting her, and when she speaks her voice is as hard as steel. "I would do anything to know the answer to that question."

Shock spears down the bond, but Knox doesn't let it show on his face as he asks, "Care to share the reasons as to why he chose you?"

She shrugs. "Not particularly."

"Have you anything useful to share?" Nolan asks, his jaw clenching.

"Expect the unexpected."

My jaw grinds as I try not to lose my temper. Before I can speak her gaze is sliding to mine once more as she swims forward.

"It's lovely to see your true self. I always wondered how

you'd look and which powers you'd possess. Do tell me, is it extraordinary?"

"As extraordinary as I'm sure it feels to return to your mermaid form. Do tell me, is it freeing?"

A light sparks in Eleanor's eyes at my sarcasm. "I see you picked up a few characteristics from me. I had hoped you'd also learn *empathy*, but—"

"If I lack anything, it's because you were never present as my supposed mother. And do not ever take credit for raising me with whatever characteristics you deem worthy. They were all from Annie. She was more a mother than you ever were."

"Who do you think was in the king's ear, twisting his arm to allow you the courtesy of having Annie and Easton in your life?" Her smile turns saccharine. "Don't forget, love, I was never your mother. Never meant to be, either. Your father twisted my fate and yours. It appears to be the bastard's specialty." Her hand waves across the room. "Take Easton, for example. That young boy was destined to become captain of the guard and now—"

"Do not speak of him! You have no right!" I scream.

"Delilah, words cannot express how sorry I am, for everything I was forced to hand you, but when I could, I truly tried to help you. I tried to be the mother you so desperately deserved, and I tried to give you the life I knew you wished for. I was never meant to be your mother and, truth be told, I know deep down I was never meant to *be* a mother, but I tried with you. I tried to give it all to you but—"

Her lips move feverishly, her violet eyes growing heavy, and I try to tune out her words as a sinking feeling settles into my lower abdomen.

"How did the king know where we were?"

My question stops her rambling. Her eyes widen.

"What?"

"You heard me."

Knox steps forward, feeling an impeding sledgehammer preparing to rise and fall and break my heart.

"Delilah."

"No. How did the king know where Easton and I were? He was meant to be in Sector Six."

Eleanor bites her lower lip, and for the first time, guilt flashes in those violet eyes. But it's nothing compared to the agony I have endured every day since losing him. "I'm sorry, he had—"

The sledgehammer strikes.

"I do not care for your pathetic excuses! Every single death the king has claimed is because of *you* and the information you told him! You could have led him astray! You could have told him a different area! Instead, you gave up our exact location and he's now dead!"

I had always wondered how he found us when we were so careful.

Now I know.

Is that why he hung his body in front of her? To torment her?

Placing my hands on the edge of the tub, I lean so far forward she's forced to pull back.

"I hope you rot in hell," I seethe.

Yanking myself away, my knees shake with fury as I march to the meeting tent. I'm grateful to find Ordelia and Phillip inside poring over maps. I ignore their looks of pity. I suppose word has gotten out that the Queen of Aloriah is a mermaid.

Lifting my chin, I allow the fire burning through my veins to erupt in my eyes. "We have a complex to burn to the ground."

Annie doesn't leave me to my thoughts for long. No sooner have I sat on my cot is she striding into my tent unannounced, disappointment in her eyes.

Guilt burns through me, but not for the reason she thinks.

It may be wrong of me, but I chose to spare her the details of Easton's body in the dungeons. She doesn't deserve the torture it would inflict upon her mind.

"Please do not lecture me on manners or kindness," I say before she can speak. "Because of her, Easton and thousands of Aloriah's citizens are dead."

She plops herself beside me, the cot creaking under our weight as she wraps an arm around me. "No. Because of the *king*, they are dead. Eleanor was nothing but another one of his prisoners."

"She had a choice, Annie. There is always a choice."

She frowns, openly stating her displeasure. "You know better than I that no one truly has a choice when it comes to him. I know you're angry, Delilah, and rightfully so. I couldn't begin to imagine having my life flipped as much as yours, but Eleanor is not entirely to blame."

She runs her fingers through my hair as a tear escapes, rolling down my chin.

"Oh, dear, I know it hurts." She pulls me closer to her side. "And I know that pain will never go away, not truly. But she did try to be a mother to you, in every way she could. She—"

"You were my mother, not her. She didn't try, because she was never there."

Annie ducks her head, trying to capture my eyes. "I appreciate the sentiment, I truly do. I see you as my own and

I have since the day you came into this world, but you cannot hold her captivity against her. She didn't choose to be captured and used."

I bite my tongue, allowing the pain to clamp down on the tears threatening to burst free from me. I also ignore the truth of Annie's words and how they want to burrow into my heart. I straighten my spine.

"How are you not angry?" I ask.

"Because for you, Delilah, you see a mother you have lost, one you never had." She sighs. "Whereas I see another battered and broken woman the king has damaged."

The words sting, not because of her displeasure for my denial again, but because she is right. Of course she is—mothers always are.

But that fire within me will not let go. "Broken or not, she is responsible for sending Easton to an early grave, and I will never forgive her for that."

"I'm not asking you to, dear. I'm asking you to see both sides. You weren't the only one abused by him."

I shrug, my cheeks burning hot with rage. "Perhaps if she didn't place the spell on me that contained my powers, I could have fought back."

Annie's sigh is deep and filled with sadness. "You aren't going to hear a word I say," she mumbles under her breath.

"No, I won't," I say, picking up on her words.

She shakes her head, despair wrinkling her brow as she places her hand atop my knee. "I will give you time to have your anger and your emotions. But there will come a day when you realize what he had to do to force those spells from her. And when that day comes, you will regret the words you spoke to her." She rubs my knee, a mother comforting a daughter. "I just hope that day isn't too far away."

Without another word, she rises, not even looking over her shoulder as she exits the tent.

And as she suspected, the second I'm left alone with my thoughts, the anger ebbs away to misery. Tears pour down my cheeks, and disgrace coats my tongue.

Chapter Thirty-Nine

I never thought it would come to this.

Sitting in the back of a wagon with shackles around my hands and feet, I begin to wonder when it all started. How I ended up here, and where exactly it happened.

Was it the in-between, the Fae I found trapped? Or was it the pendant Eleanor gave me? Or was it the moment Easton was murdered behind my back? When I was swept into the Fae lands and met Hazel? When I met Knox? The moment I walked the streets of Azalea for the first time? The moment I felt the bond snap between me and Knox, securing our hearts and souls together forever?

I believe it started long before that. Before Eleanor told me stories of mermaids, fairies, and the Fae lands. Long before my father ever hit me. No, this moment began when I started dreaming of the Fae.

It started with *my* visions.

Which is why I find it comical that I never saw any of this. That all I saw was my demise and my end in that depthless black pit.

Perhaps that's where they're leading me now.

Whatever spell Eleanor placed over the wagons is sophisticated. Not only does it glamour what's inside the wagons to those outside, making us appear to be guilty human prisoners, but it doesn't allow whoever is inside the cramped wagon to peer out. The only indication that we're still traveling through the mountain forests is the bumpy terrain jolting my body. Both discombobulating, and nauseating.

At early dawn, after excruciatingly long days of planning and allowing our magic to restore, Ace, Axel, Knox, and I set out with a small handful of soldiers, stopping along the western mountain borders with the complex and the palace lying east.

The planned pick-up went perfectly. I suppose it was the easiest task of what's to come ahead.

Knox's glamour held firm as we were all transformed from Fae to human rebels. Covered in a week's worth of mud and filth, we gave them the idea we were trying to access the palace through the mountains. To do what, we let the soldiers' imaginations run wild.

The moment we set foot on the complex parameters, soldiers came rushing down the mountain, a wagon in toe. The soldiers from our camp handed us over, claiming to have found us, a group of rebels, near their camp. It didn't take much more convincing than that. They were more than happy to take us to the capital for a hanging, but under the king's orders, they were needed elsewhere. Conveniently, the nearest cellar was in the complex.

It made me sick.

None of us spoke a word, acting as if we had accepted our fate, but it made me realize that the king never cared to hear the other side of the story.

The rebel soldiers played their part well, grimacing and hissing as they shoved us into the wagon.

Two weeks ago, I would have thought the act to be real, that their hatred ran true, but since seeing the damage of Sector Six together, friendships have begun to bloom once more, along with hope in my heart that humans will one day welcome us.

The wagon comes to a sudden halt. Everyone smashes against the back of it, our grunts of pain ringing out so loud the driver yells to zip our mouths.

I lock eyes on a young man. His build is tall and lanky, his hair hanging long past his ears, swishing against his wide shoulders. His beautiful sapphire eyes seem to glint and shine as they connect with mine.

I burst out laughing when I first saw the glamour Knox put upon himself. Even as a human, he just *had* to choose a handsome face.

Yet right now, I can't seem to conjure up the humor I felt. Not as the wagon begins to move once more, and someone barks orders outside.

We've arrived at the complex. I pull myself up to look out the window until remembering that our view outside is glamoured as well. The unknown sets my heart racing.

Where are the wards placed?

The ones that set off alarms the moment magic is used, like down in the dungeons when we transported into Eleanor's room. The type of magic wards that could make every soldier in the vicinity start shooting arrows without question at our wagon if they're set off.

The man in front of me reaches out his hand. His human skin is smooth, Knox's calluses from decades of training gone.

The four of us hold our breath as we ride over a large

bump. The moment the light shining through the bars vanishes, throwing us into darkness, panic screams for me to flee.

Knox's hand in mine tightens, while he also clutches me in his arms on the bridge between our minds.

The wagon continues, riding for what feels like hours in the dark. No more bumps or rocky terrain as we ride over the complex's smooth underground flooring. The wagon halts, the doors flinging open to reveal a dark tunnel lit by small gas lamps lining the walls. Six soldiers stand around the wagon, arrows and swords raised as they begin to haul us out.

Relief floods me as I realize the glamour is intact and didn't set off any wards. The soldiers drag me, grunting, as my weight drops in their arms from the heady rush.

As we're thrown into cells that are undoubtedly at the lowest level of the compound, the soldiers turn the key and lock us behind the bars. The ones we had planned to be behind. I smirk.

We wait for night to fall, when the fun will truly begin in this place of hell.

Ace won't look at me.

It's the only thought playing on a loop in my mind.

We've been sitting here for hours, and he hasn't made eye contact with me once. All I've had to stare at is his endless fidgeting. I don't think I've ever seen the Fae remain still for longer than twenty seconds. It's only gotten worse since Hazel disappeared.

We're about to walk into a death trap, and Ace won't look at me. Anything could happen, anything could go wrong.

Easton and I never argued, not really. I'd never seen him

cross with me, so I never knew what it would look like, how it would feel to disappoint someone who meant everything to me...but now I know. Ace is pulling the face Easton made when he spoke to his father, only that look is now because of me.

To be fair, Ace won't look at *anyone*, his focus solely on the hall beyond our cell. Like he can see through the hard material, all the way to where Hazel is being held captive.

It's an odd sight, to see the twins' roles reverse. How Ace sits pensive and quiet while Axel talks, trying to make up for his brother's lack of words.

"Do you feel her near?" I dare ask, cutting off one of Axel's many rants.

Axel tenses while Knox's eyes slightly widen. The pair seem to hold their breath as they turn to Ace and wait for his reaction.

A muscle clenches in his jaw. "No," he spits.

"It's the magic wards, Ace," Axel chimes in, rescuing me as I sit here flailing for something to say. "They don't want their loved ones banging down the door."

"Axel is right. It's probably a spell," Knox says, trying to inflict confidence no one feels.

I bite my lower lip, my thoughts stirring as I begin to form a new plan.

"Knox and I will go scope out the complex," I declare.

Ace finally—*finally*—lifts his head to mine. "That's not part of the plan. We were all supposed to wait until nightfall and then leave the cell to search for her."

Axel frowns. "Delilah, we chose nightfall because they would all be asleep."

I point to Ace. "I don't want to watch Ace continue to stare at the wall for several more hours wondering whether she is alive or not. And we can't send him out because he cannot be trusted to think clearly in this state."

Ace snarls.

"We'll scope it out, try and narrow down our search tonight," Knox says, backing me up and diffusing the fire before it starts. He stands and joins me. "We'll come back as soon as we can with details on any wards as well."

Ace frowns, jumping to his feet. "If anyone is going, it's me. I am the one—"

Knox places his hand on Ace's shoulder, halting his movements. "You are a mate who is fraught and in distress. You are not thinking clearly, and that will only get someone hurt. Let me do this for you, Ace. Let me find her."

I can see the war raging in Ace's forest-green eyes, the desire and need to be reunited with Hazel overpowering his concern for our safety. "Thank you," he finally whispers, dipping his chin to avoid my eyes.

Axel looks like he wants to protest, a similar moral war running havoc through his mind as he has to choose between his king and the happiness of his twin.

I wonder what the twins' bond feels like, if it's anything like the mating bond, where they can feel what the other is experiencing and read each other's minds.

Axel's eyes stay glued to his twin, even as Ace avoids his gaze.

His twin ultimately wins the war. "Please be careful," Axel whispers.

Knox claps the twins on their shoulders. "Always am."

Shadows swirl where Knox and I were sitting only seconds before, and as our glamours fall away like melting ice, the shadows replace the images of our human masks. My mouth falls open, staring at the new glamour. I've never seen anything like it.

I move to touch it until Knox grabs my hand gently and pulls it back.

"It will distort the image. It may appear lifelike but it's all smoke and shadows."

"Fascinating," I breathe.

"If it begins to droop, use your air to lift the shadows," Knox tells Axel before turning to me. "Are you ready?"

I swallow thickly, readying myself for the first test. "As I will ever be."

Ace and Axel's hands slide to their hips, where their swords are glamoured from sight, and every one of us holds our breath as black shadows swirl around the steel bars, sinking into the lock. A single click rings throughout the empty hall, and then a shadowed hand pulls the cell door open.

We don't dare step out, waiting to see if any soldiers come running down the halls or if alarms blare throughout the complex to indicate the use of magic.

As the seconds turn into minutes and moments continue to pass where we're still alone, my lips twitch up into a smile as I walk out of the cell.

What the king must've spent to create such a complex must be astronomical. It makes me wonder how long he's been planning this. A complex of this size wasn't created overnight, nor was it a plan thrown out in the wind.

So, when exactly did this all start?

Hidden within the depths of the capital mountains, in the belly of the complex, are tall arched hallways, crafted of impeccable stonework. Yet the essence emanating from every hall is eerie. And despite the gas lamps posted on the walls, it's dark, the shadows whispering to one another. Alive and beckoning for us to join them. Almost gleeful for our arrival. I wonder if the shadows recognize Knox, his magic a kindred spirit, but the grimace that's plastered across his lips has me thinking otherwise.

Not daring to risk using an ounce of magic in case of wards and traps against it, we try to keep our steps light and silent, though nothing can mask the echoes of our boots. Luckily, the footsteps mingle with the soldiers walking throughout the monstrous complex.

The cells we pass are surprisingly empty. Even ours is new and fresh, clear of filth and bodily fluids. It seems to be the same for all of them, meaning they haven't been used.

Where are the Fae we saw being carted in by the wagons?

Climbing stairs after stairs, hallways after empty hallways, clearing levels of empty cells, we finally hear signs of life on the third level.

The strike of swords, the clang of metal and grunts of pain, have us unsheathing the blades strapped to our legs, previously glamoured. After we climb two more levels of hallways and pass endless doors, we find the source of the noise.

The stairs open to a level completely devoid of halls or rooms. Dozens of beams arch high above, holding the structure together. The entire level is one large, open room.

Mats surround the area; walls are covered floor to ceiling with racks of weapons. The orange glow of the gas lamp flames glints off the silver of swords, daggers, knives, arrows, and axes.

A line of archer targets lines the wall. Children no taller than my hip stand poised, their tiny arms straining, muscles shaking as they pull the bow back, their practice arrows flying, zipping across the room. Landing within the targets' red ring.

I'd gasp in shock at the skill they have perfected in such a short amount of time, but when I open my mouth, the room reeks of perspiration and metallic.

A cry of agony has me whipping my head to the side. A young boy, who can't be older than nine, sobs, his tears falling down his red-streaked face. He stands, clutching his arm to his chest. It's bent at an unnatural angle.

His fighting opponent, a boy no older than he is, suddenly stops. Guilt races across his face and he reaches out to help the other boy. The trainer beside him slaps his outreached hand.

"You do not help your enemies!" he bellows, back-handing the boy.

Not one child gasps or shrieks, their pale faces unfazed. This is their new normal. This is their daily routine.

It isn't long before a stoic soldier comes and escorts the young boy out of the room. His lack of empathy for a young innocent soul is sickening.

A group of children march in the corner, rows upon rows of them. Their postures perfect, backs straight, shoulders squared as they stare at and follow directions from what appears to be a drill sergeant pacing before them.

The fear in their eyes is noticeable, their misery palpable in the air.

Knox drags me away, forcing me to leave behind the repulsive sight. I don't realize I'm crying until he pulls me into a dark corridor and wipes my cheeks, his fingers coming back damp.

Not long, Angel, not long.

Sucking in a deep breath, I dip my head, resuming our

walk. They won't have to undergo that treatment for much longer, I remind myself.

We cannot fail these children.

We cannot fail Hazel.

After a day of Ordelia's men lying low within the treetops around the building, we were able to map out where the soldiers' sleeping quarters are stationed within the building. But beyond that, everything remains a mystery, including the movements of the children and their own sleeping quarters.

It isn't long before antiseptic shoves its scent down my nose and throat. As a child who grew up spending more time in the infirmary, I know the sterilization smell all too well. I suppose it's wise, stationing the healers a short walk away, a level above that training ring.

I can't help myself, walking past the large double doors, one of them slightly ajar, I peek inside and find the little boy who broke his arm from earlier sitting on a cot.

But what's inside looks more like a hospital, not a nurse's quarter. Dozens of men and women, young and old, run around the room, tending to crying children, the metallic smell of their blood a tangible taste in the air. Despite the heavy cleaning supplies, I don't believe they'll ever be able to wash the stench away.

And the number of beds that line the room…

How often are children hurt? To imagine that this was the plan all along, that the king built a wing as large as a hospital, accurately predicting the amount of pain that would be inflicted is horrendous.

Knox doesn't have to pull me away this time. Turning on my heel from the remnants of a childhood that looks far too similar to mine, I continue on. My eyes, ears, and mind are open to what we must find.

Hazel is in here somewhere and, judging by the empty

cells we passed, they've moved her away from the children. Except the further we explore, the more I realize the expanse of this never-ending compound.

The halls have no end. No door leads to an exit, like a wild maze of mirrors, but the rooms we pass seem to be designed entirely for the children.

Circular rooms filled with small- and medium-sized chairs face a podium—classrooms for their education. Yet instead of colorful artwork and lively personalization for their young minds, everything is sterilized, bland.

What type of education are they teaching these young perceptible children? What does the king deem important?

Perhaps war games.

Considering he's an expert in them, he should be the one giving the lectures.

In what I believed was a never-ending structure, Knox and I reach the far end of the children's building, coming to a stop outside a door smelling of spices and herbs. The clangs of metal inside are for an entirely different reason as to swordsmanship and fighting.

The kitchen is full of chatter, men and women with their heads bent low as they prepare dinner. Looking at the serving sizes, it's doubtful they serve these to the guards. It wouldn't be enough to sustain a grown adult. These must be for the children.

Knox turns away from me, his eyes lingering on the end of the hall.

There must be another entrance to another part of the building. We haven't seen any soldiers besides those stationed with the children, but Ordelia's men reported hundreds coming to and from their sleeping quarters in the northern wing.

I turn to him, my brows pulling low. *You think there's an entrance they're hiding from the children?*

Have you seen an exit to the outside? His brow quirks, already knowing the horrible answer.

He's truly stolen every ounce of freedom from these children. No wonder they all appeared so pale. They haven't seen the light of day since they've been taken.

I shake my head, unable to fathom the horrid reality.

It's a prison.

Not just any prison. Knox grimaces. *Have you noticed that there are only small children present?*

My eyes widen. *They've separated them by age.*

Knox nods. *They must be keeping Hazel elsewhere too. We should have come across her by now.*

We begin walking back, our eyes sweeping over every inch of the stone walls, looking for the hidden entryway the soldiers and cooks would have to use. No wonder there aren't soldiers posted around the halls—they don't need them. This is a prison, and they know the children can't escape their cage.

This just got a lot harder, I say to Knox.

Ace isn't going to like what we come back with.

Then we don't go back. Not until we can find the answers. I owe Ace that much. Turning around in a circle, I stare at the hallways surrounding me, the feeling of the stone walls caging in. *Besides...we can't help the children escape if we're trapped ourselves.*

Knox rubs the back of his neck, his eyes pensive as he stares into mine. An emotion flashes across them, but I don't have the time to discern it before it's gone. His eyes steel as he straightens. *We use our magic. We would have set off at least one alarm by now with your invisibility if they had them.*

A smirk dances across my lips. *Gloves off?* I tease.

Knox's mirroring grin is just as devilish as he purrs, "Gloves off."

A silencing shield snaps around us as tendrils of shadows and flames dance along his wide shoulders.

My own golden tendrils swirl and it sings its praises as I let it out of the well. The golden iridescent magic sparkles against the dark contrast of the stone hallway.

"As one?"

"As one, Angel."

Chapter Forty

A blast knocks me to my feet. Sirens blare throughout the complex, the warning sound so piercing, blood trickles down the side of my face from my ears.

Soldiers scream from somewhere else in the complex.

"FIRE!"

Knox and I whip our heads to one another, our horror-filled gazes colliding. My breath stutters. Dread coils tightly in my stomach.

"It's too soon," I whisper. "It's too soon!"

Knox and I traveled every hallway and entered every room of the children's wing…twice. Our magic slithered along every crevice and crack of the space, probing for any hidden doors or compartments.

We know that the rest of the children are elsewhere, we know that the soldiers rotate shifts, we know they don't sleep here. But now I'm beginning to question if our sources are correct, or if my eyes are just deceiving me.

We should have come across the soldiers' entrance and exit by now.

Sixty seconds ago, our biggest concern was why our magic hadn't felt it yet. Now…

"We don't have a way out of here!" My eyes bulge out of their sockets as I slap a hand over my mouth. "Oh gods. We've orchestrated this plan only to set fire to trapped children."

Clinging to Knox's forearms, I shake him, screaming over the sirens. "Why did they set the fire off early?"

Knox stares at nothing as his chest heaves, the telltale glassy eyes telling me he's speaking to someone in his mind. "We have to get you out," he breathes as fear pierces his eyes.

Shaking my head, I take a step back as he moves to reach for me. "No! Tell me what's happening!"

His eyes flick back and forth, searching mine. "They got word that the king is on his way."

Ice slithers down my spine.

Knox takes the moment of reprieve to grab my hand and start pulling me through the hallway.

The plan cannot stop. The wheels are already in motion, spinning wildly with no end in sight.

I yank my arm free from his grip. "No! Ace will never forgive me if we can't get her out. Gods, if we can't *find* her…" My eyes plead with his. "We can't leave these children, Knox!"

He runs his hands through his fingers, roughly pulling the strands. "FUCK!" he screams. He rapidly analyzes the hall. "We just need to keep searching."

More sirens blare throughout the compound, bells different to the fire drill chiming wildly overhead, the sound so deafening I cry out in agony as the sound grates against my eardrums.

"Turn it off!" I scream.

Tears trickle down my cheeks, mingling with my freckles. Knox roars with pain, shooting his hand out.

Darkness consumes the hall, consumes the wing, suffocating it until…

Peace.

The sirens stop, but the screams from the children still persist.

"It's too soon, Knox," I whisper, horrified.

Knox grabs my arm, propelling us forward, making my legs move past the shock that froze my body. "We need to get out before the king reaches us."

"We haven't found a way out yet!" I cry.

Knox's footsteps are as harried and wild as my own as he says, "We're going to have to teleport!"

"There are too many children! We don't have enough time!"

The look that passes over Knox's eyes tells me that he knows we have not come in and saved them but doomed them all.

A sob claws its way from my chest.

What have we done?

None of us prepared to be taken into a fortress. We never planned to enter a hell with no escape.

They are alive and breathing…and I'm not leaving them behind.

"We're finding that door," I grit out. "The complex is large and made of stone. The plan already was for Nolan to keep the fire contained to the soldiers' quarters."

Knox's eyes are frantic, examining every stone, wall, and corner. Every square inch that we pass. Searching what we have already searched before. The panic that sweeps over his features makes me push my legs faster.

"We need to take the children before they run through their emergency drills."

Knox comes to a halt, his grip on my arm flinging me backward. Knox wraps his other arm around me as he makes the stones beneath my feet disappear. White light encompasses our bodies, and then we're floating through time and space until we touch down onto stone again.

When I tip my head back to look at Knox, I expect to see his strength to get me through this, and yet all I come to find is his features slack, face drained of color.

We've transported right into a madhouse.

In the children's cafeteria, chairs and tables are knocked over, food littering every surface. Children are crying and screaming as they run aimlessly around the room. The sound of their tiny little hearts thumping wildly in my ears, playing a song of chaos. Some even hide under tables, their small hands covering their ears and their eyes squeezed shut as if they can disappear from a nightmare that's come to reality.

But what has Knox standing in shock are the small gray puffs of smoke trickling in through the ventilation holes in the ceiling.

"We didn't account for smoke inhalation," I whisper in disbelief.

My eyes close on their own account. Another error on our part, another misstep, another wrong judgment call that will have disastrous repercussions. And then my eyes roam the room, coming up short on the ones that should be getting these children out of the burning building.

"Where's the soldiers?"

Knox's teeth clench so tightly I'm surprised they don't snap. "They left them to die," he growls.

That's what we think—until pounding boots make us spin.

Knox and I draw our blades as we hold our breaths, waiting for our assailants to round the corner but instead, two familiar warriors appear.

Axel shakes his head. "What magic did you two use?"

I rear back. "How did you know we used magic?"

Ace's eyes roam the room, searching. "You two set off the alarms. We heard about it when the soldiers ran past our cell. They were planning to leave us to be burned to death. One less hanging they had to deal with."

That doesn't make sense. We didn't *feel* a single alarm or ward. We never heard anything until the fire alarm. How did they know we used magic?

"They were silent alarms," Axel explains after seeing my confused expression, a slight grimace on his lips.

My eyes shutter closed, only to fly open with a frown. "We started using magic hours ago. Why didn't it set it off then?"

Axel blinks. "Perhaps you walked past—"

"We were on our third round of searching. We didn't cross a new area when the sirens went off."

"Someone else in the complex is using magic," Knox says coldly, marching forward without hesitation. "We need to get the children out. Now."

"We need to find Hazel," Ace barks.

My head snaps back, recoiling at the venom in Ace's words. He's always the calm one, diffusing every situation and argument. To see him in such a state…

Knox spins around. "We can't find Hazel unless we find the exit. We need to get the children out."

Disappointment and betrayal flash in his eyes, and for once, Ace does not look at Knox with admiration.

Ace marches forward, his lips curling back. "You want to leave her again?" he growls.

Knox's features soften. "Ace, they're children. They are helpless."

I shudder at the promise of violence in Ace's eyes. "She isn't here, Ace. We have searched every single inch of this fortress…and more."

Ace's bewildered gaze turns to Knox as he explains.

"There are sections to the complex. They've separated the children by age."

His eyes narrow. "Are you telling me there's a possibility we set fire to *where they're holding her*?" Ace roars.

His anger terrifies me and I'm not the only one. Axel rears his head back in shock, his mouth agape before he steps forward and attempts to calm his twin.

Axel shakes Ace until he looks at him. "You're not thinking straight right now. My brother would *never* leave innocent children to die."

The sounds of the children's coughs float to me, each one dropping a rock of guilt in my stomach. Shaking my head, I walk away. Every second we stand here arguing is another second wasted.

I rise onto the nearest table that hasn't fallen over, kicking the food and trays to the side. I soften my voice, letting my magic carry the gentle sound to every ear. It's too late to avoid the sirens now anyway. My eyes burn, threatening to shed tears as I face hundreds of terrified children.

I clap my hands to get their attention. "We're going to play a game called follow the leader! Who here would like the honor of leading their friends?"

I keep a smile of confidence I do not feel plastered to my face, the picture of serene calm to these tiny little eyes.

"My name is Delilah Covington, Princess of Aloriah."

Small gasps ring around the room and, surprisingly, a few giggles.

"I seem to have lost my helpers and am in dire need of help! Would anybody like to help me? I need a very strong person to show me where the exit is."

I wait. It's a tense moment of silence, broken every now and then by their small fits of coughing until a young girl stands on wobbly legs, her thumb in her mouth as she sucks.

She couldn't be older than five, with two braids of brown hair running over her shoulders. Her piercing brown eyes, wide and full of hope, stare up at me.

"I be princess too."

A relieved sigh rushes from my lips. "What's your name, sweetie?" I ask as I walk over to her and crouch.

Removing her thumb, she mumbles, "Annabelle." Only to quickly place her thumb back into her mouth.

I gently take the small hand that isn't in her mouth and brush my fingers over it reassuringly. "You are very brave, Annabelle. Thank you for helping me." Rising once more, my hand still clutched in Annabelle's, I let my magic carry my voice once more. "We're going to play follow the leader! Everyone get in line behind Annabelle and hold the hand in front and behind you. Now remember, we take care of our neighbors so don't let go!"

All it took was the courage and hope of a little girl's dream to be a princess, and her peers fall into line behind her.

"I want to be a princess too…"

"…what about princes?"

"Can I be a soldier?"

And then, one small voice stands out in the sea of others, quieting everyone.

"Are you taking us home?" Annabelle asks.

I swallow the lump in my throat. "I'm going to try my very best to."

The lie burns my tongue, coating it with ash at the knowledge that these children not only have no homes to return to, but no family either.

The children's small gazes shine with awe and wonder as they take in the Fae and our elongated, pointed ears. Some have called us goblins while the others chuckled, calling us big ears.

Out of everyone here, I'm surprised that it's Axel who can calm the little munchkins. He leads them with a softness in his voice and kindness in his eyes, turning our surroundings into a game.

The gentleness the silent and brooding Fae possesses is a testament to his soul.

While Axel distracts the children, keeping their small hearts calm and steady, Ace charges forward at the front, Knox and I following his lead as all three of us use our magic to probe the walls.

As we ran, we could still hear the shouts and screams from the soldiers on the other side of the complex as they try to put out a fire that will never be extinguished until Nolan is satisfied and done with them. Knox had to place a silencing shield around us to block out the sounds for the children. And he placed another shield around us, this one far heavier on our hearts.

Gray smoke swirls above us, but never enters the bubble. It didn't take long for the smoke to fill the space, even though the complex wings are enormous, the smoke shrouded everything in a haze within minutes. Any other time I would have panicked, but this seems to work in our favor. Our magic leads us in place of our sight, heightening the already sensitive sense.

After we've passed thirteen hallways, two staircases, and three levels, I halt. Axel crashes into my back as I gasp.

The skin on my chest burns, the sizzle audible as I'm marked. Yanking the silver chain away from my chest, I wince in pain, watching as the red welts vanish beneath my Fae healing. I drop my gaze to the hot pendant, a white glow emanating from the crystal.

"It's veiled," I muse.

Knox turns, his brows lowering. "We would have felt the wards used to hide it."

"No." I shake my head. "Not if the glamour wasn't placed on the door. If it was placed onto the keys, it would only be visible to those who possessed one."

Realization and shock flashes in his sapphire eyes. "Like your pendant."

Reaching out, my hand stretches the invisible shield surrounding us. It feels like nothing but air and yet I watch as it distorts, stretching to accommodate my movements.

I can't see the stone wall beside me until I take a step to the left, pushing the shield further back, the gray smoke furling away, until my palm rests on the warm stone.

The stone throbs beneath my palm as if it's a living breathing thing with a heartbeat.

I walk forward, shutting my eyes to fully immerse myself in the one sensation, feeling the energy beneath my palm. Behind me, Axel starts up the silence game, creating a competition out of who can stay silent the longest. Knox's physical presence lingers beside me the whole time, and his soul fills the doorway in my mind.

How strange that the pendant is working differently now. For the in-between, all I had to do was wear it, as with this, it seems I have to be touching it.

Step after step down the hallway with my hand on the

wall, I feel Ace's eyes burn into my flesh, inquisitive and hopeful. Until my palm tingles, and I pause.

There it is.

My feet stop shuffling. The finalization in my steps reverberates through my bones.

The wall's heartbeat turns erratic—wild. Powerful and hungry and full of anger that I found it.

My eyes flick open, my lips parting on a deep inhale as I push. A loud click rings throughout the hall, and the flood of black smoke has relief and adrenaline filling my veins.

Axel steps forward, his hands reaching out in front of him, pushing the black smoke away from us with his gust of air. The clear vision, albeit short-lived, reveals a dark passageway.

And at the end of the hallway, there's a door, golden rays of light creeping underneath it.

With a renewed sense of energy, everyone rushes for the end of the corridor. Knox doesn't hesitate, slamming black tendrils of shadow against the door. It flings open, revealing the fading sun, the stars slowly coming out to play. The children pour from the building.

I thank the forgotten gods for the small mercy that we find this side of the building empty and not a soldier in sight.

Knox pulls up Axel. "Take the children to the meeting spot. Ordelia and her men should be waiting for you there. If you see Nolan along the way inform him to help with the transport."

"What about the other children?"

Knox mulls over the question before saying, "Get these children out first and then track down Ordelia's informants. They have to know where all the exits are."

Axel's eyes slide to Ace. He swallows thickly, fear consuming his heart over leaving his brother.

He licks his lips, his gaze locking on mine for a moment, pleading to take care of him, before he dips his head to Knox and turns, ordering the children to find a buddy and walk in a line with their pair. Annabelle finds Axel's hand and clutches it tightly, but she glances around until she finds me in the crowd. A small little smile plays on her lips as her fingers lift up and down, her thumb never leaving her mouth as she waves goodbye.

We stand guard in the hallway until the very last child walks out the door, but it seems Axel can't help himself before turning back to Knox. "Bring my brother back alive."

Knox brings his hand to his heart as he nods solemnly. Not voicing a vow he doesn't wish to break.

Axel leaves without another word, his power of air overtaking Knox's bubble, keeping the children safe from smoke inhalation as clouds of darkness billow outside the compound.

Axel's shoulders are impossibly tense as the door slams behind him.

"There's another corridor!" Ace declares, shoving against the stone wall. It gives way without warning, sending Ace tumbling through the archway.

Knox and I scramble for his flailing limbs, only to stop short as we watch him barge into another bare hallway. Ace grunts, rubbing the side of his face as Knox and I stare down another corridor.

"The complex is a maze," Knox mutters.

Impending double iron doors sit at the end of the hallway, their presence looming and the silence stilting. My stomach clenches as Knox works to keep the black smoke away as we approach the doors.

Reaching the intimidating iron, I gently lay my palm flat against it, my other free hand over the pendant. But it remains cool to the touch, no beating heart or living thing here.

I shake my head, feeling silly. Iron is the very thing that detests magic.

Iron detests magic.

My eyes widen, my breath sucking in right as Ace's thoughts reach my own conclusion. He lifts his leg, bringing his boot down upon the iron door with a roar.

I stumble backward into Knox's chest as both doors fly off their hinges. He storms through the threshold, Knox and I close on his heels.

Knox creates a barrier shield to stop the black smoke from leaking into the otherwise untouched space. The darkness swirling against the clear shield where the iron doors once stood mere moments before makes me shudder.

We start heading forward but Knox pauses, the only indication he's speaking mind to mind.

"What is it?" Ace asks, looking toward a frowning Knox.

"It was an inside job." His eyes snap up. "Nolan just informed me the king was tipped off to our plans. Ordelia's informants in the complex got wind of it and let the rebels know."

"Who the hell was the leak?" Ace demands.

Shaking my head, I say, "I don't think it was a leak at all. Someone tried to attack your mind over the lake."

Knox's face pales. "He has a mind reader."

We hurry our search. The energy pulsing off Ace is one full of vengeance as we enter another wing of the complex. Another wing that needs to be searched for his mate.

Whoever he deems fit to blame for taking the one he loves will be punished, and I won't do a thing to stop him.

Our steps are light and silent, our minds open to the possibilities of traps and glamours, but the pendant resting on my sternum remains cold.

"Where are all the soldiers?" I ask.

Shouldn't we be walking into a blood bath?

"Looks like the informants weren't the only ones tipped off," Knox growls.

Pushing open another set of double doors, this one wooden and white, the men stalk through, their swords and blades drawn as their eyes and magic rove. However, mine seems to pause.

If it were under any other circumstances, I would have thought it to be beautiful, extravagant, and plucked from my imagination. However, the reality of this lying within the confines of the complex taints its beauty.

White and black checkered tiles meet my feet, the tiles so clean they shine and show my reflection as I move throughout the room. Two stories of floor-to-ceiling white bookshelves, adorned with various gold-trimmed artwork of angels, line every wall. Rows upon rows of endless stacks veer off to the sides, no doubt winding down to their own labyrinth of a maze.

I roam through the endless stacks, my gaze more focused on the books the shelves hold than what the hallways hide. And the farther I go, the more I begin to realize it's the same seven angels depicted on the shelves, crafted beautifully by hand and painted with the finest gold as they spread their magnificent wings.

I lift my head higher, my eyes climbing along with the books until they connect with the beautiful dome artwork in the center of the ceiling, the seven angels making their appearance again as they fly, hug, and whisper to one another. The mural was crafted with beautiful tones of baby pink and blue hues.

As the boys roam the library the pendant at my sternum begins to move, vibrating as if enthralled by the excitement of it all. It's different from how it usually glows, the energy pulsing out of its white crystal tantalizing in a way that guides my feet.

It leads me down three hallways and corners until I stop at a dead end. My eyes widen as I scan the titles, all shockingly about Fae, their courts, magic, and their creatures. All the books that were believed to have been destroyed and banned by the king lie here in his complex.

I gently brush my fingertips along the spines, in awe at the history that wasn't lost after all. Just kept hidden from the citizens. How nauseating that the king's belief of magic being an abomination has stolen such knowledge from young minds.

There's one book in particular that calls my name.

A symbol stands out to me on the spine of the thick black book, niggling deep within my subconscious, as if awakening a memory that sits just beyond my reach. An upside-down triangle sits in the center, whorls filling the empty space, which is surrounded by a simple circle, and at the very edge there appears to be blood dripping onto what I can only assume is a human skull.

Before I can place what is so familiar about it, Knox calls my name, pulling me away from the hidden bookcase that holds answers to all the questions I had growing up as a child. Walking back to the center of the library, I'm shocked once more at the enormity of the space. How carefully curated it is, the attention to detail that went into the design of everything.

I don't feel a trickle of sadness as we clear the library and begin to move on. Deep within my bones, I feel as if I'll see it again. My magic doesn't even wink goodbye, confirming the feeling.

Beyond the library, I expect to find more rooms similarly designed, yet it's as if the library was a reprieve. We get spat back out into a fortress of cynical, cold walls and corridors emanating a similar feeling to a prison.

How could he have built something so beautiful in the middle of a place so cold? The farther we tread, the more the hairs on the back of my neck stand on end, until I'm drawing my blade. It's become glaringly obvious we aren't approaching the children's wing.

Behind every door we pass is a room full of equipment. Tables, chairs, burners, pots, liquids, shelves, glass tubes—everything that I once discovered in the in-between is now here. Yet on a much larger scale.

This wing and compound make the in-between look like child's play.

I expect to come across some lingering soldiers, workers even, but it's silent. They must have all been herded out by the fire but what, exactly, were they *doing* in here?

What was this wing used for? What do they need all these glass jars and liquid for?

As if the forgotten gods heard my thoughts, we descend a staircase to find my answers.

Here lies hundreds of iron cages filled with every type of creature imaginable. Mermaids, Fae, pixies, brownies, griffins, gremlins, goblins, elves…there's even a tree chained to the floor, his eyes blinking rapidly amongst the bark lines of his trunk.

They even made space for a dragon. Its poor wings are curled in tight, unable to move as it bites the thick iron bars holding it hostage.

Iron. So much iron fills the room.

Slabs of it lie in the center, iron shackles dangling from

the flat surface. Needles, knives, and jars of liquid sit beside it on a roll-away cart.

Screams and pleads for help and mercy fill the once-silent room.

Knox's cry of shock joins the sounds as surprise has him pausing, but only for a moment. A sheen of tears glosses over his eyes before he takes off running right as Ace's pierced cry jolts me out of my frozen stupor.

Ace joins Knox, checking every single cage, looking at every Fae held behind the iron bars, shackles encasing their wrists tied to the roof of the cages. Knox walks beside me, his shoulders tense and eyes damp as we take in the damage the king has created. The lives he's tainted, stolen.

A gleaming door to the right catches my eye. Taking off without a word of explanation, a horrid wheezing sound tumbles from my lips as the door clangs open.

Glasses.

Thousands of glass jars line the room. Shelves are stacked like a library, yet instead of holding wisdom and knowledge, the shelves contain something far greater, something far more precious.

I fall to my knees, clutching my chest at the utter disbelief coursing through my heart.

I don't have to look to know what the jars contain, what the thousands of glasses hold. I've seen it before.

Pixies.

Thousands of trapped pixies lie within the glass bottles, the ones from the in-between that went missing, stored here in the compound like canned produce.

The king.

I grapple with my emotions, unable to form a coherent thought other than one simple truth.

The king was the one responsible for the in-between, not Emmalyn and her beasts.

It's truth, the only one that makes sense for why the vanished pixies would be here, in the king's complex of all places.

How would he be able to create this? How would he have been able to trap—

My mother.

No. Not my mother…Eleanor.

She gave me the pendant to help them, to help me see. She gave me the pendant to try and undo the wrong she inadvertently created, the darkness she was forced to build.

Forced.

No matter how you look at it, no matter that it was by my mother's—Eleanor's—hands, it was never her intention. Never her *choice*.

I blamed her for something she couldn't have fathomed, something she couldn't have even controlled because for twenty-three years, she was manipulated, her mind twisted and muddled.

Eleanor was not the one in control of her own mind, her own *body*. Her own magic.

She never was, and when she could break free of his horrible grasp, she tried to undo the horrible things she was forced to create.

Eleanor—my mother—was right.

She tried to be a mother figure to me, despite the leash the king had on her. When she was lucid, she was there, stroking my hair and telling me how much she loved me. She tried to protect me and defend me in every way she could…whether that was through the pendant or Annie.

My mother was behind it all.

She helped Annie keep her job to ensure she could be the

mother she couldn't be. She made sure Easton was allowed near me to be a companion and, thankfully, a once-in-a-lifetime friend.

She has always been there…I just never knew it.

She may not be my biological mother, but she went above and beyond for me to try and make the best of my childhood…to try and give me the tools to escape a life of misery. Because she knew all too well what that felt like…how it felt to be shackled with no escape.

She tried to save me from a life she despised.

My *mother* saved my life every day and I never knew it.

Tears fall freely down my cheeks as every horrible thing I said to her churns through my mind, how I treated her when she tried to explain things to me. Gods, I was horrible to her, and all she ever did was try to save me. In whatever capacity she could.

Eleanor could have spent what little control and energy she had on freeing herself, on escaping, but she used it for me. She showed mercy that not even many saints would give. She showed strength, courage, and compassion, and in return, I shoved it in her face and told her to rot in hell.

I swallow past the shame burning my throat and rise. Knox hovers behind me, his eyes pooling with tears.

"I guess we now know who was behind their disappearance," I say on a wobbly exhale. I shake my head, unable to look at him. "I suppose Nolan had a reason to hate me all along…the king has his sister and mother somewhere in here." I snap my eyes open. "Is she on this level?" I ask, rushing through the door to see Ace unlocking every cage with an axe he scavenged from somewhere in this hellhole. Why would they have needed an *axe* anyway? He swings it with such hatred I can feel his burning rage from across the room.

"No."

Knox rounds to stand before me, stopping me in my path. His fingers skim my cheeks, his thumbs brushing away the tears that are still rolling down my face. My eyes shutter closed as his velvety voice sends a chill down my spine. "Why are you crying, Angel?"

I nuzzle into his palm as my voice cracks. "I cannot believe I said those things to her... I cannot believe I shoved the selfless acts and kindness in her face."

"She understands, Delilah. If anyone understands, it's her," he says gently, letting his words grow taut between us until he rises, pulling back and avoiding my gaze. "Hazel isn't here. There's a lone cage left empty."

My brows furrow. "What aren't you telling me?"

He runs his fingers through his hair. "There was blood... on the floor of the cage." Knox's swallow is audible as he turns to face me, his eyes pooling with tears. "Lots of it."

Ace shouts as he runs past, not stopping, "There's more a level lower. I can hear their chains rattling against the iron bars."

Ace doesn't wait for us; he takes off down the stairwell. Knox moves forward, whistling with his two fingers to get everyone's attention.

"There's an exit a level up. You can't miss it—it's the only archway with black smoke swirling against it." Knox glances around, staring at the injured animals, the mermaids still in the tanks of water, albeit out of iron shackles. "Grab as many as you can help and get out of here. There are men helping children escape as we speak." Knox's eyes harden. "Do not, under any circumstances, harm or scare the children. They have had it as bad as you have."

"And help the pixies please," I add, pointing to their glass prisons.

Knox strides over to the mermaids. Laying his palm flat against the glass tanks, white light glows, radiating beneath his palms until it encompasses the mermaid's tail, revealing two long legs. One by one he moves, pressing his palm to six more water tanks and transforming the mermaids.

"The spell will wear off in a few hours. Make sure you have gotten to a body of water by then." Knox turns, pointing his fingers at the group of gremlins with wrath vivid in his sapphire eyes. "You stir up any trouble and I will hunt you down personally."

His voice holds the threat and promise of death, and yet the tip of his finger quivers. I wish I could laugh and tease Knox about his fear of gremlins, but there's nothing humorous about it now.

"We will come back to help as soon as we can!" I call, already beginning to run for the stairs.

Knox catches up to me moments later, his steps fast and hurried as he takes the stairs two at a time, practically flying down the stone stairwell.

As I run, my body grows impossibly slow, as if dragging through mud. My ears begin to ring with a high-pitched frequency that makes me lift my shoulders to my ears as if it can stop the pain.

Then a feeling I am slowly becoming accustomed to surrounds me, one of warmth, love, and light. A feeling so comforting it makes my body melt into nothing but a puddle of goo.

Until the feeling is ripped away from me and replaced by one I know all too well.

Panic and pain—but not my own.

Hurry!

It's that ethereal voice again, whispering urgently in my ear. *Hurry, Delilah, hurry!*

Then time resumes, hurtling my body down the rest of the stairs.

Then I finally hear it as I descend to the lower level.

The small whimpers filled with fury, the sobs and cries filled with pain.

Duke Harrison stands in the middle of the room, piercing Hazel's neck with an iron-tipped blade. Ace stands before him, trembling with fear and wrath, as he white knuckles the blade in his hand.

Duke Harrison's smile is dangerous as his eyes find mine. "How courteous of you to finally grace us with your presence, Delilah."

Chapter Forty-One

Hazel's cry of pain, red blood dripping down her neck, hits me square in the chest. My heart taking the brute force.

Ace, shaking with tears, appears to be using every ounce of willpower to not make a move for her. The moment he even twitches, Duke Harrison *tsks*, digging the blade deeper into her neck.

Hazel's wrists are bright red, the marks from the iron shackles visible, her healing power subdued. Blood dribbles from her nose, joining the dried blood on her swollen lips. One of her gorgeous blue eyes is tinged with black bruises, matching those that mar her creamy white skin. Her once vibrant red hair is dull and matted, filled with grim and dirt.

What have they done to her?

Her knees buckle as Duke Harrison pushes the knife further into her neck.

My eyes flare with indignation, fury burning through my veins.

I didn't miss the verbal jab from the duke. The last time I saw Duke Harrison, the king had said those very same words to me in the council meeting room. Moments before he beat me.

"What exactly do you wish to accomplish by this?" I quirk my brow. "You're already the king's mutt," I spit. "He has you doing his dirty work now?"

Duke Harrison chuckles darkly. "Such a filthy mouth for a princess."

I take a step forward, only for Duke Harrison to shove the knife deeper, *tsk*ing me as he elicits a scream from Hazel and a cry from Ace who kneels before me. Tears stream down his face.

I halt, raising my hands in surrender. "What do you want?"

His eyes shine, crackling with darkness. "More power."

I clench my teeth so hard I'm surprised they don't snap. The king's court members have always been snively, slimy snakes in disguise as men. Duke Harrison was the worst of them all, kissing up to the king for any scrap of power and status he could. If he could get away with murdering him, dethroning him to take over, he wouldn't hesitate to jump at the opportunity.

He has always wanted power. It's what they all want.

"Don't have enough of that from kissing the king's asshole?"

"It seems your time away has made your confidence grow. What a silly notion to have as a female," he sneers.

Female. Not woman. He only sees us as objects, whose only purpose in life is to bear a child. I'm surprised he never killed me, or worse…tried to make the heir his own.

I click my tongue. "Among other things. I don't suppose you heard the rumors?"

Interest sparks in his eyes. "About you practically wielding rays of sunshine that kill people? Why yes, dear delusional one, I did." His brow quirks. "Going to try and incinerate me now, are you?"

"I'll give you the options I so kindly gave your commanding soldier months ago." I take a step forward, a golden hand freezing Duke Harrison's knife, making his eyes widen to a comical size. Knox and Ace's menacing energies pulse behind me as I advance. "You can either remove the iron knife from her neck and live." I shrug. "Or continue foolishly believing you have the upper hand here and die." I lift my hand, wiggling my fingers as golden fire erupts along my palm. "Your choice, Duke."

A muscle ticks in his jaw before a sinister smile crawls over his lips. My heart stutters for a second. "I said I wanted power, Delilah. You forgot to ask me which type."

Dark magic, as powerful as the forgotten gods themselves, slams into me. I lose my footing, crashing to the stone floor. I raise my hands above my head, golden magic snapping in front of me, creating a shield of gold against the slimy, thick darkness.

A power similar to the one that attacked Knox's mind.

I quickly rise, my chest heaving, Knox and Ace standing behind their own shields of power, their swords raised. Hazel trembles behind the knife still poised against her neck.

"Impossible," I breathe.

I search his face, the sharp angular bone structure of his features, the dull brown eyes, bushy eyebrows, and thinning hair. Nothing appears to glow radiantly like a Fae, nor are his ears pointed. He's human, and yet…he possesses magic.

He chortles, the sound grating. "What did you think? That we merely kept the Fae and other magic bastards as pets?"

Reality crashes into me.

Suddenly the room makes sense. The burners, liquids, needles, cauldrons, beakers, cages, shackles, potions. They weren't merely studying the magic of the Fae and the creatures—they were stealing it.

I would think it impossible, but I had seen the working Fae in the in-between extracting and creating a magic potion out of the pixies' ability to deter power.

Disgust rolls through my veins.

My hand instinctively wraps around the hilt of a dagger strapped to my hip. Duke Harrison tracks the movement, and it makes a deadly spark shine in his otherwise beady eyes.

"Thank the gods," he drawls. He shoves Hazel to the ground. Oily darkness tumbles with her, wrapping around her mouth, feet, and hands. "I was growing bored playing with her."

Darkness appears, duplicating and growing into dark versions of the duke, all wielding black magic blades. This isn't anything like Knox's shadows.

It is pure darkness, and they are evil reincarnated.

Fire shadow erupts along Knox's blade, aiding him as his free hand forms a ball of fire. He doesn't hesitate as he lunges forward, throwing the ball of fire into the shadow's chest while his blade, dancing with flames, swipes for the head.

It does nothing but blow through the darkness like a cloud.

I am grateful beyond reasoning for our lessons. Because as Ace wields his water magic, forging blades and knives that only scatter through the darkness and hit the wall behind the duke with a resounding splash, I know that our pure magic is powerless against the dark magic running through Duke Harrison's blood.

Ace and Knox quickly come to the same conclusion and raise their steel, whirling against something not wholly there.

With my golden power dancing along the steel blade in my hand, I raise it to the black ink. An inch before it can touch, it recoils, revealing Duke Harrison standing before me. The snarl I'm greeted with makes the demon hounds and soul eater look like child's play.

Rage consumes me as my gaze locks on him. Rage for the little girl he watched be beaten every day. Rage for the man who would do anything for power. Rage for the man who held a knife to my friend's throat, and rage that he has the audacity to come at me with a blade at all.

I let my own snarl tear from my throat, baring my canines, before I pounce. I pivot at the last second, whirling away as a dagger flies through the air, just narrowly avoiding my neck.

Lunging only to fake right, I smirk as the duke falls for the trap, pivoting to where I want him. My blade drags across his stomach, the steel ripping through flesh and muscle, like butter.

My victory is short-lived as a foul rotting smell spills down my throat and nose, making me gag so violently that tears spring to my eyes. Black blood oozes from the wound, but it doesn't make the duke stop at all. It's as if he doesn't feel an ounce of pain. The duke's iron blade meets mine again.

Knox roars so loud I'm fearful my ears will begin to bleed. He tries to charge for me, but the duplicates of Duke Harrison shove him back with black magic and blades of darkness. He slams his own shadows into the duplicates, but it's no use. Nothing is against dark magic.

The duke lunges, swiping for my arm. I whirl and dance away, striking another exposed side. I rip right through his forearm, but he simply lets it bleed. It doesn't even seem like he notices.

When I dodge again, he growls with rage and throws the steel in his hand to the floor, running at me with his fist cocked back. I try to block the blow, but he doesn't feel it. His fist flies at my face.

The punch jolts me, knocking my head to the side so forcefully stars swim in my vision, momentarily destabilizing me. But that split second I'm weakened is all he needs.

He knocks the dragon sword from my hand. I feel the moment my fingers lose their grip, and by the time my vision comes back to me, the duke is already upon me.

His outstretched hands lock onto my shoulders and smash my body into the stone. The air is knocked from my lungs. I gasp, only to choke. Then Duke Harrison is atop me, pinning my legs to the ground and wrapping his large hands around my throat, squeezing.

Blind panic encompasses me, and I thrash. My feet kicking wildly and my arms smashing his face over and over and over. He barely moves.

I begin clawing his face. Skin peels under my sharp nails, and I pull away blood and tissue to no effect. His chest is wide open, black blood oozing, and if I had my sword, I would have gladly plunged the steel into his rotting heart.

I'm wheezing in earnest now as tears roll down my cheeks. My head grows fuzzy, dizziness clouding my mind as death waits eagerly on the sidelines for me.

Duke Harrison's face swims in front of me as I keep thrashing, trying wildly to escape his clutches. My eyes search around me frantically, even as I feel the blood vessels in my eyes pop from the pressure. Knox and Ace are pushed far into the corner by the duke's shadows.

Knox wails, thrashing like a wild beast as shadows after shadows pummel the duke and his clones. Only, the duke's darkness is stronger, unaffected. They return Knox's hits double fold, and he crumples to his knees.

Knox rushes through his mind to the bridge. He sobs, screaming and pleading with every forgotten god there is.

I try to comfort him, to hold him, but it's no use against his pure anguish.

Hazel lies near me screaming, her face as red as her hair as she wails my name over and over as if the word can free me. But the shadows hold her. Clutching her as tightly as his fists clutch me.

Running to my magic well, I skid to a stop, utterly panicked to find it near empty again. Months. My magic has been building for *months*. Knox has been training me every single night on how to control such a power within me. To not allow it to consume me, and in the moments when I need it most, it's simply gone? Vanishing as quickly as my life is fading.

Eleanor is not the cause of this siphoning. Could this be the duke's work?

Standing in my mind, gaping at the empty well, something within my sternum rumbles, vibrating loudly as if banging on a door I cannot see nor feel.

But I don't have time to search for it. Once more, time is used against me. It won't stop for me today, and as my vision begins to darken and my lungs seize, burning, I know there's not much left.

I keep trying to reach out to my magic, but it remains just beyond my fingertips. No matter how much I scream and plead and stretch myself thin, I cannot reach it.

The last thing I see before my vision goes black is Duke Harrison's snarling face, spit frothing in the corners of his mouth as he snarls, "You do not deserve the title. You are not even from this wo—"

Steel flashes, his grip loosens, and air rushes for my lungs.

My lungs jolt into action, greedily gobbling down air as light and color and the world returns to me.

Knox roars, holding the dragon sword that slices through Duke Harrison's neck, his lips curled back in fury. He's panting, clothes tattered, but nothing could've stopped him while his mate slipped between his fingers.

Black blood sprays my face, as dark as the night, covering my body as his head goes flying to the side. His sneer is permanently etched onto his face as the smell of death and evil itself fills the room.

Turning my head to the side, I retch.

I thought the Tree of Life was horrid—I thought nothing could smell worse than that.

I think I begin screaming. All I know is my throat is burning and I keep staring at myself covered in demonic blood, the smell so strong my nose begins to trickle with blood. And then Knox is there beside me, his eyes wide with fright as water pours from his palms, washing off the demonic blood as quickly as it arrived.

"My angel," Knox croaks, his voice strained from screaming. "You're all right, Angel, I've got you now."

Ace rushes to Hazel's side, his hands glowing with blue light as they run over every inch of her body. The bruises begin to fade, the cuts and abrasions healing as Ace whispers into her ear.

The tears that flow over Hazel's cheeks are ones of pure relief.

Chapter Forty-Two

In the dead of night, under the shining light of the moon, thousands of pixies fly around us, their elation a tangible feeling in the air as they feel the breeze against their wings for the first time in decades. Shining as bright from the inside out, their bodies lighting up like a thousand fireflies.

Victory against the King of Aloriah.

We still need to get everyone to a safe spot that isn't hidden within the mountains; however, we did get them out of the complex. Thousands of children and creatures stand at the meeting spot, hidden under the thick canopy of trees and makeshift tents within an endless cave system.

Thanks to the rebels and Ordelia's informants, they were able to open the emergency exits and lead the rest of the children to safety.

Where the soldiers from the complex went is a mystery for tomorrow.

Knox has already relayed the events to Lenox and Harlow, sending memories and mental notes.

Axel's face was one of pure joy, breaking into a beautiful wide smile, once he laid his eyes on Ace walking amongst the throe of creatures, his arms wrapped tightly around Hazel.

The trio embraced for so long my eyes began to burn before Ace carried her off to the nearest healers.

Family. That's what we are to one another.

Despite the wariness around the magical creatures, medics and soldiers within the rebellion stepped up to treat those who needed it.

No one expected to find the creatures, nor half the missing Fae.

Nolan wept with relief to see them all, which made it even harder when I had to tell him, "They're not here." He crumbled before my eyes, and all I could do was watch as Knox held him while we wondered where else they could be kept.

Nolan continues to be handed hope, only for it to be yanked from his grasp moments later.

Knox ordered those who could fly to depart. The command was directed more toward the dragon, who under even the best glamour and highest tree would still be noticeable. The beautiful creature flew back with those that were able to heal themselves, along with messengers to Lenox, stating to keep the ruling courts away from the human lands.

Once word gets out about the tortured and imprisoned Fae, war will be inevitable. What the king has been planning, what he has been gathering magic for, is not a war against the human race.

Through the crowd of gremlins, Fae, humans, and small flying pixies I spot Ordelia's second-in-command, Lucca. His face is a welcome sight and as his harried expression morphs into relief at seeing Knox and me, I search his body for any injuries. He was one of the soldiers that went along with Nolan to oversee the fire.

There are no injuries on him I can see. His nose lies crooked, but it's been like that since I met him. The break he told me he got while serving the king in the capital.

"What's wrong?" I ask.

"When all the creatures came crawling out and you two didn't, I began to worry."

Duke Harrison's sniveling face flashes into my mind. "Nothing to worry about." I crane my neck, looking past Lucca. Ordelia stands unharmed next to Phillip, tending to the children. Yet when I don't see who I want to speak to the most, I frown.

"Where is Eleanor and Annie?" I ask.

Lucca barely flicks his eyes to mine, too busy sorting the children and small goblins into groups. "When the Fae and creatures came out after the children, we had to prioritize men." He looks down at a small herd of pixies, no taller than his boot. His eyes widen, before he says, "You can follow the gremlins to the left."

Knox coughs. "I would send them off with the Fae."

Lucca doesn't have to repeat Knox's suggestion, but he does look up for a moment, gratitude shining in his eyes as he mouths, *Thank you.*

My brows lower; they're still hidden in the forest?

It was Eleanor's idea, to remove herself from the camp in case anything went amiss. After all, if the king were to try and retrieve her, he would follow the herd of children. Annie insisted on going with her, as long as they were stationed with a group of soldiers. The plan was to pick them up the moment we escaped.

"Have any men left to retrieve them?"

Lucca shakes his head, flicking his gaze between the line

of creatures and myself. "No, we can't send any until the first group of soldiers come back." He grimaces. "It might take a while."

"That's all right, we'll go and retrieve them."

"Is there anyone else in the surrounding areas that needs to be escorted?" Knox asks.

Lucca's shoulders slump, his eyes softening. "Thank you. No, it's just them in the western forests."

I'm glad they're not here yet. It gives me a chance to think about what I need to say, a quiet moment to apologize to Eleanor—to my mother—before we drag them back to the absolute chaos we have encountered.

Knox stares at me out of the corner of his eye. "She will forgive you."

"How do you know that?" I ask.

I try to swallow past the thick lump in my throat, wiping my clammy hands on my leather pants. I can't believe how nervous I am to face her. I never even asked if she sees herself as my mother. If she wants to remain a part of my life. There are so many questions I should have asked her and yet I was so selfish, wrapped up in my own feelings, that I didn't have the decency to ask if she was *okay*.

"Because she's your mother," Knox answers simply, reading my thoughts.

Sweeping me into his strong hold, Knox's black iridescent wings shoot out behind his back, spreading to their full width before he bends and takes off skyward. The flight is peaceful with the knowledge that the thousands of children are finally safe.

"How did he have magic?"

Knox shakes his head in astonishment. "That's one of the many, many questions I want answered myself."

"The royal courts are going to strike back, aren't they?"

Knox's jaw tightens. "I pray to the forgotten gods that they do. That bastard needs his head removed."

Silence grows between us as the night sky shines down upon us, the stars twinkling and winking hello.

"The magic the duke had…it was so similar to the one that attacked your mind. Do you think it's possible he was the one behind the attack?"

"I think it's more than possible."

It isn't long until Knox lands, setting me down on my feet, his fingers brushing my hand as we walk through the forest tree line. We emerge from the canopy of trees into the small, secluded field Axel had scouted earlier.

As I squint into the darkness, the moon not reaching the forest grass, I understand why he chose the location. Even with my Fae sight it's hard to make out my mother and Annie standing huddled together at the other end of the field. No human set of eyes would ever be able to spot them.

I raise my hand in a wave as the two figures in the dark become visible, the soldiers kneeling around beside them. I can't even blame their tiredness—they've been stationed here for hours.

I keep waving, waiting for someone to wave back, until I realize that none of them possess Fae sight. They have no idea who we are.

"Maybe we should call out to—"

My steps slow to a stop, my hand lowering.

It's not two figures standing in the darkness…but three. And the soldiers that are kneeling around them are still, so impossibly still the sight makes my stomach clench.

Knox and I unsheathe the swords strapped to our backs. The king could have found out our plan and used our movements as a distraction to take my mother back. The possibility sends ice down my spine.

I try to home in on them with my heightened Fae senses, but it's like the darkness is working against me. Their faces remain shrouded in the forest's shadows.

"Can you see?" I ask Knox as we crouch, every step calculated.

He shakes his head. "Not even my shadows can."

Knox's shields slam up, the strength behind them impenetrable. The only way we're going to find out is if we approach and, even then, it could all be a trap.

Yet even as I think it, a part of me knows it's not.

Especially when I notice that none of the shadows are moving, including the three standing. Knox notices at the same time. His feet stop for a moment, the stumble barely noticeable, but he can't hide his tells from me. And he can't stop me as I take off running.

Every thought that was churning through my consciousness disappears, as if they too decided to run.

The adrenaline pumping through my veins disappears just as quickly as it arrived, leaving me a shell of a person, trembling as I sprint through the grass. I push my feet to fly, wielding air to make me faster. I wish I knew how to use my wings, that I could spread the sensitive golden skin and fly.

My breathing is hollow and jagged, and although I feel another burnout looming none of it matters as I reach the dark shadowed figures.

This—*this* was the real reason the ethereal voice urged me to hurry.

The shadowed figures are not bodies. They are thick spikes.

And impaled on top of them are the heads of Annie, my mother, and Easton.

A note is pinned beneath Eleanor's unseeing violet eyes,

with a scribble of handwriting I have detested since the moment I learned how to read.

To my dearest Delilah, happy birthday.

Chapter Forty-Three

Everything within me grows numb.

Standing there as a shell of who I used to be, I don't feel, or think, or move.

I get jolted to the side as a figure moves to block the heads. I push Knox out of the way, the movement catapulting my body forward. Knox tumbles to the side with the force of my strength.

The numbness that spread within me recedes. As if a wave, the ocean called it back.

The next wave to crash isn't numbness—it is a catastrophic tsunami filled with emotions.

The pure agony that builds within me is not something you can stop. It demands to be felt.

I look to Annie's head. Her vibrant red hair hanging, her signature white bow missing. Her gold-ringed eyes now dull and lifeless. I stare at the woman who raised me, who cared for me, who showed me what unconditional love is…and my heart simply breaks.

The last conversation we had plays on an endless loop, and I curse myself for that being the last time I spoke to her.

For allowing my anger to override my pain. The last time she looked at me had been with disappointment.

A sledgehammer swings down upon my fragile heart. It forms a crack in the very foundation of love she built.

Then my eyes flick to my mother, the woman that I berated and verbally abused. I will never be able to apologize to her now. She gave up twenty-three years of her life to protect me, and now, her unseeing gaze just stares at me.

As if mocking that I will never get the chance to tell her how I truly feel. That I will never get to ask her questions or tell her how much I cherished the moments she was lucid or thank her for the riddles I mistook as ramblings or the fairy tales she introduced to me. I never got to thank her for putting Annie and Easton in my path.

I will never be able to tell her that I love her, nor take back the hateful words I said.

The sledgehammer comes down a second time, splintering the cracks.

And the man that meant the world to me, my dear, dear Easton—his decaying head lies on a spike next to them.

Perfectly preserved, as if the king placed a spell on him to make sure his head stayed intact. To truly break me. And it works.

Because the sledgehammer comes down once more, and when it does, it shatters my heart completely.

My three loves.

My people, my *family*.

Dead.

My knees buckle, taking me down to the forest floor with a wail so potent with pain Knox smashes his hands over his ears.

The tidal wave crashes into me, consuming me with grief so heavy I drown. The tears roll down my face with abandon, never ending. It doesn't amend or fix my shattered heart. Nothing will.

My hands reach out to them on a sob, the piercing cry shrill and full of agony I have never felt before in my life.

I'll never hear their voices or see them smile or hold them again. I don't even have their cold dead bodies to touch one more time. When that truth strikes, I ignite.

With fury. With anger so potent my roar can be heard for miles upon miles. And as all the power I have felt building and beckoning inside my body for the past two months begins to rise, I pound my fists against the ground, where it shakes and splinters, and I unleash everything with a mighty cry.

The wave of magic that explodes out of me is unending, the force of its power so turbulent Knox is sent flying backward. The land beneath my hands will be seared for as long as this world stands, on this final spot that tore my heart into ribbons.

My golden light erupts, marking its pain in this godsforsaken place.

Because I never reached burnout, not truly. It was building day in and day out and that niggling feeling earlier, where I could feel it just on the horizon, hiding within the depths of my heart, is now in my hands and I am unleashing hell on this world.

The shock waves will be felt not only across all of Aloriah but across the world. The universe.

Everyone will feel my agony, my rage, my hatred for the king. Everyone will know what was taken from me.

Night turns to day. The golden power is so bright it's as if I'm a shooting star, a meteor encasing Aloriah as it lights it up, forcing the corrupt to *see* what they have done.

The king may be everything that is wicked and cruel and

has shrouded his kingdom in the clutches of his darkness, but he will never truly win. I will never let him.

Because amidst darkness, light will always persevere.

Knox wraps his arms around me, breaking whatever power was flowing from me. It retreats just as wildly as it arrived, and it is only until I feel the warmth of Knox, his voice against my ear, do I allow myself to fully come undone.

My heart lies dead next to my three loves, and I fear it will never be resuscitated.

My eyes keep straying to them. To Easton, who had planned for years to free me and never saw his end results and the dreams he had built. To Annie, who lived in fear of the king but fought with the rebels silently and courageously. To my mother, who finally tasted liberation and the chance to be reunited with her family of mermaids, only for the king to steal her away again.

Knox pulls me against his chest, turning my head away from the sight.

"Oh Angel, my angel, I'm so sorry," he croaks, rocking me side to side.

Pain engulfs me. No amount of time will heal this wound.

"He took them from me." My hand grips his leather vest. "He keeps taking away the people I love." A sob flies from my mouth. "He broke me every day. Was that not enough?"

Heavy wings beat behind me, not enough to turn my head, but then Aurora's cry pierces the air. I lift my red-rimmed eyes to her, but her golden eyes latch on the sight behind me. When she turns to me, sympathy and pain in her expression, I wonder if that's what I look like. If that is the sight of destruction and heartbreak.

Aurora kneels, showing her condolences…and the sight turns my weeping into wails of grief.

As if I needed clarification that what I saw was real. That it wasn't a game or a trick of the mind.

No matter that Knox has turned my head away, all I can see are their heads. It keeps flashing in my mind, and I shake my head to make it stop but the image continues hounding my mind and soul.

He has taken everyone I love and killed them.

I cling to Knox as tightly as I can, as if the premonition of him dying, another person to lose, can be broken by how closely I hold him.

Chapter Forty-Four

I lost track of how long I've stayed in this bed. The days and hours and minutes began blurring the second Knox ripped me away from Annie, Easton, and my mother. He had to pin me to Aurora's back when I tried to jump off and return to them...when we were thirty feet in the air.

When Knox told me that I had to leave before the king came after my magic explosion, the paralysis took over.

My mind is working just fine, which is torture in itself, not being able to move, cry, or scream.

I do, however, know that enough time has passed for Lenox and Harlow to arrive. They tried to speak with me, offer condolences. Lenox at one point entered with what appeared to be homemade doughnuts in the shape of a pentagon. I could barely muster a blink at the kind act. Even Harlow—strutting, smirking, and witty Harlow—was somber after that.

I heard their whisperings. It's as if in this catatonic state they've forgotten that I possess Fae hearing.

I heard the damage my magic caused, what it did when it

erupted. The stories they've collected as they traveled through the Fae courts and Aloriah.

Whispers of the animals that paused and bowed their heads, whispers of the currents that stopped to listen to my agony, whispers of the trees that shed their leaves in sympathy.

The people of Aloriah didn't just hear me—the *planet* did, and she paid her condolences.

That's why Lenox and Harlow came running in the first place. They *felt* the blast.

Everyone has been taking care of me, taking shifts on who cooks, entertains, and tries to *heal* me, as if what is wrong with me is something that can be healed.

Hazel and Knox haven't left my side. While a blessed sight to see her healed, I couldn't muster any relief. The only time Hazel leaves me alone is when she's cooking. She's tried to shove food down my throat, but no matter how delicious it smells, it always ends up tasting like cardboard against my lips. And every time Hazel's eyes lock on mine, I find a speck of guilt shining in them, along with fear and sadness. I have always taken on the burden of others' guilt and it appears Hazel is doing the same.

Hazel chooses to sleep in a rollaway cot on the floor beside me and Knox…just doesn't sleep.

The pounding in my head hasn't subsided, courtesy of Knox attempting to bash down the door to my mind. A part of me locked myself in here, impenetrable even against Knox's magic. I'm not sure when I did it and I wouldn't know how to break it down, even if I had the mental capacity and strength to do so.

I suppose I truly do fail everyone. I couldn't even keep my promise to not lock him out.

When we first arrived, I couldn't see, the tears constantly pooling in my eyes. But when I had finally cried myself hoarse, when the well of tears within me dried up and there were no more left to shed, I saw where they had taken me.

The cabin.

The one Easton had built for me, the sanctuary he created for us. The one Annie had found a refugee in…her personal oasis.

I knew before I saw it because the smell of Annie surrounded me. Creseda and Henry nickered outside the log cabin.

I understand they did it out of safety, for me to be far away from the palace, but it's another kind of torture to know that Annie's smell still lingers while she herself is gone. How dare her scent continue to exist without her.

That only further shut down my mind.

So that leaves me here: unknown of what day it is, unknown of what I feel, and unknown of whether I'm still alive because I certainly do not feel like I am.

How do you continue to live without the people that gave you the courage to breathe? Without the people who helped shape who you are today? How do you continue living with chunks hacked out of your heart?

And yet, there's a small flicker.

A kernel.

Deep within the nothingness, in the darkness that has overtaken my body, there is a glimmer. Not of hope—no, I lost that long ago. But it is a glimmer of something far greater, something that I know if I reach out and touch it, allow it to grow and burn brighter, it will give me a reason to move. A reason to blink, to speak, to cry, and to breathe.

I have not breathed freely since my breath was stolen from me when I saw their three heads on a spike.

He stole it from me.

And that is how I know what the small kernel is.

Rage.

It is not determination, or a will to live for them. It is hatred, it is rage, it is disgust, and it is the only thing that will keep me from dying. The one thing that will keep me from falling deeper into this black hole of nothingness.

But rage is a dangerous game to play. It'll make me become the very person I despise most of all, the very person that put me in this situation.

How could I become the thing he wished to create?

Then Knox walks in and pinewood surrounds me. Our bond tugging, the tether checking my pulse, and when I see the sigh of relief in his eyes, I ponder.

Could I do it? Could I become a monster…just for a short amount of time? To get through this, to get through to the other side…

I'm not sure what's on the other side, but all I know for certain is that I can't stay like this. I cannot remain catatonic, and I cannot continue to do this to Knox.

So, when I see his sapphire eyes fill with fear and pain when I spot the love shining in their depths—the love that I will forever be afraid to declare to his heart—I lean toward the kernel and reach out a hand.

I stroke it and let the savage indignation engulf me.

Because my father was right—the *king* was right.

No matter how far I run, no matter how long I hide, I will never escape him. His damage will forever leave scars on my heart, and until he's six feet underground, he will always have the power to destroy me.

He will always have the power to take away the people I love most in this world.

There is only one solution, like there always has been.

I need to destroy him first. I will become the monster he wished to create, and I will make him pray that I was never born.

Because the first death my hands will take will be the one of Peter Bartholomew Covington.

Chapter Forty-Five

Hazel and Knox's heads are bent together just outside the door. Their whispers are barely audible, but it doesn't take a genius to know what they are discussing. They're so engrossed in conversation about my wellbeing that they don't notice when I leave the bed, nor when I take my first steps and stand behind them in the doorway.

"She won't want to leave this place," Hazel urges.

Knox glowers. "I highly doubt she wants to be constantly reminded of all the people she lost."

"Then why bring her here?" she quips back.

"It wasn't my idea, and you know that. Besides…it's all she has left in the human lands," Knox whispers.

My mate, forever knowing my heart's true desire and what I need most in this world.

Hazel's exasperated face would have made me smile, chuckle even…but I don't think I possess humor any longer.

I'm surprised neither of their Fae senses have picked up on me yet. I suppose even a Fae can become exhausted to the point of delirium. Because that's exactly what's swirling in their eyes.

When I open my mouth, my throat's raw and as dry as a desert. "How long has it been?"

Hazel and Knox jump at my strained and cracked voice. Their eyes widen to a comical size before they both lunge forward. Knox's hands are on me in an instant, wrapping me in his arms as his chest heaves on a deep exhale.

"Thank the gods," he whispers under his breath.

Hazel's eyes quickly flick between Knox and me. I expect them to say that it's been weeks or perhaps even months with how ragged I feel so I'm shocked when Hazel says, "Three days."

Three days isn't even long enough for them to bury her. The royal court's mourning process and funeral preparations will still be ongoing.

The funeral.

Pulling back, a plan begins to form in my head, unbeknownst to the people standing before me.

Swallowing thickly, I put that plan in motion. "I want to stay here," I lie.

Knox's eyebrows rise in shock.

I don't let him see the truth.

"Delilah, you don't have to. The children are safe now, so we can go—"

"I'm happy to hear they're safe but I am not leaving."

Large stomps shake the hallway and before I know it, Lenox is barreling toward me, engulfing me in his arms. "You're back! I mean, you were never gone...but you know what I mean. You weren't exactly *here*. I wonder where our minds go when we shut down like that." He puts me down, his hands never leaving my biceps as if he's the one who needs physical contact. "You know, my mind shut off once. I was trapped and, ugh, it felt like the best thing to do. Well…I suppose I didn't actually have a choice in the matter because you know how it—"

"Lenox, shut your fat mouth. The last thing Delilah wants to hear after three days is your nervous ramblings," Harlow *tsks*.

"It's all right, Harlow, he's just worried," I say.

Lenox frowns. "Could you hear the whole time?"

I shrug, words suddenly growing heavy again.

Knox brushes past everyone, wrapping his arms around me. "I think that's enough for one day. We don't need to bombard her."

"In other words, shut the hell up and get out of her room," Nolan calls from the hallway.

To my surprise, they all listen to him, and to my further shock, Nolan lingers, his eyes roving me as if checking on my wellbeing. I would think that's a thoughtless conclusion, one made by pure exhaustion and restlessness, but when his hazel eyes lock on mine, I see worry in them. Nolan pulls away, joining the others in the living room. And that's when it dawns on me who is missing: Ace and Axel.

"Where are—"

"They went for a walk, chopping firewood," Knox answers.

I dip my head slowly, stroking that kernel within me to breathe life of rage into my heart. Enough to make me push my next words out, setting forth the plan I created in motion.

I just hope when this is all over, Knox can find it in his heart to forgive me.

"I want to take a bath."

Knox starts down the hall to the washroom. "Of course, I'll come and set—"

"Alone," I blurt. "I need to process a few things and I've always done that best in the water."

Not a lie.

A flicker of hurt crosses his eyes, and I hate myself just that little more, but I must do this. No matter if it makes me a monster. I will carry the burden of it, happily, if it stops the suffering of those around me.

"Of course, Angel, whatever you need."

My body second-guesses itself moving forward as if it knows the choice, I'm about to make will change everything. Despite no turning back, I peer into his eyes, soaking up every minuscule detail of his face and body. The soul that I know shines as bright as a star. I take it all in and rise onto the balls of my feet and brush a kiss against his lips.

Gentle at first and then frenzied with panic, because what if this is the last time I see him?

I'd risk this being our last time if it meant his safety, if it meant that Knox remained unharmed.

Pulling back, I rip my gaze away before Knox can see the tears glistening in my eyes and shut the door to the bathroom. Not bothering to heat the buckets of water I begin pouring them into the tub, my ears straining for the sounds beyond the wooden door.

Knox hasn't moved, that tug between us growing taut as it tries to warn him. It has been growing tighter over the passing days with worry, and I must hope he will simply play it off as his nerves.

I wait, counting down the seconds, holding my breath as I do.

Let me go, Knox. You must let me go just this one time.

Although I know he can't hear me—the seal around the door in my mind holding strong—I still beg him, and as his footsteps move down the hall and join those in the lounge room, I exhale deeply, the air tinged with a mixture of relief and regret.

Guilt joins the party as I form water with my magic, pouring it loudly into the tub to hide the noise of the window sliding open and my boots landing on the ground behind the cabin. Guilt probes me in the back as I don't say goodbye to Creseda or Henry, my heart not daring to face those it feels I have failed. I even ignore the bond between Aurora and me, tugging and pulling as it begs me to ask for her assistance just a mere few feet away.

That is another set of eyes I don't dare look at.

I cannot put anyone else I love on the line. I refuse to.

Guilt follows me down the mountain, continuously snapping at the heels of my feet as if encouraging me to run faster.

Guilt becomes my best friend, my companion, as I teleport across the mountains, moving under the cover of darkness, the stars twinkling down on me.

All the way to the edge of the capital border.

Nolan and Ordelia were right, their words echoing through my mind even now.

When it comes down to it, you either choose yourself or you allow others to decide your fate. And as I race for the palace, I choose myself. Not caring about burning out or fretting over the usage of my magic. All I need is enough to kill the king. Beyond that, I don't care if I burn out like a shooting star.

Chapter Forty-Six

There is a funeral being held at the palace. Citizens are mourning in the capital. Wakes are being thrown in taverns and restaurants. There are royal ceremonies arranged to commence throughout the day. And yet none of it is for their beloved queen.

They're for *Duke Harrison*.

The king isn't mourning his wife. He isn't mourning the woman who raised his daughter, and he certainly isn't mourning his horrid crimes. I wonder if he even told anyone that their queen was deceased, or if he will simply replace her and ignore the whispers among the capital.

Duke Harrison was his partner in crime, the one he could count on in the council to have a mind as wicked and twisted as his own. He is most likely in mourning for him, just not for the woman whose life he had stolen.

If I had to guess, I would say he even smiled as he put their heads on those spikes.

I bet he watched from afar and found joy in the amount of misery it caused me.

So, as I strap my long black cape around my neck, the

hood hanging loosely over my hair, I feel not an ounce of guilt as I shift. My very molecules change and distort with a single thought, the golden well of my magic limitless.

With days of not moving, my magic was able to recuperate, and it sings its praises today as it basks in its true depth.

It's astounding and yet frightening how limitless it is.

My long chocolate hair glows as it lightens, turning into sleek blonde strands. My ice blue eyes become as warm as sunlight, my freckle-covered cheeks turning opulent beneath the new golden honey color.

I feel no guilt as I pull my hood off and descend into the middle of the capital, a faux sadness covering my new features to blend with the citizens' sniffling and tears.

These people have no idea how much of a monster the man truly was. He never protected them; in fact, he despised them. These people are wasting precious tears on a man who not only killed them but took joy in the blood that was spilled, the fear that was created, and the terror that he spread.

I join the crowd in the mourning march through the city, knowing that those who stand at the front lead us to where I need to go—the palace.

The only time the palace opens its doors is to join the citizens in mourning.

So as the soldiers stand on guard, unmoving as I walk through the arch of the palace gates, I smirk.

My smile doesn't last.

As the sobs ring hollow in my ears, the smell of salty tears and drooping shoulders begin to overwhelm me, and I start to contemplate their authenticity. None of these people knew Duke Harrison. All they knew of the man was that he was the king's right-hand man, his most trusted companion. They barely saw him. He was more familiarized in the palace among the soldiers than the citizens.

So as the woman who's hunched beside me begins to wail as if she's just lost her firstborn, I begin to wonder if he's moved on already, found a new captive to do his magical bidding, because none of this is real. This is an image he has created and molded to fit his personal views and feelings toward the duke.

The only dry eyes in the crowd belong to the soldiers, who scan every individual face with a keen scrutiny. These soldiers aren't simply on guard, protecting their King—they are *searching*.

It's been three days, and he already possesses a new captive that wields magic.

The kernel that turned into a pitiless blazing fire scorches my skin as rage builds to an all-new high within me, and I realize this for what it truly is—the crying, the soldiers.

The king is expecting me.

Swiping the nearest canteen from the clutches of a weeping woman behind me, I hunch my shoulders and sniffle as I drip water down my now tanned cheeks. I let out a keening wail, which isn't hard to do when I imagine the ones I'm mourning.

The soldier I pass stares me down, taking in my tear-streaked cheeks. He does a onceover, then glances away, not detecting the princess that lies hidden beneath.

I'll hand it to him, he was clever. Using whatever magical spell or curse placed upon these innocent people to search for the one person who wouldn't be enthralled by this procession.

The king will go to dark lengths to find me, as evidenced by the thousands of people around me, but it only makes my decision easier. It makes my steps lighter, and my conscious freer.

If he has someone who can control this many people, he can do anything. And it needs to be stopped.

With every step I take, I repeat the names of the lives the king has stolen like a mantra—Eleanor, Annie, Easton, the thousands of people he killed in Sectors Seven and Six. The thousands of children he captured to turn into puppets, the hundreds of creatures he kept hidden in the complex, and the thousands of lives before that.

The people he hung at the gallows every evening at five o'clock to spread fear throughout his kingdom and keep control.

The hundreds of women, men, and children hidden and caged underneath my feet in the dungeons, tortured like traitors.

The three thousand rebels he butchered.

I think of all the people he hurt, and most of all, I think of how he hurt me. I think of my childhood and the façade he created. I think of every hit, kick, punch, and cruel word he spat at me. I think of the detested look on his face when he stared at me—his daughter—as if I was an abomination. Every ounce of hurt he inflicted makes the speck of guilt slide off my heart like a drop of blood.

I may have to become a monster to take him down but, in the end, it will save the lives of many.

It is retribution. It is retaliation. It is karma. And I will act like the gods that forgot us to take it upon myself and claim it.

The King will die tonight by the hands of his Heir. The one he brought into this world only to inflict suffering and the one he has spent years trying to destroy.

This is my final act of rebellion.

Chapter Forty-Seven

Stalking the halls of the king's personal quarters, the sound of my footfalls are muted as I lift my chin high, back straight, and shoulders wide. The hours spent training with Knox pay off as I walk the halls not as Delilah Covington, heir to the throne, but as Hector, the king's butler for fifteen years.

It's odd to be in this body, to force my very being to shift and mold into something other than what it is. I presume it will take its toll on me later, but I do not care nor am I worried about the aftermath. All I can focus on is getting into his room.

I thought it may have taken more work than this, that I'd have to spend hours inside this hellhole they call a palace. But to my dismay and surprise, nothing has been easier. Sneaking into the kitchens under the cover of my invisibility, I immediately found the butler, and he was just how I remembered him.

His mustache combed and styled, regardless of the time. His dull eyes, no matter the request of the king. The coldness wafted off him in waves. The way he didn't bat an eye to a hand slap or a booted heel. Most of all, I memorized the sound of his feet. How soft they were despite his size, how his heel rang hollow on his left as opposed to his right. Mostly because if I heard his footsteps, the king wouldn't be far behind.

So, as I watched him rush around the kitchen, impassive and cold as ever as he prepared the king's food, I didn't have to study him for long to take the form of his body.

I did, however, struggle to get him alone.

It wasn't until he was walking down the empty corridor on his way to the king's chambers did I find the reprieve I needed.

I didn't feel an ounce of guilt as I stole the air from his lungs, my hands grabbing the silver tray in his hands before it crashed to the floor. Then, I dragged his unconscious body through the nearest door and bound him.

But when I stood to my full height, peering down at the butler with his hands and feet tied together, I pieced together where I was.

Which room I stood in.

The rage that consumed me was so intense I had to continually extinguish the flames that erupted along my clenched hands.

To the right of the throne against the back wall, a dark blood stain caught my attention.

The mark and the proof of Annie's words. That he laid Easton's head atop the throne as a message, and from there, it was easy to pick up the silver tray once more and transform myself.

It took very little effort to make that left heel ring hollow as I walked the long and lonely corridors of the palace.

Perhaps that makes me a shapeshifter, or means my magic is powerful enough to make the glamour of the butler true, or maybe my power is just as hurt and grief-stricken as I am and is willing to do anything to exact its revenge.

Whatever the reason, I am grateful, more so as I round the corner and, for the first time since leaving Easton and Annie's cabin, tremble in fear. The only thing to keep my feet moving is the power thrumming through my veins.

The king's personal suite.

Six soldiers standing by the double mahogany doors step aside as I near the entrance, never once questioning the perception I weave for their eyes.

I was always curious how he could sleep at night, with dozens of soldiers in his wing and only one stationed in his daughter's. He certainly made it easy for an assailant to attack me, leaving me out in the open to protect myself.

Although, who I truly needed defending from lies behind this door.

I pray to the forgotten gods that the soldiers ignore the slight tremble of my hand as I reach out and latch onto the golden handle and stride inside my enemy's room.

I have traveled for hours, bending and shaping who I am to get to this moment, and as I round the corner of the king's suite, I realize through it all I forgot to prepare myself to face him. I knew my intentions coming here, but maybe a part of me didn't believe I would make it this far. My eyes lock onto him for the first time since the lake, and fear paralyzes me.

A shock so jarring I wonder whether lightning struck my body.

It takes my mind a moment to process everything around me, to process *him*.

How peaceful he looks, sitting there comfortably in such a calm and pleasant room as if he didn't just slaughter my mother and Annie three days ago.

He doesn't lift his head from the book he reads before the

fire, and it gives me a reprieve, a moment to try and simply breathe against the fear suffocating my lungs.

No matter the time spent away from him, his face will always elicit such a response in my body. That will never change, and it does not surprise me as I quickly swipe away lone tears that escape.

With the heavy tray in my hands, I continue, my footsteps heavier than before, my body begging to turn around and run. I peer at the king out of the corner of my eye as I lean forward to place the tray on the table.

"Hello, Delilah."

I'm startled by the sound that's chased me in my waking dreams, the voice that makes bile rush for my throat. The tray in my hands falls, clanging loudly onto the table.

I snap upright and slide the mask in place, the one made of steel—the one that will get me through this ordeal. My hands tremble as I drop into the chair adjacent to him, not in fear but in *rage* as I remind myself of Easton, of Annie, of my mother.

"I've been waiting for you."

A deadly smirk lifts my lips, my eyes devoid of the person I once used to be. My body shifts, transforming back to my original Fae form. My long chocolate brown hair hangs loosely over my stomach as I tuck a piece behind my elongated ear, putting my abilities on display.

"Father dearest," I say, using the endearment he signed the birthday card with.

He places the book down beside his lukewarm cup of tea. "You'll have to do better than poisoning my food if you want me dead."

I hum, flicking out a small dagger from beneath my sleeve as I begin to clean my nails. "I know," I answer simply.

"To what do I owe the pleasure of your presence?"

"Trust me, the pleasure is all mine," I deadpan. "Clearly you need to send more soldiers to the cellars. They're not competent enough to keep your enemy out of your room." The taut tastes sour on my tongue. I remind myself that no one will be going to the gallows or the dungeons by the end of the night. That is, if everything goes right.

I cock my head. "Unless you're losing control. Lost your touch, have you? Run out of children to steal and people to butcher? Perhaps you can create a holiday in your name where you torture people. It would certainly stop—"

The king slams down his cup of tea, smashing the porcelain with the force. "I do not enjoy childish games. Spit out whatever you wish to say!"

I smirk at the cord I've struck, my eyes sparking with delight as the blue irises turn to chips of ice. "There's the temper I know. I was wondering how long you could pretend to be calm." I grimace. "It doesn't suit you, by the way." I wave my hand in front of my face. "Niceties look horrible on you, so worn out on your stark features."

His jaw clenches.

I click my tongue. "May I also remind you, dear Father, that *you* have been the master of these games for some time now. Far too long in my opinion."

His nostrils flare. "Have?"

There is nothing more this man hates than his ego being hit.

I smirk. "There's a new player…haven't you heard?"

He leans back further in his chair. "Knox is the name of your mate, isn't it?"

I don't let the smirk on my face slip or a hint of shock show. I will not give this man an inch to run with. Not with Knox's life hanging in the balance. The spies he would have had to acquire to learn that information sends a chill down my spine.

He lifts his hand, his fingers about to click, no doubt to call for one of his guards outside. Without moving an inch, golden hands fly for him, capturing his in a death grip, squeezing the fingers until the skin turns bone white.

"I wouldn't do that if I were you," I sing-song.

"It seems Eleanor taught you a few things while she was out on her little excursion."

"Mother," I spit. "She was my *mother*."

His eyes spark at the past tense. "Ahh, yes. I see you received the birthday gift I sent you."

Clenching my jaw, I let the words simmer in my mind. My movements need to be slow and calculated, not rushed and hasty. This is a game of chess.

"Did you ever possess a heart?"

My eyes blaze as I watch his own widen a fraction, the only sign of his shock. It's a fleeting moment, there and gone, one that I would have missed if I so much as blinked.

I wonder if he expected me to throw a fit like a child. To scream and cry and beg for him to apologize.

I wonder if he expected the child that used to turn to her father to right the wrongs he inflicted. If he did, he'll be sorely disappointed because that child is long gone, her naivety is dead, and in her place sits a woman he should be *terrified* of.

"I don't wish to play your foolish games."

"And I didn't wish to play yours either, but here we are. My mother and the ones I love are dead and you are soon to join them."

The king chuckles darkly, the sound holding no humor. "That's a very far-fetched dream you have there, child."

My lips curl into a smile as his hands begin to tremble in the grasp of my power. "I don't believe so."

If he had wards around the room preventing an attack they would have been activated by now. Perhaps the wards placed died along with my mother. Or they're silent like the ones in the children's complex and an array of soldiers are marching to this room right now to kill me.

"You will die tonight, and every drop of blood spilled will be to avenge the lives you have taken."

He jumps to his feet, only to wobble, his stance unsteady. His eyes flash with fury, blazing, as they land on me. I lounge back further into the chair.

"What have you done?" he spits through clenched teeth.

"What should have been done long ago." I flick the blade in my hand around the room carelessly. "I must say, for a man so paranoid of death, your routinely nightcap of tea was surprisingly easy to poison."

Considering the number of soldiers that guard the bastard, it was surprisingly easy to slip arsenic poison into the tea the cook set out for him. After all, no one looked twice at the face I adorned.

His beady eyes jump to the smashed teacup, the liquid dripping down the side of his table. He reaches for it, his hands trembling and spasming as his knees buckle. In desperation, he grabs it with his fingertips and hurls it at me.

Golden tendrils fly for it, maneuvering the large teapot over my head, and slamming it into the wall. The silencing shield snaps up around the room just in time for his outraged roar.

The longer his gaze bores into mine, the darker his beady eyes become. I sit back and watch it one last time…the moment they change to the soulless black pit. The moment the beast within him is uncaged.

His nostrils flare, a low growl leaving his lips as he moves to lunge for me, only for his legs to fail him.

"That, my dearest father, are the effects of poison." I rise out of the chair slowly, circling him.

He tries to stand again, wrestling against the poison flowing through his bloodstream, but only falls haphazardly against it. I soak up every moment of his struggles.

Pushing off his chair, I peruse around the room, absent-mindedly admiring my nails. The stumbling brute king behind me bangs his feet against the marble tiles, shallow curses tumbling from his sharp tongue.

Golden magic wraps around his arms and legs, silencing the incessant noise.

I wondered the entire journey what I would say to him when the time came. Rehearsing all the points I didn't want to forget, the words that have been hanging in my mind for over twenty years. The words that wish to be set free.

But I don't need to remind myself of them now. They simply tumble from my lips as the power scale falls in my favor. I stand taller. My years of training paid off, just not in the way he had thought.

"You have never once taken accountability for your actions." Hate-filled eyes snap to mine, incredulous at the words I speak. I snarl. "You are in this position because of your choices and yet you stare at me as if you're shocked that I've taken these measures. You killed my mother, you killed Annie, and you quite literally slit Easton's neck behind my back! And you dare look at me as if I am the one that has wronged you?" I shake my head in bewilderment. "Are you truly that delusional or do you just believe the narrative you've told yourself over the years?"

I bore into his eyes, watching them for any sign of emotion. Even just a small glimpse—a flicker.

It never comes.

"You took everything that I loved and cherished and broke it. You made my very existence miserable, and now you have the *gall* to look at me as if I'm the villain in your story?" I lower my face to his, my lip quivering with rage. "You didn't even give her a *funeral*!"

His face flushes red, turning a sickly shade of purple as his lips thin.

"Every action and choice you have ever made was to further your own agenda, to serve yourself. You are the most selfish, miserable bastard I have ever come across in my life and I hope the afterlife makes you pay for the thousands—no, *hundreds* of thousands of lives—you have taken for your own power-driven needs.

"You were meant to be my father," I croak. The door that I keep locked opens, the emotions pouring out of me with a vengeance as the tears I've been trying to hold back break free.

The fury that had been building within me for days comes to a head, flushing my cheeks and encasing my skin with heat. The words that have been trapped, silenced by this man, pour out of me with abandon as the hand lifts for the first time in twenty-three years.

The words flow freely, finding freedom.

"You were my father and you stared at me with such disgust that I wondered for years if I was broken—if something was wrong with me. You made me question whether I was worthy of love; you made me believe I didn't deserve it. All because you don't know the first thing about being a father—a decent human being. You broke the spirit of a three-year-old girl."

I pounce, flipping out a blade and holding it against his

Heir of Broken Kingdom   495

neck. He can't even squirm against the hold of my magic and the poison.

"Do you remember the first time you hit me? Because I do. I remember it like it was yesterday. I was three years old, and you backhanded my little face." I wipe away the tears that fall off my cheeks. "I still wanted to run to you for comfort. I thought it was a mistake, that I must have been ill and imagining what happened because my daddy would never hurt me."

I chuckle, yet the sound is devoid of emotion and humor. His face remains impassive, eyes inspecting the golden magic holding him captive. He doesn't care to hear me speak—but I do. This isn't for him, it's for *me*.

"I look back at that moment and realize how much of a monster you truly are. When I came running to you crying, even after you hit me, you looked at me with such revulsion. You stared at my tear-streaked face like I was filth and *that* was what broke me."

"You were an overly sensitive child. Your tears were useless to this kingdom."

I shove the blade into his neck harder, trying to shut his mouth but it's no use against his stubborn thin lips.

"I made you strong. Without me, you were a weak girl worth *nothing*. You should be thanking me for all I have done for you."

All he has done for me?

I lower my head, my chin wobbling with pure undulated hatred. "You should have never been a father, let alone a king. You don't deserve either title. You treated those people as if they were disposable, as if this country and kingdom were your playground. You lied, cheated, stole, and were unfaithful to the crown—to your people!" I let my words hit their mark before whispering, "You are an abomination to the word *king*; I know that now."

"Yes, your little pet Knox took care of solidifying that belief. Do you think galivanting in the streets of Azalea and mingling with poor citizens makes someone a king? That *child* doesn't know the first thing about being a king!"

His squirming body slowly deflates as the very life drains from him. Each word he spits takes seconds off his withering life.

He knew where I was all this time. How does he have men in the Fae courts?

Disgust rises in my throat at the idea of this sick evil man knowing about Azalea and its purity.

I shake my head, my brows furrowing. "Out of everything I just said, your only takeaway was Knox? The only thing that you care enough about is to check your overinflated ego is bigger than his? And to prove what? That you have spies at your disposal to do your dirty work? That you kill more people? You've killed more people than the Grim Reaper himself and that is not something to be proud of!" I bellow.

He truly doesn't care. He never has.

His eyes begin to droop, the lids growing heavy with every passing second. His hands and feet grow lax, his thrashing wilting to mere spasms. His chest slows, his breathing ragged, and I know I don't have much time.

"You broke me every day." My words rumble throughout the room like a crack of thunder, illuminating the pain that I try to keep hidden. I may whisper the words, but they strike with as much force as a scream. "You broke my heart. You were the one that was meant to comfort me when boys broke my heart, but instead, I ran to them and cried about you."

Tears roll freely down my cheeks. "I broke my spirit trying to mold myself into a version that you would be proud of, perhaps even love, but it was never enough. Nothing I ever did was good enough for you. As a parent, you should be ashamed of yourself for tearing me down when you were meant to build me up, and I will *never* forgive you for that."

His eyes lift to mine, still devoid of emotion.

"You made me hate myself. You made me wish I was never born. My own father, the one who gave me life, hurt me so deeply that you drove me to thoughts of harming myself. You made my life so bleak and hopeless that instead of hating you, I hated myself. I see the way fathers stare at their children in the capital. I see the tenderness in their gazes, the gentle touches and hugs that I never received, and it makes me wonder what I did to deserve being given such a malicious father."

His eyes turn murky, glazed. Similar to how my mother's eyes would turn unfocused. I couldn't have planned a more perfect retribution, making him suffer being trapped within your mind while your body disobeys your commands.

He sputters, drool dripping down his chin as his head lolls back and forth.

"The sight of you sickens me. I know what love feels like now. I know how it warms your heart and spirit. How it lifts you up, not tears you down. How it feels to be held with warmth and care. I know the sounds of words spoken with tenderness and I know what unconditional love truly is. It was the way in which you were supposed to love me."

I swallow thickly as his eyes snap to mine. Though bleary and unfocused, I know he is listening. "You destroyed my heart when you placed their heads on those spikes, so in return, I'm going to break yours."

Before he can register my movements, I pull the dagger back from his neck and plunge it into his chest, an inch from his heart. Red blood spills from his side, his mouth gaping open with shock that I walked through on my promise of violence.

Unsheathing the dragon sword strapped to my back, my lip quivers and my hands tremble as I wedge the blade against his neck. The shallow pulse I feel thumping faintly against the sword has tears springing to my eyes, mourning the father I never had.

This is the part I will never utter, the secret I will take to my grave.

Because despite everything, despite the pain and heartache this man has inflicted…he is my father. He will never love me enough to stop hurting me, and I will never be good enough to be loved by him, but there is a small part within me that still clings to that hope. That he will change into the father I've been dreaming about since I was three years old—the father I deserved.

The little girl who had her innocence stolen is the one who clings to hope. She prayed every night before sleep that her father would come to tuck her into bed and read her a story. She prayed to the forgotten gods to go back in time and make her daddy never hit her.

Throughout all the abuse, throughout all the years of mistreatment, she clung onto that sliver of hope, wishing upon every fallen start she saw…until three days ago when she saw the three heads.

She handed me her battered heart with tear-stained cheeks, her tiny voice full of utter despair as she whispered, "You can have him now."

He took my family away from me, and with it, he took away that little girl's hope for change. So, in honor of her, the dream that I will never see to fruition, for Annie, Easton, and my mother—I lower the sword to his neck. A small ounce of satisfaction runs through my veins that he will die at the hands of Easton's spirit in the same way he killed him.

"This is payment, Father. You must face the consequences of your actions, for you have gone unchecked for far too long. You are a sinner, the worst this world has ever seen, and I refuse to let you take away anyone else's loved ones because you don't have a soul."

Behind his beady eyes, behind the glassy haze covering them, I can see the monster within him pacing, snarling to be let out.

"Goodbye," I whisper to the fantasized version of him in my mind, to the imaginative father I had dreamed of.

And drag the dragon sword across his throat.

Crimson blood soaks me, marking me as I take his life.

This will be my penance. For as long as I live, I will breathe with the title of a murderer.

This title is worth fighting for, because for every drop of blood that spills from his neck, the light vanishing from his eyes, the monster within them disappearing, I seek retribution for the lives he took.

And as my father sits before me, bleeding out, I know I am not losing a loved one, because you cannot lose what you never had.

Chapter Forty-Eight

The sounds of chaos still haunt me. As if the commotion of the palace is ten steps behind me and not hundreds of miles. The flurry of panic that consumed the royal soldiers was a sight to behold, and yet I could have sworn in their eyes lay something I thought I would never see in the eyes of Aloriah's citizens again —hope.

It shouldn't take long for word to spread throughout the kingdom, that the once mighty and unstoppable king has fallen. Slayed by an assassin in the night, found by his royal butler of fifteen odd years.

It had felt strange to shift, making the blood and grim disappear from my clothes as my body took on the king's butler once more. It had felt repellent in a way, a thick layer of disgust coating my tongue as I covered my tracks.

I told myself it was just one more mask, the last I ever had to wear, the last time I ever had to pretend to be anything other than who I am in the walls of the palace.

The chess game had finally come to an end.

I thought I would feel elated, celebratory even. But there's just numbness. The fire within me that propelled my feet forward and got me through the last harrowing days has now extinguished, and all I'm left with is a hollow feeling.

For a moment after the monster within his eyes had faded and he was lying lifeless in his chair, I felt like his punishment had been served. A small speck of retribution had been paid. Revenge for what he had done and taken from not only me, but every citizen in the lands of Aloriah. But that feeling only lasted a moment.

I thought it would make things better, and in retrospect I know it has, but even knowing this fact, it hasn't changed the hollowness within me.

When I transformed back to my true form, I was surprised that the blood still smeared my skin and clothing. Clinging to me for dear life, like how the king had grappled for a way to stay alive. Or perhaps it was just my magic's way of reminding me of the murderer I had become.

My steps are slow, my feet dragging through the darkened forest. My body navigates me by instinct, my mind whirling too much to focus on where I'm going.

It knows where I would be safe.

Because without realizing it, in the next heartbeat, I hear whispers. Hushed, crazed voices, weariness lining the words as they argue back and forth.

I stumble through the clearing. Creseda and Henry nicker as they trot toward me, the clever sentient beings always seeming to know.

Axel and Lenox snap their mouths closed as they run for me, my name falling from their lips. "Delilah!"

Their happiness is evident until they stop abruptly, taking in my haggard appearance.

Stepping out of the shadows, I hold out my blood-drenched hands. My body is covered head to toe in crimson, as if a beacon in the night, signaling to all to stay away from the king slayer.

"I couldn't let him hurt anyone else," I croak.

My words break the curse on my mind. The numbness fades as the ramifications of what I'd just did hit me square in the chest.

"The king is dead," I whisper.

Not for Lenox or Axel, but for myself. As if to try and wake me from a dream.

Lenox steps forward. His mouth opens and closes, words forever lost. It isn't until Axel lays his hand gently on my elbow does Lenox move, taking off into the sky.

Axel's voice is impossibly soft. "Delilah, what did you do, sweetheart?"

I drag my gaze to his, surprised to find understanding and…compassion. How can Axel have compassion for a murderer?

"I slit the king's throat," I say simply, as if it will answer the questions flashing through his eyes.

A thunderous boom lands behind me, the forest ground shaking beneath my feet as a guttural roar pierces the night sky. I turn to find Knox charging for me, his face a readable mask of hysteria as Aurora lands shortly after him. Her golden eyes are just as frenzied.

Lenox lands last, rushing for his king as every one of Knox's long and powerful strides eats up the distance between us. He is dressed in his leathers, covered head to toe in silver.

The concern in his eyes is enough to bring me to my knees. Axel catches me as they buckle, and the pure terror that covers Knox's features reminds me of the reason I became a murderer.

"It's not my own," I try to say to him, but Knox can't hear

me, not over the thunderous pounding of his heart, not over the fear clutching his body. His hands tremble, searching every part of my body for the wound he thinks lies beneath my fighting leathers.

I don't even have a scratch.

I slit the king's throat and I walked away completely unscathed.

Axel removes his hands only to stop Knox. "It's not her blood."

His second's words penetrate, making Knox's head fly up, gaze snapping to mine. His eyes, then soften.

"Angel," he murmurs.

The pet name tastes sour. *I'm not an angel anymore, far from it. Angels don't take lives.*

"You locked me out," he chokes out. "You vowed you wouldn't."

My heart pinches. "I couldn't let him keep hurting people."

I couldn't let him take you away from me, I whisper, daring to crack open the door in my mind, both to Knox and Aurora's bridges.

Knox gently caresses my face, his fingers coming back red. The sight makes bile churn in my stomach.

Aurora walks up behind Knox. Where her golden eyes were filled with fear moments ago, they are now filled with betrayal. She puffs her chest out, a breath rushing from her snout as she stomps her right foot.

"I couldn't risk losing anyone else. My heart couldn't take it," I say as if that is answer enough as to why I killed my father.

I killed my father.
I killed the king.

"The king is dead," I whisper under my breath. "The king is dead," I repeat.

The past twelve hours come crashing down upon me as I repeat the saying over and over and over.

"The king is dead." *No.* I shake my head. "My father is dead."

The door flies open in my mind, Knox's starlight soul charging in to find me hugging a younger version of myself. That little three-year-old girl sobs in my arms in my mind. Sobbing for the life she dreamed of, the family and father she thought she would have one day. The innocence that was stolen from her.

Knox kneels before us, gently reaching out to pull us into his awaiting arms. The move has my resolve crumbling, that tidal wave of grief and guilt overtaking me.

Large arms catch me as my body gives out on itself. Knox carries me into the cabin, the thick blood covering my leathers now smearing his clothing and skin. He holds me tightly to his chest while he comforts that little girl in my mind.

Through it all, all I can utter is, "I killed my father."

Behind us, I see my loved ones.

I look at them and know I made the right decision… although it just might kill me to live with it.

Chapter Forty-Nine

I don't stop uttering the phrase until Knox peels the thick layers of leather drenched in the king's blood from my body. His movements are gentle and slow, like if he moves too fast, I'll crack and break. Perhaps I will, or perhaps the pit within my stomach will swallow me whole.

Knox peels off his own clothing, our gazes never wavering, the connection never breaking as he walks toward me. Gently scooping me into his arms once more before lowering us into the scalding water he prepared.

I close my eyes on a deep sigh.

I want to scrub my skin until it bleeds raw. Until it's a new layer of skin that didn't kill the king, that didn't kill her father, that didn't lose her loved ones.

Instead, Knox lathers a washcloth with my vanilla-scented soap and gently rubs it over my skin, not scrubbing it raw like how I crave to do. But he knows that, he always knows what I want or need.

I close my eyes, praying that by the time I open them once more the layer of dirt and blood will be gone.

It's silent for what feels like hours before Knox finally speaks, his voice hoarse. "Tilt your head back."

The moment reminds me of just a few months ago, after the hours of the Phoenix Rising spell, after I came to, my body struggling to function. Knox had taken care of me in such a similar way. It makes me realize just how drastically my life has changed since that moment, and in such a short amount of time.

Grief strikes as it wishes.

Sometimes it's sporadic and other times a whirlwind, where you can only clutch onto something steady and wait out the turbulent winds that try to knock you off your feet.

I feel as if I'm slipping, my grasp on reality shifting as the wind begins to lift my feet off the ground, its current seconds away from taking me forever.

Doing as Knox asked, I savor the warmth of the water trickling down my hair, running over my shoulders, as if caressing the soft skin.

I can feel Knox's eyes on my back, on the scars the king left there long ago. The scars that I will forever carry, the ones that are visible. The burns and slashes.

"I know you wanted retribution for what he did," I say softly.

Knox's hands graze my jaw, cupping it to gently turn my head to the side so I can see his face as he lowers it to mine.

"You did what you needed to do. Nobody is judging you for that." Knox's voice softens. "You needed to take your power back, especially after everything he had done to you."

Looking away, a lump lodges itself in my throat.

"What do you think life will look like now that the king is dead?"

Knox picks up the washcloth once more, lathering the

soapy rag over my skin. "I think people will need a lot of time to heal."

I know he's not only talking about the citizens.

"And I think it will look peaceful…in time," he goes on.

We both fall silent as I look to the small window at the top of the bathroom, just enough to let the steam in the room out.

The night sky is begging to give way to the sun. The shining stars fading as dawn fast approaches. Birds chirp and animals stir in the depth of the forest beyond.

Just a mere few hours ago, the kingdom lost their horrid king, and yet the world continues to move on without him—regardless of what he said about how he was the only one fit to rule the kingdom.

The moon departs and the sun rises for another day, moving on without my family.

Time is a cruel thing.

"I'm not going to be their queen."

Knox's hand stops moving. "You are the only living heir. No matter what anyone says the crown will go to you. Everyone on the council will know that you are innocent. The bounty the king placed on your head was his personal agenda, not because you're a traitor—"

"I am a traitor. I killed the king."

Knox is silent for a moment. The only ones that know I slit the man's throat are those in this very cabin, and none of them would tell a soul. To the soldiers and to the kingdom of Aloriah, I am a princess whose father despised her for her rebellious act of welcoming Fae and journeying to their city.

I saw the look on the maids and nurses' faces as they rushed through the halls, and I heard the hushed whispers and the sobs of relief.

The king's death was a blessing. As if their prayers, lost in the wind for years, were finally answered.

Even if they found out I was the one to take his life they would still rein me queen, purely out of gratefulness for taking down such a gods-awful man.

As for his loyal men...I ignored the sound of their panicked screams.

My voice is as heavy as the words I speak. "I'm not taking the throne. I'm going to appoint Ordelia."

My confession silences him, his body freezing behind me, the cloth in his hand pausing on my shoulder.

"Ordelia is a fair ruler. She had one moment of lapsed judgment, an error made during turbulent grief, and she rectified the situation instantly."

"With the help of my overbearing presence," Knox mutters under his breath.

"She's a fair ruler, Knox. She would never hurt her people the way he did," I say, ignoring his statement. I turn to face Knox in the tub, water splashing. "I will name Ordelia the new queen. I know the whispers will spread of why I didn't take the throne, why the only heir of the king has become a deserter, but after all that my bloodline has done to this kingdom...I can't stand to be here. I may have stood up to my father and stopped him, but that does not stop the memories from chasing me at night. It doesn't stop the memory of those I have lost from haunting me to the point of debilitation."

I wouldn't be able to breathe if I had to live in that palace again.

I close my eyes as a lone tear snakes down my cheek. "I need a fresh start. This place is no longer my home—it never was. These people deserve time to heal without the reminder of his daughter ruling over them." I feel Knox's soft lips press against my forehead as I ask, "If you will have me, can Azalea be my home?"

I'm shocked the question unnerves me as much as it does as I open my eyes to Knox's piercing gaze.

"You are my home, Angel. I will go wherever you go."

Relief threatens to drag me under. "Azalea," I murmur. "Azalea is my home."

The smile that overtakes Knox's face is one of pure joy and for the first time in days, I feel it flicker within my heart. A small beat for joy, a beat for the happiness I found again. Perhaps time will eventually heal the cracks and dents of my heart. It will never be the same, nor will it be whole again, but maybe it can heal enough so I can smile again.

"I just have one request," I whisper.

Throwing the last sheet over the couch has my heart pinching with pain. I look around the packed-up cabin that was once bursting with life with Annie and the remnants of hope. The whispers of a dream Easton had envisioned. It's sad to see it so cold, empty.

I'm sorry I couldn't make a home here, Easton.

Picking up the writing gear on the table overlooking the window, I carefully place it in my satchel, along with the small trinkets. What's left of the beautiful memory of Annie and Easton.

"Angel."

I turn, following Knox's voice to the front entryway, trying to discern the look in his eyes. I hold my breath, crossing my fingers behind my back as I pray and hope for one last time that the lands of Aloriah bless me when they never have.

The one request I had of him.

The soft dip of his head has air rushing from my mouth.

"Lenox and I found them this morning."

"Where were they?" I dare ask.

Knox's swallow is audible. "They're safe now. Lenox has already begun traveling home."

Knox is saving me from further pain, so I choose to believe his carefully crafted words as he dodges my question. Annie, Easton, and my mother are safe now. They found their bodies so we can lay them to rest.

The least I can do is give them a peaceful afterlife and a burial that's deeply deserved.

Turning away, I say a silent goodbye to the cabin…for now. I could never say goodbye forever, could never let go of this piece of history. The tether of my old life. So, I memorize it as it is and pray that I will see it one day soon. Hopefully I'll be able to fill it next time with joy and happiness.

I close the door behind me and take the steps one at a time, focusing on the relief on Knox and his court's faces that we overcame this hurdle together.

I look to Nolan and Harlow as they mount Creseda and Henry, preparing for the long journey back to Azalea.

I point to Nolan. "Do anything to my horses and I'll throw you in the cellar."

Harlow smirks. "I'll report *everything* that transpires, trust me."

"Gods," Nolan mutters, shaking his head atop Henry.

Our relationship may always be strained but we both relate to something far greater than pettiness. We both know what loss feels like and I won't stop until we find his sister and mother. After all, he deserves to be reunited. I didn't get my happy ending, but perhaps it isn't too late for him.

News arrived while I had been in the palace. The Fae and

creatures we rescued from the complex only accounts for half of the missing lives. The other half that needs to be found... that's tomorrow's problem.

Nolan doesn't say he blames me...but I know that when he stares at me, he sees my father. His look is a reminder of why I will never take the crown.

Ordelia took the news of her position in stride. It'll be a big adjustment, but one she's ready to fulfill.

Striding toward me, Knox wraps an arm around my shoulders. "We'll see you two in three weeks."

Thanks to Harlow and her strong teleporting abilities, she will be able to cut the otherwise two-month horse ride trip into three weeks.

I run my hands down Creseda and Henry's snouts, looking into their eyes as I say farewell for now. Thankful that through it all, they are still standing before me, safe.

"Please take care of them," I whisper to no one in particular.

But it surprises me when Nolan's gruff voice answers me.

"We will protect them, Delilah."

Pulling back, tears pool in my eyes as they take off, sparks of light flashing, disappearing and then reappearing hundreds of feet away. Henry and Creseda's joyful nickering can be heard even as they disappear from sight.

Axel spreads his glorious wings, beating wildly as he takes off into the night sky beside his brother atop Zephlyn. Hazel's worried frown pierces into me as they fly.

Aurora stalks forward. Her gaze has been more assessing than others, more cautious, as if waiting for the moment I will flee again. I hate that I've placed that distrust in her, but it was for the better, and for everyone's safety, that I went in alone.

Lowering her head, she allows me to mount her, Knox

choosing to sit behind me, trading closeness for the freedom of flying. Because we don't have to hide anymore, our bond can be shouted from the rooftops of every building in Aloriah without the worry that the king will destroy us.

Destroy him.

Knox wraps his arms around me and I dig my heels into Aurora's soft sides, signaling to her that we're ready. I crane my neck and watch the cabin grow smaller with every passing second as we begin our journey home.

To Azalea.

Chapter Fifty

Beneath Easton's tombstone lies the message, *Together forever.*

Three weeks later I finally get to say my goodbye as I stand in Knox's backyard on the ocean cliff and bury Annie and Easton—all parts of them, thanks to Lenox. Knox stands behind me, his presence and strength felt through our bond. Unyielding as I kneel between the two white headstones. The dates on them are too close together.

A small cherub angel statue stands between the two, forever standing guard, overlooking fellow angels laid to rest.

Perhaps they would have wished to be laid to rest in the country and lands they had known their whole life, or perhaps I made the right choice by bringing them here. To a land and court filled with hope and happiness.

To give Easton the chance to experience the Fae lands like he was meant to. A chance to experience the sound of beating dragon wings, the way it seems to vibrate in your bones. Here, he can also enjoy the music drifting from the ocean city below.

Easton dreamed of the magic I did throughout my life too,

a life outside of the palace. I couldn't give it to him in his lifetime but this I can give him. A final resting place where he will be safe for as long as I live.

This isn't the funeral he deserves. He deserves to have his mother here to mourn for the loss of her son. But I know her sudden disappearance is because of the king. So, I will be his family, for I always was, and he was mine.

Family doesn't mean blood. Family means love and loyalty.

As for Annie, to bring her here was a selfish decision. I'm not sure where she would have wanted to be laid to rest. She saw me as a daughter, and I saw her as a mother, and with that thought in mind, I was quick to bury her beside Easton. The other person in her life who she viewed as her own.

She will forever be close to us, and perhaps the happiness emanating from the city below will drift to her, carried on the ocean winds and fill her soul with the joy she deserved to experience in her lifetime.

Laying the bunch of peonies and dahlias across the upturned grass I fix the white bow that holds the bunch of flowers together, courtesy of Ace's kind touch.

My eyes glisten.

For the mother who showed me what it felt like to be cared for and loved, for the friend who showed me how to create joy in my life, and for the two people who always had my back.

Rising to my feet, I stare at the names engraved ever so carefully in the white stones and know without a shadow of a doubt that this is a heartbreak I will feel for eternity.

Knox comes up beside me, his heart as heavy as mine as he softly passes me two white lanterns, waiting to be lit.

With a simple blink, my power lights the flames, and as I

stare into its golden tendrils, silver pools in my eyes as I bestow the flame with memories.

The sound of Easton's voice, the way the corner of his eyes would crinkle as he laughed, how the deep timbre sound could fill my heart with such joy. The way Easton knew exactly what my heart needed with a single glance, the way his chest would puff up as he stood before me in front of danger. My trainer, my fighter, my protector, my friend, and my soulmate.

And most importantly, my first love.

My first love was born of friendship. Because before Easton, I never believed I was worthy of love. If it weren't for Easton, I would have never allowed Knox into my heart; I wouldn't have allowed his beautiful court and family in either. It is because of Easton that I stand here today with my mate and an open heart.

It may be cracked and scarred, but it is open.

And Annie…beautiful, courageous Annie.

I have my life to thank for her.

The woman who was always by my side. For the moments where my strength wavered, for the times where my heart desired to stop beating. She filled my heart and soul with tender words of wisdom and love, bestowing upon me the courage and the will to live. To keep fighting for another day. I am standing here today because of her and it is a tragedy in itself that she is not by my side.

If anyone deserves to continue on out of the three of us it certainly isn't me.

It is not fair nor kind what they went through, but that does not mean you don't deserve to live, Knox swears vehemently.

Knox stands beside me, holding me as we watch the two lanterns float up, joining the twinkling stars in the night sky.

Others are soon to follow, his court standing behind us, lighting their own lanterns in respect and tribute to those lost.

I stand watching the lanterns until I can no longer see them, the twinkling stars blurring together to create a hazy landscape of sparkles.

I don't dare blink until Knox whispers, "It's time."

Ripping my gaze away, grief swallows me whole for another reason entirely.

We walk back inside, passing Creseda and Henry as they frolic in the new paddock Knox built for them. They run down the fence line, chasing what they think are shooting stars, but are just Annie and Easton's passing lanterns saying their final goodbye.

Zephlyn and Aurora lie beside one another, Aurora's golden eyes never leaving mine until the very last moment I round the corner of the house and we trail down the side to the entrance.

Knox's court already waits there, carrying a large white coffin.

Eleanor.

I have been dreading all the burials for twenty-one days and sixteen hours, but this is the one that truly crushes my heart.

I couldn't be selfish with her, not after all she had done for me, the risks and pain she endured to try and protect and warn me. She deserved to be set free, returned to her home and loved ones.

I just wish doing the right thing didn't have to hurt so much.

We don't need to summon the mermaids. Like last time, they already know and when we land in the grass meadow, we find them all waiting, the entire mermaid pod on display with emotion shining in their usually cold gazes.

Walking closely behind the men, I'm grateful that I don't have to be the one to carry my dead mother and grateful to magic for preserving her on the long journey from the human lands.

Not one of the mermaids look at us, their piercing gazes glued to what holds their long-lost sister. Their faces are wet, presumably from something other than the river's water.

The men lower Eleanor gently into the water, her coffin bobbing, then step back, Knox not too far behind. Always close enough to save me.

And what happens next is one of true wonder.

Violet light shines through the crack of the coffin until it explodes, encompassing the entire casket in that vibrant light. I take a step forward, my hands reaching out as if to stop what I know is the end.

The mermaids circle the violet light, joining hands as they begin swaying side to side, words rolling off their tongue in a language long forgotten by humans and Fae. Their timbres drop as they start chanting louder. I don't understand their sorrowful words, but it seems to speak to my magic, making it rumble and quake inside of me, shedding tears for the soul it has lost.

The water between the mermaids and the coffin begins to swirl, twirling the coffin around and around until a hole forms, and before I know it, the water is swallowing the coffin whole, taking my mother with it.

Returned to the seas, a gift upon this world now returned to the universe, she will forever feel the water gliding past her hair and gills.

My largest regret in life will stay with me, the words left unspoken, until I am reunited with her on the other side, wherever that may be. My heart will not know peace until I speak the apology she deserves. I will carry the burden that despite being returned to her sisters at last, and being reunited with the ocean, she will never swim through the current of her home again.

As the last of my mother's light begins to fade, the violet winking out beneath the water, I take a tentative step forward, kneeling on the riverbed. Naia's eyes finally connect with mine. She swims forward, her white hair cascading down her back. The turquoise jewel that always sits on her forehead barely shines today, as if its light is dimmed, winked out as she mourns her loss.

Sitting where I was mere months ago, facing the revelation of my vision, I once more allow the soft strands of grass to soothe my aching heart and ground my restless soul. Clearing my throat twice to stop the crack from breaking my voice, I finally ask the question that has haunted me since the moment my mother's tail sprang free.

"Why couldn't you tell me?"

Couldn't, not didn't.

Taking a play from the mermaids themselves, I'm careful with my words. I try to hone the accusatory lint to my voice and as her eyes soften, those hard edges smoothing out, I know I've succeeded.

"It was not our premonition to share. Nor were we tasked with the information." Her voice lowers along with her chin. "The king made all the eyes unable to see past the veil of darkness he blanketed himself and Eleanor with."

"You never knew?"

Naia shakes her head slowly while a fire ignites in her eyes. "Not until the moment she was taken from this world.

When the spells were lifted." My arms threaten to lose their purchase as tears fill her eyes, glistening as bright as a star. "Thank you for returning our sister."

My mouth opens to apologize—for what, I'm unsure. The fact that I didn't keep her safe, that in retaliation to my actions, she was butchered. That she was even in the palace at all because of someone I shared blood with. I want to apologize for it all, to help bring whatever peace I can, but I'm stopped as her eyes snap to the court behind me and widen. She backs away suddenly, all softness removed from her face. That impenetrable wall slams closed once more, and the stone-cold Naia returns.

My brow furrows deeply as I whip my head behind me, expecting to see demonic creatures with the amount of hatred not only in Naia's expression but in her sisters' too. But there's only Knox's court, now shifting with unease.

Knox strides forward, his hand reaching out to help me stand. He keeps an eye on Naia and her pod.

"Naia, what did you see?" I dare ask.

Turbulent red eyes lock on mine. Trying to convey a message I will never be able to decipher.

"Fate, it seems, has a lot planned for you, my dear."

Before I can utter another word, they disappear, taking the small orb of violet light that was pulsing beneath the water along with them.

I rush forward, sinking my hand into the water as I watch the violet orb disappear around the lake's bend.

Goodbye, Mother.

Chapter Fifty-One

The letter in my hand singes my skin, the unknown words in its confines burning me. The ones that undoubtedly could either destroy my soul or revive it. I turn it over in my palm for the thousandth time since Knox handed it to me when we returned and stare a hole into my name written across the top of the letter, in Easton's handwriting.

The letter Knox found in the cabin.

Through it all, I shoved it into the corner of my mind and forgot about its existence, and Knox, keeping to his word, gave it to me in the end.

I've been locked in his study for over an hour, just staring at the parchment that holds Easton's sentences, thoughts, and emotions.

It's a precious gift, a blessing, and yet I am petrified.

So much so that I open the top drawer of Knox's desk and lay the parchment down gently inside before slamming the drawer closed and bolting the lock with magic. Only Knox and I will be able to access it.

It's been several hours after the strange encounter with

Naia and her pod, and I still cannot shake the gaze that pierced my soul, the warning she was trying to convey. No matter how hard I try to coax my magic into giving me a premonition, I come up empty-handed. And we're no closer to solving or stopping what my premonition showed before. All I have to show for our journey are the deaths of Annie, Eleanor, and thousands of Ordelia's men.

A small voice in my mind keeps reminding me of all the children's lives we saved, along with the creatures that were held captive. It will never outweigh what I lost but I am thankful for their safety.

Shoving out of the chair, I lock the door in my mind of Easton and the emotions that come with him and join Knox and his court in the dining room. Lenox is shoveling chocolate into his mouth until it's bursting at the seams, taking full advantage of the kind gift Knox set up for me. As a tribute to Easton and his uncanny obsession with the dessert.

I had wanted to take a nap, hoping to spur on a premonition, and yet Knox, forever the tender and caring man, had changed my plans and mind the moment I walked through his front door to find he had set up a wake for all three of my loved ones.

The chocolate fountain and dessert table were just the tip of the iceberg.

Knox had added a shelf dedicated to Annie, to all the books she raved about reading—medicinal texts, herbal books, papers on healing techniques. At my teary gaze and the knowledge that she would never read them, Knox went on to tell me how important it is in the cycle of life and the demise of grief to live for those you love. The joy, he found, is doing what his past loved ones adored before.

Perhaps it will bring me comfort and make me feel close to her to read such books, or perhaps I will pick up the pages only to bawl my eyes out. The answer is for another day where my bones do not weigh down my body with the heaviness of their loss.

The token for my mother was one that brought me to tears.

Naia had given Axel my mother's headpiece in the short moments he landed before me, ordering him to give it to Knox and pass it to me at a more appropriate time. It had been the one she wore before she was taken by the king. The beautiful purple, amethyst stone used to lie on her forehead.

Knox pulled me aside into his room to give me it, bestowing upon me the story of my mother, her origin in the pod, and how Naia was her second-in-command.

Eleanor, it seems, was taken for a reason. Being the finest mermaid seer, her gifts were ones sought after for many years, and her power was one of beauty and grace. I'm honored to have known her and yet heartbroken under the circumstances of our forced meeting.

How she was taken is still a mystery to me, but the only two who can answer that question are dead.

So that leaves me here, trying to conjure up a small smile at Lenox choking on said chocolates shoveled into his mouth, all the while Hazel and Harlow stick to me like glue, offering what they deem words of wisdom.

"It brought me comfort to celebrate Luna's life. You just need to find what way brings you the most sense of peace," Hazel offers.

"Life is too short to wallow," Harlow adds.

"Harlow!" she snaps, reprimanding the half-witch.

I know her words are crass, but they do hold an element of truth. Life is unbearably short, especially for humans. Immortality makes Fae cocky and careless with their lives, but it's a precious thing, a gift, no matter how much I want to gag at the cheesy sentiment. It almost sounds like something Annie would say.

"Life is precious and fragile. It should be celebrated while we are still breathing," I finally say.

Hazel smiles as if her words are finally taking root, whereas Harlow rolls her eyes and chugs the faerie wine in her hand.

"I need more alcohol for this." Taking a single step she pauses, her eyes narrow, assessing. "So do you."

"Alcohol is not a good coping mechanism," Hazel mutters under her breath.

"Neither is sex, but it sure feels good," Harlow calls over her shoulder, not sparing us a glance as she does so. Hazel scoffs.

Axel stalks into the room, his brows furrowed and face ashen, but he only has eyes for one person. He cuts through the room like a sharp blade, only stopping until he reaches Knox's side. I leave Hazel and Lenox, picking up the pace of my steps toward them.

"I'm sure he's just out with Zephlyn," Knox assures him.

Axel shakes his head vigorously. "No, I already checked." The fear tinging his voice makes the hairs on the back of my nape rise. "Knox, there was a trail of blood in his room."

The music stops, the chatter dies, and every Fae ear in the room snaps to Axel's strained voice. Then chaos ensues. Everybody shouts, their questions piling up until one voice breaks through the masses of Knox's court.

"Did you say there was blood?" Hazel asks quietly.

Axel turns to her then, the panic clear in his eyes. "Did you not feel anything?"

Hazel puts her hand on her heart, as if she can physically yank the bond that tethers her to Ace. "No. He was here a short while ago. He said he wanted to go get Delilah and

Knox's gift." Her gaze jumps to mine. "I hid the gift in his room."

Harlow shoves forward, waving her hand in Hazel's direction. "Can you not feel where he is?"

Hazel's eyes glass over, unseeing. Then she whispers, "No."

Axel pulls away, his breathing ragged as all the color drains from his face. Knox steps forward, placing his hands on his shoulders, trying to calm him.

"I can't lose him, Knox, not him. Please not him," he chants.

As Knox tries to get more information out of Axel, my eyes stray to Hazel, the way they remain glazed, how her hands tremble by her sides. In the next blink, her body sways, and I rush forward just in time to catch her fall.

"Deep breaths, Hazel. When did he go to get the gift?"

"Two drinks ago," Hazel mumbles.

Right, everyone has been tracking time by the drinks. Axel's head pops up at her quiet answer.

"That couldn't have been too long ago." Axel shoves Knox's hands off him. "We need to all split up and find him."

"Delilah and I will go with Hazel. Nolan, Lenox, and—"

Axel cuts in, pointing to Hazel. "I'm not separating from the only other person who can feel him."

Hazel jolts. Whether the twins had telepathy or not was just answered in the throes of Axel's panic. The years-long secret revealed. But no one seems surprised.

"Can you feel him?" I ask slowly.

Axel's jaw grinds, his teeth the only grating sound as we all hold our breaths.

"No."

Knox jumps in, his shoulders squaring as he changes his

orders. "Nolan, Lenox, and Harlow, you go off with Zephlyn. His bond should help you locate him."

"And if three people with a bond to Ace don't feel anything?" Nolan dares to ask.

"That won't happen," Axel growls before storming out of the room.

Harlow whacks Nolan in the gut. "Gods, you can be so cruel!"

Nolan feigns innocence. "I was simply asking for an order."

Ignoring the pair, I take off after Axel and Knox, pulling Hazel along with me, trying to coax her out of her shock. It's as if she's a shell of a person.

I expect Axel's wings to unfurl immediately outside, and when they don't, his movements turn frenzied, his steps zigzagging in the backyard.

"You can smell his scent."

Axel doesn't look at me as he responds. "Yes."

Zephlyn's roar is a hoarse cry on the wind, his wings flapping wildly as he takes off into the sky. I hand Hazel off to Knox as Axel begins pulling out Henry and Creseda.

Running for Aurora, I slide to a stop, my hands splayed in front of me as her wings spread, readying to take off.

"Stop!"

She moves to charge past me, but I slam a wall of golden light in front of her. The act doesn't harm her, simply shocks her out of the vengeful glare she's sporting.

"We need someone to stay back and guard the house, to wait in case he turns up."

Steam puffs out of her snout as she narrows her golden eyes.

"Please, we need someone who can fly to stay back."

I'm about to get on my hands and knees to beg when she seems to roll her eyes and flop onto her behind. A tantrum.

I run off without a backward glance as I call over my shoulder, "Thank you!"

Axel and Hazel are mounted on Henry while Knox waits for me on Creseda. Without waiting to see if we're following, Axel takes off into the night.

Creseda picks up into a gallop, and Knox stretches out his hand, his fingers brushing mine before he grips my forearm tightly and pulls me onto Creseda's saddle.

If the passing months have taught me anything, it is that time is not on your side, and unfortunately, Ace needs all the time in the world until we can find him.

Chapter Fifty-Two

It isn't until we've been riding for an hour does Axel begin to let up on Henry, slowing the horse's pace from an outright gallop to a canter. As I take in my bearings, my surroundings become eerily familiar. Memories assault my mind, one after the other, more unpleasant than the last.

A chilling slither of ice and darkness snakes down my spine. The feeling so ominous it makes me pause. The last time I was here, I let the demon hounds track me to the abandoned library doors and capture me, only so I could gain access to their den.

But when I was here, I never felt this. The library itself feels like it's emanating fear, warning those who pass to not enter, trying to save those it can. Everyone else must feel it too, because they stop…even Axel.

"He's in there," Hazel whispers.

Axel's eyes harden, his head shaking as his gaze roams the area.

"You don't feel anything?" Knox asks Axel.

I wonder if the Fae king knew of the twins' telepathy, the power that binds the two souls. The questions Knox has been constantly asking makes me believe that only the twins know the depths and details of their power, what it's capable of.

A muscle ticks in Axel's jaw before he grinds the word out. "No."

Hazel puts a hand on Axel's arm. "He's alive, I can feel him."

Axel shrugs out of Hazel's grasp before dismounting Henry and storming for the building. "I'll believe it when I see it."

Running after Axel, we rush through the double doors he throws open, sprinting past the threshold just before they ricochet off the wall and bounce back, slamming behind us with a resounding bang that shakes the floor beneath our feet.

The difference in the library from the last I entered makes me stumble to a stop.

The library has always been a whirlwind of chaos, with its abandoned shelves, shattered wood, and layers upon layers of dust. Despite it all, the library's architecture was still beautiful, with the spiral design creating endless levels and rows of books.

A labyrinthian maze of knowledge.

I cannot find the beauty in it now.

The stacks have always contained shadows, the darkness seeming to swallow up the endless levels of the library, and yet when I creep forward, placing a trembling hand on the banister and peek over the side, the shadows that greet me make me shiver in revulsion.

Something is horribly amiss, and when I turn my head, Axel now walking cautiously and Knox unable to hide the disgust on his face, I know I'm not the only one who feels it.

The only one who seems to be unaware of the horrid feeling is Hazel, who rushes past Axel screaming, "I can feel him! I can feel him!"

The words snap at the heels of our feet, forcing us to run past the fear encasing our bodies. Level after level we sprint down the library, the endless curving making my head grow dizzy.

It isn't until we reach the eleventh and final level, where even the shadows are afraid to linger, where we are plunged into darkness as black as ink, do we finally give into our instincts and stop—and finally piece together what makes the shadows something to fear.

The wicked corruption of dark magic.

Its unsettling power calls to us, slithering through our ears, coaxing us to the other side. Trying to lure its next victim.

We stand frozen in place, the feeling enthralling even Knox, until we hear a moan of pain. Axel is already sprinting, taking off around the corner. I summon a glowing ball of golden flames above our heads, illuminating the surrounding area to reveal…an empty pit.

Axel stops running, his chest heaving as he spins in a circle to search for what we all heard—the cry of agony.

Time pauses, working in my favor for once as it slows around me, but not for much longer.

The sound and feeling of home that I've come to wish for and yet despise for its warnings greets my ears again. But instead of its soft melody of whispered words, it screams with a ferocity that makes my heart stop beating.

RUN, the ethereal voice chants.

It doesn't let up and it doesn't quiet. Until the sound is cut off mid-sentence and time plunges me into the present.

My golden fire scatters for the walls, illuminating the cobblestone pit.

"Axel, get back," Knox says, deadly calm.

Axel ignores his king's command as his wild gaze

searches every crack and crevice, as if his brother might lie beneath one of them. Knox is forced to grab him around the collar of his shirt with a shadowed hand and yank him back.

He opens his mouth to protest, only for the sound of death to interrupt.

At first, I think I'm hallucinating. It couldn't possibly be. It must be my imagination, magic, a spell, even someone that just sounds familiar.

But that laugh, that dark, twisted, laugh—I lived with it for my entire life, and there was not one moment where I forgot that chilling sound. It immobilizes me even now as it turns into a wickedly cruel drawl.

"Delilah, how lovely of you to grace us with your presence."

Spinning around, the blood drains from my body as I come face-to-face with that voice. The voice of the man whose throat I slit merely a month ago.

My father.

Chapter Fifty-Three

Shadows swirl, darker than the night sky, and the tendrils that lingered against the cobblestone wall come together before us to form shapes. It isn't until a body appears does Knox snap out of the trance of shock. In a blink, he steps in front of me, a protection shield snapping around all four of us. I stand motionless, my heartbeat slowing, because there he is.

I stare at my father, who holds an unconscious Ace dangling from his grasp, with a knife poised against his neck.

His eyes flash, and the whites of them disappear beneath blackness until they resemble two pits of hell.

The sight is so disconcerting the four of us stay frozen, too late for us to realize he has always been a master of illusions. I should have known better. It was all an act, a show.

Because as we stare at the monster transforming before us, we are captured by another source entirely.

Iron.

A cage comes down around us before we can move. The whites of his eyes and the normal brown irises return to him with a dark rumble of laughter.

"You're no better than pigs. They at least have the intelligence to not look me in the eye."

A pierced cry falls from Axel's lips when his eyes lock on the image of his twin—his battered body, bruised and dripping with blood under the hands of the king. I don't turn to Axel at the agonized sound, not when I'm focused on the sight of my father standing before me, very much alive and digging an iron-tipped knife into Ace's throat.

Hazel stands beside me shaking her head, shock cascading through her body. She's not even aware she's standing outside the iron cage, oblivious to the danger. She only has eyes for Ace.

"Impossible," I breathe, blinking rapidly as if the sight before me will simply disappear, a trick of the mind due to adrenaline and exhaustion. But every time I blink, my eyes only focus more clearly and the picture never fades.

"Lovely to see you again, Delilah, and without a dagger this time. What a shame, I was hoping you could pull that little party trick again."

"I *killed* you," I gasp in stunned shock. "I was covered in your blood. I killed you!"

He has the audacity to roll his eyes. "Clearly not."

Knox steps in front of me. "Let him go and we'll let you leave here in one piece," he growls.

"That's humorous. You're speaking as if you have a choice," the king sings as more iron and darkness come down upon us.

I scream out in shock as inky darkness flings me back against the wall at my back. Cold iron shackles clamp down upon my wrists and ankles. My eyes widen, searching high and low for who he has performing dark magic, only to find Hazel standing, shell-shocked, still the only one not shackled.

"Run!" I scream. "Find the others and run!"

But I'm begging the wrong person.

When Hazel turns to face me, I don't find shock or pain in her features or worry in her gaze. Instead, guilt lines her blue eyes. And she doesn't walk toward me; she walks toward my *father* and steals the very life beating within my heart.

Eyes. They whisper to you, and if you pay attention, you can hear the words they speak.

It's how I learned when my father would hit me. It's how I learned when my mother was lucid. It's how I know, now, that I trusted the wrong person.

Hazel was never the one who needed protection, but instead, the one we needed to be protected *from*.

I blubber, tripping over my own words, "W-what are you doing?"

Hazel turns away from me, her steps ever so light and yet every one of them so impactful.

"Hazel!" I scream as if my voice can change the direction of her footsteps.

Axel's face has drained of all color. "No."

Knox *burns* next to me, rage so fierce and potent at the betrayal, I can practically taste the waves of revenge and indignation.

I shake my head, refusing to believe such a horrid thought. He simply has her under a spell. Yes, it *has* to be a spell, mind control. He had someone place a spell over Hazel so that…

My thoughts trail off, my delusions falling away as my mind finally stops churning and begins to process the possibility before me.

With every step she takes toward him, I know she will never come back to this side.

My eyes lower to my chest, expecting to find a dagger plunged into my heart, but there's not an ounce of blood trickling from me. It isn't a knife wound I'm feeling, it's betrayal. One that will cost me dearly.

Glee shines in my father's beady eyes, as Hazel takes her final step and stands beside him.

"Why?" I croak.

"The signs were always there; you just didn't want to see them," Hazel says simply.

"Do not blame me for your horrid actions." My voice grows hoarse as I bellow with rage. "Don't you dare blame my trust as a reason for not seeing the monster you truly are!"

The shattered heart she tried so hard to heal crumbles into nothing but ashes in the wind.

Pieces of the puzzle fall into place, slowly and then all at once.

The hours upon hours in which she spent poring over every dark magic book. How she always volunteered herself to be around the horror-filled pages. She always knew when something within me changed, I could never get anything past her, and she was always demanding to know what was going on within me, especially when it came to my magic.

I was naïve and foolish enough to believe that we were friends and that her care was simply that of a worried companion.

Why the creatures and soldiers never killed her when they attacked Knox's home. They had ample opportunity to; the demonic hounds were hovering over her and then the creature in charge fell under a milky, glazed look, and they let her run away. They all knew she hid in the cellar, yet not one of them came after her.

Because they all knew she wasn't their enemy.

Then the final piece clicks, the one that was so glaringly obvious. *The signs were always there.* The book. In those early days in her cottage, Hazel had a book on demonic creatures. I believed her when she said it was morbid curiosity about her daughter. How foolish of me to believe the words of a *stranger*.

I know she can see it in my eyes, the moment realization strikes, because she shrugs as if to say, *I can't believe you didn't notice.*

"I won't bother asking for your forgiveness," she says, "but I do want you to know that I never did any of this from a malicious heart."

Rage contorts Axel's face as he spits, "We don't give a shit what you think your heart holds."

"You will in time," she replies calmly. Her voice as smooth as silk, not a single tremor to be found. "It may not be today, but you will thank me for answering the questions you will have someday, as opposed to leaving you to ruminate."

I watch with my own eyes as her very demeanor changes —her shoulders and back straighten, her voice grows stronger, her eyes steel. It was *all* an act. The woman who cried in my arms, the one who consoled me over Easton, who laughed with me and helped train my magic, was never real.

My heart not only crumbles…it *weeps*.

"Most of your questions can be answered with a simple word: grief. I wasn't prepared or ready to let go of Luna." She scoffs at the horrid notion. "We're Fae. We have immortality in our blood, and yet my baby girl only got to experience seven years of her life…SEVEN!" she snaps, a temper rushing to the surface that we have never seen in her.

She clears her throat, regaining control of her carefully curated mask. "I simply refused to let her go, and when I overheard the house goblins in the taverns whispering about the dark magic that had leaked into the Fae lands and courts once more…I researched and researched and researched until the answer was glaringly obvious. I could have my baby back again one day."

My breath stutters.

The flowers.

The flowers she would kill and then revive during our journey. That wasn't a simple trick of magic, nor was it to pass the time. Hazel had been practicing.

"It was right in front of us all along," I whisper to no one in particular.

"It wouldn't be her, Hazel," Knox says gently, trying to appeal to her logical side. "Dark magic is corruption at its core—it would alter her very soul. That's if it was even able to bring her back which it can't, not truly."

Hazel's jaw tightens. "I've seen what it can do with my own eyes. Yes, it can."

My gaze flicks to my father. I shake my head, refusing to believe it, my brain not wanting to consider that possibility, but I can't help but ask.

"D-did you?" I stutter.

My father laughs, the sound grating and full of venom. "No, that's where you lack intelligence, but fear not, child. No one has been able to reveal my true identity."

My head rears back. *True identity?*

"You see, Delilah, no matter how many times you kill me, it will never be my true self." As the last word leaves his mouth, darkness swallows him whole, swirling around his form before it, too, vanishes, revealing my mother. "You can kill whatever form you wish." My mother vanishes behind a cloud of darkness, dread coiling in my gut when Easton pops out. "Yet none of them are my true form." Easton laughs, that cold sound, before changing into a young teenage boy I have never seen before, and then an old man. A young beautiful woman. A Fae, a dragon, and a griffin. Until he changes again, taking on the features of the man I grew up my entire life hating. "You will never know which mask is real or which one is fake. Nobody knows what I truly look like. Perhaps I myself have even forgotten what I look like..." He clicks his tongue. "What a pity, I suppose I can never be killed."

There's only one form of magic as wicked and powerful that can create the shapeshifter before me, that can grant true immortality—*dark magic.*

"How long have you taken on the mask as king?" Knox grits.

He claps his hands. "Finally! Someone with the interesting questions!" He begins pacing, leaving a form of darkness to hold the blade to Ace's neck as a devilish smirk plays across his lips. "Fifteen reigns, give or take."

Utter shock silences my mind, my heart, my breaths...me. It's a silence so loud it is deafening. A gasping wheeze breaks the hold of time and I peer around the room to find the source, only for my vision to blur with tears at the realization that it's me who is wheezing and I cannot breathe.

Our reactions fuel his hunger for power and attention.

A memory flashes through my mind, when we were passing the river a short few months ago. When I turned back and thought he could see me, see through the shields of magic. I thought it was my fear and anxiety that put that sickening feeling in my stomach. I thought I was being preposterous, but now I know—he saw me all along. He knew where we were, and he allowed us to pass.

He allowed us through...

He planned for it to end this way.

And the oily darkness that attacked Knox's mind as we passed. It was never the duke...it was him.

All my life I wondered how his army could perform his

disgusting orders. I questioned why his men followed him blindly and why the council kneeled before him, begging for attention and power. But what if all of that had never been a willing decision?

Hatred burns my tongue as I ask coldly, "How do you control your army?"

His eyes flash with praise. "I see you're finally understanding. A simple compulsion spell, marvelous thing."

"That's how you controlled my mind? Under the compulsion of dark magic?"

He rolls his eyes. "No need for magic when my fists will do the work for me."

Bile burns my throat at how callous and cruel this person is. I suppose you can't even call him a person anymore. His dark magic, the power he has been using for *hundreds* of years—he would have had to sell his soul to obtain it.

"You were the one behind Emmalyn."

Knox's murderous voice makes me snap my head up, my chin wobbling and heart stuttering at all the revelations. His magic thrashes between our bond, trying desperately to fight against the iron weakening us.

"Couldn't very well have you horrid Fae with your *oh so pure* magic sniffing me out." He smirks. "Your parents came close—they had to be dealt with."

Axel growls as Knox roars, a small flicker of fire and shadows jumping between his fingertips. The king's eyes widen a fraction.

Knox thrashes wildly in his restraints, murder and retribution promised in his eyes. "*You* were the one that killed them. You took their pure magic!"

His smirk widens with pride. "Well, it isn't pure anymore." He flicks his wrist, as if waving off his words. "Honestly, I got bored over the last passing decades. Everything was growing so dull, I wanted something to entertain me. And I admit, my control slipped a little after some of the ruling courts began to catch on to who I am." He shrugs, not caring for his ramblings. "I was tired of playing nice."

I swallow thickly. "Why are you telling us all of this?"

He's going to kill us, I realize.

Perhaps if I distract him long enough, Knox's magic can build and get past the iron. I know the notion is hopeful and naïve, but it's better than cowering and shivering in this iron box wondering when he will strike…when my last breath will be.

I didn't spend my last few months fighting, only to back down when it counts most.

He steps forward, and with the movement, I lock my gaze onto the cold beady eyes of the man I have despised and feared for as long as I can remember. He crouches in front of us, cocking his head as he studies me.

Knox and Axel thrash in their iron cages. I, however, don't. I don't cower, and I certainly don't avoid eye contact.

This monster has taken everything from me—my innocence, my childhood, my mother, Annie, Easton, the lives of the innocent citizens of Aloriah. I'd say he's taken Hazel, but clearly, she was never truly my friend.

He has taken so much from me, and in this moment, I find the strength to not cower.

If this is my last moment I want to go out with strength and courage in my heart.

"You were such a pesky thing, always running around asking for attention and hugs," he says, surprising me. His body shivers with repulsion. "You were a nuisance that needed to be put down, but a king must have an heir." He sighs. "It's an annoying part of the process, finding a woman and child to play the part of my doting family, but it must be done to continue passing the title down the line."

Finding *a child.*

The words that I thought would be music to my ears, the relief at knowing I don't share blood with this vile and vicious monster, is short-lived. Eleanor wasn't my birth mother, and if this man isn't my real father…

Who are my true parents, and what did he do to them?

It's why he hurt me, why he never cared about the blood he spilled from my veins. I was never his, and I was never the heir of Aloriah.

"Why me?" I rasp. "I'm not even yours. Why would you do this to me?"

He pulls out a pocket watch, flippantly saying, "That is a question for another day. For now, we need to hurry along."

"You had power all along—you have the power to control. Why hurt so many people?"

A light brightens his otherwise dark eyes. "How do you think I obtained such power in the first place, Delilah?"

Out of the corner of my eye I see Knox drop his head, his eyes shuttering closed.

I rack my brain over everything I read about dark magic, watching it float through my mind until it slows to a stop. A single passage is all it takes to bring me to my knees. When we learned how the entrapment spell had been put up in the first place. I shake my head, tears welling in my eyes to the point that his figure blurs, giving me a small reprieve until his grating voice slithers down my spine again.

"I don't kill for sport, Delilah. I kill for power. Every death gives me more." He splays his palm across his chest. "I thank the lives I've sacrificed, truly. I wouldn't be where I am today without their deaths."

I gag, bile burning my throat.

For the first time since it happened, I wish I could go back in time and slit his throat again.

"Why are you telling us this?" I ask again.

He pins me with his sharp gaze. "Because I want you to go about living your days, watching me rule my people from afar, and know that you will never be able to do anything to stop me."

Tears roll down my cheeks. For a small heartbeat, one small moment, I had been ready to die. To end the suffering that he has inflicted. He broke me down so thoroughly I had wanted to die.

And he knows that. He knows all my deepest and darkest secrets…I had poured my heart out to him when I slashed his throat. He knows every single emotional sore spot for me—where to strike.

"You can't go back as king. Everyone already thinks you're dead," Knox growls, bearing his canines.

"That's where you're wrong." He cocks his head. "Why do you think you haven't heard of my funeral?"

I stumble backward, my back hitting the cold cobblestone wall, the iron shackles digging into my forearms and calves. The cold metal isn't enough to shake me from my stupor. How selfish could I have been to walk away from my own kingdom and not *check* on the merging of titles? Lost within the depths of my grief, I haven't even thought to see if Ordelia has been receiving my ramblings of letters.

And then a horrid thought occurs to me.

The king is alive and well, but is Ordelia? Has she been receiving my letters, or is she no longer with us?

I suppose there is no kingdom for her to take over. She must have thought I'd gone mad with the grief, to be writing to her about a dead king and kingdom ownerships and crowns.

Where are the children of the complex now? We had left knowing they were safe within the sectors once more, knowing that the king was dead.

Then the most appalling thought of them all occurs to me as I remember the rebels and all that they'd done to help us get into the complex. The *reasons* why we entered the complex.

My eyes slide to Hazel. "Were you ever held captive?"

Hazel's mouth opens but is cut off when the king throws his head back on a deep belly laugh. "Captive! My dear child, you are ignorant. Who do you think relayed to me all your marvelous plans?" His eyes roll as if exasperated. "The very detailed, boring, mundane plans."

"You gave the location of the rebels?" Axel asks dangerously low. "You were the one who leaked the complex plans?"

In Hazel's blue eyes, I see the truth.

From the moment Hazel entered my life, she has been a spy for my father. Every word uttered and action taken made their way back to the king.

My body reacts without my permission. I grit my teeth to hold in the tears, to try and keep the hurt and betrayal from shining in my eyes, but it's fruitless. My throat burns with the exertion of withholding my emotions. As if the dam is banging on my senses, demanding its release as I face down who I once called my friend.

Then the kernel ignites once more, burning in the background, offering support that Hazel never will. An inferno to help me burn through this. Adding coal to the flames of hatred.

"*You*," I spit.

Hazel's eyes widen a fraction, unable to hide the shock of my loathing.

"You were the one who revealed their location! You are the reason they are DEAD!" I roar, spit flying from my mouth as rage curls deep within my gut.

They are dead because of Hazel.

There and gone in an instant, a small flicker of guilt. And that's the moment I know it was her. Those lips that whispered caring and thoughtful words to get me through Easton's death had also uttered the words that would slay my mother and Annie.

I had seen the guilt back at the cabin when she took care of me.

They wouldn't be dead if we hadn't gone after her, if we hadn't changed Ordelia's original plan to save the children.

If it weren't for Hazel, Eleanor and Annie would be alive today.

The tidal wave of emotions chokes me, and I wail. The betrayal and hurt filling my heart, a pain so undeniable and potent, makes my chest wrack and cave in on itself.

I *trusted* her.

My heart trusted her. I thought we helped each other heal —her comforting me over Easton, me helping her over Luna. I thought we were there for one another, but I was nothing but a stepping stone in her grand scheme.

I ran away from the palace, but I was foolish enough to believe I had escaped being a pawn.

The tears won't stop falling and I clutch my chest as I slide down the brick wall, the iron shackles rattling with the movement. My hand squeezes my clothing and skin, as if I can try and keep my heart intact and inside my rib cage. As if I can stop Hazel from ripping it apart, her betrayal burning brighter than all the other revelations. I always knew my father was a monster but Hazel…sweet, loving Hazel was a lie, an illusion.

She preyed on my weaknesses and vulnerability and used it against me.

She is the reason they are dead.

"Was any of it real?" I ask, my chin wobbling as I stare into her clear blue eyes.

"My pain and grief were real."

"Why work with him?" I choke. Because that's what this is—an exchange of power. She chose him over the new life she could have had with us.

"He can give me what I want most."

Ace stirs at the sound of her voice, a pained moan falling from his cut lips. Axel thrashes, his eyes burning with fear before they snap to Hazel, pleading. "What about my brother? You love him! He's your mate! If you do this to him, it will break him." He shakes his head. "It will break *you* to walk away from him in this state."

Hazel swallows thickly, avoiding our eyes. Pink tints her cheeks.

Axel's face falls with disbelief. "I-impossible. You can't just *fake* a bond."

"No, but dark magic can," the king sings, taunting.

My tears fall for Ace now, turning into pain and agony at the betrayal he will feel for the rest of his life. The betrayal of making him feel something that is to be cherished and magical. For tricking his mind into thinking he had found his mate when in reality it was just a desperate woman.

But then—

Another piece of the puzzle slides into place. It was why Ace couldn't feel Hazel when she was taken. She was never his mate, and she was never in any danger.

On my next sob, golden light encircles my hands and fingertips, trying to explode, trying to escape the agony these people have caused my pummeled heart.

Heir of Broken Kingdom

The king's eyes widen, and I could have sworn for a moment there was fear in them, but it's gone before I can truly discern it.

"Why do this? Why do any of this? None of us asked for this. We were never even suspecting you!"

"Revenge," he breathes. As if the word is meant to make sense to us.

I can see it in his eyes. He may not be my father, but I lived with him for the majority of my life, and I know when he has a card up his sleeve he isn't willing to share. So instead of pestering for answers, I croak, "You win. Now let Ace go."

The king smirks, a delightfully cruel grin that spreads so slowly I question whether he can alter time. "I thought you would never concede. As you wish, Delilah."

His darkness curls, spinning into a frenzy. And I realize too late—

What happens next plays out in slow motion.

My stomach falls along with Ace as the king lets Ace go but not the sword.

Then my nightmare, the one that has been chasing me since Easton's death, plays out before my very eyes.

The fourth, and final, strike of the sledgehammer.

Ace's head separates from his body as he's dropped onto the sword.

The scream that rips from Axel is one I will hear for the rest of my life, one that I will *feel* for the rest of my days.

A wave of pain blasts throughout the room as Axel explodes with agonizing misery and heartbreak. He claws at his chest, as if he can physically reach inside and clutch onto the bond between him and his twin and keep him tethered to this world.

Pain blasts the bridge between me and Knox, so powerful

that it flings me backward, throwing me into the garden of my mind. Grief's agonizing talons rip into him, killing every last plant between our gardens.

The iron bars disappear, along with Hazel and the king. There and gone in an instant, as if none of this ever happened. But it did, because Ace is lying on the floor, unmoving, and crimson blood is filling the now-empty room.

It's unnerving to see Ace not move. The Fae was always restless. Even in sleep, his fingers and hands would twitch. To see him *deathly* still, it's what cements the notion that he is never coming back, and he will never move again.

Axel runs to him, jaw hanging open on a scream. Tears run down his face as he tries put his brother back together. His hands shaking violently with the effort.

Sweet, beautiful Ace, murdered in the same manner as Easton. I know it was on purpose, I know the king noticed his uncanny resemblance to him.

He most likely ordered Hazel to prey on him because of it.

Kind and caring Ace, who saw a room full of people and knew how to soothe their hearts. Ace, who has a deep love and bond for Zephlyn, who would risk his own life for the creature. The one with the soft demeanor, so tender and kind to those around him. The one who brought me chocolates because he knew it reminded me of the good times with Easton.

The man who proclaimed to be my family at the discovery of our griffin's mating bond.

The man who came to me to plan a proposal for a woman that, despite the illusion, he loved. The man who was excited to start a life and a family, the one who uttered sweet words of hope.

And now, he will never experience the love he so kindly bestowed upon those around him.

Knox wraps his arms around Axel, pulling him away as he tries to put Ace's head back.

"He's gone, Axel…he's gone," he says gutturally, his own tears running down his face.

Before Axel can speak, Ace just…disappears, taken away from his brother by darkness.

Every power in the room lashes out to stop it, but it's no use. He's already gone.

"NO!" Axel screams. "Give him back! Give my brother back! GIVE HIM BACK!" Axel's body crumbles into his brother's crimson puddle. "Please give him back," he weeps.

Knox and I jump at the sound of pounding footsteps, drawing our useless blades behind our backs. Axel remains kneeling in his brother's blood, uncaring of the threat that lies beyond.

Nolan rounds the corner, Lenox and Harlow soon to follow, and the look that overcomes their faces…

True horror.

Harlow swallows. "What happened? Whose blood is that?"

"Where's Ace and Hazel?" Lenox asks.

At the sound of her name, Axel breaks down, laying his forehead on the ground, not caring for the puddle of blood, not as his chest shakes with the force of his sobs. The fight utterly leaves him.

Knox's voice croaks as he says, "Ace is dead."

"Hazel…" I force the words, spitting each one. "Hazel betrayed us."

You can feel the moment the words are processed. It changes the air, electrifying it. Charging it with suffering so raw Harlow gasps for fresh air as she heaves.

"He warned me there was a traitor." Nolan's face has turned ashen. "I-I didn't…I didn't believe him."

Harlow stands shell-shocked. She shakes her head, once, twice, her red-streaked hair swaying. "H-he—what do you mean Ace is dead?"

A deafening roar shakes the ground, joined by a smaller howl.

Zephlyn and Aurora.

The roof above us rumbles, dirt falling from the cracks of the old cobblestones as a thunderous boom echoes throughout the library.

Lenox frowns, his pale face stricken as he whispers, "Are they…?"

Another thundering crash slams into the library, this time the force so impactful it knocks us to the ground, dust filling the air.

Covering my mouth with my elbow, I squint through the falling debris and dirt, coughing wildly. "Zephlyn will bring this building down if we don't get out!"

He can't fit in the library, and he knows something is wrong. Nothing will stop him from getting to Ace, to where his blood now lies.

He'd be able to smell how much there is.

A hand at my elbow lifts me, Harlow covering her mouth with her hand as she starts ushering me out.

I turn in time to watch Lenox and Knox trying to drag Axel away, and the fight he puts up, thrashing against the two Fae. "No, please!" he begs. "I want to be with him. He's coming back! I know he's coming back…he would never leave me." Axel's chest heaves with a sob as he repeats. "He would never leave me."

Nolan rushes to them as another boom sends debris flying through the walls of the library. Zephlyn's roars fill the halls.

Nolan grabs Axel's squirming legs while Lenox and Knox take his upper body.

The moment we step outside the library, the sunrise streaming across our harried, sorrowful faces, a piercing screech thunders through the forest. I drop to the forest floor and smack my hands over my ears, squeezing my eyes shut.

Zephlyn's wail will be heard for miles.

No one had to say a word. A simple glance at the usually silent, broody twin will tell anyone with a set of eyes what he has lost.

The moment my eyes close, the deafening sound evaporates, along with the ground below me, replaced by the sight that has haunted me for months.

The premonition of Knox dying, although now that I'm watching it play out once more, I realize who is missing— Ace and Hazel.

Though this premonition is the same, the world and the land of Aloriah burning to the ground, people screaming for mercy, I'm patient this time, watching and listening closely for any difference I can see.

The dragon flies toward me with Knox's decapitated head in its mouth, and then it happens.

Two shadow figures appear, their darkness falling over me as one moves forward in the black billowy robe and taps a lone finger against the glass holding me captive. The simple light tap smashes the glass into tiny fragments.

I wait for them to move, to leave as they usually do in this premonition, but instead, they stand there floating, staring back at me. It isn't until the dark abyss calls my name, sucking me into its clutches, does the one who tapped the glass move.

I hold my breath, waiting for the moment to suffocate me with its truth.

I'm not disappointed.

The shadow figure removes the hood off their head, revealing a man with brown peppered hair, beady eyes, and a face that haunts my every waking moment.

The king stands on the other side of the glass, a cruel smile on his face, as I'm swallowed into the black depthless pit of the universe.

The last thing I see as he throws his head back on a deep sinful laugh is the demonic dragon bringing him Knox's head.

Coming out of the trance, Zephlyn's grief pierces my ears again. My chest heaves, unable to calm the buzzing of anxiety thrumming through my veins.

The premonitions finally make sense, the reason why the mermaids sent us into the human lands and to Annie, who led me to the rebellion leader. This was always their plan, because the path led me to the true source of black magic, the darkness plaguing this world.

The king.

The king has been manipulating my fate from the moment I was born. My fate has always been broken. My life was never mine to choose. None of it was.

Knox rushes forward, his gentle hands cupping my ashen face.

"What is it? What did you see?"

His question captures the attention of his court. Even Axel deigns to lift his head, his bloodshot eyes capturing mine.

My voice is full of sorrow as the revelation lies upon my heart.

Because as the king returns to his broken kingdom, there is one thing I know without a shadow of a doubt.

"The king is not done playing with my fate."

A Note From The Author

It is with awe and gratitude that I say thank you. For not only reading book one but for picking up the second and supporting me.

Heir of Broken Kingdom is a book very near and dear to my heart—as they all. But this one is special because in writing Delilah's story, it healed a part of my own and I hope that Delilah's story will do the same for many.

If not, I hope you loved the action-packed drama and brooding Fae.

I said with the first that it was a shock that I wrote it, that if I could tell my younger self that I wrote a book she would die of shock and that remains to be true but…to write a second, to be able to live out my dreams…that I owe to you and to the many readers who continue to support me.

Thank you for allowing me to tell the stories that run havoc through my mind and heart.

Thank you for reading them.

To my fur baby Lola, who will never read a word of my stories but is there for me every step of the way…I love you. You are not only my soul mate but my soul pair.

And most importantly…Charlie…thank you for being my anchor in this world. I love you the most.

Printed in Great Britain
by Amazon